Beneath a Silent Moon

Beneath a

ALSO BY TRACY GRANT

Daughter of the Game

Silent Moon

TRACY GRANT

WM
WILLIAM MORROW
An Imprint of HarperCollins*Publishers*

This is a work of fiction. The characters, incidents, and dialogue are products of
the author's imagination and are not to be construed as real. Any resemblance to actual
events or persons, living or dead, is entirely coincidental.

FIRST EDITION

Designed by Renato Stanisic

Printed on acid-free paper

Library of Congress Cataloging-in-Publication Data
Grant, Tracy.
Beneath a silent moon / by Tracy Grant.— 1st ed.
p.   cm.
ISBN 0-06-621142-5 (hc.)
I. Title.
PS3607.R423 B46   2003
813'.54—dc21   2002026425

03   04   05   06   07   WBC/QW   10   9   8   7   6   5   4   3   2   1

FOR JIM,
one in five billion

The chariest maid is prodigal enough
If she unmask her beauty to the moon.

SHAKESPEARE, *HAMLET*

Acknowledgments

Once again my deepest thanks to my editor, Lucia Macro, and my agent, Nancy Yost, for their insightful advice and boundless support during the writing of this book. Thank you to Michael Morrison, Carrie Feron, Lisa Gallagher, Richard Aquan, Leesa Belt, Donita Dooley, and Kelly Harms at Morrow/Avon, and to Marion Donaldson, Shona Walley, Sherise Hobbs, and Amy Philip at Headline for supporting my books at various steps along the way. Thank you to Pam LaBarbiera for her careful copyediting. And thank you to Honi Werner for a beautiful cover that captures my vision of the book to perfection.

Thank you to Penny Williamson for countless plot brainstorming sessions; for stopping along a very windy stretch of the Perthshire coast because I absolutely had to have a picture "right here"; for exploring endless (and beautiful) Scottish castles and country houses, listening patiently to questions such as "What if part of Dunmykel looked like this?" "Could you hear the sea from here?" "How long would it take to get from the scullery to the nursery?", and not laughing too hard at my trepidation at climbing a thirteenth-century keep; for yet more discussions of plot and logistics over numerous (and delicious) Scottish dinners and drams of whisky; and for giving Dunmykel its name.

Thank you to jim saliba for fun and invaluable plot and character discussions; and for always remembering to ask me "How's it going?" and listening to my answer, no matter how overwhelmed he was with his own work.

Thank you to the 2001 participants in the Merola Opera Program for a wonderful *Così fan tutte* (of which I saw all four performances), and to the Oregon Shakespeare Festival for a fabulous *Hamlet* in the 2000 season. Both productions helped to inspire this book.

Beneath a Silent Moon

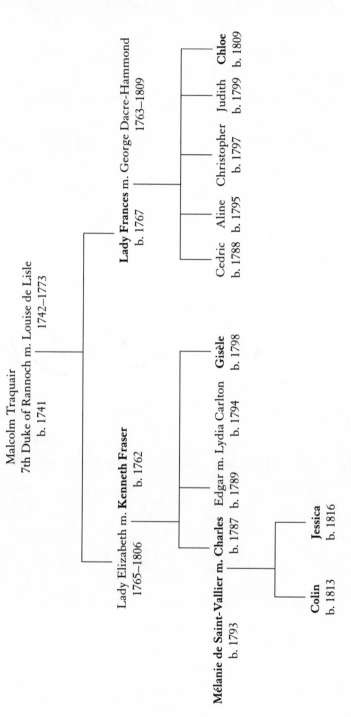

The Fraser Lineage

Malcolm Traquair
7th Duke of Rannoch m. Louise de Lisle
b. 1741   1742–1773

Lady Elizabeth m. **Kenneth Fraser**   **Lady Frances** m. George Dacre-Hammond
1765–1806   b. 1762   b. 1767   1763–1809

Edgar m. Lydia Carlton   **Gisèle**   Cedric   Aline   Christopher   Judith   **Chloe**
b. 1787   b. 1789   b. 1794   b. 1798   b. 1788   b. 1795   b. 1797   b. 1799   b. 1809

Mélanie de Saint-Vallier m. **Charles**
b. 1793

Colin   **Jessica**
b. 1813   b. 1816

The Talbot and Mallinson Lineage

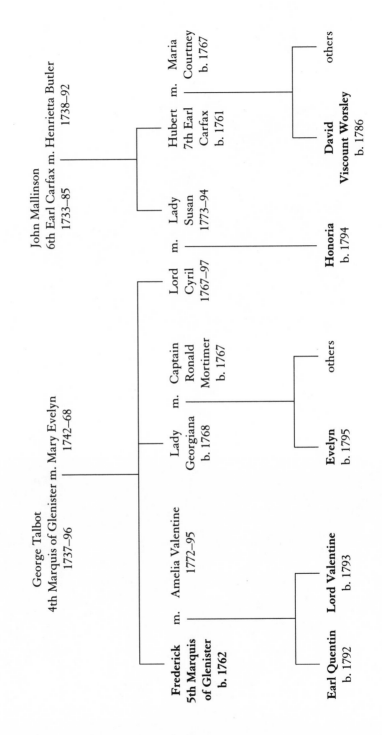

Prologue

The London Docks
June 1817

The night air was like a lover's touch. Cloaked in mystery, beck-oning with promise, sweet at times but quickly cloying. And underneath, rotten to the core.

He had forgotten what a foul whore the London night was. The river stretched behind him, a smooth dark expanse, shimmering where it caught the fitful moonlight. But the breeze off the water was choked with the stench of sewage and offal and remnants from the knackers' yards. The air was heavy with soot from thousands of fireplace grates and coal-oil lamps. It clogged his throat and clung to his skin and no doubt was turning his cravat and shirt cuffs more grimy by the minute.

He turned on the quayside. The greasy water lapped softly against the boat that had brought him across the Channel and down the Thames. Nearer at hand, the man who had sailed the boat fixed him with a gaze that was the ocular equivalent of a pointed pistol.

He fished a purse from the pocket of his greatcoat and pressed it into the boat owner's hand. "As agreed."

The boat owner tugged open the drawstring on the leather bag, tested one of the coins between his teeth, and began to count them with ponderous precision. Strange to pay three times more for twelve hours huddled in a tiny hold with barrels of brandy and tins of tea and crates of turbot than one would pay for a comfortable cabin on the mail packet.

The boat owner nodded, satisfied with his payment. The man who had paid him strode away from the river. He turned up the collar of his greatcoat and drew the folds of wool about him against the night chill. Pity his sojourn in London wouldn't allow for a visit to a tailor. One of the few things he missed on the Continent was a coat to equal those made on Bond Street.

A faded tavern sign with peeling gilt paint reminded him that he hadn't had a proper meal since before dawn. He peered through the smoke-blackened glass of the tavern windows. Greasy sausages. Potatoes soaked in lard. Meat pies filled with God knew what and those infernal mushy peas that had been a staple in the nursery. It was going to be the devil of a challenge to get a decent meal during his stay in London. But on the plus side, it was a long time since he'd had a pint of good dark stout.

The tavern door opened to admit three men on the shady side of forty, tradesmen of the middling sort judging by the quality of their coats and the modesty of their shirt points. They were engaged in a heated discussion that appeared to concern the effect of excise taxes and smuggling on the tea trade. The rhythm of English was harsh and unfamiliar to his ears. A strange way to feel about one's mother tongue.

Long-buried memories teased at the edges of his mind. The smell of ripe oranges on a birthday visit to Astley's Amphitheatre. The whack of a cricket bat. The syrupy sweetness of the treacle pudding he had actually once had the bad taste to like. The shapely calves and provocative mole of the Covent Garden opera dancer who had captured his attention at fifteen.

He shoved the memories aside and strode forward along the cobblestones. He had a job to do. The sooner it was done, the sooner he could leave this dank, smoky city that had long since ceased to mean anything to him.

He'd wait until he was closer to Covent Garden before he stopped to eat. There was always the chance of finding a passable coffeehouse run by a French émigré. He walked on, keeping to the shadows, and set his mind to the task that awaited him. The task that had begun in a shadowy past playing cricket and eating pudding and never dreaming that this sceptred isle would ever cease to be his home. The task that had taken shape in the present, thanks to the end of a war, the vengeance of a restored monarchy, and the inconvenient way secrets had of bubbling to the surface.

He hadn't had such a challenge in some time. It went without saying that it was going to be difficult.

But then murder always was.

Chapter 7

I wish he'd never come back to England, damn him."

The words, delivered in the light voice of a nineteen-year-old young lady of quality but with the intensity of a hardened soldier, hung incongruously in the rose-scented air. Evelyn Mortimer turned her gaze from the swirl of dancers on the black-and-white marble of her uncle's ballroom floor below to study the speaker. She'd had a feeling when she awoke this morning that this bid fair to be the longest day of her life. At the moment, it was looking as though it might be rather worse.

"It's no good trying to create a stir with your shocking language, Gelly," Evie said. "I'm the only one within earshot. You wish *who'd* never come back to England?"

"Who do you think?" Gisèle Fraser's kid-gloved fingers tightened round the etched crystal of her champagne glass. "My odious brother."

Evie gripped the gilded wrought-iron balustrade in a vain attempt to still the unease roiling through her. The candlelight shimmered over the scene below, glinting indiscriminately off real diamonds and paste copies, flickering over painted silk fans and starched cravats, playing off polished silver trays and crystal glasses, tapestry-hung walls and classical friezes. Yet she could feel the tension rippling beneath this spun-sugar world. A tension that stood to shatter the peace of the evening.

She spotted the tall, lean figure of Gisèle's brother on the far side of the dance floor, talking with two other black-coated gentlemen. At first glance, Charles Fraser appeared little different from any other man at the ball. His coat was cut less extravagantly than some, though he wore it better than most, and his shirt points were not as ridiculously high as the style some of the young gallants affected. But something else marked him out from the throng, a restless intensity in the set of his shoulders and the angle of his head. Like an actor who is giving a creditable performance of Goldsmith but would much rather sink his teeth into *Hamlet.*

Alarm prickled the back of Evie's neck. Of all the complications of the evening, it was Charles Fraser's presence that chilled her to the bone. "Odious isn't exactly the word I'd use to describe your brother," she said.

Gisèle tossed back the remaining quarter of her glass of champagne. "He doesn't belong here."

"At Glenister House?" Evie continued to watch Charles. He was leaning an arm against one of the pillars with casual ease, yet she had the sense that even here he was ready to spin round and disarm an attacker. "I hate to argue, but I went over the invitation list myself, and I can assure you he was invited."

"In Britain," Gisèle said. "I'm sure Wellington and Castlereagh still need him in Paris, stealing documents and unmasking traitors and shooting people and that sort of thing."

"Is that what diplomats do?" Was it too much to hope that Charles might decide to leave the ball early? Yes, it probably was. "And here I thought they filled their days with dull things like signing treaties and shuffling papers."

"Charles wasn't a normal diplomat. Only he won't talk about what he really did during the war and I'm not supposed to ask questions. Not that I want to talk to him. After nine years, we really don't have anything to say to each other. Which is why I wish to heaven he'd stayed on the Continent, instead of coming home and dragging that wife of his along from Spain—"

"Portugal." Evie mentally cursed herself for allowing the conversation to take this turn. Discussing Charles Fraser's marriage was like stumbling into an ever more treacherous mire. "He was at the embassy in Lisbon when he married her."

"But she's Spanish. And French. She has those exotic looks that gentlemen find annoyingly attractive." Gisèle twisted one of the pink silk roses on the left shoulder of her gown. "Everyone says she married him for his money."

"It's always difficult to know why one person marries another," Evie said. The words seemed to hang in the air, cutting like a knife through the pastel fabric of the evening.

"I can't imagine why Charles married *her*," Gisèle said. "She's very pretty, but he treats her more like a junior attaché than the woman he loves. I've scarcely seen them within ten feet of each other all evening. Of course, the whole concept of Charles being in love seems self-contradictory."

Evie glanced down at the ballroom again. Even amid a fair share of London's Upper Ten Thousand, Mrs. Charles Fraser stood out like a poppy in a posy of hothouse roses. It wasn't her looks, though her dark hair and pale skin were undeniably dramatic. Or her gown, though she had plainly brought the narrow, clean-lined creation of spider gauze and silver satin with her from Paris. It was the way she held herself, with a graceful ease that seemed out of place in an English ballroom.

It wasn't easy to be an outsider in this world, as Evie knew to her own cost. For an instant her mind was flooded with the memory of her uncle's crested black traveling carriage, arriving late one night to take her away from the crowded, dingy house that was the only home and family she'd ever known.

She swallowed, so hard that she felt as if the life was being choked out of her. Absurd. It wasn't the past that mattered now, it was the present. She needed her wits about her to get through tonight with all the key players still in one piece.

"Do you think she has a lover?" Gisèle said, her gaze on her brother's wife.

"Honestly, Gelly, they've only been married—"

"More than four years. I should think she'd want *someone* to pay romantic attention to her, especially if she only married Charles for his money. Everyone else in the Glenister House set has a lover. Or two. Except the unmarried girls. It's so boring being a virgin."

"Speak for yourself. At the moment I find life quite complicated enough without any lovers to muddy up the situation." Evie studied Charles Fraser's wife. Mrs. Fraser was standing alone, beside one of the archways. Charles seemed to have disappeared. Oh, poison. If he'd gone where Evie feared he had, the evening was rapidly unraveling.

Gisèle rested her elbows on the balustrade, heedless of the way she was creasing her ecru gloves. "Of course, I suppose it could be worse."

"How?" Evie scanned the ballroom for the golden-haired figure who, she had a sinking feeling, had gone in search of Charles Fraser.

"Charles could have married Honoria."

"Charles Fraser, you wretch. Wild horses shouldn't be able to drag you away from your lovely bride."

The voice, a woman's voice with the melodious sweetness of Schubert played on a well-tuned pianoforte, drifted beneath the Corinthian pediment of the library doorway and reverberated against the robin's-egg-blue plaster of the corridor. Mélanie Fraser paused, a half-dozen paces from the library door. She had come in search of her husband, who had a habit of vanishing into the library at large entertainments. But evidently someone else had come in search of him first.

"Mélanie's well able to fend for herself in a ballroom. She wouldn't thank me for hovering."

That was her husband, but the teasing familiarity in his voice hit her like a shock of rainwater down the back of her neck. Prudence, good manners, and common sense indicated she should beat a hasty retreat. Instead she stayed where she was.

The woman in the library gave a brittle laugh. "I still can't believe you actually went through with it after all the times you've sworn yourself blue in the face that you'd never do anything of the sort."

"Anything of what sort?" Charles said.

"Getting yourself leg-shackled, as my cousins would put it."

"You expect me to be consistent, Honoria? I thought you knew me better than that."

Of course, Mélanie realized. The musical voice belonged to Honoria Talbot, the Marquis of Glenister's niece and ward and the hostess at this evening's entertainment. Charles had scarcely seen Miss Talbot since he left England when she was in her early teens— or so he had led Mélanie to believe.

Her guardian is my father's oldest friend. We grew up together. Charles hadn't elaborated, but then he rarely did. Mélanie sometimes forgot just how much about her husband she did not know.

"You're the most consistent man I know, Charles Fraser," Miss Talbot said. "You have been since the age of seven."

The swish of a silk skirt sounded from the library. Mélanie could see the scene as clearly as if the plaster wall of the corridor were replaced with glass. Charles sprawled in a chair, probably with a book in his lap, long legs stretched out, brown hair falling untidily over his forehead, cravat slightly askew. Miss Talbot crossing the room toward him, her white satin skirts swirling about her graceful figure, her swanlike neck curved above the gathered tulle on the bodice of her gown, the smooth golden coils of her hair shining in the candlelight.

" 'I'm not cut out to be anyone's husband.' " Miss Talbot mimicked Charles's quietly emphatic voice with spot-on accuracy. "That's a direct quote, Charles."

"It sounds like the sort of categorical thing I might have said in my undergraduate days."

"Then you went off to Lisbon and spent the war having all sorts of mysterious adventures—"

"I don't know what you're talking about." That was the voice Charles used to deflect any comment on his work during the war.

"And now suddenly you're back in London turned all domestic with a beautiful wife and two adorable children in tow. While I'm three-and-twenty and practically on the shelf." Miss Talbot gave a laugh that was part rueful, part self-mocking. "You told me once that one day I'd meet the right man and fall in love. I sometimes think I should have given up years ago and settled for someone charming and agreeable."

"Marriage isn't anything to rush into, Noria."

"Now you sound like Evie. She's always giving me maddeningly sensible advice. Sometimes I grow tired of being sensible."

Evie must be Evelyn Mortimer, the chestnut-haired girl who had made a point of stopping to speak with Mélanie and ask after her children earlier in the evening. Miss Mortimer was also Lord Glenister's niece. She and Honoria Talbot had both been raised at Glenister House, almost like sisters, from what Mélanie had heard.

"Besides, you're a fine one to try to be sensible," Miss Talbot continued. "As I hear tell, you'd known your wife less than a month before you married her."

"We were in the middle of war," Charles said. "One doesn't have the luxury of time to wait."

Or to think things through.

"Confess it, Charles," Miss Talbot said. "You took one look at that ebony hair and those sea-green eyes and all your qualms about marriage went out the window. 'Love wrought these miracles.'"

The pause that followed could not possibly have been as long as it felt to Mélanie, standing motionless in the corridor. Her fingers closed on the molding, so hard she could feel the plaster chip beneath the silk of her glove.

"I've never been one to believe in miracles," Charles said with the practiced lightness of an actor playing Sheridan. "And God knows in our world love and marriage often have very little to do with each other."

Something twisted in Mélanie's chest, like a piano wire stretched to the breaking point. But what else could Charles have said? He was honest to a fault.

There was a rustle of tulle, as though Miss Talbot had turned her head. "It's odd the things one misses. Sharing apples at harvest dances. Wading through tide pools and getting sand between our toes. Sitting on the edge of the cliffs and watching the sun sink into the sea on those incredibly long Scottish evenings. Picking wildflowers. Rosemary for remembrance. We can't go back, can we?"

"To the people we were then? Hardly. We can't forget what we've learned in the interim. I don't know about you, but for myself I wouldn't want to."

"No? Perhaps not. But sometimes it seems life would be so much simpler if we could. In those days I never thought—"

"What?" Charles's voice sharpened, the way it did when he scented danger.

"Nothing. Nothing that makes any difference now. And yet—I can't help but think how my life might have been different if we'd made different choices."

"There were no different choices to make, Honoria." Mélanie knew that tone of her husband's voice as well. Stripped to nothing but honesty. And she knew the look in his eyes that went with it. A tenderness all the more devastating because it contained no artifice.

"You can't know that for a certainty, Charles. Neither of us can." Miss Talbot drew a quick breath, like the shattering of glass. "When you told me that one day I'd meet the right man, you also said that you'd bring me nothing but unhappiness. Do you remember when you said that? And where?"

The silence was so thick Mélanie could feel the pressure reverberating against the walls. The crystal girandoles on the sconce overhead might just as well have been the sword of Damocles. "Yes," Charles said in a harsh voice that was wholly unlike him.

"You practically told me to get me to a nunnery. I've often wondered—" Mélanie could almost see Miss Talbot stretch out a white-gloved hand and then let it fall. "You're right, we can't go back to the people we used to be. The girl I was in those long-ago summers believed in fairy tales. A prince who'd place a slipper on my foot and take me to his beautiful, safe castle in his mythical kingdom."

"You never needed a slipper to make you a princess."

"It wasn't the princess part I wanted. It was the prince. But now I know such endings don't exist."

"Honoria." The wood and leather of the chair creaked, as though Charles had leaned forward. "If something's the matter, you know you can turn to me, don't you? No questions asked, nothing expected, no secrets revealed. I'll do whatever's in my power to help you."

"Dear Charles. You're far superior to a prince with a glass slipper. But some plights are more complicated than what one finds in a storybook."

"For God's sake, Noria, if you're in some sort of trouble—"

"Nothing you can do anything about. Just go on believing in the girl I was, Charles. And look at me sometimes the way you're looking at me now. When no one else can see."

Intimacy pulsed through the air. Mélanie knew with absolute certainty that something had passed between her husband and Honoria Talbot. Images raced across her mind. Fingers twining together. A hand brushing tousled hair. Lips against a hand, a cheek, a forehead. A mouth claiming another.

She turned away, betraying tears stinging her blackened lashes, and cursed herself for a bloody fool.

Gisèle ducked into an alcove on the edge of the dance floor and tugged at the folds of her blond lace scarf, which had become hopelessly twisted. She never could get it to lie smooth, the way some women did. Women like Honoria Talbot and Charles's intimidatingly lovely foreign-born wife.

She'd very nearly made a hideous mistake with Evie just now and told her things she had no business revealing. It was difficult, keeping secrets all the time. How on earth had Charles managed when he was having adventures on the Peninsula and no doubt telling lies to everyone he met? Just one evening of pretending to feel and think things that were alien to her left her with a pounding headache and a hollow ache in the pit of her stomach.

Or perhaps that was the number of glasses of champagne she'd swallowed. It had seemed to help at the time, but now she felt the alcohol churning in her insides. She pressed her face against the cool plaster of a convenient pillar.

Picking her way through the tangle of people and relationships at Glenister House was as difficult as negotiating the yew hedge maze on her grandfather's Irish estate. But tonight she'd swear there was something more. Some tension she couldn't explain rippling beneath the polished surface of the evening, pressing against the candle-warmed air like the heaviness that warns of a thunderstorm about to break.

A man lurched into the alcove, shoes thudding unsteadily against the marble floor. Gisèle drew back against the pillar. The man clutched a potted palm. "Sorry," he muttered, "I didn't—oh. It's you, Gelly."

His voice was thickened and his face shadowed, but Gisèle recognized William Talbot, Earl Quentin, Lord Glenister's elder son. "Hullo, Quen," she said, stepping away from the pillar.

"Hiding from the gorgons, child?" Quen's eyes glittered in the shadows. He always seemed one step short of punching his fist through a window.

"Only trying to recover my defenses." Gisèle peered at him. Perhaps it was a trick of the light, but his face looked green. "Are you all right?"

He gave a strangled laugh. "'All right' is a relative term, but I assure you I'm perfectly—" His face turned chartreuse. "Oh, Christ, I'm not. Profoundest apologies." He pushed past her and proceeded to be sick into the potted palm.

The smell nearly made her vomit herself. Her instinct was to run, but the memory of the boy who'd rescued her favorite doll from the duck pond made her stand her ground. She put a tentative hand on his back. He was shuddering as though he had the fever. "It's the champagne," she said. "I don't feel very well myself."

"It's the champagne and the claret and the brandy and all the damn—" He retched again.

"There you are, Gelly, thank goodness, I've—" Evie swept into the alcove and went stock still. "Oh, Quen, you're foxed."

"I should think so." He straightened up, gripping the palm tree for support. "How else am I supposed to get through a family party?"

Evie tugged a handkerchief from her puffed sleeve and wiped his mouth. "You couldn't have waited until afterward?"

"After—oh, right. Forgot this is an important night."

Gisèle looked from one to the other. "Important how?"

Quen stared at her with eyes that suddenly seemed to focus. "Lord, infant, they haven't told you?"

Something in his gaze made Gisèle go as cold as if a champagne bucket of ice had been dumped over her head. "Told me what?"

"Oh, God, you'll never—" Another spasm of retching brought him to his knees.

Evie bent over her cousin, arms round his shoulders. "Gelly, could you find one of the footmen and ask him to have coffee sent into the book room as soon as possible?"

"But what—"

"Quen doesn't know what he's saying. *Please,* Gelly."

Gisèle fled.

Chapter 2

Mélanie held the spider-gauze skirt of her gown in one hand and gripped her beaded lace shawl taut with the other to prevent telltale rustling as she retreated along the mirror-hung corridor. Mercifully, the thin soles of her satin slippers made barely a whisper of sound on the oak floorboards.

Her mind went back to an airless sitting room in the British Embassy in Lisbon, choked with the heat of a December fire. The embassy chaplain, hurrying through the wedding service with the speed of one eager for his dinner. Charles's firm, level voice as he repeated his marriage vows, his fingers steady on her own as he slid the hastily purchased gold band onto her finger, his hand neat and even when he signed his name to the marriage lines.

Their marriage had begun in a crucible of war and personal turmoil. Even now she could not be entirely sure of his reasons for offering for her. And God knew her own reasons for entering into the marriage had been less than pure.

In Lisbon and war-torn Spain, in the thickly layered intrigue of the Congress of Vienna, in Brussels before Waterloo and Paris afterward, they had been consumed by the needs of the moment. To think of the future, let alone plan for it, had been an impossible luxury. As for the past, it had been a minefield round which they'd both learned to tread with caution, respecting each other's scars. Charles had volunteered little more than cursory details about his family and friends and childhood. With more than enough reasons to avoid discussing her own past, she hadn't pressed him.

But now they had stepped back into the warp and weft of Charles's old life. The life of a man who was grandson to a duke, educated at Harrow and Oxford, connected to half the noble families in England and Scotland. A life of alliances stretching back generations, of unwritten rules and uncrossable boundaries. A life that Honoria Talbot exemplified. A life to which Mélanie was alien in every sense of the word.

Without Charles, she would be alone in this strange world. She needed him, she who had once prided herself on not needing anyone. Words like *love* belonged to fairy tales and lending library novels and balconies in Verona. Was it folly to want to believe that something more than desperation and chivalry, physical need and yellowed marriage lines bound them together?

A laugh sounded from one of the anterooms off the corridor, followed by a stir of fabric and a furtive sigh that was unmistakable in its implications. Some of the guests had stolen away from the ball for reasons other than talk. Mélanie hurried on and then realized she should have reached the ballroom by now. She must have taken a wrong turn in the maze of corridors. A faint whisper of music drifted through the air, but she wasn't sure of the direction.

"Don't tell me my son has abandoned you. I'd say I thought I'd raised him better, but I'm afraid I can take little credit or blame for his upbringing."

Her father-in-law, Kenneth Fraser, stood ten paces away. He must have emerged from one of the rooms that lined the corridor, though she hadn't heard any sound until he spoke.

The cold glass of the mirrors that lined the corridor threw their reflections back at them—a black-coated man with graying hair and a bearing that radiated power, a pale, dark-haired woman in a silver dress. Fraser's fine-featured face was set with its habitual mask of sardonic amusement. One of the tapers in the sconces on the left wall had gone out, leaving him half in light, half in shadow. Fitting. In a fanciful mood, she'd have called him equal parts Sun King and Prince of Darkness.

"I may be new to London society, Mr. Fraser," she said, "but I know very well that a husband and wife are not expected to live in each other's pockets."

"To say the least. I'll wager there's more intrigue at a London ball than you've found in all your years in Continental diplomatic circles." His gaze seemed to slice through the gauze and satin of her gown and the linen of her chemise to expose the flesh beneath. "You've learned the ways of London society very quickly, my dear. You have the look of a daughter of the game."

She lifted her chin a fraction of an inch but otherwise held herself still. "What game is that, Mr. Fraser?"

"The oldest game of all, Mélanie. And the most enjoyable." He strolled toward her with the easy confidence of a roué striding across a courtesan's boudoir. "I'm sure you have all the requisite talents to excel at it. You're obviously an excellent actress. You play the devoted wife to perfection."

She gave him a smile designed to be as hard and brilliant as the mirrors. "That depends on whether or not one considers it acting to portray the truth convincingly."

"You see what I mean? You're superb." He offered her his arm. "May I escort you back to the ballroom? It's a sad shame for you to hide yourself away from your admirers."

She didn't allow herself to hesitate before she set her ivory-silk-gloved fingers lightly on the black superfine of his sleeve. They walked a few paces down the corridor in silence.

"I'd give a great deal to know why you married him," Fraser said.

"If you have to ask that, Mr. Fraser, you don't know your son."

"Ah, there you speak the truth, my dear. And I know you even less. But then in the final analysis, who's to say why anyone chooses a marriage partner? Often even the person's spouse is quite in ignorance."

"Oh, Mr. Fraser," Mélanie said. "Sometimes ignorance is bliss."

"One must find bliss in marriage somehow." His gaze drifted over her face and throat and settled on a point just above the twists of silver satin at the neck of her gown. She felt it like a rapier point against her skin. "I advise you to remain in the ballroom, my dear. I think you'll find the events that are about to transpire to be of interest."

They stepped through a blue damask-draped archway into a long, barrel-ceilinged white-and-gold chamber. The room was an assault on the senses. The brilliance of burning wax tapers and sparkling crystals, the lively melody of a country dance, the smell of perfumes and oils and fresh-cut flowers.

Gauzy pastel gowns, feathered headdresses, ringleted hair, and sober coats of coal black and midnight blue swirled on the dance floor. Strange to see so few redcoated officers, riflemen in green, staff officers in sky blue. Mélanie was reminded, with a jolt that was almost physical, that she was no longer in Lisbon or Vienna or Brussels or Paris. The war was over and danger had supposedly been left behind on the Continent. This unfamiliar world was home now. It was supposed to be safe. Though holding her father-in-law's arm, she didn't feel safe.

The Marquis of Glenister, Honoria Talbot's uncle, was leaning against one of the columns on the gallery that ran round the top of the ballroom. His silver-streaked dark head was bent close to that of a fair-haired lady in a peach gown who was young enough to be his daughter. Lord Glenister and Kenneth Fraser had been friends since their school days at Harrow and were said to have shared every manner of debauchery. According to rumor, Glenister had once bought a mistress from Kenneth Fraser for the sum of five thousand pounds. The lady and her husband were said to have been witnesses to the contract.

"There you are, Kenneth. Might have known I'd find you with a pretty girl on your arm."

The speaker was a tall lady with a thin, imperious face, sharp blue eyes, and a quantity of auburn hair piled high on her head and adorned with three orange ostrich feathers and a diamond clip that would have kept a company of soldiers in rations for a month.

"My daughter-in-law, Mrs. Charles Fraser," Kenneth said. "Lady Winchester. A friend of my late wife's."

The woman's gaze swept over Mélanie as though she were inspecting a horse she suspected of being unsound. "So you're the gel who finally brought Charles Fraser up to scratch. I always thought his taste ran to blondes. French, aren't you?"

"My father was French. My mother was Spanish." That much of her history was the truth.

"So confusing, these Continental alliances," Lady Winchester murmured in a tone that implied if foreigners had the least sense of breeding they would confine themselves to marriage partners of the same nationality. "And your father was——?"

The inevitable question. The question that defined one's place in this world. "The Comte de Saint-Vallier," Mélanie said, the lie coming easily to her tongue.

Lady Winchester pursed her rouged lips. "Haven't heard the name. But then I understand they do things differently in France. Nearly everyone has a title."

Kenneth had been drawn away by a gentleman in a snuff-stained coat. Mélanie gave Lady Winchester a smile that had all the sweetness of lemon ice. "Not quite everyone. Or perhaps we wouldn't have had a revolution."

"Outspoken, aren't you? Continental manners won't do in London, you know. You met Charles in Lisbon?"

"In Spain. In the Cantabrian Mountains. Charles came to my rescue after my maid and I had been stranded."

"My word. I would never have thought to find Charles Fraser taking part in such scenes of high romance. You obviously have quite an influence on him, my dear."

Lady Winchester's expression suggested that this influence was no doubt compounded of black magic and a thorough knowledge of the writings of the Marquis de Sade. Mélanie summoned up her best demure Desdemona look. "I'm afraid I can't take credit for Charles's adventurous side. It was well entrenched before I met him."

Lady Winchester unfurled her fan and wielded it vigorously. "I understand you've already managed to produce two children."

She knew, Mélanie realized, looking into Lady Winchester's hard gaze. She knew precisely how many months into their marriage their son had been born. She thought Mélanie had worked her wiles to capture a wealthy husband. If only she were aware of the full truth.

Lady Winchester closed the ivory sticks of her fan with a snap.

"The Frasers aren't an easy family to marry into, as my friend Elizabeth, Charles's mother, learned to her cost. You should—"

"Mélanie. I've been looking all over for you. Pray excuse us, Lady Winchester. I promised to present Mrs. Fraser to the Duke of Devonshire."

It was David Mallinson, Viscount Worsley, Charles's closest friend and a blessed voice of comfort and sanity. He bowed to Lady Winchester, took Mélanie's arm, and steered her toward an ivory satin settee set in an alcove between two columns. "I haven't the least idea where the Duke of Devonshire's got to. Do you mind? It was the only story I could think of to extricate you from that gorgon."

"I'm eternally grateful." Mélanie squeezed his hand and smiled into his kind brown eyes. "Thank you, David."

David grimaced. "It's the least I could do. I must apologize for Lady Winchester. I always suspected she wanted to catch Charles for her own daughter. When someone connected to as many powerful families as Charles suddenly comes home with a wife it's bound to make people curious. Particularly—"

"When the wife is the penniless daughter of a minor French aristocrat who lost what little fortune he had in the Revolution."

David's well-cut features twisted with discomfort. "That's not it. Not with everyone. But it would be foolish to pretend people don't think—"

"That Charles ought to have married a nice British girl."

"Anyone who really cares for Charles only wants him to be happy."

Which would be a bit more comforting if she could be confident that Charles *was* happy. Mélanie forced her gloved fingers to unclench and cast a sidelong glance at her husband's best friend. David, she acknowledged with a pang as sharp as a knife cut, knew Charles far better than she did herself. David was also Honoria Talbot's cousin. His father, Miss Talbot's mother's brother, shared her guardianship with Lord Glenister, her father's brother. If anyone could explain what Charles and Miss Talbot had been to each other, no doubt David could.

"Very unsporting of him to leave you to fend for yourself," David said in a lighter voice. "Where's he got to?"

Mélanie swallowed. "He's in the library."

"Of course, where else? I'd have sought refuge there myself, but I had to help Evie deal with Quen. He was dipping a bit deep and he ended up being sick into one of the potted palms."

"You're a kind cousin, David."

David shook his head. "We're a hopeless tangle, aren't we? Talbots and Mallinsons and Frasers. It must give you a headache trying to sort us all out."

"It's not nearly as complicated as diplomatic protocol at the Congress of Vienna." The country dance had ended and the musicians were striking up a waltz. Mélanie was swept up in a memory of waltzing with Charles at a ball given by Count Stackelberg in Vienna. She still couldn't say what made that night different from any other—the haze of champagne, the blur of candlelight, the seductive strains of the music. She'd looked at Charles and for a mad moment they'd both been transported to a world of girls in white muslin frocks, ardent young men just down from university, and tentative, breathless first kisses in moon-drenched gardens. Then they'd laughed, a little too quickly, because such a world was so wholly alien to them and what they meant to each other.

Mélanie spread her hands in her silken lap and glanced at David. "You and Charles must have seen a lot of the Glenister House children growing up." Even as she framed the words, she hated herself for being weak enough to need to ask the question.

"Good Lord, yes, we were all in and out of each other's houses. Charles and I taught Quen and Val how to hold a cricket bat, when we were ten and eleven and they couldn't have been more than four and five." David's gaze fastened on a young man with artfully tousled blond hair and a girl with golden brown ringlets who were waltzing together closer than some lovers embraced. The young man was Lord Valentine Talbot, Lord Glenister's younger son. The girl was Charles's sister, Gisèle.

"Val's as bad as Quen in his own way," David muttered. "I'll have to say something to him. Gisèle's only nineteen."

Mélanie studied her young sister-in-law. Gisèle's gaze was fixed on Val Talbot with an expression that seemed to be equal parts adoration and defiance. "I imagine interference will only make her more determined."

David shot her an appraising look, his level dark brows raised.

"Charles was right. You're good at reading people. Gisèle's always had a willful streak. Quite the opposite of Honoria."

"I don't suppose you and Charles taught Miss Talbot how to play cricket."

"Hardly. Honoria knew exactly what was proper even then. She and Charles used to play and sing duets, though."

Memories of joining Charles at the pianoforte in a deliciously flirtatious rendition of "Il core vi dono" tugged at her mind. "I should have guessed. Miss Talbot has a lovely voice."

David nodded. "I remember one afternoon in Lisbon—"

"Miss Talbot was in Lisbon?"

David's gaze darted over her face. "Honoria, Val, and I went to Portugal on a visit with my father six years ago. Before you came to Lisbon."

Miss Talbot would have been seventeen, as lovely as she was now but less polished and self-assured. Charles would have been three-and-twenty, perhaps not yet quite as self-contained or numbed to feeling as the man Mélanie had married. "That explains it," she said. "They're better friends than I would have expected if they hadn't seen each other since childhood."

"Look, Mélanie, I don't know what you've heard—"

"What is there for me to have heard?" The question slipped from her lips with a woeful lack of finesse.

"Nothing." David squeezed her hand. "You said it yourself. We all grew up together. It was only natural—" He broke off, his fair skin flushed with color.

"That everyone expected Charles to marry Miss Talbot one day?"

"People are always trying to marry off their children to each other," David said.

When you told me that one day I'd meet the right man, you also said that you'd bring me nothing but unhappiness. Do you remember when you said that? And where?

"Mélanie." David's fingers tightened on her wrist for a moment. "Sometimes the past is best left in the past. For everyone's sake."

His words quickened the alarm that had been coiling inside her all evening. Sometimes the past couldn't be left in the past, or one had no hope for the future.

"Escaping to a quiet corner, wife? You're picking up bad habits from me." Her husband had materialized from the crowd and was leaning against one of the pillars beside the settee. Like his father, he could move soundlessly when he chose. Mélanie suppressed a start, as though he'd caught her with a lover rather than his oldest friend.

"You're impossible," David told Charles. "Where have you been? It's one thing for a bachelor to hide from the throng. It's another for a married man. You have responsibilities."

"On the contrary." Charles was smiling, cheerful, and to his wife quite obviously playacting. "I'm well enough versed in the matrimonial rules of engagement to know a husband isn't supposed to get in his wife's way at a ball." He met Mélanie's gaze for a moment, but the Fraser armor was well in place. He didn't appear remotely concerned or apologetic at having left her alone, but then he rarely acted protective toward her. Why should he, when she had been at great pains throughout their marriage never to let him think that she needed him?

"Oh, dear, darling." Mélanie got to her feet. "Only four and a half years and you've quite lost interest in whom I choose to flirt with. Goodness knows what I'll have to do to get your attention when we've been married a decade." She reached for Charles's champagne glass and took a sip. A blatantly proprietary gesture. It should have been beneath her.

Charles didn't seem to notice. "I hear you stopped Quen from making a scene," he said to David as he took the champagne glass back from Mélanie.

David grimaced. "I did my best. I don't know why the devil he always—"

He broke off. A sudden silence had rippled through the room and settled over the crowd. Charles raised his brows. Lord Glenister had walked halfway down the stairs. Honoria Talbot moved up the stairs to join her uncle, a slender column of white and gold.

Near the base of the stairs, Evie Mortimer stood smiling like a waxwork figure at Madame Tussaud's. She was holding Lord Quentin's arm, as though in an effort to keep him upright. Mélanie caught sight of Charles's sister in the crowd. A shadow of fear flickered across Gisèle's face. She cast a look of inquiry at Lord Valentine, who was beside her. He avoided her gaze, his own fixed steadily on his father and Miss Talbot.

"My friends," Glenister said, "the time has come for me to confess that there is another reason for our party this evening. As you know, for the past eighteen years my niece Honoria has graced Glenister House with her presence. It is hard to believe the time has gone so quickly. You must allow me a father's feelings on this happy occasion."

He paused for a moment. He might have been recovering from an attack of fatherly sentimentality or relishing the drama of the moment. Or both. "My friends, I have an announcement that it gives me great pleasure to make. Please join with me in celebrating the betrothal of my niece Honoria to my best and oldest friend, Kenneth Fraser."

The silence from the crowd in the ballroom lasted just a fraction of a second longer than one might have expected after such an announcement. Then it gave way to the requisite applause. Kenneth climbed the steps to stand beside Miss Talbot, took her hand, and raised it to his lips.

Gisèle looked as though she had only just comprehended that someone had slapped her across the face. Lord Valentine dropped a hand on her shoulder, in comfort or in warning. Lord Quentin jerked away from Miss Mortimer and lurched from the ballroom.

Closer at hand, Mélanie heard the crack of broken glass. Charles was staring straight ahead, his expression unreadable. He seemed quite unaware that he had shattered his champagne glass.

Chapter 3

A light drizzle was falling as the guests emerged from Glenister House. The flambeaux at the base of the steps let off puffs of acrid smoke, as did the pine torches carried by the linkboys to light the carriages. The departing guests huddled beneath the Ionic portico while their coachmen jostled in the street below to pull up close to the pavement.

Charles was quiet, scanning the street for their own carriage. The flickering light gleamed against the white of the handkerchief Mélanie had bound round the gash in his hand when he broke his champagne glass. He had said little since Lord Glenister's startling announcement of his father's betrothal to Honoria Talbot. Mélanie was holding his arm, but he seemed even more remote than he had in recent weeks. She had an impulse, an absurd echo of the naïve romantic girl she had never been, to press her face into the warmth of his shoulder. Instead, she pulled the swansdown-edged folds of her cloak closer about her. The night was cool for mid-June.

Long practice made her adept at catching words in a crowd. Beneath the shouts for carriages and the stamping of horse hooves and the jangle of bridles, certain phrases echoed through the night air.

"What a delicious surprise! It quite makes up for the Season being so sadly flat!"

"Never thought he'd marry again."

"Always thought Honoria Talbot would end up married to a Fraser, but Kenneth wasn't the one I had in mind . . ."

Charles tugged at her arm. Randall, their coachman, had drawn up their lacquered blue barouche a short distance down the street. They descended the steps and turned along the pavement. The other houses on the square were long since shuttered for the evening, lamps turned down and candles snuffed. The moon had gone behind a cloud, and the street was dark between the pools of lamplight. Mélanie was concentrating on keeping her footing on the rain-slick pavement when a hand shot out from the area railings and gripped a fold of her cloak.

She jerked back and reached for her pistol, but of course this was England and she didn't have a pistol with her. Charles whipped round and put himself between her and the assailant.

"Please, I don't mean any trouble." The voice was harsh and had the unmistakable lilt of a French accent. A woman in a patched brown cloak sprang up from the area steps.

Charles wrapped an arm round Mélanie and reached for his purse.

"I don't want your money." The woman's face was a pale blur beneath the hood of her cloak, but her eyes burned with the intensity of torchlight. "Are you Charles Fraser?"

"I am. You have the advantage of me, madam. You know my name but I don't know yours."

"Mine doesn't matter. I have a message for you, Diego."

Charles's arm tightened round Mélanie. Diego was an alias he'd used in his days in intelligence on the Peninsula. "A message from whom?"

"Francisco. Francisco Soro."

Another name from the past. The name of a man Mélanie had last seen in Vitoria, face black from cannon smoke, eyes glinting with a reckless love of danger that ought to have lost him his life a dozen times during the war but somehow had helped him survive instead.

The sound of a man shouting to his coachman carried through

the air from the Glenister House steps, bringing home the proximity of observers. The cloaked woman glanced round with the wariness of a frightened deer. Mélanie dropped her reticule with sufficient force that the silver filigree clasp snapped open, spilling the contents over the paving stones.

"Oh, dear. How clumsy of me." She crouched down over the scattered objects. So did Charles. So did the woman, who seemed to understand Mélanie's intention. Which she would if she'd spent any time at all round the sort of work Francisco Soro engaged in.

Charles picked up Mélanie's scent bottle and handed it to her. "How do you know Francisco?" he said. The war might be over, but the old instinct to trust no one was still in place.

The woman reached for an enamel box of lip rouge that had rolled toward the area railing. "We met in Paris."

"You're lying." Charles gathered up loose coins as he spoke. "I was in Paris myself until three months ago. Francisco would have sought me out."

"It was too dangerous."

"And now?"

"He has information for you." The woman handed Mélanie her silver nail scissors. Her hood had fallen back, revealing matted hair in an artificial shade of gold. Her face had the pert, heart-shaped prettiness of a Boucher painting, but her eyes had a hunted look and her mouth was set with fear. "He says it's important. Not just for him. For you as well."

Charles reached for a stray half crown wedged between two paving stones. "Why didn't he come to see me himself?"

"He couldn't."

"Is he ill?"

"No."

"Then why send you instead of coming himself?"

"Because someone's trying to kill him."

The words should have sounded incredible, delivered on a neat stretch of Grosvenor Square pavement, with the cream of London's *haut ton* climbing into their carriages just yards away. But in the world in which Mélanie and Charles had lived, such words were far more normal than a request for a dance or an invitation to take tea.

Charles dropped a handful of coins into the reticule in Mélanie's lap. "Who?"

"I can't—" The woman cast a sidelong glance up and down the pavement. A couple and two young girls in white were approaching on their way to their carriage. "He wants you to meet him tomorrow night at the terrace overlooking the river, off Somerset Place. Twelve o'clock."

"Take me to him now."

"No." She scrambled to her feet. The lamplight caught the blaze of terror in her eyes. "It has to be exactly like he said."

Charles sprang up. "But—"

"The Somerset Place terrace. Midnight." She whirled round and ran down the street in a swirl of dun-colored cloak and pale hair.

Charles took two steps after her, then stopped with a muttered curse.

"Mr. Fraser?" The gentleman with the wife and two daughters called out to them from beside his carriage. "Did that person accost you and your wife?"

"No, Sir Hugh." Charles reached down to help Mélanie to her feet. "My wife dropped her reticule and the lady was kind enough to help us retrieve the contents. A good evening to you."

Randall had caught sight of them and jumped down to lower the steps of the carriage. Charles handed Mélanie up and climbed in after her. Randall closed the door, and they were encased in the artificial safety of watered silk and polished mahogany and plate glass.

Mélanie leaned back against the squabs. Images of Francisco Soro raced across her mind. Passing a stolen dispatch to Charles beneath the scarred wood of a tavern table. Bending over her hand with a friendly spark in his eye while rifle shots sounded not fifty feet away. Helping a wounded Charles up the steps of a ruined Spanish farmhouse. "Do you believe her?" Mélanie said, settling the folds of her cloak.

"I don't see any reason not to."

"Charles!" She swung her head round to stare at him in the shadows, as though he was one of the children and was sickening with something. Was this her rational, analytical husband talking?

"Only someone who knew me in the Peninsula would have known to call me Diego."

"For God's sake, darling, that includes French soldiers and spies of all stripes and Spaniards of every possible allegiance. They aren't all friends."

"And it's not an alias I used with everyone."

"The message could be a trap."

"Set by whom? A French agent angry because they lost the war? A Spanish Liberal who thinks our government abandoned them? An *afrancesado* who wishes the French were still in power in Spain?"

"That doesn't exhaust the possibilities, but it's certainly a start."

"Don't overdramatize, Mel. I admit there are plenty of people with cause to be angry at our government, but no one's likely to come seeking revenge on me. I wasn't important enough."

Mélanie's fingers closed on the velvet folds of the cloak. This was dangerous ground to be treading with Charles, but she should be used to it by now. She just had to remember to avoid the obvious traps. "Don't sell yourself short, darling. You were more important than you'll admit."

"I may have had my uses during the war, but the war's over."

She flinched inwardly. "The war isn't over for everyone, Charles."

"I owe Francisco my life. I have to meet him."

"I wasn't arguing that you shouldn't. Only that we should take precautions."

She felt the force of the glance he shot at her.

"Don't look at me like that, Charles. There's not a chance in hell I'm letting you go without me."

He laughed, a warm, genuine sound. "I'm relieved to hear it. Francisco was always more inclined to listen to reason from you than me."

Mélanie released her breath. Danger had always been the common ground in their marriage. So much easier than negotiating the thorny briers of day-to-day life. "What do you think Francisco was doing in Paris?" she said, falling back into the comfortable rhythm of investigation as though she had pulled on a pair of well-worn boots after days in too-tight slippers.

"That depends on whom he's working for at the moment. He's always been a bit elastic about which side he'll take. He's the sort of man who thrives in war and doesn't know what to do with himself in peacetime."

"When he wrote to us in September he said he was in Andalusia. Which doesn't mean that's actually where he was."

"Quite. Francisco wasn't overfond of King Ferdinand. I could see him leaving Spain for France if excitement beckoned. If he got mixed up with Bonapartists he might have felt it wasn't safe to tell me as a British diplomat. But as to what the devil brought him to England and why his life would be in danger—"

"Whoever the woman is, she was terrified. You could see it in her eyes. And Francisco doesn't panic easily."

"Quite the reverse. He's absurdly confident in the most precarious of situations." Charles's voice was thoughtful, but there was a hard edge underneath. "That's one thing I'm sure of."

"What?"

"If Francisco says someone's trying to kill him, the danger is real."

The carriage drew up before the house in South Audley Street that David Mallinson had hired for them before they returned to Britain. After three months, it still felt more alien than their myriad of Continental lodgings. Even the smell, a peculiarly English combination of lemon oil, lavender, and beeswax, jarred as they stepped into the entrance hall.

Michael, the footman, a boy from Charles's grandfather's estate in Ireland, was dozing on the settle by the door. Charles touched him on the shoulder and told him to lock up. They lit candles from the Agrand lamp on the hall table, climbed the stairs, and peeked into their children's rooms. Jessica, six months, lay on her back in her cradle, a tiny fist curled against the embroidered coverlet, downy head flopped to one side. Colin, almost four, was sprawled beneath his quilt, one arm flung above his head, the other stretched across the pillow. Mélanie straightened the covers. Charles patted Berowne, the family cat, who was curled up on the foot of the bed.

They closed the door softly and made their way to their bedchamber. Charles shrugged off his coat and loosened his cravat. Mélanie removed her cloak and dropped her lace shawl on a chair. The rattle of the crystal beads echoed through the quiet.

Neither of them had mentioned Charles's father's betrothal to Honoria Talbot. The fact of it hung over the room, a heavier burden than tomorrow night's rendezvous with Francisco Soro. She could be no more certain of how Charles felt about the betrothal than she could of the reasons Francisco claimed his life was in danger. As for Charles, he was doing what he always did when he didn't want to talk about something. Pretending it hadn't happened.

"Thank God," Mélanie said. "At least this proves you don't expect me to dwindle into a conformable wife."

"I never wanted a conformable wife, and well you know it."

"Dearest," she said before she could think better of it, "you never wanted a wife at all."

"With my family history?" Charles picked up a tinderbox to light the lamps. "I'd have been mad to do so."

The air between them seemed to thicken, as though a host of unspoken words had rushed in to fill the silence. "I should look at your hand." Mélanie moved to the cabinet where she kept her medical supplies.

A flint sparked against steel. "Leave it, Mel, it's only a scratch."

"Even scratches can fester." She crossed back to him, carrying a flask of brandy, scissors, and a roll of lint.

Charles grimaced but held still while she unwrapped the makeshift bandage. The handkerchief was matted with dried blood, and an angry red gash stood out against his palm. "I didn't realize how bad it was," she said. "It must hurt."

"If you keep pulling at it." He winced as she dabbed at the cut with a length of brandy-soaked lint. "Quite like old times."

"If this were old times, I'd be more likely to be digging a bullet out of you. Hold still, Charles."

His gaze shifted to a hunting print on the wall opposite, a relic of the previous tenant. She snipped off a length of lint. The ticking of the gilt clock on the mantel and the patter of drizzle against the windows sounded preternaturally loud. The weight of the silence was so heavy she could feel it pressing through the thin silk of her gown and reverberating through the hollowness in her chest. The room was filled with echoes of a conversation she wasn't supposed to have heard, with ghosts of a past she didn't understand and Charles wouldn't talk about.

"Father asked me to call round at five o'clock tomorrow," Charles said, so abruptly that she nearly dropped the bandage. "I think it's the first time he's requested a private interview with me since I left Harrow."

Mélanie placed the fresh bandage over the wound. "If he wants to warn you about his betrothal, he's left it a bit late."

"I should have known he might remarry." Charles's voice was matter-of-fact, but his gaze slid away. "I don't know why the announcement took me by surprise."

Mélanie knotted the ends of the bandage. "Perhaps it's not the fact that he's remarrying so much as *who* he's marrying."

He went still for a fraction of a second. "Honoria deserves better," he said in the same careful voice. "But she's a grown woman. Presumably she knows what she's about."

Mélanie set down the scissors and the ends of lint and looked up at her husband. He returned her gaze, but his eyes had turned as impenetrable as the weathered rocks of the Scottish coast he loved so well.

At such moments, there was only one way she knew she could reach him. She wondered sometimes if such tactics cheapened what they had between them, but at the moment she hungered for any affirmation of their bond the way a battlefield amputee longs for laudanum. She curled her hand behind his neck and pressed a kiss against his throat.

A wall of flame shot up before him. Panic closed his throat. A woman screamed. He ran, stumbling through a dark, unfamiliar landscape, and caught her in his arms. She clutched him tightly, as though she was caught in an undertow. He thought it was his sister, but the hair he was stroking was a paler gold. Honoria. She lifted her head from his shoulder and looked at him, her eyes fevered with desperation, her face contorted with fear.

Someone grabbed his shoulder, trying to pull him away from her. He shook the attacker off and clutched Honoria more tightly.

"Charles." The attacker grabbed him again. "Darling, wake up."

He loosed one arm to strike his assailant, but some part of his brain registered that the voice belonged to his wife. He opened his eyes onto darkness. He was sitting up in bed, his heart pounding, his skin slick with sweat, his arms wrapped over his chest, his fingers digging into his bare flesh.

Mélanie touched his arm with cool, steady fingers. He flinched away from her all-knowing gaze. He couldn't bear to have her understand something he couldn't make sense of himself. Not to mention the risk of revealing secrets that weren't his to share.

"I'm all right." He hunched forward. He was chilled to the bone despite the sweat drying on his skin.

He pressed his shaking fingers against his temples. Usually Mélanie was the one with nightmares. Usually he held her. For the first time he wondered if she ever found being held an intrusion.

Mélanie said nothing and didn't attempt to touch him again, but he could feel her concerned gaze on him. He turned his head and managed a smile. "Lobster patties and whisky. Always a fatal combination. It's a wonder my nightmares weren't worse."

In the shadows, her gaze moved over him the way she checked for signs of physical damage over his protests that he was unhurt.

He touched his fingertips to her face. Difficult to believe he'd been kissing it only a few hours before. He flinched again, inwardly, at the memory. He might not be a paragon of a husband, but he'd like to think he was above using his wife to exorcise his own demons. He'd failed at that tonight. He'd buried himself in her heat and let the touch of her fingers and lips and the taste of her skin turn his blood to fire, seeking an oblivion that was all too temporary. "I'm all right, truly. Go back to sleep, Mel. Sorry I woke you."

The Irish linen and Portuguese silk coverlet rustled as she lay back against the pillows. He lay down beside her, resisting the impulse to retreat to the far edge of the bed. The sliver of black between the curtains told that dawn was a long way off. He listened to the even sound of his wife's breathing and tried to sort through the question of why he had been dreaming about the woman who was about to become his stepmother.

Chapter 4

Mélanie stared at the jumble of gilt-edged vellum on the writing desk before her. Invitations requesting the pleasure of Mr. and Mrs. Charles Fraser's presence at balls, routs, receptions, dinners, musicales, breakfasts, and fêtes champêtres. Written in the flowing, governess-trained hand of ladies she had never met, half of whom were connected to one branch of Charles's family or the other, the other half of whom had no doubt rolled hoops round Hyde Park with Charles's mother or played dolls with Gisèle or Mozart duets with Charles himself.

Charles had said that as far as he was concerned she could pick the ones she wanted to attend or decline the lot of them. But she knew it wasn't that simple. Charles was in Parliament now, and entertaining and being entertained were an important part of a political career. The part that was supposed to be managed by the politician's wife.

She glanced at the hearthrug where Colin was building a block tower. Jessica, propped against a cushion, watched him with a rapt gaze.

She and the children were in what was optimistically called the library, a glorified name for a back downstairs parlor lined with bookcases and now also filled with crates of the books they hadn't been able to fit on the shelves. As lady of the house she should choose a decorous room on the first floor where she could do her correspondence, but she found the musty smell of the books and the chaotic jumble a great comfort, familiar from years of living in cramped quarters.

Jessica snatched up a bright red block and tried to stuff it in her mouth. Fortunately it was too big for her to swallow. Colin reached for the block. Jessica screamed. Half the blocks fell over.

"Mummy!" Colin said.

"I know it's frustrating, darling. Let her have that one and move the tower away a bit. She can't crawl yet."

Colin began to shift the blocks away from his now smiling sister. "When's Daddy coming back? He said he'd read us a story."

"And I'm sure he won't forget. He'll be home before dinner. He had to see his father."

Mélanie glanced at the mantel clock. Charles's interview with Kenneth Fraser was in half an hour's time. Charles had left the house after swallowing a hasty cup of coffee this morning and stayed out the whole day. Neither of them had got much rest the night before. Charles had tossed and turned and kicked at the coverlet and muttered unintelligible phrases and finally broken out in a cold sweat of terror. He'd jerked away from her proffered comfort as though she'd struck him. For the remainder of the night, he'd lain stock-still, trying to control his breathing so he wouldn't disturb her. She knew, because she'd been doing precisely the same thing.

She forced her attention back to the invitations. The rules of social intercourse had been freer on the war-torn Continent. The British *ton* was uncharted territory, and she was woefully ignorant of the rules of engagement.

A rap sounded at the door, and Michael stepped into the room. "Miss Talbot has called, madam." His shoulders were punctiliously straight, but his dark gaze was warm with sympathy. "Are you at home?"

Mélanie cast a swift glance round the room. Her first instinct was to have Miss Talbot shown into the drawing room, but on reflection she would far rather greet Charles's old friend—or whatever else she was—on her own territory. She had five minutes to twitch her sarcenet skirt straight, rub at the ink on her nails, smooth Colin's hair, and scoop Jessica into her arms before Michael announced, "Miss Talbot."

Honoria Talbot swept into the room with a whisper of violet and hyacinth and a stir of jaconet muslin and primrose satin. Her face broke into a smile that sparkled with just the right amount of informality bounded by good breeding. "I was hoping to meet the youngest members of the Fraser family."

"My son, Colin, and my daughter, Jessica. This is Miss Talbot, Colin." And then, because Colin was going to find out soon in any case, Mélanie added, "She's going to marry your grandfather."

Colin, who had been introduced to the Duke of Wellington, the Crown Prince of the Netherlands, Talleyrand, Metternich, and the Duchess of Richmond, stepped forward and bowed. "Does that mean you'll be my grandmama?"

Miss Talbot laughed and crouched down to his level, heedless of the way she was crushing her flounced skirt. "I suppose it does, but I'm afraid I'm still getting used to being a wife, let alone a grandmama, so perhaps you'd best call me Honoria."

"Noria," Colin repeated. A smile broke across his face. Apparently Miss Talbot's charms were effective on three generations of Fraser men.

Miss Dudley, Colin's blessedly efficient governess-nurse, arrived to take the children into the garden, and Michael brought in a tea tray. Mélanie and Miss Talbot settled themselves on the green velvet sofa before the fireplace.

Miss Talbot began to undo the pearl buttons on her limerick gloves. "What lovely children. You must be so proud. I believe Colin has Charles's eyes and mouth."

Colin couldn't look remotely like Charles except by sheer luck. Miss Talbot was either being exquisitely tactful or sending a particularly effective dart in Mélanie's direction.

Mélanie lifted the teapot, which had a chip in the spout from one of their various moves. "Milk or lemon?"

"Lemon. And two sugars. I have a shocking sweet tooth." Miss Talbot accepted the cup and took a graceful sip. "It seems so odd to think of having children of my own, though I've wanted them for such a long time." She set the cup and saucer down, barely rattling the bone china, and turned her Wedgwood-blue gaze full on Mélanie's face. "There's no sense in pretending. Last night must have come as a shock, especially to Charles."

Mélanie reached for the milk jug. "It was certainly a surprise."

"I thought about warning him. I couldn't begin to find the words. So I took the coward's way out." Miss Talbot smoothed her gloves in her lap. "I own to a craven relief that Charles isn't at home."

"He's gone to see his father."

"Today?" Her fingers tightened on the gloves. Her diamond betrothal ring caught the light from the windows. "I didn't realize Kenneth—Mr. Fraser—would tell him so soon."

"Tell him?" Mélanie set down the milk jug, splattering white droplets over the satinwood table and silver-rimmed saucer.

Miss Talbot laid the gloves atop her shell-shaped reticule. "I wish—but it isn't my place. Only do be kind to Charles when he returns—oh, but that's nonsense. I'm sure you're always kind. And I'm sure he'll tell you directly. You seem so admirably devoted."

Mélanie took a sip of delicately scented tea, longing for café au lait. "I'm sure Charles will tell me whatever he wishes to." She held out a plate of biscuits.

Miss Talbot accepted a biscuit, but set it on her saucer untouched. "I do hope we can be friends. It's bound to be awkward. I'm sure you know that Charles and his father aren't on the terms of intimacy one would hope for between a father and son."

"You have the makings of a diplomat, Miss Talbot."

"Perhaps it's presumptuous of me, but I hope in some small way I can help to put things right between Charles and Mr. Fraser. I don't know the whole of it, of course—no doubt he's told you more. But I do know it was dreadfully hard on all of them when Lady Elizabeth—Charles's mother—died. It could hardly fail to be so, especially considering the *way* she—" Miss Talbot's gaze skimmed over Mélanie's face. "Oh, dear Lord. He hasn't told you?"

The weight of unmade confidences pressed against Mélanie's chest. "Only that his mother died just before he left Oxford. I assumed it was illness or an accident."

"Charles doesn't make confidences easily. But I was sure—usually he'll confide in those he's closest to—but then you were abroad, away from the family. It must have seemed easiest to him to ignore it." Miss Talbot reached for her cup. "When I was a little girl, I thought Lady Elizabeth Fraser was the most beautiful woman in the world. I remember her coming into the nursery to say good night to us once during a house party in Scotland. She was wearing a dress embroidered with silver acorns and a diamond tiara. She looked like a fairy princess. But her marriage to Mr. Fraser wasn't happy. She used to have dreadful bouts of the blue devils and then at other times she'd be quite giddy and—well, I don't suppose the rest matters and I hate to repeat gossip." The little silver teaspoon trembled in Miss Talbot's fingers. "Lady Elizabeth didn't die of illness or an accident. She shot herself in the head a week before Christmas when Charles was nineteen."

Mélanie's images of her husband's childhood shifted and tumbled in her head. She'd guessed, from his careful reticence, that his mother's death was still a raw pain, but not the full extent of the reason. "Dear God."

"Charles's brother—Edgar—was in the room with her when she did it. I don't know the particulars, but I know that he and Charles haven't been the friends they once were since."

Edgar was one of the few members of Charles's family Mélanie had met in the early days of her marriage. A soldier in Wellington's army, he'd been in and out of Lisbon on leave, in Brussels before Waterloo, and now was stationed in Paris, where Charles and Mélanie had lived themselves until a few months ago. Edgar had welcomed Mélanie to the family with laughing good humor and was a devoted uncle to Colin and Jessica, but he and Charles always treated each other with careful constraint. Mélanie, used to being able to read people, was baffled by the relationship between the Fraser brothers. Miss Talbot's revelations went some way toward explaining it. "It must have been hell for all of them."

Miss Talbot nodded. "Charles finished up at Oxford and then took a post as an attaché and went off to Lisbon. Gisèle was only eight. She went to live with Frances Dacre-Hammond, Lady Elizabeth's sister. I suppose the last thing any of them dreamed was that Mr. Fraser would marry again one day."

"I'm sure they all want their father to be happy."

Miss Talbot's mouth curved with unexpected irony. "Now who's talking like a diplomat, Mrs. Fraser?" She set her tea down again. This time the spoon clattered against the saucer. "Does Charles despise me?"

"I can't imagine why he would do so."

"I don't think I've become the woman he thought I could be."

"Charles isn't one to pass judgment on anyone."

"No. That's what I—that's why his good opinion matters so much to me." Miss Talbot reached for her gloves and reticule. "You're a lucky woman, Mrs. Fraser. There aren't many men like Charles."

"And his father?" Mélanie said before she could think better of it.

Miss Talbot smoothed on her gloves, one finger at a time. "Kenneth Fraser is the choice I've made. For better or worse."

Chapter 5

Charles paused beside the black metal of the Berkeley Square railing, beneath the spring-green late-afternoon shade of the plane trees. A nursemaid and two small boys were descending the steps from one of the houses, and a smart yellow racing curricle with a showy pair of bays was drawn up near the pavement. Otherwise, the square was empty, most of the residents no doubt out paying calls or making a circuit of Hyde Park at the fashionable hour of five o'clock.

He stared at his father's house, to which he'd been summoned the evening before. The house of which Honoria would soon be mistress. Smooth walls of gray Portland stone, graceful ivory moldings, lacy filigree lampposts framing a polished front door. Despite the classical elegance of the pediments and columns, despite the delicate fanlight and the greenery spilling from the window boxes on the first floor, it had the look of a fortress.

He'd never thought of it as home, not like Dunmykel, the estate in Scotland, which had been in his blood since boyhood. The Berkeley Square house had been the mysterious place to which his parents vanished after their infrequent visits to their children in Scotland. On rare childhood stays in London he had felt like an unbidden guest, curious about the life in this mysterious place but under no illusion that he belonged and not quite sure he was welcome.

Which, of course, was completely irrelevant now that he was nearly thirty, a husband and father himself, gone from his father's roof for nearly ten years. Yet as he climbed the sand-scoured steps and rang the bell, he couldn't shake the sensation of powerlessness, as familiar and unchanging as cambric tea in the nursery. In a few hours, he and Mélanie were to meet with Francisco Soro, but in its own way the interview with his father promised as much danger as whatever Francisco was about to drag them into.

Most of the servants he'd known as a boy were long gone, but the footman on duty recognized him from his handful of visits in the three months he'd been back in Britain. "Mr. Fraser's in the study, sir. If—"

"Thank you." Charles handed the footman his hat and gloves. "I know the way."

"Yes, sir, but he's with—"

"Your sister." The cool tenor voice came from the hall beyond. A golden-haired figure rose from one of the velvet benches, a newspaper rustling in his hand.

"Hullo, Val." Charles walked toward Lord Glenister's younger son. "What the devil are you doing here?"

"I drove Gisèle round in my curricle. Your father wanted to see her." Val tossed the newspaper onto the bench. "Did you think you were the only one of his children he'd summoned?"

"I long since gave up trying to puzzle out what Father might or might not do."

Val regarded him, arms folded across his light blue coat and striped silk waistcoat. "Strange to think this farce of a marriage is going to make us—what? Stepcousins once removed? Of course, to all intents and purposes Honoria's a sister to me, which means to all intents and purposes I'll be your stepuncle. You'll have to start showing me some respect."

"What odds on hell freezing over?" Charles said with his pleasantest smile.

"A few days ago, I'd have given those same odds on the chances of Princess Icicle marrying your father. I swear, I think she accepted him because he's the one man in London we'd all be shocked at her getting herself leg-shackled to."

"Honoria doesn't do things simply to shock people."

A cold smile curved Val's mouth. "So sure you know her, Charles? After all these years?"

"Val, I'm—oh, Charles." Gisèle swept into the hall and stopped short, a pair of lilac kid gloves clutched in one hand, her gaze as still and cool as a Highland stream on a windless day in January.

"Hullo, Gelly," Charles said.

She tugged on her gloves and began doing up the buttons. "I suppose Father wants to talk to you about it, too."

"*It?*"

"This ridiculous marriage of his." She walked over to Val and tucked her hand through the crook of his arm. "Not that he really explained anything. He never does."

Charles looked down at her, seeking echoes of the little girl he'd built dollhouses for and scooped up for rides on his horse. The top of Gisèle's head still barely reached his shoulder, but the round-faced, bright-eyed child was gone, replaced by a modish young woman with plucked brows, sharpened cheekbones, and fashionably cropped hair. She looked as polished and frozen as one of the porcelain dolls she'd played with as a girl. "I know it's odd," he said, "for Father to be marrying one of your friends—"

Gisèle's chin jerked up, making the ribbons on her bonnet rustle. "You've been gone a long time, Charles. Honoria and I haven't been friends for years. If we ever were."

Her green eyes were as hard as glass. Nine years of mistakes and broken promises, unspoken words and unvoiced failures hung like dust motes in the air between them. "Childhood companion, then," Charles said.

"Assuming you call being odiously superior companionship. Whatever we once were, I don't imagine Honoria's any more eager to have me for a daughter than I am to have her for a mother."

"Don't worry, my sweet." Val smiled down at her. "Now when she really makes you cross you can call her 'Mama.'"

Gisèle tilted her head back to look up at him. For a moment, the reckless glint in her eyes was so like their mother's that Charles's throat tightened with fear. "Do you know, that almost reconciles me to the whole sorry business."

Val flicked his fingers against her cheek. "I'd give a monkey to see Princess Icicle's face when you try it."

"If you're good, perhaps you will." Gisèle tightened her grip on his arm and tugged him down the hall. "You'd better not keep Father waiting, Charles."

"Val's seeing you back to Aunt Frances's?" Charles said. Gisèle had made her home with their mother's sister since their mother's death.

"No, he's sweeping me off to Gretna Green to marry me over the anvil. And before you go all glowering, that was a joke."

"Oh, I don't know," Val said. "It would drive Honoria mad if we got married first and stole her thunder."

Charles bit back a number of blistering comments that would only have made the situation worse and suppressed the impulse to wrest his sister from Val's grasp and plant Val a facer.

Gisèle paused midway down the hall and looked back at Charles over her shoulder. "I'm sure this is harder for you than it is for me, Charles. I didn't even like Honoria. Let alone love her."

She dragged Val from the house with a swish of muslin skirts. Charles swallowed, counted to ten, and strode to face his interview with his father.

As infrequent as his visits to the Berkeley Square house had been, his visits to the study had been even more rare. Only when he or his brother Edgar did something so extreme that their father couldn't ignore it, as he did most of their actions, were they called into the study to feel the sting of Kenneth Fraser's tongue, sharper than any birch rod.

"Ah. Charles. Good." Kenneth Fraser looked up from behind the mahogany ramparts of his desk. A pen and penknife lay on the blotter before him, and a stack of papers rested at his elbow. A Renaissance bronze that had the look of Cellini served as a paperweight.

Charles closed the door and advanced into the room, negotiating the Axminster carpet as though it were a battlefield. "I saw Gisèle in the hall. And Val."

"I thought you might. I suppose Gisèle could do worse, though Val's not exactly the match I'd choose for her."

"You don't fancy the thought of your daughter marrying a younger version of yourself?"

Kenneth's gaze hardened. "Even at four-and-twenty I flatter myself that I had rather more finesse than Valentine Talbot."

"He hasn't offered for her, has he?"

"Not yet. Stop scowling, Charles, you've scarcely seen Gisèle for nine years. I shouldn't think you'd have much interest in whom she married."

"And you do, sir? I never thought you had much interest in any of us."

"On the contrary. I've always been very fond of Gisèle. Sit down, Charles," Kenneth added as Charles continued to stand before the desk.

Charles glanced about the room. He couldn't remember actually sitting in it before. Two high-backed velvet chairs were drawn up by the fireplace. Instead he moved a ladderback oak chair beside the desk, less commodious but better positioned to join whatever battle his father was about to begin. "I haven't had a chance to offer you my felicitations."

Kenneth Fraser leaned back against the claret-colored damask of his armchair. "It must have been a surprise. You were always very fond of Honoria yourself, as I recall."

Charles dropped into the chair in one motion. Images from last night's nightmare teased at the corners of his mind. "Of course I'm fond of her. We grew up together."

Kenneth's mouth curved in a faint smile. "You learned the art of diplomacy well." He regarded Charles for a moment. "No questions? You must have been as surprised by the announcement as Gisèle was."

Charles's hand must have clenched, because he felt a stab of pain through the bandage on his palm. He met his father's gaze, willing his defenses not to slip. The least he owed Honoria was to protect her from the implications of the past. "You made up your mind exactly what you were going to tell me long before I walked into the room."

"Perhaps. But even I know the value of improvisation. I didn't expect to marry again. My first experience hardly left me with a favorable impression of the institution. I certainly didn't expect to marry my oldest friend's niece. But I didn't bargain on the woman Honoria would grow into." Kenneth spoke in the tone Charles had heard him use to describe a da Vinci drawing or a Fragonard oil he'd found to add to his collection. "I intend to make her happy."

"Most husbands do," Charles said, perhaps unwisely.

Kenneth raised his brows. "The voice of experience? Your own wife is a diamond of the first water. And as I've remarked before she seems genuinely devoted to you. Though I understand from amateur theatricals that she's proved herself an excellent actress."

Charles pushed himself to his feet, scraping his chair against the carpet. "You can say anything you like to me, sir. But if you're going to insult my wife or my children I'll take my leave."

"Sit down, Charles. I didn't ask you here to enact a scene out of *King Lear*."

"There's little fear of that." Charles put his hand on the chair back and let himself down against the hard wooden slats. "I won't toady to you like Goneril or Regan."

"Or profess pure devotion like Cordelia. Gisèle didn't, either. If nothing else, this family has always managed to avoid false sentiment."

Kenneth surveyed Charles with a gaze as incisive as a scalpel. Charles forced himself to sit still beneath his father's regard. "When you took yourself off to Lisbon," Kenneth said at last, "I wasn't sure we'd ever see you again. I doubted you'd have the guts to come back."

The words carried a weight that went deep beneath the surface. Far deeper, surely, than Kenneth could realize. "So did I," Charles said. "It seems I can surprise myself as well as you."

"And here you are following me into Parliament—if I may use the word 'follow' in its loosest sense." Kenneth picked up the ivory-handled penknife and tapped it against the blotter. "I have to admit you speak rather well, though I'd be the last man to agree with anything you say."

Charles fixed his gaze on the bronze sculpture, which appeared to depict a naked Triton ravishing an equally naked Nereid. He gripped her, either in conquest or supplication, while she looked away and yet curved her body into his own. "If you ever agreed with one of my speeches, I'd fear for my sanity. Or yours."

"Quite." Kenneth traced a line in the blotter with the point of the knife. "I don't expect to argue you out of your Radical convictions. Or to attempt to convince you that the ideas you advocate would destroy our way of life and lead to the sort of disaster we've seen in France. It's never been any concern of mine if you choose to make a fool of yourself. Suffice it to say, I believe I'm not overstating your views when I say you don't believe in primogeniture?"

Charles stared at the point of the penknife. "You aren't overstating my views."

"Good." Kenneth set down the knife and aligned it on the desk before him. "Then you'll have no objection to agreeing to change the entail on Dunmykel."

Charles had thought he'd armored himself against anything his father might say to him. But these words were like a dagger in the back when one has come prepared for a duel. For a moment he was robbed of speech or even breath. As with a wound, the pain would be sharper when he could fully comprehend it. "No," he said. Such a simple word, to carry away with it something he'd loved as long as he could remember.

"Just like that?" his father asked. "No objections?"

"As you pointed out, sir, I could hardly object without looking like a hypocrite." Charles drew a breath. The air scraped against his throat and lungs. "I assume you want to settle the estate on your and Honoria's first son."

"You're quick, boy, I'll give you that." Kenneth inclined his head. "Yes. I want Dunmykel to go to the first son Honoria gives me. You'll still have this house and the Italian villa and your mother's property in Bedfordshire, and your grandfather's Irish estates."

"Far more than I have any right to." That was perfectly true. It was also true that none of the other properties meant to him what Dunmykel did. But that was his problem. "It's your house after all, sir. You bought it."

Kenneth's head jerked up, and Charles saw that he had drawn blood. One wouldn't think it to look at Kenneth Fraser now, but he had come from a minor branch of the Fraser family. Orphaned early, he'd grown up as a poor relation, shuttled between various relatives. Dunmykel had been the property of Kenneth's godfather and distant cousin. Thanks to an unexpected legacy, judiciously invested, Kenneth had bought the estate after his godfather's death.

"I don't know whether your equanimity is a sign of strength or weakness," Kenneth said. "Whatever your views on inheritance, you don't want to pass the estate along to your own son?"

Charles looked into his father's eyes and forced every muscle in his body not to betray him. "My son has enough of a heritage. As do I." He pushed his chair back with deliberation. The sound of the wood scraping against the carpet echoed through the room. "If that's all, sir, I promised Colin and Jessica I'd read to them before supper." Not to mention the fact that he and Mélanie had a midnight rendezvous with Francisco Soro.

He walked from the room without sparing his father another glance. There was no way, he told himself, no way on earth, that Kenneth Fraser could have even a glimmering of the truth behind Colin's birth. Just as there was no way Kenneth could know the exact story behind Charles's sudden departure for Lisbon nine years ago or what had transpired between Charles and Honoria Talbot in that city three years later.

And yet the look in Kenneth Fraser's eyes had told Charles that his father was aware of far more than he admitted.

The cobblestones gleamed blue-black in the moonlight. The glamour of night, Mélanie thought as she and Charles made their way on foot along the broad expanse of the Strand. They had directed Randall to set them down in Tavistock Street and were now proceeding on foot the rest of the way to ensure that they weren't followed.

It was close to midnight. The banks and shops and warehouses were shuttered and bolted, but the street was crowded with carriages and pedestrians. Candle and lamplight spilled out the doors of chophouses, taverns, coffeehouses, and brothels. Tobacco smoke and snatches of ribald songs and bawdy rhymes drifted through the air. She must have heard half the score of *The Beggar's Opera* as they made their way along the street.

Instead of holding her elbow, as he would in Mayfair, Charles had his arm wrapped round her shoulders. Never let it be said her husband didn't know how to play a part. He could be far more demonstrative in the service of some charade than in his own person. He turned his head, his lips brushing her temple. "Anyone following us?"

"I don't think so, and I've been watching carefully."

They'd spent dinner discussing the best way to approach the meeting with Francisco. Charles had said nothing about his interview with his father, but she could read how difficult the meeting had been in the shadows in his eyes, the tension in the set of his jaw, the extra glass of wine he'd drunk with dinner. She'd mentioned Honoria Talbot's visit but had said nothing of Miss Talbot's cryptic hints about whatever matter Kenneth Fraser meant to broach with his son. Yet Charles's failure to confide in her was as palpable as if he'd returned home from a journey of several days and failed to kiss her.

Last night's rain had cleared the air. People were tossing dice and playing backgammon on chairs and benches pulled out onto the pavement. She was used to such scenes in Paris, Lisbon, or Vienna, but this was the first time she had been in this part of London at such an hour. The noise, the color, the smells, the need to use all one's senses quickened her blood. She hadn't realized how she'd thirsted for such activity.

They were wearing their plainest clothes, but Charles had already had to remove a quick-fingered lad's hand from his pocket. They drew to the side as two men in corduroy jackets and homespun breeches staggered out of a tavern. A few paces on, Charles pulled her into the street to avoid a man who was relieving himself against the wall. From one of the dark courts off the Strand came grunts and murmurs strikingly like the sounds she had heard from the anteroom at Glenister House the previous night. The man involved might be little different from the gentleman at Glenister House, but the lady was undoubtedly one of those who plied her wares up and down the street.

At last they turned into the quiet of Somerset Place. The breeze carried the sound of lapping water and the rank smell of the river. Mélanie gagged and turned her face away. There was a time when she would barely have noticed the stench. She must be turning into a lady.

The river terrace was in shadow, a long, dark, seemingly empty line. They'd debated having her hang back while Charles went to meet Francisco, but Charles had pointed out that Francisco wouldn't be surprised to see them both and that there'd be more risk if they separated.

Mélanie drew another breath, recovering from the first gut punch of foul air. She and Charles descended the steps to the terrace. The crumbling, moss-covered stone stretched about them, empty of life save for a small rodent that scurried toward the balustrade.

She heard the slide of metal against fabric and knew Charles had reached for the pistol in the pocket of his greatcoat. He stood still for a moment, scanning the terrace. His gaze focused on a point in the far corner, close to the river's edge. "Francisco, you bastard, come out of the shadows and tell me why we're meeting like characters in a lending library novel instead of having a whisky in my library."

His words were greeted by silence. Then a dark figure vaulted over the railing. Booted feet thudded against the stone. "Melly, my sweet, are you still following this madman into danger? I should have asked you to meet me instead of Charles."

The voice belonged unmistakably to Francisco Soro. A tension Mélanie hadn't been aware of eased from her shoulders. "I'm flattered, Francisco, especially as I'm now the mother of two. But you know Charles and I have a tiresome habit of looking out for each other. He wouldn't have let me come alone."

"To meet Francisco? I wouldn't have dared," Charles said.

"Wise man, Fraser." Francisco strode forward, kissed Mélanie's hand, and clapped Charles on the shoulder. "I think the last time we met I said I'd see you next in hell. It seems I was mistaken."

"Depending on one's definition of London," Charles said.

Francisco's gaze moved to Mélanie. His curly, coal-black hair fell over his forehead as it always had, but his face was thinner than she remembered, and his dark eyes held a wariness that was new. "With everything else, you've found time to produce another Fraser?"

"A daughter, last December. Her name is Jessica." She scanned his face for clues to the past months. "I wrote to you after she was born."

"I know. That is, I don't know. I haven't been in Andalusia as I told you." He cast a swift glance round the empty reaches of the terrace. "We don't have much time. I went to Paris last autumn. Why doesn't matter now, but when I got there—"

A rifle report drowned out his words. He slumped against Mélanie. She caught him as he fell, staggering beneath his weight. His breath whistled against her skin, and hot blood spurted between her fingers.

Chapter 6

Charles caught Francisco beneath the arms before he could collapse on the ground and take Mélanie with him. A second gunshot ricocheted off the paving stones. A sliver of rock hit him in the leg. He dragged Francisco into the shadows of the staircase. Mélanie followed.

Charles sank to his knees, supporting his wounded friend. His hands were sticky with the blood spurting from the wound in Francisco's back. Mélanie gave him her shawl and he bunched it up against the wound, but Francisco shook his head.

"'Not so deep as a well.' Isn't that what you'd say, Fraser? ''Tis enough, 'twill serve.' All too damn well."

"Don't try to talk," Charles said. He could feel the blood leaching through the cashmere of Mélanie's shawl.

"Have to." Francisco's voice shook with insistence. "Not much time. Manon. Covent Garden—find her—before they do. *Promise*."

"Of course," Mélanie said. She was holding Francisco's hand.

"Le Lion d'Or—in the morning—seven o'clock. Said I'd meet her."

Mélanie glanced at Charles. Le Lion d'Or was a coffeehouse near Covent Garden. "We'll be there." She leaned forward and brushed her lips over Francisco's own.

Francisco released her hand and reached up toward his neck. His arm collapsed on the paving stones as though he didn't have the strength to lift it. He gave a hoarse curse.

Mélanie unknotted his neckcloth with quick, gentle fingers and pushed back his shirt collar. She reached inside his shirt, carefully so as not to brush against his wound, and drew out a handful of papers.

Francisco's eyes glinted in the shadows, coin-bright with relief. "Important."

"We'll take good care of them," Charles said. Blood seeped between his fingers, and he could feel the spreading chill in his friend's body.

"Listen." Francisco grabbed hold of Charles's neckcloth and pulled his face close to his own. "Els—" The word was swallowed by a cough. Blood dripped from his mouth.

"Else? Something else?" Charles said

"Elsinore. League."

"Elsinore League?"

"Have to stop them." Charles's shirt collar bit into his skin under the force of Francisco's grip. "Before they kill again."

Charles searched his friend's pain-twisted face. "But—"

"It all comes down to honor . . ." Francisco's grip on Charles's neckcloth tightened like a vise, then went slack. His head fell back against Charles's arm. The brilliant, reckless light fled from his eyes.

Charles put his fingers to Francisco's throat and then to his wrist, but he felt no pulse. He looked up at Mélanie. Her eyes were like dark glass. She nodded.

Charles looked beyond the shadows to where moonlight slanted against the paving stones and swept over the stairs above them in a cool, all-too-bright wash. No sound save for the lapping of the water, but old instincts, honed in the Spanish mountains, told him they were being watched.

He lowered Francisco's body to the paving stones. "I'll draw the sniper's fire. He'll have to reload. That should give us at least thirty seconds to get to the top of the stairs."

Mélanie touched her fingers to her lips and brushed them over Francisco's forehead. Charles closed his friend's eyes and squeezed Francisco's cold hand for the final time.

He stepped into the light, angling his body so it made the smallest possible target, then sprang back just as a bullet struck the stone where he had been standing. He caught Mélanie by the wrist and they raced up the stairs, shoes scrabbling over the crumbling stone. As they reached the top of the stairs, a bullet whizzed by his shoulder, so close he could feel the vibration through his coat. He fell back against the wall at the top of the stairs, shielding Mélanie with his body.

"That wasn't thirty seconds," she said.

"No. Whoever he is, he has a rifleman's skill at reloading."

They inched along the wall and rounded the corner. Out of range of the sniper. The moonlight picked out the gates of Somerset Place. They ran toward them. A whistle sounded from behind, where the gunman must still lurk. The report of a rifle echoed through the cold air in front of them. Pain stabbed through his left arm.

He kept running through the gates into the bustle of the Strand before he stopped to lean against the wall of a shuttered shop and draw a breath. "My apologies. I didn't reckon on a second gunman. Weren't you saying it would feel like old times if you could dig a bullet out of me?"

"Don't overdramatize, Charles, the shot only winged you." Mélanie pushed back his greatcoat. "At this rate I'm going to run out of handkerchiefs," she said, knotting one round his arm. "Try not to move it too much."

"Right." He tugged his greatcoat over his shoulders and winced at the stab of pain. "If we have to do any brawling I'll leave it to you."

Even the boldest assassin should know better than to risk gunfire in the crowded precincts of the Strand, but he cast a cautious glance up and down the street. Then he wrapped his good arm round Mélanie and they made their way back through the crowds toward Tavistock Street, taking two detours to ensure they weren't followed.

Randall was waiting where they had left him with the carriage. He jumped down from the box at their approach, let down the steps, and opened the door, his face schooled not to ask questions. Bless the

man. He was getting a taste of life in the Fraser household sooner
than Charles had bargained. "Don't move the carriage yet," Charles
said. "We may not be going home directly." He unhooked one of the
carriage lamps and climbed in after Mélanie.

Harsh breathing filled the carriage as he closed the door. He
couldn't separate Mélanie's breath from his own. He put his hand
over his face and realized he was shaking.

Mélanie reached up and wrapped her fingers round his own. "I
thought we'd seen the last of our friends killed." She drew his hand
down to the seat between them. "I keep remembering Francisco
tossing Colin up on his shoulders. *Those bastards.*"

"Quite. The question would seem to be which particular bastards this time." He drew a breath, suppressed the impulse to smash
something, and steadied his grip on the lamp. "Let's look at the
papers."

Mélanie pulled the papers from the bodice of her gown. Two
sheets of foolscap, spattered with blood but mostly legible. Two sets
of writing, one neat and even, the other a flowing scrawl. Neither
appeared to be Francisco's hand. Especially as Charles didn't think
his friend had been familiar with ancient Greek.

"Your Greek's better than mine," Mélanie said, "but it looks like
a code."

"It is." Charles peered at the letters in the flickering lamplight
while he did automatic calculations.

"We can't go home before we meet Francisco's friend," Mélanie
said. "They may be watching the house."

Charles opened the carriage door and handed the lamp to Randall. "The Albany."

"David and Simon will think we're mad," Mélanie said as they
pulled away from the curb.

"David and Simon have been convinced I'm mad for years. But
we can trust them." David had shared rooms with Simon Tanner
since they came down from Oxford. Unofficially, they shared a great
deal more, a circumstance to which David's family turned a blind
eye, though maintaining the polite fiction grew more difficult as the
years passed without David marrying and producing an heir to the
earldom he would one day inherit

"Charles, this is *London,*" Mélanie said. "Not Burgos or Salamanca or Vitoria in the middle of the war, with the British and the French and God knows how many Spanish factions at each other's throats. A sniper killed one of our friends and shot at us in the middle of the city in peacetime."

And not just any city. The city that was now home. The city he'd brought his wife and children to, thinking it was safe. God help him, last night he'd actually relished the call of adventure. Guilt welled up on his tongue, sour as spoiled milk. "And the sniper had a second gunman in place in case they lost their quarry," he said. "Which argues money. And power."

"And desperation. Whatever they were trying to conceal was worth considerable risk. To themselves as well as us."

He stared at the yellow glow of the streetlamps through the carriage window. "If I'd known—"

"We couldn't have done anything differently, Charles. Francisco chose the meeting place. Unless we've both lost any instinct for avoiding pursuit, we weren't followed. Someone must have followed him. Or got wind of it some other way."

"Save your cosseting for the children, Mel." Her sweet reasonableness grated on the guilty, dark core inside him, rubbing raw places he had never let her glimpse. "I'm old enough to live with my mistakes."

She drew a breath that had a harsh rasp to it. "If there's blame to go round, I'm just as much to blame as you."

"No sense in wallowing." He locked his hands together. "They didn't just want Francisco. They wanted whatever he might have told us. Whatever's in those papers."

Mélanie turned her head to look at him. "Do the words Elsinore League mean anything to you?"

"Other than echoes of a corrupt court in Renaissance Denmark? No."

Randall turned the carriage into the forecourt of the Albany. Charles had had bachelor chambers in the Palladian building himself in a brief interval between Oxford and Lisbon. The sight of the brown-brick walls slapped him in the face with the memory of one of his greatest failures. He swallowed the bitterness and handed Mélanie from the carriage.

Simon Tanner opened the door of his and David's flat, evening coat rumpled, neckcloth gone, shirt open at the neck. "Oh, Lord," he said, steadying his grip on the lamp he carried. "I knew things had been quiet for too long. What is it this time, politics or family?"

"Politics, as best we can tell." Mélanie stepped into the shadowy entrance hall and smiled at David, who stood behind Simon, as meticulously dressed as if he was at the start of the evening rather than the end of it.

"Sorry for the late hour," Charles said, "but we have to be at Covent Garden at seven and it isn't safe for us to go home first."

David's gaze swept over them as they moved into the light of the entryway. "My God, what have you done to yourselves?"

"Grown careless in our old age," Charles said.

"But—"

Mélanie glanced down at her gown. "Most of the blood isn't ours."

David regarded Charles with the misgivings of one who'd known him since boyhood. "You're hurt."

"No," said Charles.

"Yes," said Mélanie, "but it's not serious. I need lint and alcohol, a good light, and someone to make Charles hold still."

David went down the corridor in search of medical supplies while Simon led the way to the book-strewn sitting room. He went straight to the drinks table and poured two whiskies. "We just got back ourselves," he said. "I dragged David to the Tavistock to make sure the actors weren't mangling my dialogue too atrociously and then we had a late supper at the Piazza." He pressed the whiskies into Charles's and Mélanie's hands. "Wait till David returns for the story. No sense in telling it twice."

Charles curved his fingers round the glass, relieved to find that his hands had stopped shaking. Mélanie took a long swallow and drew a breath. She was several shades paler than usual. In the light from the tapers on the Pembroke table, he saw splashes of blood on the lace at the neck of her gown. He could feel the weight of Francisco's body in his arms, smell the sickly stench of blood, sense the chill of dying flesh. If the gunmen had been a few inches off with any of their shots, it might have been Mélanie who bled to death in his arms. He set his whisky down before he could smash yet another glass.

Mélanie pulled Francisco's papers from her bodice and set them on the table. Charles took a step toward the table, but at the same moment David returned to the room, a medical supply box in his hands.

Mélanie set down her glass. "Take off your coat, Charles."

He complied, because it took less time than arguing with her. While she cut away his shirtsleeve and cleaned and bound the wound, he gave David and Simon an account of the evening's events. When he finished, David stared at him as though he had just announced foreign troops had invaded English soil. "Charles, you have to go to Bow Street with this."

"With what? A story about mysterious warnings and coded papers and secret organizations that sounds as though it's straight out of a gothic novel? Any Bow Street Runner worth his salt would laugh in our faces. And assuming a runner did take it seriously and began asking questions, how far do you think he'd get among the polite world?"

"This isn't a game, Charles. You could have been killed. *Mélanie* could have been killed."

"Christ, don't you think I know that?" Charles glanced at Mélanie and drew a breath. "I'm sorry. But I know the stakes, David. *Believe me.* If I thought I could safely turn this over to Bow Street, I would."

David returned Charles's gaze. Twenty years of shared history hung between them. Sipping scalding cups of chocolate and pouring over dog-eared books during late-night discussions at Harrow. Pressing iced towels to bloody noses after unequal fights. Drinking cheap wine in an Oxford tavern, drunk on ideas. Sobbing with a raw despair one dared reveal to no one else.

"Damn you," David said. "You always end arguments by asking me to trust you."

"Do you?" Charles said.

"Far more than is good for me. Or you, I sometimes think."

"Were they trying to kill you as well or just scare you?" Simon asked.

"I'm not sure," Charles said. "We didn't give them many clear shots. But they were certainly prepared to use lethal force. A few inches off and any of those bullets could have killed either of us." He glanced down at Mélanie, who was snipping off a length of lint, and fought an urge to touch her for reassurance. She'd look at him as though he were mad. "Knot the bandage and stop fussing, Mel. I want to look at Francisco's papers."

"You'd find it dreadfully inconvenient to develop gangrene, Charles." Mélanie set down the scissors. "Try to keep your arm elevated."

Charles moved aside a playbill and a sheaf of papers that appeared to be notes for Simon's latest play, and spread Francisco's papers out on the table.

"Look at this." Simon pointed to a dark red splotch at the top of one of the sheets that Charles had taken to be a blood spatter. Now he saw a matching spot at the bottom of the paper. A red wax seal, snapped in two when the papers were opened. He turned the page over and folded it, bringing the two halves of the seal back together, and held it to the light of the lamp. It appeared to be some sort of castle.

"Probably from a signet ring," Charles said. "But it's not a crest I've ever seen."

"The Elsinore League?" Simon asked.

"Very likely."

David stared down at the writing on the two papers. "It looks as though it's a good thing I still have my dictionaries of ancient Greek."

"The Greek's just an added flourish." Charles ran his finger over a line of text. "It's numbers, written out in word form in ancient Greek with a few extra letters thrown in to confuse matters. The trick is going to be turning the numbers into words. We'll need a pen and ink and rather a lot of paper."

To turn the two blood-spattered pages of ancient Greek into a sequence of numbers was time consuming but not difficult. Charles studied the results. "They've only used numbers between one and fifty, so this isn't some sort of *Grand Chiffre,* where we'd need multiple messages before we had a prayer of breaking it. Assuming the original message was written in English or French, the most commonly occurring number should translate to 'e.' Which looks to be forty-two. Mel?"

"Right." His wife had already drawn up a chair beside him and was sketching out the beginnings of a table.

It took a little over an hour—during which time Charles wondered more than once that the cipher was not more complex—to decode the two papers Francisco had given them. In the end, the plain text lay before them, in Mélanie's swift, slanted hand.

The first message read:

Remember the past is never dead, only temporarily buried. And I can resurrect it whenever I wish.

And the second, which had been written in a different hand:

We have no choice but to eliminate the evidence.

"The first sounds like a blackmail threat," Simon said. "And the second could be an order to kill the blackmailer."

"Francisco told us they had to be stopped before they killed again," Mélanie said. She was perched on the edge of the Pembroke table, her fingers smeared with ink. "The question is, what on earth is this past that the Elsinore League fears could be resurrected?"

Charles smoothed the edges of the papers. "We can only hope Francisco shared some of the secrets with Manon. In any case, we have to find her at Le Lion d'Or at seven and warn her. She's in danger herself."

"And you?" David asked.

"We weren't followed from Somerset Place, but if the assassin knows who we are, someone might be watching our house."

"I don't suppose there's a chance you'll let mere civilians help you," Simon said.

Charles and Mélanie exchanged glances. "As a matter of fact," Charles said, "we can't make our plan work without you."

.   .   .

The rhythm of French assailed Charles's ears as he and Mélanie stepped into the smoky, dimly lit interior of Le Lion d'Or. For a moment the swift, musical pattern of speech swept him back to their days in Paris. Mélanie's gaze darted about the crowd, but he felt her almost palpably relax, as though the sounds took her home.

He caught a phrase or two in Spanish, one in Viennese German, and finally an English-speaking voice, from a corpulent man at a table by the fire giving his order in a voice three times louder than necessary, as though that would make the waiter—who very likely spoke fluent English—understand better.

Even the smells were different. Coffee that was strong but not bitter. Creamy cheese. Meat and vegetables soaked in butter rather than lard.

The coffeehouse was crowded with an assortment of émigrés. Actors and musicians who earned their keep at the nearby theaters, no doubt, writers and journalists scribbling in notebooks, and some men in leather aprons who were probably taking a quick break from the bustle of the market.

Fewer women were present, but there was a mix of actresses and shapely ankled opera dancers, flower sellers with baskets on the floor beside them, and some women who probably sold not flowers or fruit but their own bodies.

"Charles." Mélanie tugged at his sleeve and nodded toward the far corner, away from the light of the fire. Even in the shadows, the woman's hair gleamed guinea bright.

They started forward. When they were a half dozen steps away, Manon's head jerked up. For a moment she stared at them. Then she sprang to her feet, tipped over her chair, and bolted across the room.

She was fast, but Charles had glimpsed her intention in the flicker of her gaze. He sprang forward and caught her by the back of her cloak. "It's all right, Manon. We're here to help you."

"*Help.*" She gave an incredulous laugh. With a wrench of torn wool, she pulled out of his grasp.

She didn't so much as look at the door. She made straight for the windows. Charles ran after her, skidded on the floorboards, and nearly fell.

Manon knocked over a bench, pushed aside a man reading a newspaper, and jumped atop a table to window height. Without hesitation, she hurled herself at the window, breaking the latch on the casement.

A cry went up from the coffeehouse, half amazement, half admiration. Charles was already atop the table. He shouldered through the broken casement and sprang down after Manon into the empty yard beyond.

Charles landed on the hard-packed ground with a thud. Manon was halfway across the yard, her faded blue skirts billowing about her. Charles ran after, dodging round barrels and slop buckets and piles of refuse. He was still a half dozen paces behind as he stumbled into Maiden Lane and then rounded the corner into Southampton Street.

A jumble of carts and barrows clogged the street. A donkey's bray split the air. Manon plunged into the throng of costers and apple women, flower girls and greengrocers. She veered right round a donkey barrow. Charles flung himself to the left, into a narrow gap between an excursion van and a whitewashed step piled high with rhubarb and broccoli. The move gained him a pace on his quarry.

"Thief!" Charles yelled in his best Harrovian accents, with a mental apology to Francisco's friend. He couldn't protect her if he couldn't stop her. "The woman in blue."

Heads turned. Hands reached out. A man in a green-stained apron caught Manon by the arm. Manon twisted, gold hair tumbling about her face, and delivered a jab to the aproned man's ribs. The aproned man staggered backward into the arms of a stout woman wearing a head basket.

Charles lunged at Manon. Manon hurled herself toward the nearest doorway and kicked over a stack of turnips. The turnips careered into a sack of potatoes. The potatoes struck a pile of cabbages. The whole mess of vegetables spilled over the cobblestones.

Manon dodged round a bricklayer's cart. The horse pulling the cart neighed and skidded to a halt as the torrent of produce rolled into its path. The cart swung sideways, blocking the road. Bricks thudded to the ground. Someone screamed. Someone else let loose a string of invective. Charles jumped over the stream of vegetables, dropped to the cobblestones, and rolled beneath the cart.

He scrambled up from the slimy, green-stained cobblestones and fought his way through the crowd to the square. Covent Garden Market spread before him in all its tumultuous glory. He sprang up into the back of a nearby donkey barrow, amid crates of apples and bunches of carrots, tossed a coin to the startled coster, and scanned the likely avenues.

His gaze honed in on the blue dress and bright hair against the basket-hung railings of St. Paul's. Manon must have paused for a moment to get her wind back. Charles sprang down from the cart and set off at a run, dodging, twisting, pushing through the crowd. Past the chirp of the bird catcher's stand, past the whir of a knife grinder, past the sweet violet scent of a flower seller.

Manon had seen him coming and was off again, along the west side of the square, toward the Piazza. Oranges and turnips sailed overhead. People shouted. Charles banged his knee into something hard and shouldered on, not stopping to look, to wonder, to apologize. Manon started up the steps of the Piazza, a dozen paces or so ahead, with a press of people between them.

A line of coffee stalls ran beneath the shelter of the Piazza. Manon made straight for the nearest one. A knot of people were clustered about the entrance, but she didn't waste precious seconds picking her way through them. She hurled herself at the makeshift cloth wall, ripping through the sheet and tipping over the wooden clotheshorses that supported it.

Charles lunged after her, through the broken wood and torn linen, into the wreckage of the stall. The floor was strewn with spilled coffee, soggy slices of brown bread, slimy pats of butter. The steaming air was thick with the scent of chicory and angry voices. A fist slammed into his head, accompanied by a curse in Irish Gaelic. He skidded on the slick floor and grabbed hold of the nearest support. It proved to be someone's arm; he didn't look to see whose. Manon was a half dozen feet away on the opposite side of the stall, half concealed by a man in a gray coat, her escape blocked by a deal table. A knife flashed in the man in gray's hand, aimed at Manon's ribs.

Charles hurled himself forward in a desperate attempt to reach Manon before the man could stick the knife in her back. As he moved, a stream of scalding coffee caught the man in gray in the back of the neck.

The man screamed. Manon twisted away. Charles glimpsed his wife, holding a coffee can. The man in gray plunged through the white sheet of the near wall. Charles skirted a broken chair and an overturned can and ran after him into the next stall. The would-be assassin knocked over a paper screen, tipped over a can of coffee, and fought his way through the angry customers, back toward the Piazza steps.

Charles ran out the back of the stall after his quarry. He dodged round one of the pillars of the Piazza, narrowly avoiding another blow to his head. He reached the steps in time to see the man in gray make a flying leap into the back of an apple cart in the square below.

Without hesitation Charles jumped after him. It was a wild jump, but he might have made it. Yet even as he sprang forward, he felt the sole of his boot, slick with butter, slip out from under him. He had a moment to realize he did not have enough distance and to curse himself for a bloody fool. Then he crashed into the steps.

Mélanie dropped the empty coffee can and caught Manon by both arms as she twisted away from the assassin. "Please. Trust us."

Manon's blue gaze raked Mélanie's face. She jerked against Mélanie's hold. Mélanie, used to holding squirming children, tightened her grip.

The assassin raced out of the stall in a blur of movement, Charles close on his heels.

"It's simple," Mélanie said. "That man wants to kill you. We want to help you."

Manon held Mélanie with her gaze for a moment, drew a breath, and nodded. She and Mélanie ran toward the Piazza steps in time to see the man in gray jump into an apple cart and Charles crash into the steps.

By the time they reached him, Charles had pushed himself to a sitting position. His gaze went straight to Manon. "You're not hurt?"

Manon gave a shaky nod. Mélanie tightened her grip on the other woman's arm. She didn't trust Manon not to run. God knew she had more than enough reason to do so.

Charles scrambled to his feet, winced at the pain in his head, and glanced round the square. "Christ. He's gone?"

"I think the man in the apple cart was a confederate," Mélanie said. Charles wasn't staggering too badly, which probably meant he hadn't done serious damage to his head when he fell. She'd have to wait to check for bruises, she couldn't risk letting go of Manon.

Shouts came from the Piazza behind them. In another minute they were going to have angry coffee stall owners demanding compensation.

Of one accord, the three of them ran down the steps and slipped into the concealing chaos of the crowd. This time Manon made no protest. "We'll send payment and an apology later," Charles said, stopping for a moment beneath the shelter of an orange seller's stall. He looked at Manon. "We have to go somewhere we can talk."

Manon's gaze slid round the market. She was tense, poised for flight. "They may know where you live."

"We're not going to our house." Charles took her arm. "We have friends waiting. This way."

They made their way through the market to a narrow alley and a side door of the Tavistock Theater. Simon was waiting at the door, holding a lamp as he had been in the Albany a few hours before. His gaze went from the fresh damage to Charles's face to the woman at Charles's side.

"Manon, I presume. I'm glad they found you. I'm Simon Tanner. I write plays, but I'm reasonably sane and quite good at keeping secrets."

He led them into the darkened theater, round looming canvas flats and shadowy pieces of furniture, and opened a door onto a white-painted dressing room that smelled of face powder, lily of the valley scent, greasepaint, and wilting bouquets. He pushed aside a peacock-blue brocade robe that hung from a clothesline strung across the ceiling. Costumes were everywhere—pinned to the clothesline, draped over the Chinese dressing screen, flung across the dressing table bench. The room had no windows, but a multitude of candles were lit. David sat on a chipped gilt settee amidst this incongruous jumble with a hamper of food at his feet, brewing tea over a spirit lamp.

"We thought you might be hungry," Simon said. "It's all right," he added in response to a nervous look from Manon. "I own a share in the theater and the leading lady's a friend of mine. There's no rehearsal today. We're quite safe."

David got to his feet, manners undimmed by the bizarre nature of the scene. Charles murmured a quick introduction.

Manon sank down on a wicker crate, arms crossed over her chest, and looked from Charles to Mélanie. Her gaze was still wary, but she now seemed armored not against what might be done to her but against what she might hear. "He's dead, isn't he? I can see it in your eyes."

Her voice cracked on the last word. The mother in Mélanie wanted to put her arms round her. But simple comfort couldn't ease this hurt. Mélanie glanced at Charles and thought of what might have happened if the snipers' bullets had been a few inches closer, if Charles had been a fraction of a second less quick to jump out of the way. She thought of all the other times in the past four and a half years when he might have been killed. Her hands locked together.

She sat on the crate beside Manon, not so close as to intrude. Simon lifted a ruby velvet robe from the settee where David was sitting and dropped down beside him.

Charles perched on a stool opposite Manon and told her, gently and succinctly, what had transpired with Francisco the night before.

Manon scarcely blinked throughout his account. Her gaze was trained on his face, her mouth set against betraying anything. When Charles finished speaking, she was silent for a long moment. The hiss of the flame from the spirit lamp filled the small room. "I should have known," she said at last. "He promised he'd meet me at Le Lion d'Or this morning. He was careful about making promises, but when he did he always kept them. He's the only man I've ever known who did." She rubbed a hand over her eyes. "When I saw you I could only think he'd been wrong to trust you and you'd come after me. We've been running for so long . . ."

A sob shuddered through her. This time Mélanie put her arm round her. Manon seemed scarcely aware of the touch. Mélanie wasn't sure she was even aware of her surroundings, aware of anything save the fact that Francisco Soro was no longer part of her world.

David poured a cup of tea, stirred in plenty of sugar, and gave it to Mélanie, who pressed it into Manon's cold, numb fingers. Manon's hand closed round the warmth of the cup. She took a sip, choked, then swallowed some more.

Charles watched her with a gaze that was warm yet implacable. "Talking must be the last thing you feel like doing, but we need to know the truth if we're to protect you."

Manon's gaze flew to his face. "You didn't protect Francisco."

Charles's mouth hardened. "No. I failed Francisco. I don't want to fail you as well."

Manon's shoulders straightened beneath Mélanie's arm. "Francisco knew the risks. He didn't come to you for protection. He came to you because he wanted someone to know the truth."

"About what?"

Manon stared down into the teacup. "I don't understand it. Not all of it."

"When did you meet him?" Mélanie asked. "And where?"

"Last December. At the Café des Arts. In Paris. I'm—I was an artist's model." She gave a rough laugh and touched her tangled hair. "Difficult to believe anyone would want to paint me now."

"You have the face for it," Simon said.

She shot him a quick glance. "My mother was an artist's model," Simon said. "I'm not sure which my grandparents thought more unforgivable—that my father went off to Paris to paint or that he insisted on marrying her."

Manon gave a faint smile. "I'd gone to the café one evening with some friends. Francisco came in and we started talking." Her hands tightened round the teacup. "He was—kind. And clever. And—"

"Devastatingly handsome," Mélanie said.

Manon twisted her head to look at Mélanie. Tears glittered in her eyes, but her mouth curved slightly. "Yes. I'd never met anyone quite like him. He had so many stories about Spain during the war—I knew half of them were made up, but I always suspected that the most outrageous ones were the truth."

"Very likely," Charles said. "I doubt even Francisco could invent anything more outrageous than a lot of the things he actually did. Did he tell you why he'd come to Paris?"

Manon's face went closed again. "He said he'd come to France on business. He told me once that he'd liked the people he worked for better during the war, but beggars couldn't be choosers." She stared into the teacup. "Things are bad in Paris now. The war's supposed to be over, but no one can forget. Soldiers are everywhere— British, Prussian, Russian, Belgian." She looked at Charles, chin lifted with defiance.

"And soldiers don't make the best of guests in a foreign country," Charles said. "It can't be easy to watch one's city overrun. I didn't find it very easy to watch as a British diplomat."

Mélanie blinked back her own images of the foreign uniforms crowding the streets and quays and squares of Paris.

"It's not enough for the Royalists that the emperor's gone," Manon said. "It's not even enough to reclaim their land. A lot of them want revenge. For the war. For the Republic. For—"

"Everything that's happened since the Revolution," Mélanie said.

Manon nodded. "So many people have been imprisoned, so many executed. Friends. Men whose only crime was to fight for the emperor when he escaped from Elba." She cast another quick glance at Charles.

"I worked against the French in Spain," Charles said, "but I don't approve of what's happening in Paris now. Even Wellington thinks the reprisals have gone too far."

"But he couldn't stop them from killing Marshal Ney."

David opened his mouth, then closed it.

Manon pinned him with a gaze that read far too much in his

ingenuous face. "A man I was close to—a man I loved—died fighting in Russia. If he'd lived, he'd have rejoined the emperor when he
escaped. And if he'd survived Waterloo, he could have been executed for his loyalty."

Charles leaned toward her, his gaze steady. "When did you
become entangled in what Francisco was doing?"

Manon shrank back against the wall, dislodging a beaded mask
that hung from a nail. Mélanie picked it up. "Sometimes Francisco
would leave Paris for days on end. I didn't ask where he went. I
knew it was dangerous, but—he could take care of himself. I
thought." She choked. "*Mon Dieu,* I thought the way he lived was
exciting."

Mélanie met Charles's gaze for a moment. It could be exciting.
Headier than champagne, more addictive than opium.

"He came to my room in the middle of the night," Manon continued. "Dripping blood all over the floor and bed. He'd been shot. He
wouldn't talk about what had happened. Even then I didn't realize—
But he said he needed help."

"What sort of help?" Charles asked.

She tightened her grip on her teacup. "Letters would be delivered to me at the studio where I modeled and I'd take them to Francisco. I never read them. A few times he had me go to the
Conciergerie."

Charles cast another quick glance at Mélanie, and even Simon
and David looked alert. The Conciergerie, located within the Palais
de Justice, had been one of the most formidable prisons in Paris for
over five hundred years. Many Bonapartists were now held within
its walls.

"Whom did you visit?" Charles said.

"A man named Coroux, a former Bonapartist officer."

David was several shades paler than usual. Even Simon, used to
dreaming up fantastic flights of fancy with his pen, looked as though
he couldn't quite believe what he was hearing. *Welcome to the world
your friends have been living in.* Sometimes Mélanie forgot that any
sort of other world existed.

"Do you have any idea of the content of the messages?" Charles
asked.

Manon shook her head. "The papers were always sealed. Once

he opened one and I caught a glimpse of the writing—I can't be sure, but I think it was in a code."

Charles looked at Mélanie and inclined his head. Mélanie unbuttoned the cuff of her gown and pulled out a drawing of the seal that she'd made while they waited at David and Simon's for it to be time to leave for Covent Garden. "Do you recognize this?"

Manon studied it. "It's a seal. I saw it on the letters I carried and sometimes on papers Francisco brought home."

Charles nodded. "What was he like, this man you visited?"

"Courtly. He used to kiss my hand and tell me he liked my bonnet or my shawl or the way I'd dressed my hair. He had kind eyes."

"When did you leave Paris?"

Her face twisted. "Ten days ago. In the middle of the night. Francisco dragged me out of bed and said I had to listen. He kept pacing up and down the room, saying he couldn't believe he'd been so deceived. At first I thought he was accusing me of being unfaithful. Then I realized he wasn't angry with me at all."

"Whom was he angry with?"

"Whomever he worked for. I couldn't make it out, because he was raging so much and he'd start saying whole sentences in Spanish, but he seemed to be saying they'd tricked him. That he'd never forgive himself for what he'd done. What he'd helped them do. He said we had to leave. He said it wasn't safe now that they knew he knew and that I wouldn't be safe, either. I'd have to come with him. He said it as though he was apologizing, but—" She swallowed, then lifted her head and looked directly at Charles. "I'd never have forgiven him if he'd left me behind. I loved him. I don't know what he felt for me. Affection, duty, responsibility. Maybe even love. Now I'll never be certain."

Mélanie flicked an involuntary glance at her husband. Even if one woke every morning in the same bed and shared morning coffee and visits to the nursery, could one ever be certain?

Manon took a sip of tea and stared into the cup. "We left Paris that night. I only had time to pack a small valise. We stayed outside Paris at a farm where the people knew Francisco. During the night, someone came searching for us. We had to hide in the hay bales."

"Who was searching?" Charles asked.

She shook her head. "I don't know. I heard voices, but it only seemed to be one man and he spoke quietly. I couldn't make out the words. I don't think it was soldiers. There would have been more of them. We made our way to Dieppe and took a fishing boat for England. We landed on the coast. Sussex, he called it. We got a ride to London in a coal cart. Francisco said they had to be stopped. He said he had to get word to someone who could help." She looked at Charles again. "You."

The failure to help sat heavily in Charles's eyes. "He told you my name?"

"Eventually. The night he sent me to find you." She shook her head. "It's odd. For all the danger, he seemed happier those last days. Only two days ago, he said to me that it was good to know which side he was on again."

"Did he ever mention something called the Elsinore League?"

"No."

So Francisco had been working with Bonapartists. That wasn't surprising. He hadn't liked the French when they were overrunning Spain, but he was hardly a Royalist. Was that what he'd come to warn Charles about? A Bonapartist plot? Mélanie's blood chilled. Surely not another attempt to help Napoleon escape.

"Do you know the contents of the papers he was bringing us?" Charles asked.

Manon shook her head. "He said it wasn't safe for me to know more. But—" Her gaze darted from Charles to Mélanie. "He took papers with him when we left. Some he gave to you. The rest—" She reached inside the bodice of her gown and drew out a handful of creased papers. "He gave to me."

Charles took the papers. In the candlelight, Mélanie glimpsed the same ancient Greek characters as on the papers Francisco had given them. "Did Francisco ever mention any names?"

"No. That is, yes, I suppose it's a name. In the middle of one of his rants." She frowned in an effort of memory. "He said with all they'd done, it was ironic that the people he worked with feared most of all for Honoria."

Chapter 8

"What?" David sprang to his feet, knocking over the three-legged table that held the spirit lamp and teakettle.

Simon grabbed the lamp before it could start a fire and threw a sheet over the spilled tea.

"You're sure he said Honoria?" Charles asked Manon.

"Yes." She looked at David. "Is she your sister?"

"My cousin." David ran a hand over his hair. "She's just become betrothed to Charles's father."

"*Nom de Dieu.*" Manon's gaze flickered between Charles and David.

"But the betrothal was only announced the night before last," Charles said. "When did Francisco mention Honoria?"

"The night we left Paris. Less than a fortnight ago." She shook her head as though she could not believe how much had happened in that span of time.

Charles turned to David. "When did Father offer for Honoria?"

"A week since. At least that's when my father heard of it."

Mélanie looked at Charles. "Francisco's last words—"

"Yes. 'It all comes down to honor.' I should have known he
wasn't talking about 'honor' as a concept. That wasn't Francisco at
all. He was trying to say a name. 'It all comes down to Honoria.'"

David frowned. "But—"

A knock sounded on the door. Fear ran through the room like a
palpable current.

"It's all right, it's only me." A woman opened the door and
stepped into the room with proprietary ease. She wore a stylish chip
straw bonnet over her glossy auburn ringlets, and her figured muslin
gown was cut along the lines of the latest Paris fashion plates.
"Simon, love, I hope you realize only you could have got me out of
my bed at such an ungodly hour. Don't you know actresses are supposed to spend the morning lolling in their boudoirs?" She brushed
aside the half-curtain of costumes hung from the ceiling and
advanced into the room. "Actually, I was supposed to go down to
Roehampton and see the children, and they're going to be thoroughly cross with me, but I shall simply have to—" She stopped
short, taking in the assembled company. Her exquisitely groomed
brows rose in inquiry.

"Cecily Summers," Simon said. "Who has an uncanny knack for
bringing a playwright's words to life with a depth he never knew
was there. Cecy, we need your help."

Mrs. Summers looked from Charles and Mélanie, whom she
knew, to the unknown Manon, who had huddled back against the
wall, arms folded defensively across her chest. The actress's mobile
face altered subtly, from woman of the world to supportive friend.
She dropped down in the nearest chair. "Tell me."

Mélanie had met Cecily Summers a handful of times in the
months she'd been in Britain. She knew Mrs. Summers had a quick
wit and a kind heart, but she hadn't realized how generous or com-
passionate Cecily Summers was or what nerves of steel she possessed. She listened to Simon's and Charles's account of Manon's
plight without a blink and jumped to Simon's suggested solution
before he proposed it himself.

Manon balked. Mélanie gripped her hands and fixed her with a
firm, frank stare. "You can't go back to Paris. Not yet. Even if we
could find a way to get you there, it's one of the first places they'd

look for you. You won't be safe with us. We promised Francisco we'd look after you. Please let us do this for you. For him."

She expected more argument, but at the appeal to Francisco's memory, Manon went still. She flicked an appraising glance at Mrs. Summers, looked back at Mélanie, and gave a cautious nod.

Half an hour later, Manon, dressed in a brunette wig and a suit of boy's clothes normally worn by Cherubin in *The Marriage of Figaro,* left the theater in Cecily Summers's carriage, accompanied by Simon and Mrs. Summers. They were bound for Mrs. Summers's villa in Roehampton until such time as the threat had been dealt with. Mrs. Summers's husband and children were in residence at the villa, and Mrs. Summers would join them there when the theater had closed for the summer. Mr. Summers, a former rifleman, should be able to cope with any unexpected incidents.

When Simon and the two women had left the theater, David stared at the dressing room door with the expression Mélanie had seen on Charles's face when she went into danger without him.

"The best thing we can do for them is stay here out of sight for half an hour," Charles said. "No one should know we're at the theater, but if we show our faces there's always the chance someone will make the connection."

David grimaced and nodded. Then he spun round to face Charles. "This settles it. I'm going to my father with what we know. Honoria may be in danger."

"David, listen—"

"No, you listen." David strode across the room, kicking over a basket of fans and sending a gold brocade robe and a red velvet gown fluttering on the clothesline. "This is my cousin we're talking about. I care about what happens to her, even if you—"

He broke off, his face suffused with horror at his own words.

Charles looked back at him, white-faced but steady-eyed. "Believe it or not, I'm not entirely lacking in concern for Honoria's happiness myself."

Mélanie sat stock-still watching her husband and his best friend engaged in a silent duel she could only begin to guess at. Echoes of whatever had happened on that long-ago visit to Lisbon reverberated between them, quickening the air and chilling Mélanie's soul.

David swallowed. "I'm sorry. But—"

"Damn it, David, if you go to your father, what then? One man's dead and someone shot at Mélanie and me last night and made a very creditable effort to kill Manon just now. If you go to your father with our suspicions—and he doesn't laugh in your face or commit you to Bedlam—he'll storm about and tell half the Cabinet. Our unseen enemies will know what we know and we'll lose what little leverage we have, along with any chance to investigate quietly. Not to mention that it will be twice as hard to protect Manon."

"Then what do you suggest we do?" David demanded.

"It's entirely possible the 'Honoria' Francisco referred to has nothing to do with Honoria Talbot. Still—" Charles drew a breath. "Did Honoria ever say anything that could connect to any of this? Anything to indicate she might know about danger, that she was afraid of anything—"

"We may be cousins, but we're hardly confidants." David drew a breath. "You always knew her better than I did."

"Once, perhaps. I haven't seen her for a long time." Charles ran his fingers down a silver tissue cloak that hung from the clothesline.

"She's never been one to reveal a great deal of herself," David said. "I own I was shocked when—"

He bit back the words. The subject he and Charles had not discussed since the Glenister House ball hung between them like gunsmoke. For a moment Mélanie was afraid that if she drew a breath the pressure in the air would hurt her lungs. She was afraid that if she looked into Charles's eyes, what she saw there would cut even deeper.

"She didn't say anything to you about why she's marrying my father?" The question seemed to burst from Charles's lips in spite of himself.

"Only that it's what she wants. You know Honoria when she makes her mind up."

"Yes." Charles glanced away. "I can't imagine your father was overjoyed at the match. In fact, I'm surprised he agreed to it."

David shot a glance at him. "He didn't at first. According to my sister, Mr. Fraser called on Father, and Father lost his temper and ordered him from the house. Then Father stormed over to Glenister House and reminded Glenister that Honoria has two guardians and he wasn't about to agree to the match, whatever Glenister said."

"What changed his mind?" Charles asked.

"Honoria. She said she was of age and if Father wouldn't give his consent she'd marry Mr. Fraser anyway. He could withhold her dowry, but given your father's fortune that was hardly much of a threat. By the time I was sent for, Father had calmed down a bit, but he kept asking Honoria if she wanted more time to consider. She laughed and said she was three-and-twenty and it was high time she got off the shelf."

"Old wishes die hard."

David raised his brows.

"David, I'm not blind. Your parents have always wanted you to marry Honoria."

David took a turn about the small room. He always moved as though holding himself slightly in check, as though he carried the weight of the earldom he would one day inherit. "Honoria never showed the remotest interest in me as anything but a cousin. They couldn't have had any serious hopes that we'd make a match of it."

Because they'd expected her to marry Charles. Mélanie stared at a splotch of dried blood on the braided cuff of her gown.

"Whatever her reasons for marrying your father, it's difficult to see what it could have to do with the Elsinore League," David continued. "In fact it's impossible to see what Honoria could have to do with intrigue in postwar Paris. Except—"

He looked at Charles. Charles looked back at him. "Honoria's father," Charles said.

"Yes. There is that."

Charles turned to Mélanie. "Honoria's father, Cyril Talbot, had Bonapartist sympathies. Of the romanticized, undergraduate sort. He liked to make shocking pronouncements round the dinner table or in the coffee room at Brooks's."

"It drove his father and his brother—the current Lord Glenister—and my father mad," David said.

"Which I suspect is the chief reason he did it." Charles stared at a jeweled mask on the wall. "But I suppose it's possible that the same motivation led him to get entangled with a Bonapartist organization. The secret society bit would appeal to a young man thirsting for adventure. But even if he had been linked to the Elsinore

League, why would his former associates be afraid for Honoria so many years after his death?"

"He died when Miss Talbot was quite small, didn't he?" Mélanie said. "What happened?"

"He had an accident with a gun during a shooting party. A shooting party my father was hosting at Dunmykel. Honoria was three."

Mélanie drew in and released her breath. "You're sure it was an accident?"

"No one's ever suggested otherwise."

"Good God," David said. "You're not suggesting Cyril Talbot was murdered?"

"I'm only asking questions in an attempt to arrive at some sort of answer. Whatever the circumstances of Lord Cyril's death, if—and it's still a big if—he was involved with the Elsinore League, perhaps some of his comrades promised to protect his daughter."

"While someone else is threatening her?" David said.

"The papers we decoded last night imply that someone was threatening to reveal the past. Perhaps part of the threat was for Miss Talbot to learn the truth about her father." Mélanie kept her voice even. She knew full well how great a threat the revelation of the truth could be.

"And you think there's some unknown Bonapartist who feels so great a debt of friendship to Cyril that his primary concern is Cyril's daughter all these years later?" David asked.

"One can accumulate a lot of debts in the course of a friendship," Charles said.

David returned his gaze for a long moment. "Point taken."

"It's still just supposition," Charles said. "But at least it's one theory that links the pieces together." He pulled his watch from his pocket. "It should be safe for us to leave the theater now."

Mélanie waited until they were in a hackney bound for South Audley Street before she voiced the concern she hadn't wanted to mention in front of David. "You didn't tell me David and Miss Talbot visited you in Lisbon."

"Didn't I?" Charles was looking out the cracked glass of the window. "There was no reason for it to come up, I suppose."

Most people would have been deceived into thinking his tone was perfectly normal. Most people didn't know him like she did. "I thought you hadn't seen her since she was a child."

"Does it make a difference?"

"There's quite a difference between fourteen and seventeen." The difference between a girl and a woman.

"David's father was sent to meet with Wellington and the ambassador. Honoria and David and Val came with him. They weren't in Lisbon long. I didn't see a great deal of them."

"Charles, I'm stumbling in the dark if you won't tell me everything you know about Miss Talbot."

Charles swung his head round. His gaze met hers, black and impenetrable. "I don't know anything about Honoria Talbot that could connect to any of this. Trust me."

"It's not a question of trust, Charles. I think you're being blinded by—"

He continued to stare at her, an aristocrat who wouldn't dream of being so ill bred as to suggest a commoner has been overly familiar.

"Your feelings," she said.

He gave a brief laugh. "A novel argument, considering a lot of people think I don't have them."

"Don't talk rubbish, Charles."

He turned his gaze away. "I know her, Mel. You don't." He didn't sound angry. It would have been better if he had.

"You knew her once, Charles. You don't necessarily know her anymore. Unless you know her better than you've admitted."

"I know her enough to know that whatever game she's involved in, she's a pawn."

"Damn it, Charles." She caught his hand and gripped it. "We don't even know what the bloody hell the game is that's being played."

He looked down at their hands. He didn't attempt to extricate himself from her grip, but nor did he return the pressure of her touch. "You're not sounding much like yourself either, Mel. You're not usually so quick to rush to judgment."

Mélanie bit her lip and released his hand. "I'm not making a judgment, Charles. I don't know enough to do so. I'm trying to make sure we have all the facts at our disposal."

"And I'm telling you that we do."

She stared down at the hackney seat. Their hands were now inches apart on the water-stained leather. Only the night before last his fingers had moved over her flesh and she had licked the sweat from his skin and wrapped herself round him and taken him into her body. For a moment, when he shuddered in her arms, his self-control shattered like crystal, she had been able to delude herself that he was hers.

But that was folly, of course. People didn't belong to other people. If one was lucky, one could touch a proffered fraction of another's soul, like fingers twining together across an expanse of cool sheet in the dark. But these days, no matter how tightly she gripped her husband, she seemed to touch less and less of him.

They pulled up in South Audley Street and climbed the steps without speaking. Difficult to believe they had left the house a scant twelve hours ago. Colin would be upset that they had missed breakfast in the nursery, and Jessica would have had to make do with one of her silver feeding bottles. The pull of her bloodstained gown across her chest reminded Mélanie that she was still a nursing mother. If she'd known they'd be out all night, she'd have used her breast exhauster before she left the house.

They'd faced danger before. They'd always been able to protect the children. Surely they still could.

"You have a visitor," Michael said when he opened the door. "A Mr. Barrington. He insisted on waiting. I've shown him into the sitting room."

She and Charles looked at each other, the constraint between them forgotten. The name was unfamiliar and that, coupled with the events of the past thirty-six hours, was enough to set them both on edge.

Charles opened the sitting room door and cast a glance inside before stepping aside to allow her to precede him. A man stood by the windows. A slight, sandy-haired man of middle years, dressed in tan breeches and a dun-colored coat. Mélanie, used to choosing clothes for their effect, decided that he had dressed with the intention of creating as little notice as possible.

His gaze flickered over them, reminding her of the blood and coffee spatters on her gown, the smears of dirt and green vegetable stains on Charles's coat, the scrapes and stubble on his face.

"Mrs. Fraser." He gave her the briefest of nods, then turned to Charles. "I don't believe we've met, Fraser. I was at Oxford before you, and then I spent some years posted in Brazil. Like you, I've only recently returned to Britain." He fixed Charles with a cool, level gaze. "The Foreign Secretary sent me. He wants to see you immediately."

Chapter 9

"Sit down, Charles."

Charles closed the door of the Foreign Secretary's office, crossed the worn carpet, and lowered himself into a ladderback chair. The use of his given name was a reminder that the Foreign Secretary had known him since he was a boy, but he suspected Castlereagh had employed it more to put him in his place than to reassure him.

"Why am I here, sir?" he asked.

Castlereagh surveyed him across the surface of his desk, which was uncharacteristically disordered, piled high with papers and sheaves of foolscap, ledgers, and today's edition of the *Morning Post*. His brows rose slightly at the picture Charles presented. Charles's hand was still bandaged, and he had a bruise to the jaw from the fracas in the coffee stall at Covent Garden. He'd taken the time to shave and change before he left South Audley Street, but he'd nicked himself twice with the razor. Haste and lack of sleep. Not to mention nerves.

"I understand you and your wife were involved in an incident last night," Castlereagh said.

Charles tensed. This was quick even for Castlereagh. "Where did you hear that?"

"I'm not at liberty to say. But I am aware that your friend Francisco Soro was shot yesterday evening."

"Do you know who shot him?"

"No. Though I may perhaps know more about the matter than you do." Castlereagh aligned the papers on the desk before him so the tops of each stack were level. "I don't think you quite realize what you've got involved in, Charles."

Charles looked from the Foreign Secretary's aristocratic face to the slender hands creating order out of the chaos on the desktop, much as Castlereagh would like to impose his vision of order on the rest of the world. Charles had worked closely with him at the Congress of Vienna. Castlereagh had been quick to employ Charles's talents, both official and unofficial, before the peace negotiations had been brought to an abrupt halt by Napoleon's escape from Elba. But when it came to the course that was best for Britain and Europe, they had sharply divergent views.

Dissatisfaction with a view of the world that placed paramount importance on stifling all dissent for fear of revolution was a large part of why Charles had left the diplomatic service. In fairness, Castlereagh had always listened to Charles's arguments, though he had never given the least sign of being persuaded by them.

"Perhaps you'd care to enlighten me about what I'm involved in?" Charles said.

Castlereagh tightened the buff-colored ribbon that held a sheaf of foolscap closed. "You were in Paris until recently. You know the situation there is still anything but calm, for all that the war's officially over. The Comte d'Artois and his followers have been somewhat—ah—excessive in the zeal with which they've sought retribution against members of the former regime."

"Revenge might be a more appropriate word."

"Perhaps. Semantics aside, it would be foolish to deny that Bonaparte's followers and Bonaparte himself still constitute a threat." Castlereagh replaced the lid on a jar of ink. "A few weeks ago, I received reports from Paris concerning a secret organization with the unlikely name of the Elsinore League. An organization of former Bonapartist officers, some in prison, some still free."

"Reports from whom?"

"Agents of mine." Castlereagh wiped a trace of ink from the side of the jar. "You didn't know every agent in my employ, Charles."

"I never thought I did, sir."

"Two of my agents had managed to infiltrate themselves into the fringes of the Elsinore League some months since. It's risky work, as I'm sure you appreciate based on your own experience."

Charles nodded. "Risky" was no doubt a massive understatement. "Where does Francisco fit into this?"

Castlereagh moved a paper from one stack to another. "I know Soro was a friend of yours and that he was very useful to us in the Peninsula. But since the war he seems to have found himself at loose ends. He went to Paris last autumn and apparently fell in with the Elsinore League. A bit surprising when he'd worked against the French in Spain, but perhaps his quarrel was more with French occupation of his country than with Bonapartist ideals. You'd agree?"

Charles shifted his position in his chair, his gaze on Castlereagh. "Yes," he said in a guarded voice.

"According to my agents, Soro was acting as a courier. He probably wasn't aware of the full extent of what the group was planning."

"What were they planning?"

"We haven't been able to determine that, not for a certainty. At first we thought it was simply the rescue of former Bonapartist officers from prison, but now we suspect they have something bigger in mind." Castlereagh picked up his penknife and picked at a piece of sealing wax on the tooled green leather of the desktop. "As you well know, the alliances between the French monarchy and our government and the Russians and the Prussians are not entirely harmonious. We've done our best to paper over the cracks, but if something were to happen to disrupt things, the sort of incident that would have everyone blaming everyone else and demanding someone pay—"

Charles straightened his shoulders. "An assassination attempt? That's what you're afraid of? On whom?"

"A member of the French royal family. A foreign ambassador.

We haven't been able to determine with certainty." Castlereagh pried the wax loose with a vicious twist of the knife. "Soro may have learned what the group was planning. He came to England to hand over information on their activities. To you, it seems. One of the group followed him and killed him last night. And very nearly killed you and your wife as well. My God, Charles, what were you thinking?"

Castlereagh fixed him with a firm, parental stare. Either his words were true or he was a very good actor or he believed the lie. His story fit the facts. Almost. It didn't account for how the devil Honoria Talbot fit in with Francisco's activities in France.

Charles hesitated, searching for time, answers, a way out. "Can you show me evidence of any of this?"

"My dear Charles. You worked in intelligence. You understand about secrecy. My word as a gentleman will have to suffice."

"With all due respect, my lord, without seeing the evidence myself, I can't be sure that you haven't been misled."

"I'm not misled easily," Castlereagh snapped in the tone of one who had faced down monarchs. He gripped his hands together on the desktop. His knuckles were white. He couldn't abide being out of control, an attitude Charles could sympathize with. "Soro must have arrived in Paris when you were still there yourself. He never made any attempt to contact you?"

"No." For some reason, the admission made Charles feel like a traitor.

"That should at least confirm that he was involved in something he didn't want you to know about. He didn't say anything to you before he died? Or give you anything?"

The last question set off signal fires of alarm in Charles's head. "You think he meant to give me something?"

"Assuming we're right that he sought you out to give you evidence against the Elsinore League."

"He was shot before he could tell me anything," Charles said. That much was true. He neglected to add that Francisco hadn't died immediately upon being shot.

Castlereagh leaned back in his chair and tapped his fingers on the ink blotter. "We haven't always agreed, Charles, but you did us able service during the war. I know you understand what's due to

your country. I know you'll understand what I mean when I tell you
not to pursue Francisco Soro's death further."

Charles stared at his former superior. "Surely if what you've told
me is true, there's every reason to continue to investigate."

"But you're not the man to do it."

"Sir—"

"Soro's assassin is no doubt halfway back to Paris by now. Where
my agents are still in place. That's how we'll uncover what the Elsinore League are planning. Any questions we ask here will only
reveal that we're on to them and put our people in Paris at risk."

"That assumes we can't investigate here without them getting
wind of it."

"You're a clever man, Charles, but you're not infallible. Or
invulnerable." Castlereagh pushed his chair back and got to his feet.
He stared down at his desktop for a moment, then wandered over to
the window and looked out into Downing Street. He seemed to be
seeing something beyond the clutter of midmorning traffic. "I know
it's difficult, believe me. Coming home after all these years. Leading
a domestic life after living on the edge for so long." He cleared his
throat. "I don't know the details, but I'm aware that your relationship with your father has not always been what one might wish.
You're living in proximity to him for the first time in nearly ten
years, and he's just announced his intention to marry again."

Charles stared at the Foreign Secretary's aristocratic profile, outlined against the light from the window. In all the years he had
known and worked with Castlereagh, the Foreign Secretary had
never touched so directly on his personal life. "I left boyhood behind
long ago."

"I don't know that one ever leaves one's childhood truly behind.
But whatever the temptation, this is no time to go tilting at wind-
mills. You have a family of your own now. For God's sake, you
dragged your wife into this."

"I didn't drag her, she insisted on coming with me. Francisco
was her friend as well."

Castlereagh turned to look at Charles. "I'm aware that Mrs.
Fraser is a woman of somewhat unorthodox talents, but you can't
wish to risk her life. This isn't your fight. Leave it to us. For her sake.

For your children's sake. We'll learn the truth, and Francisco Soro's murderer will be brought to justice. You have a parliamentary career to think about. I can't say I agree with most of the things you stand for, but you obviously take your beliefs seriously."

"I knew Francisco," Charles said. "I understand the way his mind worked. Surely—"

"Damn it, Charles." Castlereagh strode forward and slammed his hands down on the desk. The ink jar rattled, and a sheaf of foolscap thudded to the floor. "This isn't about your friend or your theories or your damned need to fix everything. If you won't stay out of it for your family's sake, then have the goodness not to risk the lives of my agents."

Charles shifted against the hard wood of his chair. Castlereagh's words rang true and cut close to the bone. And yet—he looked up into Castlereagh's intent eyes. "The Elsinore League is an odd name for a group of French soldiers. Could they have any connection to people here in England?"

Something flickered in Castlereagh's gaze for an instant. Something Charles would have sworn was fear, a fear he had rarely seen the Foreign Secretary display. Castlereagh drew back and straightened his shoulders. "No," he said. "To my knowledge their activities are confined to France."

But the fear in Castlereagh's gaze belied his words. He knew more than he'd admitted. Perhaps he knew what linked the Elsinore League to Honoria Talbot and possibly her father. Charles gripped his hands together, assimilating the fact that the Foreign Secretary of Britain, a man he had worked with, a man he trusted, had just lied to him.

The question was where the truth left off and the lies began.

"Charles?" Castlereagh tugged his coat sleeve smooth. "Do I have your word that you won't pursue this matter further?"

Charles looked into the Foreign Secretary's eyes. "You do," he said, returning lie for lie.

"So the question," Mélanie said, "is whether Castlereagh's being fed misinformation or whether he's part of the plot himself."

"In a nutshell." The chintz cushions creaked as Charles dropped down on the nursery window seat beside her. He closed his eyes for a moment and leaned his head back against the white-painted window frame. He looked like he had after the third day of cannon fire shaking their house in Brussels during Waterloo, his skin ashen, his gaze vacant.

He didn't agree with Castlereagh's politics, Mélanie knew, but he had trusted the Foreign Secretary. For all Charles's skepticism, betrayal hit him hard. He wasn't as familiar with it as she was herself.

She touched his arm. He jerked and turned back to her, leaving whatever had troubled him in some far-off region of his mind where she couldn't follow him.

Jessica stirred at Mélanie's breast and made a protesting sound at the disruption. Charles gave a half smile, his distancing, attempting-to-reassure-her smile, and cupped his hand round Jessica's head. "The story Castlereagh told me was perfectly designed to explain away what we've learned," he said.

"Except that whoever designed it didn't realize how much we know."

"Quite. The story doesn't explain why the Bonapartists would fear for a woman named Honoria, who may be Honoria Talbot." Charles frowned at Jessica's downy head. "When I asked if the Elsinore League has connections to Britain, Castlereagh looked frightened. He may not know the whole story. He may believe some of what he told me. But he knows the story he told me isn't the complete truth."

Jessica reached up to pat Mélanie's breast and released her nipple. Mélanie rocked her in her arms. "Whether Castlereagh designed the story or someone fed it to him, it was structured to convince you to tell him anything you'd learned from Francisco and to hand over anything Francisco had given you."

"And to convince me to stop asking further questions." Charles handed her a flannel from the basket on the window seat between them.

Mélanie draped the flannel over her shoulder and lifted Jessica against it. "Did he believe you on either count?" She patted Jessica's back. "That you hadn't learned anything from Francisco and that you'd stop asking questions?"

"I'm not sure. I thought so at the time, but I was followed home from the Foreign Office."

Her arms must have tightened round Jessica, because her daughter made an indignant noise. Mélanie kissed Jessica's head, breathing in the milky sweetness of baby. "Did you get a good look at—him? Was it a man?"

"I think so. Brown coat, middling height, beaver hat. I could have given him the slip, but that just would have alerted him to the fact that I was on to him. They could find us here easily enough in any case."

Mélanie smoothed down a wayward curl on Jessica's forehead. "Is he still watching the house?"

"He was a quarter-hour ago. I glimpsed him across the street from the half-landing window."

They looked at each other, the extent of what they were involved in hitting both of them like a hammer blow. Of one accord, their gazes went to Jessica. She looked very small nestled in the curve of Mélanie's arm, her skin soft and translucent against the rose-striped lustring of Mélanie's dress, her tiny limbs wobbling slightly. Jessica looked from one parent to the other with bright, curious eyes and stretched out a hand. Charles held out a finger, and she clenched it tightly. "It's hardly the first time we've faced an unknown enemy," he said.

Mélanie nodded. "This means we can't trust anyone connected to the Government, doesn't it?"

"Including the Home Office," Charles said while Jessica examined each finger of his hand one by one. "We were right not to go to Bow Street. Word would be sure to get back to the Home Secretary."

Mélanie swallowed. Given her background, it was not so strange to think of the British Government as an enemy, but she had never thought to find her husband in this position. "Charles, how far do you think this goes?"

Jessica was fidgeting. Charles took her from Mélanie and balanced her on his lap, her fingers curled round his own. "Difficult to guess when we don't even know what it is."

Mélanie did up the buttons that closed the flap on the nursing bodice of her gown (designed to "enable Ladies to nourish their infants in the most delicate manner possible"). "Castlereagh wouldn't lie lightly."

"No, if he's involved he thinks the country's interests are at stake." Charles touched his forehead to Jessica's. Jessica giggled with glee. "The question is, what did the Elsinore League hire Francisco to do, what made Francisco turn against them, and what the devil does it have to do with Honoria?"

Mélanie took the flannel from her shoulder and carefully folded it. "Charles, I decoded the papers Manon gave us."

He swung his head round to look at her. "And?"

She put the flannel back in the basket and twitched it smooth. "I'm not sure what it means. It's a list of names with numbers next to each one that I realized were map coordinates. I worked out where each one is." She walked to the white-painted writing desk and lifted her notes from its rose-splashed surface. "Marseilles, Lyons, Calais. All French. All but the last."

She held the paper out to Charles. The last name on the list was British. The name of the place that, Mélanie well knew, meant more to her husband than anywhere else on earth.

Dunmykel.

Chapter 10

Charles stared down at the deciphered list, a dozen new questions tumbling in his head.

"It's odd that Dunmykel is the only British place on the list," his wife said. "But considering we suspected the Elsinore League was connected to Britain and perhaps to Miss Talbot's father—"

"It's not Dunmykel. It's the name next to it." *Giles McGann.* Another piece of the past he thought he'd left behind, which seemed to be closing about him in an ever tighter web.

His wife was watching him with the gaze that often saw far more than he wanted. "Of course," she said. "You must know everyone at Dunmykel. He's someone you grew up with?"

"One of the tenant farmers on the estate. He taught Edgar and me to fish." For a moment, Charles could hear Giles McGann's cheerful voice in his ear. *Steady, lad, don't pull on the line.* His throat tightened.

Jessica wriggled in his arms and pressed a damp kiss against his shoulder. Charles smoothed her hair. "I suspect this is some sort of network rather than the membership of the Elsinore League itself," he said, returning his attention to the list. "If Francisco was acting as a courier, perhaps he'd been to visit these people."

"Do you think this is what Castlereagh knew? He didn't want you involved because he knows you care for Giles McGann?"

"Giles McGann is a scholarly man of liberal principles, fond of Rousseau, who supported the French Revolution until it turned into a bloodbath and who admired Napoleon Bonaparte until he made himself emperor. So, as a secret Bonapartist agent—it's difficult for me to imagine." Charles shifted Jessica against his shoulder. "And yet—" The words stuck in his throat like a betrayal, but he could not but deny the logic of the connection. "This could explain the link between the Elsinore League and Honoria Talbot."

"Mr. McGann knows her?"

Charles began to circle the room, jiggling Jessica in his arms, though he couldn't have said which of them he was trying to soothe. "Honoria often visited Dunmykel as a child, along with Quen and Val and Evie. McGann was kind to all of us. But he had a soft spot for Honoria."

"Did he know Cyril Talbot well?"

"Cyril visited Dunmykel, but he was the younger brother of Father's friend. McGann was a tenant. In Father's set, the two groups rarely mixed. But if McGann and Cyril Talbot were both connected to the Elsinore League, the visits would have given them a chance to communicate."

"And if Francisco had been to Dunmykel on business for the Elsinore League and met Mr. McGann, Mr. McGann could be the person he worked with who confessed to a fear for Honoria Talbot. Fear she'd learn the truth about her father?"

"Or fear for her safety. Other members of the League could have held either one over McGann's head." Charles looked down at his daughter, nestled against him with boneless trust. He remembered the day Mélanie had told him, over the gleaming linen of the breakfast table in their lodgings in Paris, that she wanted to have another child. He stroked Jessica's soft, sparse hair, fingers trembling with the same wonder and terror he'd felt that morning in Paris. He had no doubt Mélanie loved Jessica as fiercely as she did Colin, but even now he wasn't sure what had motivated her to want another child. A need to prove that the bond between them was more than convenience? A sense that she owed it to him, for all he'd insisted from the first that she didn't? Or an uncomplicated longing that was hard to imagine in their very complicated lives?

"I'll talk to Honoria," he said. "See what if anything she knows about what's going on. I think I can do that without giving the game away. Unless I've completely lost my edge."

He summoned up a smile and looked into his wife's eyes. Her gaze had the impenetrable darkness of deep, still water. He wondered what she suspected about his relationship to Honoria. Probably something more obvious than the truth and yet not nearly as bad. He wondered how much she'd mind if she knew the whole story. They had the sort of marriage where they never asked those questions.

The door burst open without even a preliminary rap to reveal Gisèle, her straw hat askew and her cheeks flushed with color. "Have you heard? It's too awful and I won't go." She slammed the door shut and leaned against the white-painted panels. "He can't make me."

"Who?" Charles studied his sister. In the three months he'd been back in Britain, this was the first time she'd come to the house unannounced. "Go where?"

"Father." Gisèle tugged off her hat and tossed it onto the nearest table, stalked over to a striped chintz armchair, and flung herself into it. "He wants to have a house party at Dunmykel to celebrate this ridiculous betrothal of his. Honoria's family and our family in the wilds of Perthshire for a fortnight. Can you imagine anything more ghastly?"

"Yes, actually, if I put my mind to it," Charles said. *Such as the events of the last couple of days.*

"It's going to be hideous. You don't know what you're in for, Mélanie." Gisèle cast a brief glance of acknowledgment at Charles's wife. "You've never seen us all gathered together full force."

Mélanie took Jessica from Charles's arms. "I own it doesn't sound the pleasantest way to spend the summer, but I shouldn't think you'd find it wholly distasteful. I presume Lord Valentine will be there."

Gisèle started. "Oh. Yes." She smoothed her fingers over her crumpled skirt. "Of course."

Charles studied his little sister. For a moment, he'd swear Gisèle had forgotten that the man she'd been outrageously flirting with all season even existed.

"Have you quarreled?" Charles asked. Though surely a quarrel would have generated more passion.

Gisèle pleated the patterned white fabric of her skirt. "No, nothing like that. But you know what it will be like—Honoria looking superior and criticizing me. And sitting down to dinner with the same people every night—"

"Disagreeable, but hardly enough to justify this sort of panic."

"I'm not panicked, I'm—" Gisèle glanced round the room, looking everywhere but into the eyes of the people present. If her hair had been a shade paler and her face a fraction thinner, she might have been their mother. She gave the same impression of volatile emotions welling up beneath the flushed eggshell porcelain of her skin, ready to break free in a myriad of unexpected directions. "Aunt Frances says we have to go for the sake of the family."

"Typical of Aunt Frances," Charles said. "She always picks the most inconvenient moments to turn conventional."

She looked up at him the way she had when she was a little girl who'd thought her elder brother could fix anything. "I can't go to Dunmykel, Charles. Don't ask me to explain why. Just help me. Please."

Charles dropped down beside her chair. "Do you want me to talk to Father?"

"You can't. He's already left."

"What?" Charles was hardly in his father's confidence, but Kenneth had said nothing about leaving town when he summoned Charles to Berkeley Square the previous day. "For Dunmykel?"

"This morning. Lord Glenister and Honoria left as well. Evie and Quen and Val are following in a couple of days."

Odder and odder. "How long had this been planned?"

"It hadn't been planned at all, as far as I know. If you ask me, something happened to send them all haring off to Scotland at a moment's notice, but I can't think what. The rest of us are to join them as soon as possible. It's not like a normal house party at all, where one has time to plan and make arrangements properly and choose the right clothes." Gisèle's breath caught with panic, belying the frippery nature of her words. "It's bad enough Father's making a fool of himself by marrying a girl young enough to be our sister without dragging us all into it as well."

Charles laid a hand over her own. "I'll talk to Aunt Frances, Gelly. Perhaps you can stay with a friend."

Gisèle smiled at him, a real, direct smile, the first she had given him since he'd returned to Britain. "Thank you, Charles."

Charles nodded, not daring himself to push further against the boundaries his sister had set. Gisèle disengaged her hand from his own and sprang to her feet. "Colin will never forgive me if I don't look in on him. Where is he? In the schoolroom? No, it's all right, I know the way." She touched her fingers to Jessica's cheek and whisked herself from the room.

Charles and Mélanie stared at each other.

"It sounds as though your father and Lord Glenister wanted Miss Talbot out of the way," Mélanie said. "Could they suspect she's in danger as well?"

"Perhaps. Or perhaps it's coincidence. Though I'm disinclined to believe in coincidence at the moment."

"So we all go to Dunmykel?" Mélanie said.

Charles looked across the nursery at his wife, a slender figure in a rose-striped dress, the strong, fragile bones of her face lit by the light from the window, their daughter nestled against her. She didn't deserve to have his problems inflicted on her. And he flinched at the thought of her seeing the sordidness of his family and his past. "Mel—"

"Charles, don't you dare turn Hotspur on me. The children and I are coming with you."

Mélanie wasn't the sort of woman who could be packed off to safety. Even assuming he had the least idea where safety from their unseen enemies might be found. "Good," he said. "At least if we're all in one place we can look out for each other."

In Scotland he could talk to Giles McGann. And he could talk to Honoria, as he had meant to do before he learned she had left London. The more they discovered, the more imperative that talk became.

Honoria's image flickered in his mind, blue eyes wide with trust and entreaty; lips parted; strands of gold hair spilling over her pale shoulders, her fragile collarbone, her firm, naked young breasts.

He blinked the image away and met his wife's unreadable gaze. "When do we leave?" Mélanie asked.

Dunmykel, Perthshire
Ten days later

The rain slapped against the granite and ran down the fifteenth-century leaded glass of the mullioned windows like rivulets of tears. The air was thick with damp and sea salt and a musty scent that was redolent of regret. The stone-floored corridor was cold, even on a July evening. Scotland was always cold, a numbing cold that soaked through layers of superfine and silk and linen to permeate flesh and bone, like a memory that could not be expunged.

Frederick Talbot, fifth Marquis of Glenister, stopped midway down the vaulted corridor and drew a breath. His chest felt as though it had been pummeled black and blue. His throat was tight, his mouth dry. Even when he closed his eyes on the guttering flame of his candle and the aged oak wainscoting of the walls, he could not hold the images at bay. But that wasn't surprising. They never really left him, even in sleep. He opened his eyes, strode to the end of the corridor, and turned the handle of the study door without knocking.

The air held the pungent scent of good tobacco and better whisky. The room was in shadow, lit only by the yellow glow of a lacquered Agrand lamp on the green baize table by the fireplace. "If you're trying to find your way to a lady's boudoir," Kenneth said, "you drank even more at dinner than I realized."

He was sprawled in one of the high-backed tapestry chairs at the table, gaze fixed on the cards spread before him.

Glenister set down his candle without sparing Kenneth a direct glance. Glass after glass of burgundy and port swirled in his brain, but he crossed to the table that held the decanters and poured himself a whisky. "I couldn't sleep. I never can north of Edinburgh."

The whiffle of a card being turned over sounded behind him. "What an admission for a Scotsman," Kenneth said.

"A Scotsman with an English name and a Scottish title and probably more English blood in his veins than Scots." Glenister tossed down the whisky in one draught. It burned his throat, but didn't drive out the fear. Or the memories. "It was a mistake to come here." He refilled his glass and turned to stare at his old friend. In the lamplight, Kenneth's face was as calm and composed as if it had been carved of marble. "If you had to have a house party to celebrate this ridiculous betrothal of yours, we should have had it in Richmond. Or Surrey. Or even Argyllshire. Anywhere but here."

Kenneth's gaze drifted over the delicate Chinese porcelain on the mantel, the elegant lines of the bronze nude in the corner, the Renaissance oil above the fireplace (Cleopatra reclining upon blue velvet, the work of some Old Master that Glenister knew he should recognize). "That would hardly have served the purpose of the visit."

Glenister crossed to the window. Through a crack between the claret-velvet drapes he could see the dark outline of a pine tree, its branches whipped by the wind. The walls were over a foot thick here, in the oldest part of the house. God knew what acts of betrayal and brutality had leached into the granite in three hundred years. Merely the events of the past quarter century were enough to turn Glenister's blood to ice and his legs to water. "The truth is here. We can't hide from it. It's soaked into the damned walls. It lingers beneath the stairs. It's lurking behind the tapestries and the wainscoting and those bloody pictures you're so fond of collecting."

Kenneth's chair creaked as though he were leaning back. "I've never known you to wax so poetic. Perhaps you paid more heed to literature lectures at Oxford than I realized."

"Shut up." Glenister didn't feel like talking about Oxford.

"If there's any truth buried here, it's a truth only you and I could recognize."

Glenister spun round. "It's a truth that could destroy both of us. You as much as me. Don't you forget it."

Kenneth turned a fresh card over and stared at it as though the suit meant something to him. "Men in our position make their own truths, Glenister. We've been doing so for the past three decades. I don't see why now should be any different."

"Damn it, Kenneth, do you realize what's at stake if it all begins to unravel? We're not boys playing games anymore."

"Of course not." Kenneth aligned the cards spread on the baize before him so the tops were exactly even. The red and the black shimmered in the lamplight. "They never were games."

The angle of Kenneth's silvered chestnut hair and the drape of his paisley silk dressing gown held unquestioned arrogance. His fingers were steady as he turned over another card. The king of clubs. Glenister wondered if his oldest friend had any idea how much he hated him. "What the hell do you want with her?" he demanded.

"My dear Glenister." Kenneth looked up from the cards. "If you can't appreciate your niece's charms you're blinder than I realized."

Glenister's fingers tightened round his glass. He almost fancied he could hear the crystal crack. "You've had your pick of women for years. Why marry again now?"

The lamplight bounced off Kenneth's pewter-hard eyes. "Is it so hard to believe I've fallen in love?"

"You?" Glenister gave a coarse laugh that held echoes of brothels and boudoirs, grottoes and glades, window embrasures and closed carriages. "Yes."

Kenneth returned his gaze to the cards. "If you disapprove, you should have withheld your consent to the match."

Glenister flinched, conscious of a guilt nothing could assuage. "You know damn well I couldn't have."

"Of course you could." Kenneth reached for his own whisky glass and took a sip. "If you were prepared to take the consequences."

Glenister's free hand curled into a fist. If he'd had one more drink in him, he'd have smashed his fist into Kenneth's face. "You bloody bastard."

Kenneth gave him one of those damned mocking looks that had cut him to ribbons for as long as he could remember. "You didn't come looking for me tonight to reminisce, Frederick. Why the devil did you come here?"

"Because it's past time the evidence was destroyed." Glenister hurled himself at the mahogany mass of the desk in two unsteady steps.

With the speed of a greyhound, Kenneth was on his feet. His fingers closed round Glenister's arm with the bite of steel. "I wouldn't touch anything if I were you, Glenister. Besides, what you're looking for isn't here."

Glenister tried to jerk away. Kenneth's fingers tightened until Glenister would have sworn he could feel the imprint on his bones. "Honoria's going to be living in this house with you. If you think I'll risk her of all people finding out—"

"My dear Glenister, if you'll recall we've gone to great lengths in the past weeks to ensure she never does. Do you imagine I'm the sort of man who can't keep secrets from his wife?"

Glenister gripped Kenneth by the lapels of his dressing gown. "Give me your word that Honoria will never learn the truth."

"I can't imagine why she would."

Glenister tightened his grip. "Your *word*. That you'll never tell her. Swear it."

Kenneth detached Glenister's hands from his dressing gown, throwing Glenister back against the desk. "I'd be a fool to tell her. Don't worry. I have what I want. So do you, after a fashion. Go to bed, Frederick. Or if you still can't sleep, go inflict yourself on one of the housemaids."

Glenister snatched up his glass and swallowed the last of his whisky. It left a raw void in his chest. He lashed out with the only weapon to hand. "What about your son? He's the sort who asks questions. He's too damn clever by half and he's still far too fond of Honoria."

Kenneth's face went still for a moment, not with feeling but with the conscious absence of it. He returned to his chair, seated himself, and spread his hands over the cards on the table. "He'll be here himself in a few days. You can leave Charles to me, Glenister. Though all things considered, it really is a pity he didn't manage to get himself killed in the Peninsula."

Chapter 77

Tension from a myriad of disquieting possibilities pulled at Charles's face as he lifted the knocker on the door of the granite cottage. But Mélanie also caught a spark of schoolboy anticipation in his eyes at the reunion with his old friend. Giles McGann meant a great deal to him. And yet until McGann's name had appeared on the list she had decoded, Charles had never mentioned McGann to his wife.

The clang of the iron knocker on the deal planks echoed through the damp morning air. Mélanie glanced round the short expanse of garden between the house and the road beyond. Someone had taken care in laying it out, but now weeds spilled over the beds of primroses and wood anemones and sprang up between the cobblestones that formed the path to the house.

Charles clanged the knocker again and called out, "Giles."

The word echoed in the fog-choked air. Charles frowned and without further speech walked round to the back of the cottage. The spreading branches and spiky needles of a Scots pine half hid the back door, lower and narrower than at the front. Charles knocked and called McGann's name again. When another minute passed with no answer, he felt about on the ledge above the doorframe and retrieved a tarnished key.

Mélanie followed him into a stone-floored kitchen. Copper pans glinted on the walls in the murky light, but no aroma of recently prepared food lingered in the air. Instead the room had a musty smell, as though it were some time since a fire had been kindled or the windows opened. She touched her fingers to the deal table. A film of dust showed on the French gray of her glove.

Charles pushed open the kitchen door and went into a narrow hall, calling McGann's name. He opened a door off the hall onto a sitting room, crossed to the window, and pushed back the faded print curtains to let in the fitful morning light. Bookshelves lined the room, crowded with books of all shapes and sizes, stuck in at odd angles and stacked crosswise to make the most of the space. Not unlike Charles's study at home.

His gaze roamed over the bookshelves, the smoke-blackened fire grate, a fire screen so faded it was impossible to tell what it depicted, a tarnished brass ink pot and penknife on the writing desk against the far wall. Each one seemed to hold a story. Part of the tapestry of memories of which Mélanie knew nothing.

A book lay open on a three-legged table beside a threadbare velvet wing-back chair. A candlestick with dried wax pooled round the pewter base and a glass stood beside the book. Mélanie crossed to the table and held the glass to the light. Sediment crusted the bottom, and it still had a faint, nutty whiff of port.

She showed the glass to Charles. "It's dried," she said. "It's been here for days. Perhaps longer."

Charles grimaced. "McGann's never been the tidiest housekeeper. But—"

He went back into the hall and quickly climbed the steps to the first floor. Mélanie followed him into the bedroom at the head of the stairs. The oak bed was made up, the quilt and sheet turned back, a faded blue wool dressing gown tossed over the foot of the bed. As though in readiness for the occupant. Save that there was a film of dust on the linens as well.

Fear gathering in his eyes, Charles opened the scarred doors of the wardrobe to reveal a full set of clothes.

He touched his fingers to the frayed gray wool of a coat, as though trying to conjure memories of the man who had worn it. "If he left of his own free will, his departure was abrupt. Perhaps—"

They both went still. A creak had sounded from the floor above that had nothing to do with the stirring of wind. Charles moved toward the door. She followed, holding her sarcenet skirts taut, sliding her half-boots over the floorboards with as little noise as possible.

They climbed the stairs to the second floor, testing the treads to avoid telltale squeaks. They hadn't brought their pistols with them. A mistake, perhaps, but experience had taught that weapons could create as many problems as they solved.

The second-floor landing opened onto a corridor shrouded in shadows. Heavy worsted curtains were drawn over the windows, letting in only meager light. Doors opened on either side of the corridor. Charles jerked his head toward the door to the left. Mélanie flattened herself against the curtains, ready to spring on anyone fleeing from the room.

Charles turned the door handle, eased the door open, and stepped into the room. He disappeared out of her line of sight. Silence followed. Her senses keyed to the room beyond, she scarcely registered the stir of the curtains at her back. Not until an arm closed round her throat and she felt the press of a knife against her ribs.

"Don't look round, whatever you do," a voice said in her ear. "Just stand still while I go down the stairs, and you have nothing to fear."

Mélanie went limp in her attacker's hold. He stumbled beneath the force of her weight. She caught his wrist and twisted away from him just as Charles lunged through the open doorway and came to a frozen stop. His eyes blazed with fear and fury, then narrowed. "Belmont, you reprobate. Get the bloody hell away from my wife."

The Honorable Thomas Belmont, second son of the Earl of Lovel, put up a hand and straightened the intricate muslin folds of his cravat. "You really ought to keep a better eye on her, old boy. You never can tell who may be skulking behind the curtains. My profoundest apologies, Mélanie."

Mélanie righted her bonnet. "You're getting shockingly lazy, Tommy. You should have known I could get away from such a commonplace neck hold."

"Not one of my more shining moments." Tommy leaned back against the faded curtains and gave Mélanie the smile he'd given her while waltzing with her in an embassy ballroom; while she was bandaging a knife cut in his arm in an Andalusian barn; while he sighted down a rifle barrel in the Cantabrian Mountains. "I don't suppose you'd believe I came to Scotland for the fishing?"

"Yes, actually," Charles said. "But not the sort of fishing one does in a lake or a stream. I take it Castlereagh sent you?"

"Not exactly a brilliant deduction, Charles, considering we both used to work for the man."

"And you still do." Charles's gaze was as hard as the knife Tommy had pressed to Mélanie's side.

Tommy grimaced. "He'd skin me alive if he knew I was talking to you. He warned me not to let you know I was here. He said you'd be difficult, which was a bit redundant—you're always bloody difficult."

"Which is why you put a knife to Mélanie's ribs and tried to make your escape."

"Should have known it wouldn't work. But I had to at least make an effort."

Charles folded his arms across his chest. "Last we heard you were in Paris."

"I still am, officially." Tommy looked from Charles to Mélanie, much like Colin when he'd been caught climbing on a chair to peek into drawers that were supposed to be off limits. "Oh, for God's sake, Fraser, stop it with the damned high-handed expression. It was tiresome before we were a year into the war. I agree that explanations are called for, but perhaps we could go downstairs? I think I saw a bottle of port in the sitting room. I don't know about the two of you, but I could do with a drink."

They trooped downstairs in silence. Charles produced three chipped glasses from a dresser in the corner, dusted them with his handkerchief, and poured out the port. Change the surroundings slightly and they might have been in the embassy library in Lisbon.

Or sitting round a campfire in the Spanish mountains on the way to meet a contact or deliver a document.

"Quite like old times." Tommy dropped down on the settee. "Charles poking his nose into inconvenient places and asking awkward questions and annoying our superiors and generally making life hellish for those of us who just like to get the job done and get on with the dancing and drinking."

"Questions are awkward only when you find the answers inconvenient, Belmont."

"Damned right I find them inconvenient. You have a tiresome habit of forgetting whom we're fighting."

"An interesting argument, coming from a man who just held a knife on my wife."

"You know bloody well I'd never have—"

"Oh, for God's sake, you two." Mélanie clunked her glass down on a three-legged table. "Stop behaving as though you're on the playing fields of Harrow."

Charles leaned against the drinks table. "Where's McGann?"

Tommy's gaze darted over his face. "You mean you don't know, either?"

"Mélanie and I just got here."

"So did I." Tommy took a sip of port. His face was leaner than Mélanie remembered, sun-weathered and set with lines that sat oddly with his boyish insouciance and white-blond hair. "I suppose now we all dance about trying to figure out who knows what."

"Or we could just make it easy and try telling the truth." Charles watched his former fellow diplomat with a steady, appraising gaze.

"The truth? Good Lord, Charles, what have we come to? Still, I suppose trying something new always has a certain piquancy." Tommy gave the sort of disarming smile that had been setting hearts aflutter in diplomatic ballrooms ever since he was first posted abroad as an attaché. It didn't, of course, mean he intended to tell anything remotely close to the truth. "I'm sorry about Francisco Soro," he added. "I never quite trusted the man, but I know he was a friend of yours."

Mélanie's gaze went involuntarily to her husband's face, as Charles's went to her own.

"Oh, yes, I know about Soro," Tommy said. "I know most of what you know, I think."

"Is that why Castlereagh sent you here?" Charles asked. "Because of Soro?"

"Indirectly." Tommy crossed his legs. The light from the window picked out a film of dust on the gleaming leather of his Hessians. "I've been involved in investigating something in Paris for some time now."

"Something?"

"A spy ring of sorts. A ring of former Bonapartist officers. Called the Elsinore League, of all things. We haven't been able to determine exactly what they're up to, but we suspect it's something serious. Soro seems to have gone to work for them when he came to France."

"So Castlereagh told me," Charles said, neglecting to comment on whether or not he believed the Foreign Secretary.

Tommy nodded. "We have a couple of men infiltrated into the Elsinore League, or at least the league's outer circle. We thought we were finally on to something."

"We?"

Tommy met his gaze for a moment. "Castlereagh had me running the operation. It's gone on for several months now."

"Since before I left Paris."

"Yes." Tommy smoothed a crease from the glossy blue superfine of his sleeve. "No one can be involved in everything, Charles. Not even you."

"And my sympathies have been considered a bit too Bonapartist since the war."

"You said it, old boy, I didn't." Tommy took another sip of port. "If Castlereagh told you that much, he must have told you Soro apparently reached the point where he couldn't stomach the group's activities. I always thought he was too soft for his own good, though I could never tell which way he'd break. He came to England, probably with evidence against his former associates. He sought you out. He trusted you."

"Which may have been a fatal mistake on his part. I didn't do a very good job of protecting him." Charles's fingers whitened round his glass. "You followed Soro to England?"

"No. I came because we'd stumbled across evidence linking the Elsinore League to contacts in Britain."

Charles's shoulders straightened, an involuntary sign of quickening interest. "Go on."

Tommy ran his finger over a chip in his glass. "Why did you come to see Giles McGann today?"

"Why did you?"

"Here we go again. This circling round really is tiresome. I'm guessing you were doing more than simply calling on an old friend. But I don't think you quite realize what McGann was involved in, Charles."

"Enlighten me."

"One of the members of the Elsinore League, a Colonel Coroux, hanged himself in his cell in the Conciergerie three weeks ago."

Charles gave a quite brilliant impression of never having heard of Colonel Coroux. "You're sure it was suicide?"

"We're bloody well not sure of anything. My agents bribed the jailer to give them a quarter-hour to search the cell. They didn't find any evidence of foul play. But they did find some papers hidden in the straw in Coroux's mattress. Part of a list. Judging by the jottings, it looked like something he'd decoded. Or encoded. It seemed to be some sort of network." Tommy looked up at Charles, his blue eyes hard as tempered steel. "Giles McGann's name was on the list."

Charles's eyes widened. Given what they already knew, Mélanie thought some of the surprise in his gaze was feigned. "What the hell would a Scots farmer have to do with a ring of former Bonapartist officers?"

Tommy shifted his position on the frayed tapestry settee. "Castlereagh didn't tell you the whole story. A number of the members of the Elsinore League are former Bonapartist officers, that's true. But we think the group itself is far older than Waterloo. Older even than Bonaparte's regime. We've traced it back to the early days of the Revolution." He rested his arm along the back of the settee. "McGann had sympathies with the Revolution, didn't he?"

"I could name you a dozen MPs of whom one could say the same."

"Fair enough. Perhaps if McGann had been in Parliament he'd have expressed his views in that way. Instead he seems to have been acting as a sort of courier for this group, relaying messages and supplies. Holding things in safekeeping for them."

Charles folded his arms. "That's a good story. But I've heard a lot of good stories lately."

"Christ, Charles, are you going to take Soro's word over mine?"

"Do you really have to ask me that?"

"Given our history? No, I suppose not. You've always been quick to trust anyone other than those in authority."

"Francisco's been at least as honest with me in the past as you have."

Tommy sat forward, hands gripping his knees. "Damn it, Charles, Castlereagh would skin me alive—"

"I can think of a number of situations where that hasn't stopped you."

"You know as well as I do there isn't always proof—"

"If there's no proof, I don't see how you can be certain of your claims, either."

Tommy grimaced, swore, and knocked back the remainder of his port. Finally, he pulled a paper from inside his jacket. "I found this locked away in a box in your friend McGann's writing desk."

Charles took the paper, glanced at it, and went still. Without speech, he held the paper out to Mélanie.

McGann,
I have a delivery for you.

In place of a signature, it bore a stamp in red ink, as from a signet ring. Not the castle of the Elsinore League, but a small picture of a falcon.

"Do you recognize it?" Charles asked Mélanie, his voice without a hint of betraying inflection.

She studied the crimson image. "It seems as though I should, but—no."

He took the paper back and stared down at it. Fear flickered in his eyes for a moment, sharp and wounding. "Have you heard of Le Faucon de Maulévrier?"

Chapter 12

Mélanie tensed inwardly as she did whenever Charles mentioned anything to do with France, but in this case she was able to shake her head without any need for deception.

Charles gave a faint smile. "I sometimes forget what an infant you are."

"Only six years more so than you," she said.

"An important six years in this case. You were a baby during the Reign of Terror. I was a young boy. And even then I probably wouldn't know about it myself if I didn't have cousins who emigrated from that part of France."

"Le Faucon de Maulévrier was active during the Terror?"

Charles nodded. "He was a *représentant en mission* in the Vendée at the height of the anti-Republican rebellion. He was very effective at keeping order, largely because he was willing to inflict whatever horrors it took to frighten the local populace into submission."

"When the guillotine proved too slow, he tied prisoners up, bombarded them with cannon fire, and bayoneted the survivors,"

Tommy said. "But his real task was to deal with a band of rebels who were hiding out in the hills, causing havoc for the local authorities. Le Faucon systematically had his men ravish the wives and daughters left behind in the village in an attempt to drive the men out of hiding."

"Did it work?" Mélanie asked, shutting her mind to memories.

"It was a start," said Tommy, seemingly unaware of the way Charles was scowling at him. "But after a few months he still hadn't caught the rebel leader, who was eldest son of the d'Argenton family, the local landowners. The d'Argenton parents were dead, but a younger brother and sister still lived in the château. Le Faucon—" Tommy caught Charles's eye at last. "Got them to talk."

"He broke into the château and threatened to rape the sister if the younger brother wouldn't tell him where the elder brother was?" Mélanie said.

Tommy's eyes widened. "How the devil did you know?"

"It's the obvious way to get the information." Mélanie glanced at Charles. "The moral dividing line is whether or not once he had the information he ravished the girl anyway and killed the younger brother."

"He did," Charles said, eyes grim. "And then ambushed the elder brother and his remaining followers in their camp."

Mélanie willed herself to relax, the way she always had to when they discussed this part of French history. "Who was he? Le Faucon?"

"That's the odd thing," Charles said. "No one knows where he came from or his real name. He always signed his papers with a signet stamp, as on the paper you see there. Some say he was a student from the University of Paris, perhaps the younger son of an aristocratic family. There are even theories that he was foreign."

"English?"

"Or Prussian or Belgian or Italian. Perhaps because a number of Frenchmen would prefer not to take credit for him."

"What happened to him?"

"Just as the Terror was collapsing, he disappeared." Charles looked at Tommy.

"We think Le Faucon is running the Elsinore League," Tommy said. "That he started the league in the days of the Terror. It may have gone on all these years, or he may have resurrected it after Waterloo."

"Do you know where he is now?" Charles asked. "Or *who* he is?"

"Damn it, Fraser, do you think I'd be in the wilds of the Highlands if I did? A lot of Frenchmen would like to see him brought to justice. A third d'Argenton son who was away at school survived the Terror and is now a friend of the Comte d'Artois. He's rumored to have offered a sizable reward for information on Le Faucon's whereabouts."

"And Castlereagh?" Charles said.

"Would like to find him first. Le Faucon may have been a wanton criminal, but his intelligence gathering was phenomenal. Whether he continued the Elsinore League through the war or started the group up again since, he has contacts with a number of former Bonapartists who were powerful men. Castlereagh's more interested in learning what Le Faucon can tell him than in exacting vengeance or retribution."

"You don't have any idea where he went to earth?"

"He could be anyone. A soldier in the Bonapartist army, a Bonapartist government official. He could even have been masquerading as a Royalist all these years. He could well not even be in France. The most persistent rumor is that he was British or at least half-British and he took refuge in England."

"But nothing was ever proved."

"No. And Castlereagh knows no more than what you just outlined. Le Faucon would have been in a precarious enough position if his past had come to light under Bonaparte. Under the White Terror, with the current Vicomte d'Argenton one of d'Artois's cronies, he wouldn't have a hope in hell of surviving."

Charles surveyed Tommy. "Castlereagh told me he was afraid the Elsinore League was planning an assassination to stir up trouble between the allies. Surely that would be a bit extreme if Le Faucon fears for his life. He's been content to lie low all these years."

Tommy shifted his position on the settee.

"That isn't it, is it?" Charles said. "You think they may be planning to kill someone but not to stir up trouble. To cover up Le Faucon's past."

"Damn you, Charles. You could always put me in check before I even had my pawns arrayed."

"Who?" Mélanie said. "Whom do you think they might try to kill?"

"That's just it." Tommy sprang to his feet and took a turn about the room. "Until we know who Le Faucon is, we can't begin to guess."

"And you think McGann might know?" Charles said.

"He was a possible lead." Tommy gave a short laugh. "Our only possible lead."

"Did you find anything else in the cottage to indicate where he might have gone?"

Tommy shook his head.

"There are no signs of violence in the cottage," Mélanie said, "but it looks as though Mr. McGann left abruptly, probably late at night."

"Could he have known you were on to him?" Charles asked, his gaze trained on Tommy's face.

Tommy stalked to the dresser and refilled his glass. "I wouldn't have thought so, but I suppose it's possible."

"What will you do now?" Charles asked.

"Keep looking for McGann. At present, he's the best lead I have."

"Let me help make inquiries among the villagers. I can do that more easily than you can."

"Can you give me one good reason why I should trust you, Fraser?"

"Not that I can think of. But I want to find McGann as much as you do."

Tommy looked at Charles for a moment, measuring Charles as Charles had measured him. "All right."

"Where can I find you?"

"Oh, no, I'm not going that far. Let's appoint a meeting time and place. Midnight tomorrow?"

Charles nodded. "There's a chapel on the Dunmykel grounds. Just beyond the birch coppice. It will be deserted at that hour."

Tommy set down his port and straightened his cravat. "I hear your father's to marry Honoria Talbot."

Charles went still for a fraction of a second. "Gossip travels fast, even when one's incognito. Yes. He is."

"She's a lovely girl." A host of different subtexts hung in the air, but Mélanie couldn't settle on any one of them. "For her sake, I hope they're happy."

"So do I," said Charles.

Tommy gave a quick nod, turned to Mélanie, and lifted her hand to his lips. "Enchanting to see you, under any circumstances. I'd say not to let Charles drag you into anything too dangerous, but half the time it seems to be the other way round."

Mélanie summoned up the sort of bright smile that went with champagne and dance cards and hid her true feelings as effectively as a silk fan. "How well you know me, Tommy."

Tommy brushed his lips over her hand, but when he straightened up his gaze had turned serious. "Let me go out through the back. Then wait a bit before you leave." He looked from her to Charles. "These people are dangerous. Le Faucon, whoever he is, is still a powerful man. We know he's ruthless, and now he has nothing to lose. Just because we're in Britain doesn't mean the world's turned safe."

Charles nodded. "Caution sits oddly on your tongue, Belmont. But I take your meaning."

A smile tugged at Tommy's mouth. "Despite everything, I really wouldn't care to see you with your throat cut, Fraser. At least not until after we get to the bottom of this."

Tommy left the room with the swish of well-cut coattails and the click of Hessian boots. Charles went to the door and looked into the hall to make sure he had really left. He came back into the room, leaned against the closed door, and nodded.

"Do you believe him?" Mélanie asked.

Charles prowled across the room. "Do you?"

"I asked you first."

He scowled at the bookshelves. "The paper with Le Faucon's seal on it looked genuine. It was certainly old. They could have faked it, but—"

"It would have been difficult."

"Yes." Charles ran a finger down the faded gilt of a book spine.

"Charles." Mélanie looked across the room at her husband, feeling the familiar rush that always came when their minds clicked together over a problem. Some couples no doubt got this feeling from moonlight kisses or leisurely caresses exchanged on sun-dappled sheets. "According to Tommy, Colonel Coroux was found dead in his cell three weeks ago, which is just about the time Francisco and Manon fled Paris. What if Colonel Coroux was murdered and that's what had Francisco so upset?"

Charles's eyes narrowed. *"They have to be stopped before they kill again.* If Tommy's right about Le Faucon trying to cover up his past, Coroux could have been killed because he knew too much."

"Perhaps the messages Manon carried were communications between Coroux and Le Faucon. Coroux was trying to blackmail Le Faucon over his past, and Le Faucon decided the only safe solution was to get rid of him." Mélanie fingered a fold of her skirt. "If McGann was involved with Le Faucon and the Elsinore League and he got wind that Francisco had escaped with the papers and the whole thing was unraveling—"

"Then Giles would have had more than enough reason to disappear," Charles finished in a cold, flat voice.

"Yes. But—"

The thud of horse hooves echoed through the dusty glass of the window. Charles crossed the room and flung open the casement. "Andrew."

Mélanie followed her husband to the window in time to see Andrew Thirle, the Dunmykel estate agent, turn his dapple gray toward McGann's gate. Andrew was the oldest of Charles's small circle of real friends. His father had managed the estate before him, and he and Charles had grown up together at Dunmykel.

"Charles. By all that's wonderful," Andrew said. "I heard you arrived last night. Is McGann back?"

"Apparently not. Where's he gone?"

"That seems to be the mystery."

"What the devil—"

"Wait a bit," Andrew said. "I'll come in."

Andrew looped his horse's reins round the gatepost and made for the door. Charles and Mélanie met him in the entrance hall. "What the hell happened?" Charles demanded.

"We aren't sure." Andrew swept his beaver hat from his unruly chestnut hair. "Mrs. Fraser. It's good to see you again."

Mélanie returned the greeting. Andrew always treated her with careful formality, though she'd told him to call her Mélanie when they met three years ago.

Charles fixed his friend with a hard stare. "What do you mean, you don't know what happened? Where did McGann go?"

"No one seems to know. He's been missing for over a fortnight. At least that's the last time anyone saw him. He took a saddle into the tack shop in the village to be repaired two weeks ago last Thursday."

"He didn't mention business to anyone? Ask anyone to look in on the house or the livestock?"

"No. It took a while to sort out that he was actually gone. Danny Alford took the horses to his house and Meg and Harry Fyfe are feeding the rest of the animals. After a couple of days I took the spare key and had a look inside the cottage to make sure he hadn't fallen ill or suffered an accident." Andrew cast a glance round the hall, as though to make sure there was no sign of McGann's return. "But as you can tell, he must have gone away."

"In the middle of the night without warning, from the look of it."

Andrew flicked a finger through the stack of newspapers on the gateleg table in the hall. "McGann never was the tidiest sort."

"Damn it, Andrew, don't tell me you left it at that."

"What else could I have done?" Andrew's mobile features were set with a wariness Mélanie didn't remember from their meeting three years before. "Look, Charles, I'm as fond of McGann as you are, but he's able to take care of himself. He wouldn't thank any of us for meddling."

"An old friend disappears without a word of warning, and it doesn't even occur to you to wonder—"

"Of course I wondered." Andrew's voice cut against the beams overhead. "I asked questions of everyone who knew him. It's the talk of the village—at least, it was for the first few days. But there's no evidence of foul play. There's no evidence he fell ill. He seems to have left of his own accord. I assume he had his reasons for doing so quietly. Which means he wouldn't want us asking questions."

"Questions about what? Is there anything to even hint at why he might have done this?"

Andrew shook his head. "He's always kept to himself, especially since his wife died. But my mother had him to dinner a week before

he went missing and nothing seemed out of the ordinary. If anything, he was in one of his more cheerful moods. He'd just received
a copy of Madame de Staël's *De l'Allemagne* from Edinburgh. We
had quite a lively discussion about it."

"For Christ's sake, Andrew, if you're keeping something from
me—"

"Why would I keep anything from you?"

Charles stared at Andrew for a moment, then slammed his hand
down on the table. "Did you write to me when you realized McGann
had gone missing? Did I miss the letter because I left London?" He
read the answer in Andrew's face. "Why the hell didn't you at least
write?"

Andrew shifted his weight from one foot to the other. He was
two years Charles's senior, Mélanie knew, but in that moment he had
the look of a schoolboy picking his way through a conversational
mire. "I thought about it. But what could I have told you? There's no
reason to suspect anything untoward has happened. Besides—" He
glanced away.

"What?" Charles said.

Andrew looked back at Charles. "You haven't wanted to have
much to do with Dunmykel or anything associated with it for the
past nine years."

"What the devil's that supposed to mean?"

"You've been back to visit—what? twice?—since you left
Britain."

"What the hell does that have to do with—"

"The world hasn't stood still here any more than it has on the
Continent. Do you have any idea what I deal with day to day?
Thanks to your father's Clearances, it's next to impossible for a lot of
the tenants to make a living with their cattle. I'm trying to repair cot-
tages without the money to do so, scrape together food to get families
through one more winter, scrounge up peat and firewood—let's just
say that the fact that an able-bodied man like McGann apparently
disappeared of his own free will hasn't been at the top of my list of
concerns."

Charles scraped his hand through his hair. "I know things have
been difficult. But I assumed—"

"That we could weather the storm better than the average Highland estate?"

"That you'd have written to me if it was that bad."

Andrew met his gaze as though they were confronting each other on the cricket field. "Did you write to me for my advice on the intricacies of Continental diplomacy? This isn't your world anymore, Charles. Any more than the embassy in Lisbon or the Congress of Vienna is mine."

"Christ, Andrew, you should know I want to know when anything's amiss at Dunmykel, whether it's the tenants starving or McGann disappearing."

"That's just it, Charles." Andrew's friendly blue eyes had turned marble hard. "You made it clear you wanted to get as far away as possible from Dunmykel and your family. I can understand. God knows I tried to run from my own family, with less provocation, though I could only afford to go as far as Edinburgh. But it hardly inspired me to come running after you with the estate's problems. Dunmykel hasn't been your concern for a long time."

"I never—" Charles swallowed. Mélanie saw Andrew's words hit home like a hammer blow in her husband's eyes.

Andrew put out a hand as though to touch Charles on the shoulder, then let it drop to his side. "Look, I didn't mean—"

Charles squeezed his eyes shut for a moment. "I'm sorry, Andrew. I've no call to take my worries out on you."

Andrew scanned Charles's face. "The last few days can't have been easy. It must have come as a shock."

"It?" Charles said.

"Your father's betrothal to—to Miss Talbot." Andrew didn't so much as glance at Mélanie as he spoke, but Mélanie suspected that had she not been present more words would have been exchanged between the two friends about Honoria Talbot. Andrew must have known Miss Talbot on her childhood visits to Dunmykel.

"My father's always had a knack for surprises," Charles said.

Andrew returned Charles's gaze as though they were passing a memory back and forth between them. "McGann didn't know about the betrothal, did he?" Charles said.

"No. We none of us knew until your father and Lord Glenister and Miss Talbot arrived. McGann will be pleased to see Miss Talbot as mistress of Dunmykel."

"I daresay. Though pardonably concerned about her marrying my father."

"He's bound to be as surprised as the rest of us. He's always had a soft spot for Miss Talbot. Mother says it's the resemblance."

"Resemblance?"

"To Miss Talbot's mother," Andrew said. "You didn't know? No, I suppose you wouldn't. I didn't know myself until Mother started reminiscing a few months ago. Apparently Miss Talbot's mother visited Dunmykel as a girl several times with her family before her marriage, before Mr. Fraser bought the estate. According to my mother, McGann was quite taken with her. Nothing could come of it, of course. The gulf between their stations was far too wide. But it's natural he'd care for her daughter."

Charles regarded Andrew for a long moment, as though searching for a trace of his boyhood friend. "You know even more about McGann than I realized. You're sure you can't shed any light on why he disappeared?"

"Quite sure," Andrew replied.

"Andrew's right." Charles strode along the worn ground of the path back to the house, booted feet thudding against the beaten-down grass as though he could pound some sort of sense out of it. "I had no call to turn my back on Dunmykel as I did."

"You were rather preoccupied, Charles. A little thing known as a war."

"I could have made more of an effort to keep in touch. I could have written to Andrew more often. I could have asked for news." He cast a quick glance at her, then looked back at the path ahead. "Andrew was reading law in Edinburgh when I left Britain. He claimed he had no desire to be immured in the country like his father."

"Did his father want him to take over running the estate?"

"His father was the sort who doesn't push. But he and Andrew quarreled when Andrew was at university. I never found out why. Andrew and I weren't—we didn't talk as much by that time. Then when I was in Lisbon he wrote me that his father was ill and he'd come home and later that he'd decided to stay on and run the estate. I never questioned why." He drew a breath. A layer of defenses was stripped from his face. It was like getting a look at the boy who had gone fishing and climbing with Andrew and borrowed books from Giles McGann. The boy she would never know. "Things were—bad—before I left Britain." He chose the words as though he were picking his way through bits of broken glass in his memory. "Andrew had every right to believe I didn't want news from home. Because it was true. I didn't want it."

Mélanie studied his profile, outlined against the blue-gray of the sky. He seemed to have been whittled down to the bones of his past, so achingly vulnerable that she was afraid he'd break if she touched him. "Even if you'd known what was happening at Dunmykel, there wasn't a great deal you could have done."

He swung his gaze to her. "I could—"

"I know you like to believe you're responsible for everything, Charles, but the estate belongs to your father." She drew a breath, struck by the unreality of the fact that one day it would belong to Charles. Easy enough to think of Charles as lord of the manor. Quite impossible to imagine herself as mistress of this house that radiated history, this multitude of art treasures, these acres of land. Cutting ribbons at village fêtes, taking tea with the minister's wife, presiding over harvest dances, reviewing menus and seating arrangements for dinners of twenty-five served on the Spode china with the Fraser crest. Playing the role Honoria Talbot seemed to have been born to play. "It will be different one day when it's yours."

Charles watched her for a moment, his gaze as dense and lightless as the sky just before a thunderstorm. "Yes," he said, "I suppose that would make a difference."

For a moment she thought he meant to say more, but instead he took two long, impatient strides along the path. "Andrew knows or suspects something about why McGann went missing. I'd stake my life on it. Something he doesn't want me to find out."

The small window of confidences was shuttered. She wanted to wrench the shutters open, but that would only make him retreat further. Instead she fell into step beside him, forcing her mind back to the investigation. "Because he's afraid for Mr. McGann?"

"Because he doesn't trust me."

Mélanie frowned at the silvery line of birch that bordered the path. "Charles—it isn't remotely possible that Mr. McGann is Le Faucon de Maulévrier, is it?"

"I'd like to say no for a hundred reasons. But the most obvious is that McGann wasn't gone from Britain long enough at the right times."

She turned her gaze from the trees to her husband's set face. "What about Cyril Talbot?"

Charles paused for a moment. "I only have the vaguest memories of Cyril. At the age of ten, I scarcely knew my father, let alone his friends. But from every description of him, he was as much of a dilettante as my father and Glenister, with rather less wit."

"That could have been a clever cover."

"So it could. And he did spend a great deal of time on the Continent. But if he was Le Faucon, Le Faucon died twenty years ago."

Mélanie pushed a strand of hair beneath the satin-lined brim of her bonnet. "You're certain Cyril Talbot did die?"

Her husband stared at her. "He's buried in Dunmykel churchyard. And no, I wasn't at the funeral—I was staying at my grandfather's when he died. But why in God's name would he have needed to fake his own death? He was safe enough in Britain as Lord Cyril Talbot."

"Suppose there were people who knew Lord Cyril and Le Faucon were one in the same. By faking his death and disappearing, he escaped them."

"But there must have been a body, even if I didn't see it. Difficult to see how he could have managed the deception without help from Glenister and my father and perhaps others at the house party."

"If Lord Cyril was Le Faucon, I could imagine Glenister going to fairly drastic lengths to avert scandal and save his brother's life. On the other hand, it's entirely possible Lord Cyril really did die and someone else has resurrected Le Faucon's network. Or that Lord Cyril wasn't Le Faucon at all."

"Except that Cyril's daughter seems to be in the middle of this."

They had reached the edge of the stream that wound through the estate. Charles stared out over the clear water, but he seemed to be seeing something beyond it. Honoria, Mélanie thought. He's remembering Honoria. He must have walked these same paths with her. She could picture Honoria, a delicate girl in a white frock, stopping to pick wildflowers, while a gangly, teenaged Charles carried a basket and pruning sheers for her. Mélanie couldn't remember the last time she'd had the leisure to pick flowers.

"Francisco was right, wasn't he?" Charles said. "It keeps coming back to Honoria." His eyes darkened with a feeling Mélanie could not put a name to, though it made her insides twist as though someone were pressing a knife beneath her ribs. "I'll talk to her tonight."

Chapter 13

"E vie?" Gisèle rapped once on her friend's door, then turned the handle and poked her head in without waiting for an answer. "May I borrow your jade earrings, they'd look quite splen—what on earth's the matter?"

Evie was sitting at the dressing table of her room at Dunmykel, elbows on the tabletop, face between her hands. The tapers on either side of the looking glass illumined her reflection. Her eyes were red, her cheeks streaked with damp.

"Just a fit of the blue devils." Evie swung round and rubbed her hands over her face. "Sorry, Gelly, what did you want?"

"It doesn't matter." Gisèle closed the door and walked into the room. "You never have the blue devils, Evie. You're much too sensible."

"Maybe I just hide them better than most. You try living with Uncle Frederick and Val and Honoria."

"And Quen."

"Yes, Quen."

"He hasn't done anything truly horrid since we've been here. I suppose throwing up at the betrothal ball was enough for the moment. All things considered, the house party isn't starting out as hideously as I feared." Gisèle flopped back on the feather bed and stared up at the plasterwork ceiling and then over at the pilasters of the window embrasure. Evie's room was in the seventeenth-century part of the house, new compared to the north wing, but even here she could feel the overlapping layers of history. "I forgot how much I love Dunmykel, even if it is hideously cold. You don't suppose that's why Honoria wants to marry Father, do you? Because she made up her mind to be mistress of Dunmykel and now that Charles is taken, Father's her only choice?"

"Honoria's never been particularly fond of Scotland."

"Yes, but Dunmykel's so—" Gisèle straightened up and drew a breath of the salt-laced air. "How could anyone not want to live here?"

Evie gave a faint smile. "It's different for you, Gelly. It's your home."

Gisèle inched back against the bedpost. "Frasers don't have homes. Just places we live for a bit. I suppose Honoria must have mixed feelings about Dunmkyel—I mean, her father died here, which is a bit gruesome, though I don't suppose she remembers him much."

Evie twitched a fold of her skirt smooth. "She doesn't talk about it. But then there's a lot Honoria doesn't talk about. I've lived with her for twelve years, and I'm not sure what she's thinking three-quarters of the time."

"But she must have had some reason for accepting Father. Especially when she's still in love with Charles."

Evie's hands closed on the chair back. "Gelly—"

"Oh, of course she is, as much as Honoria's ever going to be in love with anyone. She's been fixated on him like a lodestar since we were children. Even I could see that, though it's not the sort of thing one likes to notice about one's brother. And now she's going to marry Father. It's like a Greek myth. Perseus or Theseus or whoever's wife was in love with his son. It's asking for trouble, having all of them shut up here for weeks."

Evie picked up her comb and began to tidy her side curls. "I thought you were determined not to come at all. You were positively gleeful when you got Charles to persuade Lady Frances to let you go to a friend's house instead."

Gisèle tugged at a snagged thread in her white lace overdress. The problem with Evie was that she saw far too much and asked far too many pointed questions. Just like Charles. "You know how I enjoy doing the opposite of what people expect."

Evie continued to tend to her hair, but Gisèle could feel the pressure of her friend's gaze reflected back on her through the glass. "I thought perhaps it was something to do with Val," Evie said.

"Well, of course it's quite agreeable that he's here." Gisèle twisted her pearl bracelet round her wrist while a multitude of scorching thoughts that would no doubt make Evie look at her as though she'd taken leave of her senses tumbled in her head.

Evie set down the comb. "Do you want to marry him?"

Gisèle gave a high-pitched laugh that she managed to rein in one step short of hysteria. "Dear Evie. Why on earth should marriage have anything to do with it?"

"Because you're a nineteen-year-old girl from a good family. You have to marry someone."

"By the same logic, so do you."

"I'm a poor relation. It's different."

"Gammon. Lord Glenister will give you a dowry."

Evie's mouth twisted. "It's not very agreeable being dependent on charity, love."

"It's not charity, he's your uncle. Anyway, you'd have more of the Glenister money yourself if your grandfather hadn't—"

"If my grandfather hadn't cut my mother off without a shilling after she eloped with a half-pay officer and gave birth to me a scant five months later?" Evie smiled. "It's all right, Gelly, my mama's indiscretions are hardly the most scandalous in the Talbot family. They don't make her daughter very marriageable, though."

"Rot. A sensible man wouldn't care a rush—"

Evie turned back to the mirror. "Perhaps that's the problem, love. Perhaps I don't want a sensible man."

"You've never much wanted anyone so far as I can—" Gisèle leaned forward and nearly toppled off the bed. Sometimes she was so caught up in keeping her own secrets that she forgot other people had them as well. "Evie, is that what you were crying about? Is there someone—for heaven's sake, who—"

"Don't be a silly romantic goose, Gelly. Did you want to borrow my earrings? The jade ones?"

Gisèle sprang to her feet. "Are you crying because he's back in London? You must be, it couldn't be someone here. I mean, there's only—oh, Lord. You haven't fallen in love with David, have you?"

Evie was bent over her jewel case. Her shoulders shook. "No, Gelly, I'm not such a fool as to fall in love with David."

"Or Simon?"

"Or Simon."

"Then it can't be anyone here, because there's only Val and—" Bits and pieces of her friend's behavior locked together like puzzle pieces in Gisèle's mind. "Quen. Oh, Evie, you love Quen."

"Of course I love Quen. He's practically my brother."

"But he isn't your brother. And I suppose he is rather attractive when he isn't causing a scene. You don't just love him. You're *in* love with him."

Evie turned to her and held out the jade earrings. "Just take care you don't lose them the way Honoria always does."

Gisèle took the earrings but continued to look at her friend. "You can't simply wait about for something to happen. It never will, unless you take matters into your hands."

Easy enough to say, but as she spoke, Gisèle went cold at the thought of what her words would mean if she applied them to her own situation.

"Even if I were in love with someone," Evie said, "perhaps I wouldn't want anything to happen. Love didn't exactly turn out well for my mother."

"But—"

"Don't dawdle, Gelly. Val will be waiting for you."

"I love the air here. It's so clean. It seems any lie would be blown right out to sea and scattered to the four winds." Honoria rested her arms on the granite balustrade and looked out over the gardens below and the mass of the sea beyond, the gray water turned to lavender in the glow of the late Scottish sunset. Peach and vermilion and rose-gold streaked the sky. The warm light clung to her pale hair and the yellow fabric of her gown.

Charles stood beside her, breathing in the familiarity of a world that wasn't his anymore. "Are lies being told?"

Honoria glanced over her shoulder. Mozart and candlelight drifted through the French windows from the drawing room behind them. "Aren't lies told at any social gathering?"

"That sounds unexpectedly arch coming from you."

"Does it? Well, I've grown up a bit in six years." She glanced away and toyed with a fallen leaf that lay on the balustrade.

In the drawing room behind them, the Mozart gave way to the poignant insistence of the *Moonlight* Sonata. Charles glanced through the French windows. Mélanie was at the pianoforte, with Simon turning the pages of her music. Evie was handing round the tea. Gisèle had her head close together with Val in the most shadowy corner of the room. Quen was slumped alone in another corner, brandy glass in hand. Kenneth, Glenister, David, and Lady Frances had made up a whist table.

Charles turned his gaze to the woman who was about to become his stepmother. "I haven't congratulated you properly."

"You don't do most things by the book, Charles. Even kissing."

She looked at him. The memory of her bending down and brushing her lips against his own in the library at Glenister House hung in the air between them.

"Were you surprised by the announcement?" Honoria said.

"Very. But then I've hardly been privy to your inner thoughts in recent years."

"I'm sorry." Her Wedgwood-blue gaze turned wide and candid and earnest. "Perhaps I should have warned you. But I think I wanted to live in the past for a few moments longer."

"I didn't need a warning."

"That was presumptuous of me. I only meant—well, it's bound to be a bit awkward. You can't have expected to have me as a step-mother." She drew the flowered silk folds of her shawl about her shoulders. "I'm not very like her, am I?"

"My mother?" Charles risked a glance at the gardens his mother had designed, the hedged walkways and parterres, the fountains and statues and ornamental pools turned to dark, smudged silhouettes in the fading light. "No. But when it comes to making a success of marriage to my father I wouldn't count that as a negative."

Honoria twisted a knot of apricot ribbon on the bodice of her gown. "I saw her grave today."

Charles had an image of the vine-covered churchyard and the sea-weathered granite of the headstones. "You went to visit your father's grave?"

She nodded. "It's years since I'd seen it. I can scarcely remember him."

"You were only three."

"Yes, but I wish—he used to toss me up in the air. I remember that. But I can't see his face."

"Do you ever talk about him?" Charles schooled his face not to betray a hint of his suspicions that Cyril Talbot might have been Le Faucon de Maulévrier. "With your uncle?"

"Uncle Frederick doesn't like to discuss him. I think he feels responsible."

"For your father's death?"

"It's silly, of course. But Uncle Frederick was his elder brother. He was here when Papa had the accident with the gun. He should have kept an eye on him—or so he thinks." She turned to take a few steps along the terrace. "I imagine Quen would feel that way about Val, for all they're equally irresponsible. Wouldn't you feel the same about Edgar?"

"I expect so." Charles fell into step beside her. Fallen leaves scrunched beneath their feet. Clouds were gathering in the brilliant sky and the air held the promise of rain. "Did you think to visit Giles McGann when you were riding about the estate?"

"I rode by the day after we arrived here, but the cottage was closed up. Do you know where he's gone?"

Her eyes were as guileless as when she'd been in leading strings. "No one seems to be quite sure," Charles said.

"I do hope he's all right. I wanted to explain to him about my betrothal. He'll be as surprised as everyone else, and his opinion matters to me more than most."

"Honoria." Charles stopped, out of view of the windows from the drawing room. "Have you ever heard of something called the Elsinore League?"

"The what? Charles, I admire *Hamlet* as much as anyone, but isn't it going a bit far—"

"They aren't anything to do with *Hamlet*. At least not that we know of. They're an organization in Paris that a friend of mine was involved with. Someone shot him in London ten days ago."

"Good God!"

"He died warning me about the Elsinore League. He also said the people he worked for were afraid for a woman named Honoria."

Honoria stared at him as though he'd fired a pistol shot over her tea table. "Charles, I can't begin to understand the life you've lived, but obviously it's a different Honoria. I don't see what I could have to do with intrigues in Paris or anyone involved in them. You do believe me, don't you?"

"I believe you don't know anything about it. But humor me. Don't mention this to anyone else. And lock your door at night."

"For God's sake, we're in Scotland, in your father's house—"

"And I'm probably mad, but you've thought that for years anyway. Do I have your word?"

"Yes, all right."

Charles nodded. "Why did Father plan this house party so abruptly?"

"To get away from all the tiresome congratulations and furtive speculation on the betrothal, I imagine. I don't think he realized how bad it would be."

Charles leaned his shoulder against the age-worn granite of the balustrade and looked at his father's betrothed. The torchlight sharpened the softly curved bones of her face.

"Why, Honoria?"

"Why is the speculation so tiresome?"

"Why are you marrying my father?"

Her gaze moved over his, like the lightest brush of fingertips. "I told you. I'm tired of being on the shelf." She straightened her shoulders. A hard, brittle shell seemed to close round her. "I'll make him a good wife."

"I'm not questioning that. But of all the men you could choose—"

"Why did you marry your wife?"

He should have seen it coming, but he couldn't check his inward recoil. "She needed me." Or rather, she needed a husband. She could have done far better, but that was another matter.

"I needed you once."

"Not in the way Mélanie did. You had far more options."

"And so you threw away everything we could have had."

The possibilities of an alternative life hung before him, like the sun about to sink into the Atlantic. A life of familiarity. A life he had run from and craved and never fully considered because he'd always known it was out of his reach. "We would have made each other miserable, Honoria."

"Unlike your own marriage, which is deliriously happy?"

The words shot home like a dagger. "My marriage is my own business."

She scanned his face. "He isn't yours, is he? The little boy. Colin."

"Colin is unquestionably my son." This part was easy, because for him it was the truth.

"Because you chose to make him your son. She was pregnant. That's why you married her. Oh, Charles, you stubborn, idealistic fool. To stake your future and your happiness on protecting someone else."

"Mélanie wouldn't thank you for implying she needs protection." He gripped the balustrade. "Honoria, I told you at Glenister House that you could come to me if you were ever in trouble. For God's sake, tell me what's the matter now."

"Why should anything be the matter?"

"Because the girl I've known half my life wouldn't ally herself with Kenneth Fraser."

Honoria stared at him with eyes darkened to indigo. The sun had sunk below the horizon. The cool light bled the color from her gown and hair, turning her into a creature of shadows. "You're forgetting the half of my life you don't know."

"On the contrary. I want to know what the devil in that life drove you to this madness." He caught her hands. "This is the rest of your life, Noria."

"And I'm only supposed to marry someone to whom I can commit myself in body and soul? My dear Charles. Can you claim that's what you did?"

Guilt welled up on his tongue like blood from the lash of a whip. "I told you. Mélanie needed me. Are you claiming Father needs you?"

"Perhaps I need him."

"There are other men—"

"Your father is the man I want to marry. The man I have to marry."

"*Have* to?" He tightened his grip on her hands. "For the love of God, Noria, you don't have to do anything. I'll get you out of this, whatever it is. I swear it."

"Even you can't fix everything, my sweet."

"At least let me—"

She jerked out of his hold. "Let go of me, Charles. You don't have the right to demand anything of me anymore."

"She's afraid."

"Of what?" His wife's crisp voice was a sharp contrast to Honoria's anguished tones on the terrace.

Charles unwound his cravat from about his throat and stared at the length of muslin. "I'm not sure."

Mélanie picked up a lead soldier Colin had left on the floor of their bedchamber and set it atop the chest of drawers. "Do you think she knows anything about—"

"Francisco's death? Giles McGann's disappearance? The Elsinore League?"

"Any of it." Mélanie dropped down on the chintz-covered dressing table bench and began to unroll her stockings.

"No. But I think there's more to her reasons for marrying my father than meets the eye."

"You think she's being coerced?"

"She as good as admitted something was troubling her, but she said it was something I couldn't do anything about." Charles unbuttoned his waistcoat. The anguished plea in Honoria's eyes lingered in his memory. He looked at his wife and felt a metallic taste in his throat. Because for a moment he'd let himself imagine the life he might have had? Because Honoria's words had slapped home the fact he'd given Mélanie Spanish coin rather than the riches she deserved?

Mélanie dropped a stocking and a pink silk garter into the basket beside the dressing table. "Engagements are broken all the time. Why would she think she had no choice but to marry your father? She has a comfortable fortune of her own. When does she come into possession of it?"

He shrugged out of the waistcoat and laid it and the cravat over a chair back. "On her marriage or her twenty-fifth birthday, I believe."

"Suppose she'd run up gambling debts? One can lose a fortune at the card tables in a Mayfair drawing room on a single evening. Even I've heard the stories about the Duchess of Devonshire and Lady Bessborough."

"Yes, but—"

"You know her and I don't?"

"I wouldn't have expected Honoria to run up gambling debts." His voice sounded stiff to his own ears, like an overstarched cravat. "But then I wouldn't have expected her to become betrothed to my father, either. On the other hand, if all she wanted was access to her money she could have married any of her suitors."

"So you think she's being coerced into marrying your father specifically?" Mélanie drew her bare feet up onto the dressing table bench. "Suppose Glenister's the one in debt."

"To my father?" Charles leaned against one of the walnut bedposts. "And Honoria's sacrificing herself to redeem the debt? *La Belle et le Bête?*"

Mélanie unfastened her heavy citrine necklace and began to pull the pins out of her hair. Her garnet silk skirt was tucked up, revealing the curves of her ankles and calves. Her unself-conscious sensuality could not be more different from Honoria's cool decorum. It tugged at his senses, reminding him that in the scales of their marriage he had gained far more than he had given.

"I admit it's convoluted," Mélanie said. "Why else might Miss Talbot feel coerced to go along with the marriage? To protect someone else she cares about? Her cousins?"

Charles smoothed a hand over the openwork on the Irish linen
coverlet. The threads formed a gossamer-fine web. "She cares for
them, for all they're often at one another's throats. Quen or Val could
could have lost to Father at cards or Father could have bought up
their vowels."

Mélanie snapped open the lid of her dressing case and dropped a
handful of pins into one of the velvet-lined compartments. "Could
she be in love with another man?"

Charles stared at the snowy-white threads and the bits of flowered quilt showing beneath. "And marrying Father to protect him?
From what she said, I don't think that's her reason."

He looked up and forced himself to meet Mélanie's gaze.
Mélanie looked back at him, as though his statement carried no
more weight than anything else he'd said. But she seemed to be trying just a bit too hard to maintain the expression.

"We can make more inquiries about McGann in the morning,"
Charles said. "We won't get much farther discussing this tonight."

His wife nodded, got to her feet, and walked toward him. He
wanted to twist his fingers in her hair and cover her mouth with his
own and blot out the questions in her eyes. He wanted to bury himself in her and sever his mind from the tortures of thought. Because
he knew just how appallingly selfish he'd already been where she
was concerned, he drew back.

Mélanie curled her hand behind his neck and pulled his head
down to her own.

"Mel—"

"Don't talk, Charles. And for God's sake, don't think. We've
done far too much of that already."

She caught his lower lip between her teeth and parted her mouth
beneath his own, seeking, yielding, demanding. He closed his arms
round her, accepting what she offered, making an offer in kind.

Spanish coin or not, it glittered bright enough to blind one.

Flames engulfed him again. Honoria trembled in his arms. She was
murmuring incoherent sounds of distress, and her breath was quick
and panicked against his skin. She sobbed, a raw harsh sound that
jerked him out of the scalding fire and acrid smoke to cool linen

sheets and thick, enveloping darkness. She wasn't in his arms, she was thrashing beside him, as though caught in a snare. He reached for her, felt the sting of sweat on her skin, and gathered her to him.

The familiar scent of roses and vanilla washed over him. The texture of the hair and the curve of the bones beneath his fingers jerked him back to reality. He was in his bed at Dunmykel, holding not Honoria but his wife. Guided by instinct more than thought, he slid his hand to the place at the nape of her neck that always soothed her when she had one of her nightmares.

Mélanie gripped his shoulder and curved her body against his own, jolted out of whatever remembered or imagined horrors had tormented her.

He smoothed her hair back from her face, reassured by the more regular sound of her breathing. The trust in the way her hand curled on his chest and her head nestled in the hollow of his throat brought a familiar stab of guilt.

He'd married her because he'd thought he could protect her. Dear Christ. He'd thought of himself as a cynic at five-and-twenty, but he'd been a naïve, romantic fool. In the light of the past four and a half years, it seemed one of his more laughably arrogant and appallingly shortsighted moments. Protecting her had been an excuse, a smoke screen to cover his own selfish need. He'd gained a witty companion, a partner in adventure, an ardent bedmate. And all the while he'd been able to keep whatever he wanted of himself locked away, telling himself that they shared more than dozens of couples who made marriages of convenience.

He'd got used to sleeping with her curled against him, to not tugging away too much of the quilt at night, to all those cut-glass scent bottles and little silver and enamel boxes of powders and paints crowding his shaving things off shared dressing tables in cramped quarters. He knew how to fasten and unfasten the hooks and but-tons and laces and strings on her gowns. She'd got quite good at tying his cravats when he'd broken his arm and his valet Addison had been off for fortnight on a mission in northern Spain. They could pack a valise for each other down to the undergarments and toiletries, order each other's meals, forge each other's signatures. They both knew the exact touch that could soothe or arouse or send the other tumbling into delight.

But such intimacy existed on the still, safe surface of life. In the dark corners beneath lay the fragments of his life that he didn't care to look at himself, much less share with anyone, even Mélanie. Especially Mélanie.

He leaned back against the headboard, stroking his wife's hair, and stared up at the dark walnut bedframe, streaks of black against the pale chintz canopy. Honoria was right, they couldn't go back to the people they'd been. But they couldn't forget those people, those events, those memories. The past echoed through the present, laughing at him for the presumption of thinking it could be left behind.

One had a ghost of a chance of a future only if one turned and confronted the past. And the future had to be thought of. If having children had taught him nothing else, it had taught him that. He'd had to come back to Britain. He couldn't spend the rest of his life running. But he wasn't at all sure it was fair to have inflicted his coming to terms with family and his past on Mélanie and the children. In his darkest moments, he wasn't sure it was fair to have inflicted himself on them at all.

He was still wondering when a raw explosion of sound ripped through the silence of the night. He was half out of the bed, reaching for the pistol he no longer kept beneath his pillow, before he realized the sound had been a scream.

The night air bit into his naked skin as he jumped out of bed and fumbled for his dressing gown. Mélanie was beside him, silk rustling as she knotted the sash on her own dressing gown.

They stumbled out the door without taking time to light a candle. Moonlight spilled through the tall windows and lent a faint illumination to the corridor. Their bedroom was in the old north wing. The cry had not come from the nursery, deep in the north wing, thank God, but from the first bedroom where the corridor widened into the central block. The bedroom occupied by his father.

Charles rapped on the door. "Sir?"

Silence engulfed the corridor. Charles turned the handle and pushed open the door.

The room was cloaked in darkness. Guided by memory, he found a flint and lit the lamp on a table by the door. Yellow light outlined the mahogany four-poster mass of the bed and the dressing-gowned figure of Kenneth Fraser standing beside it. The light bounced off the bronze-green satin of the bed hangings and gleamed against the pristine white of the sheets and the pale gold hair of the woman who lay on them. The woman's face was hidden by the pillows and the fall of her hair, but that particular shade of gold unmistakably belonged to Honoria Talbot.

Kenneth didn't react to the opening of the door or the flare of light. He was staring at Honoria as though transfixed.

"Sir?" Charles said again.

Kenneth made no response, not even a turn of his head. Charles crossed to the bed in two strides. Mélanie picked up the lamp and followed him. They both saw the sight on the bed at the same moment. Charles went still. Mélanie stumbled against him and clutched his arm to keep from falling.

Honoria was stretched out beneath the satin counterpane and embroidered linen sheet, arms at her sides, eyes closed, face still. Too still. Her skin had a waxy sheen that was all too familiar from countless field hospitals. Above the lacy yoke of her nightdress, an angry line of bruising showed round her throat.

Charles put his fingers to where the pulse should have been beating in her throat. He felt nothing but the cold emptiness of death.

Chapter 14

Mélanie stared at the lifeless face of the woman lying on the embroidered sheet. The face of the girl Charles had grown up with, the woman who had almost been his stepmother, the friend and companion who had meant something to him that she couldn't begin to fathom.

Charles touched his fingers to Honoria's throat, glanced at Mélanie, and gave a slight shake of his head. His gaze was as hard and still as a window on a moonless night. He moved to his father and laid a hand on Kenneth's arm. It was the first time Mélanie could remember any physical contact between the two men.

Kenneth jerked at his son's touch. His gaze went to Charles's face, as though he could not make sense of what Charles was doing there. "Dear God, she's dead."

His fine-featured, sardonic face was drained of color, his keen eyes vacant, his incisive voice a stunned monotone.

"Yes." Charles steered his father toward a japanned armchair that faced away from the bed.

Mélanie glanced round the room. A set of decanters stood on the folding shelf of a cabinet near the fireplace. She poured some whisky into a glass and gave it to Charles. Charles pressed the glass into Kenneth's hand. When Kenneth simply stared at it, Charles guided the glass to his lips. Kenneth choked and coughed, but he swallowed some of the whisky, and a little color returned to his face.

Mélanie took a blanket from the bench at the foot of the bed and put it round her father-in-law's shoulders. Through the silk of his dressing gown, his body felt chilled to the bone. She went to the fireplace and lit the tapers on the mantel and in the gilt wall sconces. The tinderbox rattled in her hands. Hot drops of wax spattered over her fingers.

The candlelight flickered over Kenneth, hunched in the chair, and Charles kneeling beside him. They were not much alike, save for a certain hard-cut, Celtic determination in their faces. Charles's gaze was fixed on his father as though he was trying to frame a question to which he wasn't sure he could bear the answer. He helped Kenneth take another sip of whisky, then dropped back on his heels.

"What happened?" Charles's voice was completely neutral, the way it got when he was making a massive effort at control.

Kenneth stared at Charles. He seemed to be truly aware of his presence for the first time. "I came into the room. It was dark. I only had a candle." He cast a glance about, as though seeking what had become of the candle. Mélanie saw a silver candlestick and an extinguished wax taper on the floor by the bed.

"And then?" Charles said in the same steady voice.

Kenneth swallowed. "I was beside the bed before I realized—I put out my hand—her skin was so cold." He stared down at his right hand, curled round the whisky glass.

Charles closed his hand over Kenneth's before he could drop the glass. "Did you know Honoria was in your room?"

"Did I—?" Kenneth's gaze went to Charles's face. Comprehension flashed in his eyes. "What do you take me for, boy?" He clenched the handkerchief. "She was my fiancée, not my trollop."

A spasm ran along Charles's jaw. "How long had you been gone from your room?"

"I don't—most of the night."

"Where were you?"

"In the library." Fraser took another sip of whisky. "Reading. Someone must have broken into the house," he said, as though he had been too shocked at Honoria's death to think about who might have killed her until now.

"Possibly." Charles got to his feet and looked down at his father. "Sit for a moment, sir. You're still in shock."

Kenneth didn't seem to hear him. Charles took one of the candles from the mantel and exchanged a look with Mélanie. His face was gray, his eyes haunted by what they had witnessed and by the imagined horrors of what might lie behind Honoria's death. But he merely said, "Check the windows."

He went through the door into the adjoining dressing room. Mélanie cast another glance at Kenneth Fraser, but he was slumped beneath the blanket, staring at the whisky glass in his hands. She took the other taper from the mantel, went to the windows that that ran along the outer wall, and tested the latches. They were all securely bolted on the inside.

She returned to the bed and looked at Honoria Talbot, forcing herself to note pertinent details. Miss Talbot's skin, which had been so fresh and glowing, was tinged blue-gray instead of pink and white. A thin film of lip rouge stood out on her mouth, like a slash of too-bright paint. Beneath it, her lips were drained of color. Despite the violence of the mark round her throat, there was no sign of a struggle. Almost as though she'd slept through the attack.

The mark on her neck was narrow, probably made by a cord or rope rather than fingers. Mélanie glanced about. The flickering flame of her candle caught something red-tinged on the floor between the bed and the bedside table. She bent down to retrieve it and held it to the light of the candle. The red was not blood but embroidered flowers. It was a tapestry bellpull.

Mélanie touched her fingers to Miss Talbot's face, smoothed back her hair, lifted her eyelids. Her eyes had the empty, absent stare of death. Her pupils were contracted, dark pinpoints in irises that were as blue as they had been in life.

Mélanie turned back the covers. Miss Talbot's arms lay loose at her sides. Her diamond betrothal ring caught the lamplight. One leg was turned in slightly, but her nightdress was smooth, as though she had adjusted the folds when she lay down. Mélanie lifted one of her arms and pushed back the frilled cuff of her nightdress. The underside of her arm had the purply look of a bruise. When Mélanie pressed her finger against the darkened flesh, the skin blanched beneath her touch. She removed her finger, and the skin purpled again.

Footsteps sounded behind her. "Nothing in the dressing room," Charles said in a quiet voice.

No one, was what he meant. "It looks as though she's been dead for at least an hour and not more than four," Mélanie said. "I doubt we have to worry about an intruder in the house."

Charles glanced at the body of his childhood friend. "She was drugged." It wasn't quite a question.

Mélanie nodded. "I've seen morphine overdoses. I recognized her eyes. Besides, why else would she appear to have slept through it?"

"Quite. But we should make sure there's no intruder in the house all the same."

"Do we wake everyone?" Mélanie asked.

"Not yet. I'd like to hold off a scene of general hysteria for as long as possible." Charles glanced at his father, then back at Mélanie. She had seen that look on his face during the war, when a wrong decision would be paid for in lost lives. "Stay with my father."

"Charles—"

He brushed his fingers against her cheek. "I'll check the nursery myself. I promise." He turned to go, but when he was halfway to the door, he stopped and looked back at his father, who was sitting hunched in the armchair. "Sir?"

Kenneth turned his head.

Charles drew a breath. There was a raw note in his voice Mélanie had never heard before. "If by any chance she wasn't dead when you came into the room, you'd best tell me now."

The realization of what Charles had implied filled Kenneth's gaze. His eyes turned as cold and sharp as broken glass. "What I've told you is the truth. I'm damned if I'll justify myself to my son."

Charles held his father's gaze for a long, fraught moment that sent a chill along Mélanie's nerves. Even after four and a half years as Charles's wife, she could only begin to guess at the echoes that passed between the two men.

At last Charles gave a curt nod and stepped from the room.

Mélanie rubbed her arms. For all the dangerous, painful, unpleasant eventualities she had considered when they left for Scotland, that Honoria Talbot would be murdered had never occurred to her. Miss Talbot wasn't Francisco, who had lived a life on the edge for years. And yet Miss Talbot more and more seemed to be at the center of the ever-expanding web of intrigue. Francisco had said it himself. *It all comes down to Honoria.*

She drew a breath of the night air, and then returned to her father-in-law and knelt on the Aubusson carpet beside his chair.

Kenneth was staring at a painting on the wall by the fireplace. Danaë was reclining on gleaming red velvet, her head thrown back, her hand extended to clutch a fistful of gold coins. Kenneth seemed to be scouring the velvet and gold as though answers were hidden in the brushstrokes. His shoulders were hunched beneath the fuzzy merino of the blanket. The candlelight picked out strands of silver in his light brown hair and deepened the shadows beneath his eyes, the creases beside his mouth, the furrows in his forehead.

She could not be sure what he had felt for Honoria Talbot. She wasn't sure he was capable of feeling love at all, save perhaps for the works of art he collected. He had done things to her husband for which she would never be able to forgive him. Yet it was impossible to look at the numb disbelief stamped on his face and not feel pity. She touched his arm. "I'm so sorry, Mr. Fraser."

He looked down at her as though he had to remind himself of where he was and with whom, but when he spoke, his voice held a trace of the customary irony. "I pride myself on being prepared for most eventualities in life. I must say this is one I hadn't anticipated." He twisted his glass in his hands. "Charles must be pleased."

Her hand closed round the carved arm of the chair. "That's ridiculous, and you know it."

"Is it?" His gaze moved over her. She was keenly aware that the satin ribbons at the neck of her dressing gown had come open and she wore nothing beneath. "Why don't you ask him yourself?"

For a moment his blue eyes were as keen as ever. She returned his gaze, her blood suddenly still, and found herself questioning every certainty of the past quarter-hour.

.   .   .

Charles rounded the corner of the ground-floor corridor into the north wing. His candle, burned halfway down, cast fitful light on the oak wainscoting, but he was moving more by memory than illumination.

His heartbeat had slowed a fraction, thanks to a glimpse of his son and daughter sleeping peacefully in their canework nursery beds, along with his eight-year-old cousin Chlóe, his Aunt Frances's youngest child. He'd gone back to his father's room to tell Mélanie. Kenneth had seemed a bit more himself, and Mélanie had persuaded him to move to the dressing room.

Mélanie was now checking on the rest of the family and guests. Charles's estimable valet, Addison, had organized the footmen to make sure the house was secure. Charles had hastily changed into a shirt and breeches and taken the ground floor of the north wing for himself. Not that he expected to find anything. He was convinced, with a certainty that gnawed at his vital organs and turned his stomach, that Honoria Talbot's killer had come from within the house.

Honoria's lifeless face flashed before his eyes, as it had every few minutes since they'd found her, interrupting the smooth, ceaseless flow of activity. He blinked the image back to some part of his brain where it could be examined later, and turned the knob on the library door.

The door swung inward, the sound echoing off the high ceiling. A rush of cool, musty, leather-tinged air greeted him. The library was the only part of the original thirteenth-century keep to have been incorporated into the current house. The air always smelled different here, as though it, too, had absorbed the history of the room.

Charles drew a breath. The library had been his favorite room at Dunmykel as a child. But now he could not step over the threshold without remembering that this was the room in which his mother had put a bullet through her brain. He stepped into the room, holding his candle aloft so the light fell over the tall ranks of bookshelves, the high-backed chairs, the gateleg table.

And the dark silhouette of a man standing beside the table.

"You're late," the man said. "I was beginning to worry."

The speaker was of average height, bareheaded and greatcoated, his face indecipherable. His voice was educated and unaccented, wary but not surprised. Nor did he start guiltily or make any move to escape. He stood where he was, waiting for a response, a dark presence in the blue-black shadows.

Charles's gaze slid to the fireplace. Even in the darkness, he could see the outline of the bookcase that had swung outward, revealing the entrance to Dunmykel's secret passageway. He edged forward, trying to put himself between the intruder and the escape route. "I was unavoidably detained," he said, when he knew further seconds without speech would alert the intruder that something was wrong.

He kept his voice as neutral as possible, but apparently it was no match for whomever the intruder was expecting. In two strides the intruder went from the table to the mouth of the passageway. Charles was a pace behind him. The rush of movement extinguished his candle. He dropped it, caught a handful of his quarry's greatcoat as he flung himself into the passageway, and banged his head on the low lintel of the hidden doorway.

The intruder wrenched free of his grasp. Charles sprang forward in the dark. The force of the jump knocked them both to the ground. He slammed into the cold, hard rock and earth, clutching the intruder's ankles. As he tried to scramble up, a booted foot caught him in the face.

The force of the kick threw him against the granite wall. Pain sliced through his head, and what vision he had swam darkly. The click of a hammer sounded. He barely had time to feel a cold rush of fear before a bullet ricocheted off the ceiling and a hail of rock fell to the ground between him and his quarry.

Chapter 15

Mélanie was halfway across the first-floor corridor when she heard footsteps on the stairs. She turned to see her husband step onto the landing. The corridor was lit only by the candles they carried, but she'd know the lean angles of Charles's body and the graceful set of his shoulders anywhere. "Everyone on this floor is safely accounted for," she said.

Charles nodded. He was leaning against the grisaille-painted stair wall. His candle tilted precariously in one hand, leaving his face in shadow. "Did you tell them what happened?"

"No, I fell back on the oldest trick to avoid panic—I lied. I tapped on the doors and said we'd heard a disturbance outside, that we thought it was just the dogs, but I was checking to make sure everyone was all right."

"That's my Mel." An effortful ghost of a smile sounded in his voice. "The servants are all safely accounted for as well, and the house is secure."

"That's a relief, although—" She shifted her candle and got a good look at him for the first time. His face and shirt were smeared with dirt, and dried blood crusted a scrape on his cheek. "Good God, darling." She reached out to smooth his hair back from his forehead and check for further damage. "What have you been doing?"

"Securing the house."

Her fingers froze against his temple. "There was an intruder?"

"*Was* being the operative word." He caught her hand and drew away it from his face. "He escaped down the secret passage."

Her mind went to the panel with the Fraser crest he had shown her on her visit to Dunmykel three years earlier. "He was in the library?"

"Waiting for someone."

"*Waiting—?*"

"When I first came into the room, he said I was late. He thought I was whomever he'd come to meet. The fact that he was waiting calmly for whomever that was makes me question whether he killed Honoria." Charles passed a hand over his face. "We should wake David and Glenister. They deserve to hear about Honoria as soon as possible."

Mélanie rapped at David's door and asked him to come to Kenneth Fraser's dressing room, while Charles did the same with Glenister. She and Charles met back in the corridor and reached Kenneth's dressing room ahead of Honoria's two guardians.

The silence in the dressing room pressed against the Beauvais tapestry wall hangings and the mahogany fittings. Kenneth was slumped on the ivory satin settee, with the same vacant expression that he had worn earlier.

"We've asked Glenister and David to join us," Charles said without preamble. "They'll be here in a minute."

Kenneth glanced up. His gaze focused and his brows snapped together. "You—"

"They're Honoria's guardians."

Father and son regarded each other for a moment. Kenneth inclined his head a quarter-inch.

"Do you want me to talk to them?" Charles asked.

"Thank you, but I think I'm sufficiently recovered to be master in my own house." Kenneth pushed himself to his feet, staggered for a moment, and strode to the fireplace. He stood with one arm on the mantel and one foot on the fender, as though to establish control of the room and the situation. He seemed quite oblivious to the damage to Charles's face and person.

After less than a minute a rap sounded at the door, and Glenister and David stepped into the room. "What in God's name is so important it couldn't wait until morning?" Glenister demanded.

Kenneth was silent for a fraction of a second. Then he stepped away from the fireplace. He moved with decision now, and though his voice was hoarse, it had regained the familiar note of command. "You'd better sit down, Glenister. David. It's hard to see how the news could be any worse."

Neither man made any move to sit. David shot a look of inquiry at Charles, but Charles was letting his father do the talking. Glenister frowned at Kenneth. "What?"

Kenneth didn't shrink from his gaze, but again it was a moment before he spoke. "It's Honoria."

"What?" Glenister said again.

"Frederick—" Kenneth said.

Glenister paid him no need. Before anyone else could move, he strode across the room and jerked open the door to the bedroom. He took a half-dozen steps into the room, then went still.

Mélanie almost expected Glenister to catch his niece in his arms and deny that she could be dead. Instead he spun round, hurled himself at Kenneth, and slammed his fist into Kenneth's face. "My God, you bastard, what have you done?"

Kenneth grabbed Glenister to keep from falling. The two men crashed into an ormolu table and sent a Meissen chocolate service shattering to the floor in a cascade of cream and gold. Glenister drew back his arm to strike another blow.

Charles seized Glenister by the shoulders. David ran to the open door to the bedroom and let out a cry at the sight beyond. The connecting door on the opposite side of the dressing room was jerked open. Lady Frances Dacre-Hammond, Charles's aunt, stood on the threshold and surveyed the scene. "What in God's name is going on?"

No one answered her. Glenister jerked against Charles's hold. Charles tightened his grip. "That won't bring her back, sir."

Mélanie went to David and put her arm round him. From this angle, the damage to Honoria's person was all too clear. Lady Frances came up behind Mélanie and David and drew a sharp breath, but when she spoke her voice was crisp. "Close the door, Mélanie. David, you should sit down."

Lady Frances had five children, and though few would consider her the maternal type, at times her mothering instincts were surprisingly keen. She took David by the arm and steered him to a chair. Mélanie closed the door to the bedroom.

Glenister was breathing hard, still in Charles's grip. Kenneth held a handkerchief to his nose, which was streaming blood. "Thank you, Charles," Kenneth said, "but I believe I'm still capable of fighting my own battles."

"You coldhearted monster." Glenister's gaze raked Kenneth's face.

"My dear Glenister," Kenneth said, his voice muffled by the folds of the handkerchief, "if you imagine I had anything to do with—if you imagine I had anything to do with what happened to Honoria, you don't know me."

The two men stared at each other, locked in a silent duel.

"What was Honoria doing in your bed?" Glenister demanded.

"I know no more than you."

"You didn't invite her there?"

Kenneth removed the handkerchief from his face. "I was going to marry her, Frederick."

"Damn it, Kenneth, that's no answer. How the hell can you—"

Lady Frances ran her hands down the front of her lilac satin dressing gown. "Glenister, you know Kenneth and I haven't seen eye to eye since the day he married my sister. But if you think about it for a moment you'll realize that whatever else he's capable of, he wouldn't touch his virginal fiancée before the wedding night."

Glenister slowly inclined his head. Typical of their code. A code that allowed them to indulge their carnal appetites to the fullest extent of their imaginations but held their unmarried daughters inviolate.

David had leaned his head into his hands. Now he looked up at Charles. "What happened?"

"We aren't sure yet." Charles kept one eye on Glenister as he spoke. "Father found her less than an hour ago."

"The others?" David asked.

"Everyone's all right. But there was an intruder in the library."

"What?" Kenneth's gaze snapped in his son's direction. For the first time, he seemed to notice the state of Charles's clothes and face.

Charles told the story of the man he had happened upon in the library and the subsequent chase and struggle, in more detail than he had told it to Mélanie on the stairs. His voice was measured and precise, but he had his hands locked behind his back, a sure sign that he couldn't stop them from shaking.

"Are you telling us you let Honoria's killer go?" Kenneth said.

"No, sir, I'm telling you I was soundly beaten by a man with a gun. But I'm not sure he was Honoria's killer."

"Damn it, if someone broke into the house—"

"He didn't break in. He came through the secret passageway. And if he was the killer, apparently he strangled Honoria, then went downstairs—somehow managing to miss encountering you in the library—and waited about for an hour or so. Bizarre behavior for a murderer."

"How do you know—"

"He was in the library to meet someone. He thought I was that person when I walked into the room."

"Who?" David asked.

"I don't know." Charles's gaze swept the room. "Do any of you?"

"What the devil are you implying?" Kenneth demanded.

"Exactly what I said. The man was in the library to meet someone. Someone in this house. I suppose it could be one of the servants, but it's far more likely it was one of the family or one of our guests. His visit may have had nothing to do with the murder."

Lady Frances tugged at the lace collar of her dressing gown. "When I make an assignation with a gentleman in the middle of the night, I don't choose the library."

"This is absurd," Kenneth said. "Of course it wasn't any of us."

"Whatever the intruder was doing in the house, surely his business was dangerous," David said. "He had a gun."

"Which he could have used to kill me, but didn't," Charles said. "That doesn't prove he didn't kill Honoria, but it does make me question whether he's the murderer."

"Besides," Mélanie added, "some time before Miss Talbot was killed, she was drugged with an opiate."

David's gaze hardened. "So it was premeditated."

"Unless she was in the habit of taking large amounts of laudanum to help her sleep," Charles said. "Do you know, Glenister?"

"No, I don't think so." He passed a hand over his face. "No, of course not. Why should she?"

"The young have an infernally easy time sleeping." Lady Frances put a well-tended hand to her mouth. "Oh dear. Oh, good heavens. I can't quite believe she's actually—" Her angular face went pale. "That poor child."

"Could she have been drugged somewhere else and then put into Mr. Fraser's room after she lost consciousness?" David asked.

"Perhaps," Charles said. "We did only a cursory examination of the body."

"She died between one and four hours ago," Mélanie said. "The weapon was a bellpull cut from the wall in Mr. Fraser's room. As Charles said, she'd taken or been given a considerable amount of an opiate, probably laudanum." She looked from Glenister to David. "She doesn't seem to have recovered consciousness. She wouldn't have suffered."

David nodded, though his gaze said he wasn't yet ready to seize on such a shred of comfort.

"My God. I can't believe—" Glenister dropped down on the settee and covered his face with his hands. "I knew it was a mistake to come here. This damned house is cursed."

Mélanie sat beside him and put her arm round him.

Glenister looked up at her. His face, normally set in lines of bored dissipation, was streaked with tears. "She was such a pretty child. So clever. My God, who could have done this?"

David was staring at the mirrored panels of the door to Kenneth's bedroom. In the lamplight, the glass had the cold, merciless glitter of diamonds. "Even if the intruder killed her, he'd have to be working with someone in the house, wouldn't he?"

"If she was drugged, almost certainly," Charles said. "Besides, it's been raining since before midnight. The intruder left footprints on the library carpet, but none beyond."

Lady Frances put a hand to her head. She managed to look regal, despite the fact that her feet were bare and her buttery blonde hair was stiff with curl papers. "As my late husband would have said, what a bloody mess."

Kenneth raised his gaze from the stained handkerchief in his hand. "Quite."

Glenister leaned forward, hands balled into fists. "We have to move her."

Mélanie stared at him and felt everyone else in the room do the same.

"We have to move her back to her room before the rest of the household wake up," Glenister persisted, as though they were being very slow. "We can't have it get out that she was found in Kenneth's bed. Good God, can you imagine what people will say?"

Charles dropped down on the carpet in front of him. "Sir, a murder's been committed. We have to send for a bailie at first light. There will have to be an investigation."

Glenister's eyes sparked. "Damn it, Charles, I'm not going to have my niece's name dragged through the mud."

"He's right, sir," David said. "We have to find out who did this. We owe it to Honoria. We owe it to the law."

"Who the devil do you think you are—"

"One of Honoria's guardians. As my father's representative. My father is just as much her uncle as you are, sir, and he'd insist we investigate. But we don't necessarily have to send for a bailie."

"David." Charles got to his feet.

David stood to face him. "Think about it, Charles. It isn't as though we have Bow Street Runners at our disposal."

"A good point," said Lady Frances. "What sort of investigation could the local bailie organize?"

"Your faith in me is touching as usual, Frances." Kenneth had returned to the fireplace and was staring into the cold grate. "I'm the local bailie."

"I assumed you'd turn it over to someone else," Charles said.

"The only other bailie within a day's ride is Gilbert McKenzie. Not a man noted for his brilliance, and I fear a bit inclined to toady to me."

David raised his brows at Charles as though to say, *You see?*

"What do you suggest we do instead?" Charles asked. The question sounded genuine, though Mélanie was quite certain her husband knew where David was headed. She suspected he had steered him that way.

"You investigate," David said.

Kenneth's eyes narrowed. Lady Frances smoothed the lace on her sleeve, her gaze thoughtful.

Glenister stared from David to Charles as though he wasn't sure he had heard aright. "See here, David, Charles was a diplomat and now he's a Member of Parliament. He's scarcely qualified—"

"He was more than a diplomat during the war," David said.

Charles returned his friend's gaze. "I don't know what you're talking about."

"This is no time for modesty, lad," Kenneth said. "What your friend is trying tactfully to point out is that presumably someone with your skills at intelligence work would have a talent for investigation. In fact, I believe you were involved in investigating at least one murder on the Continent. Don't look so shocked, Charles. You aren't the only one with good sources of information."

It was, Mélanie thought, perhaps more interest than Charles had ever seen his father display in him. Charles looked at Kenneth for a moment, as though he wondered what his father wanted from him. Then he addressed the company in general, his voice as cool as the mirrored glass on the wall opposite. "Be that as it may, you're overlooking the fact that I have an excellent motive myself."

He had been playing the scene just as Mélanie expected, but this was a departure from the script. She stared at him. Beside her on the settee, Glenister had gone still.

Charles's jaw was clenched hard and his hands, still clasped behind his back, had gone white-knuckled. He turned back to his father. "Will you tell them, sir, or shall I?"

Kenneth returned Charles's gaze for a moment. "I assume Charles is referring to the fact that a few days ago I asked him to agree to break the entail on Dunmykel. I wanted to settle it on Honoria's and my first son."

Mélanie heard herself gasp. For all her husband and his family baffled her, she knew Charles's love of this house, this piece of land, went bone deep. She could guess what the loss of it would mean to him. And yet he'd said nothing to her of it. Even though only that afternoon they'd spoken about him one day inheriting Dunmykel.

"Kenneth, that's monstrous," Lady Frances said.

"He agreed readily enough." Kenneth glanced at Charles, as

though daring him to deny it. "He'll get his grandfather's Irish estates and his mother's property in Bedfordshire. Not to mention the London house and the Italian villa."

"True," Charles said. "But everyone knows I've always been fond of Dunmykel. Perhaps I resented losing it. Perhaps I wanted to keep the estate for my own son. Perhaps I thought that if I got rid of Honoria you'd change your mind."

"You'd have been wiser to kill me," Kenneth observed.

"Besides," said David, "everyone knows you wouldn't—"

"But that's just it," Charles said in a gentle voice. "Someone did."

Lady Frances looked at Mélanie. "Did he leave his room during the night, my dear?"

Mélanie ignored her husband's gaze. "No," she said. "I'm quite sure I'd have known if he had."

Glenister frowned. "You might not have woken—"

"I suspect she would have," said Lady Frances.

"Yes," said Mélanie.

Glenister stared at her. "But—"

"Charles was holding me."

Glenister, a roué of more than thirty years' standing, coughed in embarrassment. Mélanie didn't add that Charles had been holding her because she'd woken, gasping and sweat-drenched, from one of the nightmares that still troubled her sleep far too often.

"You see," David said. His determination had overcome his usual tendency toward prudishness.

Lady Frances pressed her hands over her silken lap. "Obviously the only solution is to turn the matter over to Charles. We need to discover the truth, and Charles is the best equipped to do so."

"Don't look to me for argument," Kenneth said. "I think it's the wisest course of action."

Charles stared at his father. Kenneth looked back at him. His own gaze gave away nothing.

Glenister nodded. "I agree. Good God, we can't have strangers—"

"Airing our dirty linen," Lady Frances finished for him.

"Whatever we learn," Charles said, "there'll be no covering up the truth, no private vengeance. We turn the evidence over to the proper authorities."

An uneasy silence hung in the air. Neither Kenneth nor Glenister was used to acknowledging any authority but themselves. David, for all his good nature, was an earl's son, bred up to lead. Lady Frances was a duke's daughter, used to having her own way at the snap of her fingers.

"Agreed," David said at last. No one argued with him, which gave the illusion of consensus.

"How do we tell the others?" David asked.

Charles glanced at the mantel clock. It was just past three. "First thing in the morning, we'll gather everyone in the Gold Saloon and tell them all at once."

Kenneth moved to the door. "I see little more to be done until then. It's foolish to think of sleep, but I'm going to one of the guest rooms."

Lady Frances got to her feet. "Kenneth—"

He looked at her over his shoulder. "Fanny, you of all people should know I'm the last man on earth who needs to be coddled. I think I've spent sufficient time in a state of maudlin breakdown for one night. You needn't fear a repeat performance."

Glenister stared at the door as it closed behind Kenneth. "I always knew Kenneth was cold-blooded, but by God—"

"He was in shock when he found her, Lord Glenister," Mélanie said. "I suspect irony is Mr. Fraser's way of controlling his feelings."

"I sometimes wonder if Kenneth has feelings," Glenister muttered.

"So do I," said Lady Frances. "But I'll vouch for the fact that he was feeling something tonight, though I can't for the life of me tell you what it was."

Glenister glanced round the dressing room, as though looking for answers he could not find in the mirrored glass and Chippendale furnishings. His gaze went to the door to the bedroom. The reality of what had happened to his niece slammed home in his eyes. His face crumpled. He gave a sob, desperate and awkward, as though he had forgotten how to do so.

Lady Frances put her arm round him. "Life can be the very devil, Frederick. Come with me, you shouldn't be alone."

Glenister clutched her arm like a drowning man clutching a spar and allowed her to lead him from the room.

David looked after his uncle by marriage. "I should cry. I can't—
I don't think I can really believe it's happened."

Charles drew a raw breath. "I told you we had time to get to the
bottom of this. I'm sorry."

"That's hardly—oh, Christ. You aren't blaming yourself, are
you, Charles?"

"Not to such an extent that I won't be able to function." Charles
crossed to the door to the bedroom and turned the handle. "We need
to examine Honoria further. Why don't you wait in here, David."

"I'm coming with you."

Charles nodded. "Mel, would you mind holding the lamp?"

Mélanie held the Italian bronzed lamp while Charles pulled
back the sheet carefully so he could check for any threads or hairs
caught against the linen. He undid the tiny row of buttons and
peeled back Miss Talbot's nightdress. If her cool, naked flesh held
any memories, he schooled himself not to reveal them. His face
betrayed nothing as he lifted her arms, pushed aside her hair, looked
inside her mouth.

It was Mélanie who noticed the slight swell of Miss Talbot's
abdomen first. Not surprising, perhaps, in a woman who claimed to
have a weakness for sweets. And yet—Mélanie reached out to touch
the curve of flesh. "Charles."

He followed the direction of her gaze. His face froze, as though
for a moment he would not acknowledge the reality of what lay
before him. He laid his hand over Miss Talbot's stomach, the way
Mélanie remembered him feeling for the stirring of their children
within her womb.

"What?" David said from across the room. "What is it?"

Charles looked up at his friend. "Honoria was about two months
pregnant."

Chapter 16

For a moment, none of them spoke. Mélanie stared at the frozen face of the dead girl on the bed before her. Honoria Talbot had broken one of the cardinal rules of her world. A lady was required to bring a spotless maidenhead to her marriage bed. Society might look the other way at what she did after she had married and given her husband an heir, but any transgression before was the stuff of scandal and disgrace. Even a rumor could mean ruin. An illegitimate child would spell social ostracism.

"That's impossible," David said.

"Improbable," Charles said. "But true."

"But—"

"Mélanie's had two children. I've seen pregnant women in the Peninsula, where there was less room for modesty. Unfortunately I've seen dead pregnant women." Charles's gaze lingered for a moment on the thatch of blonde hair between Miss Talbot's legs, as though noting what Mélanie had already seen herself. Then he drew the sheet over Miss Talbot's body and closed her eyes with a touch as gentle as a caress. "Let's go to our room. It will be easier to talk."

They closed the door on Kenneth Fraser's room and adjourned to the bedchamber Charles and Mélanie occupied. Mélanie lit the lamps. The light flickered over the rosy-cream color of the walls and the flowered bed hangings. Though the room had been theirs for less than eight-and-forty hours, she found it an unexpected comfort to be surrounded by the familiarity of her brush and comb and scent bottles, Charles's shaving kit, Colin's lead soldiers.

Charles picked up the decanter that stood on top of the chest of drawers, poured three glasses of whisky, and passed them round. If one ignored the tension about his mouth and the numbness on David's face, it might have been any evening when they had all shared a drink and discussed the play they'd seen or the party they'd attended. Yet the press of emotions in the room was more redolent of a group of soldiers swallowing rotgut after an ambush that has taken the life of one of their comrades.

Mélanie took a sip, savoring the pungent familiarity of the drink. "Miss Talbot is hardly the first young woman to find herself in such a predicament. She was three-and-twenty. That's a number of years with—"

"The needs and impulses of a grown woman," Charles said.

"But—" David bit back whatever he had been about to say. His face had gone bloodless and broken, like linen slashed with a carving knife.

Charles tossed down half his whisky. A bruise was starting to show on his jaw, but behind his eyes Mélanie caught a glimpse of raw, open wounds to his soul far worse than any damage the intruder had done. "If she was a man, no one would think twice about it. But she was a woman and she got pregnant and if the truth got out her reputation would be in tatters. Damnably unfair, but undeniably true." He slammed his hand down on the mantel, rattling the candlesticks and tinderbox. "Sweet Jesus, I've been a fool."

"You couldn't have known about this," David said.

"Last night Honoria as good as told me she was in some kind of trouble and had no choice but to marry Father."

"You think your father seduced her and got her pregnant?" David rarely even raised his voice, but he looked as though he'd rend

Kenneth Fraser limb from limb if he walked into the room. "So she had no choice but to marry him?"

"Possibly," Charles said in a voice from which all feeling had been stripped. "Or she could have been pregnant by someone else, someone she couldn't marry, and she accepted Father to cover it up."

"This could explain why she was in Mr. Fraser's bed," Mélanie said.

"Because it was his child?" David asked.

"Or because she wanted to make him think it was. If she was already two months along, she couldn't wait until the wedding night and still pass the baby off as his." Mélanie turned to Charles, knowing he had seen what she had in his last look at the body.

Charles nodded. "It also appears that Honoria had been intimate with a man at some point last night."

"What?"

Mélanie swallowed, wondering which of them David would find it easier to hear the explanation from. "There were hairs caught in the hair—between her legs. Hairs that weren't her own."

"And that tells you—"

"It's difficult to come up with another explanation," Charles said.

"Good God, are you telling me your father ravaged her in his bed—"

"No. At least, not in Mr. Fraser's bed," Mélanie said. "There was no—there was no indication that lovemaking had taken place there and she'd plainly washed afterward."

"You mean she'd been—"

"All we can say for a certainty is that she was intimate with a man at least twice," Mélanie said. "Two months ago and again last night. We don't know that either time was consensual."

Charles's gaze jerked to her face, an unspoken apology in his eyes. "Very true. If she was raped two months ago, she might have been too afraid to tell anyone."

"But surely—" David said.

"She'd have told Glenister?" Charles asked, as the words died on his friend's lips. "Or Val or Quen? It's not the easiest thing to confide in a father figure or a foster brother. If she told anyone, she might have told Evie, but Honoria doesn't—didn't—confide easily. And she'd have feared the—"

"Stigma," Mélanie said.

Charles looked straight at her, eyes dark with the desire to protect her or Honoria or both of them and bitter with the knowledge that it was too late to do so for either of them. "Yes," he said.

"She could have confided in me," David said. "Or in you. We wouldn't have judged her—Christ, as if anyone could judge a woman who—"

"A number of people do," Charles said. "We wouldn't have judged her, but Honoria might have judged herself. You said yourself that you and she weren't confidants. And she and I haven't exactly been on confiding terms in recent years."

"If she was raped that could explain how she was pregnant," Mélanie said, "but it doesn't explain whom she was intimate with yesterday."

"No," Charles agreed. "Though it's possible the same man—or even another man—assaulted her again last night."

"That would mean it's someone in the house," David said.

"Whether she was assaulted or went willingly to a lover, the man involved was almost certainly someone in the house." Charles's voice was like a lid pressed down on a seething cauldron.

"Could she have been killed somewhere else and then moved to Mr. Fraser's room?" David asked.

"Possibly," Mélanie said, "if she was moved quickly after she died. But she was strangled with the bellpull from Mr. Fraser's room, so the killer would have had to plan ahead. Or he—or she— might have drugged Miss Talbot and then moved her to Mr. Fraser's room and strangled her. But either way, I don't see how the killer could have known Mr. Fraser wouldn't be in his room."

David pushed himself to his feet. His glass tilted in his hand and splashed whisky over his feet. "If I'd had a shred of sense and understood the trouble she was in—"

"David." Charles crossed to him and gripped him by the shoulders. "You're going to blame yourself. You're going to rethink every moment you spent with Honoria from the day she was born and call yourself every name you can think of. It will get worse before it gets better. But believe me, *believe me,* you couldn't have known. Twist this how you will, it's folly to blame yourself."

His voice and face were compelling, quite as if he weren't flaying himself raw for his own inability to understand. But then Charles was always harder on himself than on other people.

David dashed an impatient hand against his face. His eyes were glassy with tears. "She needed someone and I didn't do anything to take care of her."

"Neither did I."

"And the intruder in the library?" David blinked back his tears and frowned at the basin and ewer on the nightstand. "Where the devil does he fit in? Could he have been Honoria's lover?"

"I doubt it. At least, I doubt Honoria was the person he'd come to meet. When he said, 'You're late,' he didn't sound like a man talking to a lover. And even in the dark, I don't think he'd be likely to mistake me for Honoria."

"What do the Elsinore League have to do with all this?"

"I'm not sure. But Mélanie and I learned more about it today." Charles told him about their meeting with Tommy and his story about Le Faucon de Maulévrier.

"You're telling me Honoria was killed to cover up the truth about the identity of a butcher from the French Revolution?"

"Not necessarily. According to Tommy, he and Castlereagh had intelligence that the Elsinore League were plotting to kill someone to cover up Le Faucon's past. But even if Cyril Talbot himself was Le Faucon, it's difficult to see how Honoria could know anything that would be a threat. She was only three when he died."

"Unless he's still alive." Mélanie dropped down on the edge of the bed. "But then we'd have to assume he risked making contact with his daughter after all these years only to turn round and have her killed."

"Because she was threatening to expose him?" Charles said. "In which case, why the hell hadn't she exposed him already?"

"Precisely." Mélanie drew her feet up onto the walnut bedframe. "Besides, the one thing we're sure of is that she was killed by someone in the house."

"Which brings us back to Father and Glenister. They're the only two who could realistically have known of any connection between Cyril Talbot and Le Faucon. Assuming such a connection existed."

"But even if it did, one would think they'd have wanted to protect Miss Talbot from her father's past."

"Besides," David said, "Soro told Manon the people he worked for feared *for* Honoria, not that they were afraid of her."

Charles nodded. "Quite. As soon as it's light, I want to have another look at the room where she died and also at her own bedchamber. For the moment, her pregnancy and the Elsinore League go no farther than this room. They're leverage of a sort."

Little more could be said or done until the light of morning. David gripped Charles's arm for a moment, squeezed Mélanie's hand, and went to talk to Simon before the morning gathering in the Gold Saloon.

Charles closed the door behind his friend and rested his hand on the oak panels. All the tension of the past two hours seemed to settle between his shoulder blades. "I want to take a look at the secret passage before the intruder or anyone else has a chance to come back and remove evidence."

"Darling—"

"The others won't be awake for another couple of hours. No sense in wasting the time." He crossed to the chest of drawers.

"Charles—"

"I'm all right, Mel." He rummaged in the top drawer and took out his pistol and a powder bag. His movements were swift and jerky, one step short of doing violence to whatever was nearest at hand. "I can do this. But if I stop to think, I'm not sure what will happen. So let's just keep going."

Unlike her husband, Mélanie was still wearing her dressing gown. She went to the wardrobe. Fortunately, she'd packed breeches and a shirt. Experience had taught that one never knew when they might come in handy.

She was half afraid Charles would go downstairs without her, but after he'd loaded his pistol he took hers from the drawer where she kept it and loaded it as well. She scrambled into her clothes and laced on a pair of half-boots. Charles was ready about thirty seconds before she was. Under the circumstances, she counted it as a promising sign that he waited for her.

He handed her her loaded pistol, and they made their way down the pine-wainscoted stairs. The yellow light from the lamps they both carried flickered over the grisaille paintings of the Nine Muses that lined the staircase, the framed royal charter that hung casually in one corner of the hall, the crossed swords over the fireplace.

Charles walked swiftly, scarcely seeming aware of her at his side. Tension radiated off him like heat waves. They turned into the north wing, where the thicker, fifteenth-century walls cooled the air. He opened the door to the library.

Mélanie had heard about the secret passage, but she had not actually explored it on her one previous visit to Dunmykel. She watched now as Charles walked to the fireplace without hesitation and pressed the bend in the griffin's tail on the Fraser crest carved into the pilaster beside the fireplace. One of the bookcases flanking the fireplace slid to the side with the soundlessness of well-oiled hinges. The lamps wavered in a draft of dank air. Charles glanced back at her, then ducked his head under the lintel and stepped into the passage.

The floor was hard-packed dirt, the walls granite. A tumbled pile of rock a few feet from the entrance showed where the intruder had shot rock from the ceiling to delay Charles. Charles crouched down and tilted his lamp so the light fell over the spilled chips of granite. Booted footprints showed in the dust from the fallen rock, but the intruder had neglected to drop anything convenient, such as more coded papers with the seal of the Elsinore League.

"I could have run after him," Charles said, his gaze going to where the footsteps trailed off as the dust had rubbed off the intruder's boots. "But I thought he had too much of a start. It seemed more important to go back upstairs than to indulge in a fruitless pursuit."

"Besides, he had a gun and you didn't. He might have reloaded." Mélanie cast a sharp look at her husband. In his present mood, she wasn't sure he'd have caviled at such a consideration.

"True," Charles said, and walked on without further comment. "The passage was built in the sixteenth century," he added a moment later. His voice sounded bizarrely normal, especially in contrast to the erratic breathing that underlay it.

"To smuggle priests in and out of the house?"

"In this family? Hardly. It connects to the lodge. The lord of the manor at the time was having an affair with the steward's wife."

"You don't think the intruder escaped into the lodge?"

"I doubt it. The passage branches off. One branch leads to the lodge, the other runs to a cave and the beach."

The passage diverged a few yards on. They traced one path to a wooden panel similar to the one that opened onto the Dunmykel library. This one, Charles explained, gave onto the book room in the lodge. As there was no sign that the intruder had gone into the lodge, they traced the path back and took the other fork. Mélanie scanned the hard-packed, uneven ground for further clues. Even so, she didn't glimpse the patch of red, brighter than the red-brown of the earth, until she had nearly stepped in it. She crouched down and pointed. "Blood."

Charles touched his fingers to the splotch and held them up to the lamp. "Quite a pool of it. And not yet completely dry."

"Did you wound the intruder?"

"I didn't think so. It's possible he broke his nose when he fell, but you wouldn't think a nosebleed would drip this much onto the floor, not by the time he got here."

"Miss Talbot didn't bleed," Mélanie said.

"No," Charles agreed.

"Then—"

"I'm not sure."

They went on. She caught a whiff of salt in the air. A gust of wind blew out Charles's lamp. He stopped and fumbled with a flint. They rounded a bend. The sound of the sea rumbled toward them. Up ahead a light glowed.

Charles grabbed her wrist and pulled her against the wall. They both blew out their lamps and slid their pistols from their pockets.

"Curse those miserable idiots," a voice muttered from the direction of the light. "We'll be here all night. Why couldn't they have sorted as they unloaded?"

A second voice mumbled something in reply, the words indistinguishable. Charles inched closer along the wall. His foot must have struck a loose bit of rock. The rock clattered, echoing in the stillness. Footsteps pounded in the opposite direction.

Mélanie and Charles ran forward. The passage turned and widened into a cave. A lamp set in a niche cast a wash of light over the sea-scarred walls and the stacks of crates that filled the interior. Charles ran to the mouth of the cave. Mélanie snatched up the lamp and ran after him.

Footprints in the sand beyond the cave showed where the two men had run off, but they were out of view. A rush of cold water hit Mélanie's feet. The tide was coming in.

"We can't catch them," Charles said, his gaze going from the dark, undulating mass of the sea to the cliffs above them.

They ducked back into the cave. Charles pulled out his flint and relit their own lamps.

"Did you know about the cave?" Mélanie asked, scanning the crates. More boxes than she'd used to move their household from Paris to London. Most of the crates were lined up against the walls, but a jumbled pile had been left in the middle of the cave.

"Oh, yes. But it was always empty when we played here as children." He used his picklocks to pry open the nearest crate and lifted out a bottle. He held it up to the lamplight. "Brandy."

"Smugglers?"

"So it seems. Apparently we interrupted them in the midst of sorting a shipment."

Examination of the other crates yielded tea, champagne, port, and bordeaux. "Not a bad vintage, either." Mélanie set down a bottle. "Do you think the intruder in the library was a smuggler?"

"Meeting with a confederate in the house?" Charles returned a tin of tea to its crate.

Mélanie was standing at the side of the cave. The light from her lamp flickered over the granite wall. Amid the scarring of sea and wind, a rectangular depression stood out, unexpectedly symmetrical. "Charles, what's that?"

"What?"

She reached up to touch the depression. The granite slid in her hand and a panel of rock groaned open.

Chapter 17

D amp, musty air, heavy with the weight of rock and earth, fluttered the flame of her lamp. She peered into the shadowy expanse revealed by the granite panel. Another passageway stretched before them, narrower than the main passage. "Did you know about this?" she asked Charles.

He shook his head, dragged one of the crates over, and wedged it against the open panel. Without speaking, they started down the passage.

Charles had to stoop his head beneath the low ceiling. The linen of Mélanie's shirtsleeves snagged against the rough rock as she brushed past. The path twisted, labyrinthlike. At last it widened into another cave, though this one seemed to have been carved out of the rock by human agency rather than nature.

Charles lifted his lamp and swung it round in an arc. The light fell not on granite but on age-darkened wood. A door with iron hinges, set into the rock. Instead of a conventional keyhole the lock was in the shape of a rose, with overlapping iron petals and the lock itself at the heart of the flower. Charles reached into his pocket and drew out his set of picklocks.

It took longer than usual, but after several minutes of jiggling and listening for the click of tumblers, the door swung inward. The light of their lamps spilled over the delicate blue and gold of an Aubusson carpet and the pale blur of furniture under Holland covers. Dark, gaping archways opened onto further rooms beyond. The carpet was spread over a dirt floor, but the walls appeared to have been hung with paper. Mélanie lifted her lamp, as did Charles, and realized the walls weren't papered, they were painted. With a series of floor-to-ceiling murals, depicting characters from Shakespearean plays, though no production Mélanie had ever seen featured the scenes displayed here.

Hamlet—he seemed to be Hamlet judging by the black clothing and clichéd wild-eyed stare—was ravishing a golden-haired, white-clad Ophelia against a stone wall in a bizarre perversion of the "get thee to a nunnery" scene. Gertrude disported with Claudius, Polonius, and a third man who was probably supposed to be old King Hamlet, though whether he was a ghost or in the flesh remained unclear. Romeo and Juliet were twined together in a position that appeared to defy the laws of physics. Desdemona and Othello were making the beast with two backs while Iago observed them from behind a tapestry. A black-veiled Olivia was enjoying the ministrations of an identical pair in blue doublets who must be Viola and Sebastian.

Mélanie stood still, breath caught at the sheer audacity of it, skin flushed with reluctant heat. Crude, blatant, yet undeniably arousing.

She drew a breath. As the initial assault of the pictures wore off, her other senses returned. The air wasn't as musty as in the passage. She could smell the acrid tang of recently extinguished candles, the sour bite of wine, and a pungent, smoky scent that was unmistakable in its implications.

Charles must have smelled it at the same moment she did. He strode across the room and through the nearest archway. Mélanie followed. The archway gave on to a smaller room. A carved four-poster bed took up most of the chamber, a fairy-tale creation of white and gold and gauzy hangings. Two half-empty wine goblets stood on a table beside the bed. Charles jerked back the rumpled bedclothes. The smell wafted through the air. The sheets beneath were still damp.

He cast a glance at Mélanie, then looked round the room. It, too, was painted with murals. These depicted the four lovers from *A Midsummer Night's Dream* in every possible combination. Titania's court were engaged in an orgy in a mural on the ceiling. The theme was echoed by the nude nymphs twining themselves round the table legs and the gilded bedposts. Something else gold glinted at each of the four corners of the bed. Finely wrought handcuffs and leg irons.

Charles saw the cuffs and irons a fraction of a second after she did. She felt his start of surprise. Sometimes she forgot that in many ways her husband was far more innocent than she was herself. Memories of her own past rushed through her, twisting her insides, making her skin crawl.

"Search," Charles said. "Everywhere."

They combed the room inch by inch, but it yielded no telltale strands of hair or conveniently dropped earrings. No taste of laudanum lingered in the wine goblets. The other rooms opening off the main room were decorated with variations on *Measure for Measure, Troilus and Cressida,* and *The Merry Wives of Windsor.* More beds, a chaise longue, a hamper of fancy dress—with a great many low-cut bodices and codpieces and all manner of swords and daggers—and a collection of birch rods.

But nothing to identify the couple who had made love in the first room only hours before.

They returned to the main room without speaking. Charles lifted a corner of the Holland cover on the object in the center of the room. The lamplight gleamed off the polished wood of a table. The other Holland-covered objects proved to be a set of chairs upholstered in a tapestry that echoed the theme of the murals and a marble-topped Boulle sideboard with gilt comedy and tragedy masks on the doors. The interior was filled with crystal glasses etched with more erotic scenes and bottles of whisky, brandy, claret, and port. Behind them, Mélanie found a smaller brown glass bottle filled with a clear liquid. She unstopped it and sniffed. "Charles."

He was shining his lamp beneath the chairs. Mélanie walked over to him, holding out the bottle. "Laudanum."

Charles stared down at the bottle. The light of his lamp lit the hard planes and angles of his face from below. His eyes glittered with a rage that had snapped free of the last shred of control. He crossed to the door in two strides.

She caught him by the arm.

He jerked away, but she tightened her grip. "Darling, listen. This doesn't prove anything."

"The bed. The sheets. The laudanum. Jesus, Mel, why do I even have to state the obvious." He turned to the door.

She grabbed him by both shoulders. "You want to storm into your father's room and confront him, but what then? He'll deny Miss Talbot was ever in this part of the house, he may deny he was here himself, and he'll almost certainly deny he killed her. And he may be telling the truth."

"Damn it, Mélanie, the pieces are all here—"

"You think your father brought Miss Talbot down here, shackled her to the bed, drugged her with laudanum, and raped her."

He looked at her with a gaze night black with fury. "You saw what I saw."

"And then he cleaned her up, carried her to his own bedchamber, and strangled her."

"He could have strangled her here. Probably during the act."

"With the bellpull from his own bedchamber, which he happened to have brought with him? If he killed her here, it's even more bizarre that he carried her to his own bedchamber and then conveniently screamed to wake us up. And don't tell me it's some devious plot to deflect suspicion, because it certainly isn't working."

"Except on you." His gaze moved over her face. His shoulders were taut as a bowstring beneath her hands. "I admit you have a point. Especially about not having proof to confront him with. But someone had intercourse in that bed."

"Miss Talbot could have been here with a different man, who killed her and put her in your father's room."

"Perhaps. Though as you pointed out, the killer would have had to know Father wasn't in his room. And if Father was in the library all evening as he said, he'd have seen them using the passage."

"A number of people may have made love in this house last night. You and I did." Mélanie looked up at her husband and lover. Carnal images pressed in on them from all sides. The smell of stale sex drifted through the room. She felt Charles's physical recoil from the thought that what had taken place in these rooms was at all akin to what they had taken from each other only a few hours ago. Yet didn't the give-and-take of lovemaking often come down to an attempt to hold darkness at bay, whatever the circumstances? When he pressed her into the mattress and sucked at her flesh, had he been worshipping his wife's body or trying to blot out the memory of his last talk with Honoria Talbot? When she wrapped her legs about him and dug her nails into his skin, had she been seeking communion or freedom from thought?

"Suppose your father wasn't reading in the library," she said. "Suppose he had an assignation in these rooms with one of the maids? He returned to his bedchamber to find Miss Talbot dead in his bed."

Charles drew a breath, sharp as a dagger thrust. "That fits the facts, I'll grant you. But I still don't see how the hell the killer could have known Father would be away from his room. Unless the killer was in collusion with the woman with whom Father had the assignation."

Mélanie stared at the paintings, looking for clues beyond the obvious. The characters were costumed in Elizabethan dress, but the full style of the women's hair and the way their brows were plucked and their cheeks rouged had a more recent appearance. "I'd judge these were painted about thirty years ago."

"Yes, I'm quite sure these rooms are Father's creation," Charles said in that light voice that she found so frightening. "I didn't think he even *liked* Shakespeare. I won't forgive him if I have these images running through my mind the next time we go to the theater."

Mélanie glanced from Gertrude, Claudius, and Polonius to Hamlet and Ophelia. "Several of these pictures are set at Elsinore."

"But leaving aside that it's difficult to connect these rooms to Le Faucon de Maulévrier and an organization of Bonapartist officers; there's no sign of the Elsinore League seal. Not even on the lock. Instead we get the rather heavy-handed rose symbolism."

"No. But if Cyril Talbot is or was Le Faucon, perhaps these rooms gave him the inspiration for the Elsinore League's name."

"Perhaps. That's as logical an explanation of the name as we've found so far."

It seemed bizarre and yet somehow normal to be matter-offactly discussing murder motives in a lamplit love nest with her husband, who was probably two steps away from a breakdown. "Charles—we don't know where Tommy Belmont's been since we saw him at McGann's cottage this afternoon. Could he have been the man in the library, the man you chased into the passage?"

Charles grimaced. "It's possible. I didn't see or hear enough to know with any certainty."

"Was Tommy in Lisbon when Miss Talbot visited six years ago?"

This time Charles looked at her for a moment before he replied. "Yes."

"Did they see much of each other?"

His gaze moved over the paintings beyond her shoulder. "They danced together. They flirted, the way Tommy flirted with every pretty girl in Lisbon. I saw no evidence of anything else. But even if there had been something between them, that wouldn't explain whom Tommy might have been meeting in the library. I'm quite sure the intruder was waiting for a man."

"He could have had a rendezvous with one of the servants to ask questions about Mr. McGann."

"So he could."

"Should we try to find him?"

Charles shook his head. "Tommy's devilishly hard to find when he doesn't want to be found, and the more he has to hide, the more our looking for him will put him on the defensive. Time enough to question him at our meeting tonight." He stepped back, breaking her grip on his shoulders. Control had returned to his face, but his gaze still gleamed with danger. "First we have to see how everyone reacts to the news of Honoria's death."

The Gold Saloon was already full when Mélanie entered it shortly after seven. She had gone to the nursery to visit the children, leaving it to Charles and Lady Frances to gather up the guests. Aspasia Newland, who had once been governess to Honoria Talbot and Evie Mortimer and was now governess to Lady Frances's daughter Chloe, accompanied Mélanie to the Gold Saloon.

Sunlight, battling the morning mist, spilled through the windows, gleamed against the polished floorboards, brightened the gold silk wall hangings and the gilded moldings. Save for the early hour, it could have been any morning gathering of the house party. The company seemed curious about the reason they had been called together but not unduly alarmed. They probably assumed it had something to do with the disturbance outside that Mélanie had mentioned when she knocked on their doors in the middle of the night.

Miss Mortimer was passing round cups of coffee. Lord Valentine was sprawled on one of the gold silk settees that flanked the fireplace, his arm stretched along the back, brushing Gisèle's shoulder. Gisèle was turned toward him, eyes bright with laughter at something he had said. Glenister, Kenneth, Lady Frances, and Charles stood talking by the windows. Charles was managing to look quite his usual self, if one ignored the tension in the set of his mouth. From this angle, Mélanie couldn't see into his eyes.

It seemed insane that any of the company gathered in this white-and-gold room, talking and drinking coffee, had drugged Honoria Talbot with laudanum and strangled her. But was it any more incredible than the general who could sip Darjeeling from a silver tea service the morning after he had ordered the sack of a village? Civilization, Mélanie had learned firsthand, was a thin veneer, broken as easily as one could scratch the surface of a Sheraton writing table with a hat pin.

Miss Newland slipped into a chair in a corner of the room. Mélanie went to join David and Simon, who were standing not far from the door, beneath a Canaletto landscape. David smiled at her, though his eyes were dark with everything that had happened and everything he feared was to come.

Simon squeezed her hand. "I'm afraid I'm beastly in situations where a clever remark would be tasteless."

David glanced at Miss Newland. "It was a good idea to ask her to join us. Are the children all right?"

"Blissfully unaware that anything's gone wrong. For once I have cause to be grateful that the nursery is so isolated from the rest of the house."

As she spoke, the door opened and Lord Quentin slipped into

the room. As usual, he could not have presented a greater contrast to his brother. Lord Valentine was the image of the fashionable young gallant—tasseled Hessians, elaborately tied cravat, artfully tousled golden hair. Lord Quentin had made only a token attempt to tie his neckcloth, and his dark hair was disordered not from effort but from the lack of it. His coat was rumpled, his shirt looked as though he had slept in it, and he hadn't bothered to shave. He dropped into a chair near the door and then winced, as though the movement hurt his head. Miss Mortimer brought him a cup of coffee, eyes filled with affectionate reproof.

Glenister and Kenneth exchanged glances and moved to stand before the white marble Adam fireplace with its Venus and Jupiter andirons. David joined them.

Kenneth spoke first. All signs of his shock of last night were gone, save for the drawn cast to his features. He had shaved and dressed with his usual impeccable understatement.

"My apologies for gathering you all together so early. I'm afraid I have sad—tragic news to impart." His voice was firm and resonant. He was, after all, a successful barrister and a Member of Parliament. Charles might not share his father's politics, but his skill as a speaker was a legacy from Kenneth.

Kenneth's gaze swept the company. "In the early hours of the morning, I entered my bedchamber to find Honoria lying in my bed, strangled to death."

The room went silent, the sort of silence that might follow a cannon blast in the midst of a ball.

Lord Valentine pushed himself to his feet. His cup tumbled from his fingers and thudded to the floor, spattering coffee on his biscuit-colored pantaloons. "My God. Why didn't you tell us?"

"We did," Glenister said. "Just now."

"David knew last night. If he hadn't he'd look more surprised." Lord Valentine glared at David. "She was just as much our cousin as his."

"They told me because I'm acting as one of her guardians," David said.

"But—"

"For God's sake, Val," Lord Quentin said. "She's dead." He was staring at a patch of sunlight on the Turkey rug, as though he were looking into hell. Miss Mortimer, who was perched on the arm of his chair, put her arms round him and leaned her head against his shoulder. She was shaking.

Gisèle gave a high-pitched cry somewhere between a laugh and a sob. Charles moved toward his sister, then checked himself as Lady Frances went to her.

Lord Valentine transferred his gaze from his father to Kenneth. "I knew it was madness for Honoria to marry you." His eyes narrowed. "What the devil was she doing in your room?"

"Valentine." Glenister's voice had the snap of a whip.

"By God, sir, we have the right to know. Honoria was practically our sister."

"Certainly you have the right to know," Kenneth said in a voice as cool as carved ice. "I haven't the least idea what Honoria was doing in my bedchamber. I'd like to know myself."

Lord Valentine's chin jutted out. "She can't have gone there willingly."

Gisèle lifted her head from Lady Frances's shoulder. "We never can do anything like a normal family." She looked at her father. "Honoria didn't even survive to the wedding. At least Mama was married to you for twenty years."

"Don't be ridiculous, Gisèle," Kenneth said.

"Ridiculous?" Gisèle's voice cracked on the word. "You can't deny your women have a short life expectancy, Papa. Perhaps I should have warned Honoria—" She gave another laugh that teetered on the edge of hysteria.

Lady Frances slapped her across the cheek. Gisèle drew a sharp breath. "Is that how you dealt with Mama, Aunt Frances?"

Miss Mortimer looked at Glenister. "Uncle Frederick? What happens now?"

Glenister exchanged a look with Kenneth and David, and then explained their arrangement with Charles about investigating the murder.

Lord Valentine's face darkened as his father spoke. "You mean we have to answer any questions Charles chooses to ask us?"

"Better him than the bailie," Lord Quentin said. "Or Bow

Street." He scraped a hand through his untidy hair. "Surely what we need to do is find this intruder who was in the library last night."

"It's not that simple," Charles said, and went on to explain about the laudanum and the implications of the intruder waiting for someone in the library an hour or more after the murder.

Miss Mortimer was frowning in silent concentration. "One of us killed her." She gripped her hands together in her lap. "That's what you're saying, isn't it?"

The ugly truth no one had yet dared voice hung in the air. Disbelief reverberated against the silk-hung walls and echoed off the gilded ceiling. "It's beastly," Miss Mortimer said, "but there's no sense pretending otherwise."

Lord Quentin shot a look at her. "I suppose we could try to pin it on the servants. That's customary in the circumstances. But it doesn't make a lot of sense."

David cleared his throat. "I'm sure Charles will want to talk to all of us individually. I need hardly say that it's in all our interests to cooperate with him. The sooner we learn the truth, the better for all of us."

"Except the killer," Lord Quentin said.

"Quite," said David.

Simon leaned against the wall beside Mélanie, watching David with a concern that for once he didn't take the trouble to mask. He must, Mélanie realized, be as worried about the strain on David as she was about the strain on Charles. Then, too, whenever David stepped into his official role, as now, Simon was forced to remain in the background. They had to maintain a fiction that they were just friends who shared lodgings, though they were closer than half the married couples Mélanie knew. Closer, by far, than she and Charles.

"The intruder was in the library waiting for someone," Charles said. "Presumably someone in the house. It may have had nothing to do with Honoria's death. If so, the simplest thing would be to explain now."

No one volunteered such an explanation.

"Did anyone hear anything last night?" Charles asked. "Or see anything?"

"Other than Mrs. Fraser knocking on our doors with a story about an outside disturbance?" Lord Valentine said. "No."

Miss Mortimer pushed a strand of hair behind her ear. "Honoria came into my room to talk about dresses for tomorrow—today, that is." A spasm of realization crossed her face. "That was the last time I saw her."

"Do you remember what time that was?" Charles asked, his voice gentle.

Miss Mortimer frowned. "I suppose—it was a quarter past midnight when she left the room. I heard the clock in the corridor striking when she opened the door."

"Did anyone see her after that?" Charles asked.

Silence reverberated through the room once again.

"Do any of you know if Honoria was in the habit of taking laudanum?" Charles asked.

"Laudanum?" Lord Quentin stared at him. "I shouldn't think so. She was a confounded heavy sleeper."

A crossfire of surprised looks darted his way.

"As a child, I mean," Lord Quentin said. "I remember having the devil of a hard time waking her from naps on picnics."

"Val?" Charles said. "Evie?"

"Good God, I don't know." Lord Valentine took a restless turn about the room. "I expect Quen's right. He has a better memory than I do."

Miss Mortimer drew a breath. She looked as though she was using every ounce of willpower to concentrate rather than burst into tears. "It's true Honoria was a heavy sleeper, especially when she was younger." She hesitated, her dark brows drawn together.

"But?" Charles said.

Miss Mortimer looked up at him. "She'd been complaining of restlessness in the last few months. She never told me she was taking laudanum, but—I suppose it *is* possible. Oh, dear. All I've done is muddle things more."

"The truth is frequently a muddle," Charles said. He turned to Honoria's former governess. "Miss Newland? Do you know if Honoria ever took laudanum?"

"Not to my knowledge." Her voice was level, though her numb eyes gave the lie to her composure. "But I left Lord Glenister's employ five years ago. I can't speak to Honoria's habits in recent years."

Lord Quentin pushed himself to his feet. "Can we see Honoria?"

"Of course," Charles said.

"Good God." Glenister stared at his son. "You can't have any idea—"

"She was strangled. I don't see how it could be anything but horrific. She's my cousin. I want to see her."

Miss Mortimer stood beside him. "So do I."

"For God's sake, Evelyn—" Glenister said.

Miss Mortimer lifted her chin and straightened her shoulders. "I'm not a baby, Uncle Frederick. I haven't been for a long time."

Charles exchanged a look with Mélanie. She nodded and felt in the pocket of her gown for her vinaigrette. She, Charles, the Talbot brothers, and Miss Mortimer went upstairs. Outside the door of Kenneth's bedchamber Charles turned to Miss Talbot's cousins. "She's been dead for several hours. I don't know if you've ever seen a dead body, but with time—the appearance changes."

Miss Mortimer looked up at him and forced a smile to her lips. "It's all right, Charles. If I don't see, I expect my nightmares would be worse."

But when they filed into the room, Miss Mortimer gave a sharp cry. Lord Quentin put his arm round her and she pressed her face into his shoulder. Lord Valentine cast one look at the bed, then spun away, crossed to the washstand, and vomited into the basin.

Mélanie took a step toward him. Lord Valentine waved her away. He stood gripping the dresser, gaze fixed on the wall.

Miss Mortimer lifted her head from Lord Quentin's shoulder and looked again at her dead cousin. "I don't think I really believed it until now." She looked at Charles. "You were right. I'm glad I saw." She drew a deep breath, walked over to Lord Valentine, and put her arm round him. Lord Valentine pulled her to him in an awkward, brotherly hug.

Lord Quentin looked down at Honoria for a long, silent interval. "Fraser," he said at last.

"Yes?" Charles said.

Lord Quentin turned his head and fixed Charles with a hard stare. "Can you find the bastard who did this?"

"I'll do my best," Charles said.

"Good." Lord Quentin stared back at his murdered cousin. "And then you can leave it to me to finish him off."

Chapter 18

Silence echoed the length of the servants' hall when Kenneth Fraser finished his account of Honoria Talbot's death. The walls were whitewashed rather than hung with gold silk, the furniture covered in black horsecloth rather than figured damask, the rugs loomed in Yorkshire rather than France and Persia. But the horror and disbelief on the faces of the assembled crowd were the mirror image of that of the guests in the Gold Saloon.

Hopetoun, the butler, looked as though he took it as a personal failure that such a tragedy had occurred in a household of which he had charge. Mrs. Johnstone, the housekeeper, stared at Kenneth as though he had announced that fleas had got into the linens. They were sitting at the front of the room. The cook, the underbutler, the chief housemaid, and the valets and ladies' maids of the various guests were ranged about them. The more junior members of the staff stood at the back of the room.

Kenneth, Glenister, David, and Charles faced the assembly. Mélanie stood to one side. Her role was to observe reactions. The servants often knew what was going on in the house far better than the guests and family.

The silence was broken by the swish of starched skirts and an abrupt thud. One of the kitchen maids had fainted. Mélanie hurried to the girl's side, fumbling in the pocket of her gown for her vinaigrette.

"What is that?" Kenneth's voice came from the front of the room, sharp with impatience.

"It's all right, Mr. Fraser. One of the girls was overcome by the shock." Mélanie waved the vinaigrette beneath the girl's nose. She was a freckle-faced child of no more than fifteen. Mélanie's maid, Blanca, knelt beside her and chafed the girl's wrists.

Hopetoun, in a voice still racked by shock, offered condolences on behalf of the staff. While he was speaking, David's valet got up from his chair and came over to Mélanie, Blanca, and the girl who had fainted.

"Please don't fuss about me, Mrs. Fraser," the girl murmured as Mélanie and Blanca helped her to her feet. "I'm quite all right."

"I'm sure you are, but you'll do better if you sit down for a bit. What's your name?"

"Morag, ma'am."

"Morag. Marston is kindly offering you his chair. It would be bad manners not to accept the offer."

Morag gave a shy smile and sank into the chair. A little color had returned to her cheeks, but she plucked at her cotton skirt with nervous fingers.

A sob from the front of the room cut short Hopetoun's speech. Mélanie looked up from Morag to see Miss Talbot's maid, a straight-backed young woman in a stylish poplin dress, dissolve into tears. Kenneth drew an exasperated breath.

Charles knelt before Miss Talbot's maid with the same gentle smile he had given Evie Mortimer. "Fitton, isn't it?" He offered her his handkerchief, as her own was thoroughly drenched. "What time did you leave Miss Talbot last night?"

Fitton twisted the handkerchief between her fingers. "Just before midnight, sir. I helped her into her night things and brushed out her hair. She told me she'd wear the striped lilac sarcenet the next day with her violet spencer and her new half-boots."

"She didn't ring for you again?"

"No, sir. That—" Her voice caught with realization, as Miss Mortimer's had done. "That was the last time I saw her."

"Do you know if your mistress was in the habit of taking laudanum to help her sleep?"

"Laudanum?" The surprise was plain in Fitton's voice. "No. That is, I suppose she might have done without telling me. She'd sometimes complain she'd had a restless night."

"How long had you been with Miss Talbot?"

"Just short of two months, sir." Fitton brought the handkerchief up to her face. "I couldn't imagine a kinder mistress."

Charles asked if anyone had seen or heard anything out of the ordinary during the night. No one offered any information. There was little to be gained from prolonging the scene. Kenneth, Glenister, and David went to make arrangements about Honoria's burial. Charles and Mélanie climbed the stairs in silence. They had had no time to talk since the scene in the Gold Saloon. Charles opened the door to their bedchamber, steered her inside, pulled the door to, and leaned his shoulders against it. His face was set in firm lines, hard, polished armor buckled over the raw pain of last night. How the wounds beneath the armor were festering was another question. "Whoever killed Honoria is a damned good actor," he said.

Mélanie sank down at her dressing table. She was suddenly aware that she'd had only three hours sleep the night before. The few sips of coffee she'd swallowed roiled in her stomach, and her limbs ached from the exploration in the secret passage. "The servants seem even more bewildered than the guests."

Charles strode across the room. "I seriously doubt she was killed by one of the servants."

Mélanie looked at him sharply. It was unlike Charles to make a blanket statement based on class. "Why?"

"Because as kind a mistress as Honoria may have been, she was the sort who doesn't look at the household staff as flesh-and-blood human beings. I can't imagine her getting close enough to any of them for them to have had a motive."

Harsh words to use about a woman for whom he had seemed to care so deeply. She continued to look at him.

Charles returned her gaze. "I was fond of Honoria. I wasn't blind to her faults."

A direct answer which at the same time left a vast array of feelings unexpressed. "If her death had something to do with the Elsinore League, Le Faucon or whoever's behind them could have hired one of the servants."

Charles's face tensed with the impulse to defend the Dunmykel staff, then went still. "Yes. There is that. Addison and Blanca can make inquiries among the staff better than we can. But my instinct is to focus on the guests."

The guests. As though they were people he scarcely knew. While his impulse was to defend the staff, he seemed determined to give his friends and family no quarter. Mélanie rubbed the sore muscles at the base of her neck. "I wouldn't exactly say any of them gave themselves away."

"No." Charles passed his hand over his eyes. "I'll say this for Quen and Val and Evie. None of them lack courage."

"I'm glad they saw Miss Talbot," Mélanie said, thinking of the deaths of her own parents and sister. "It makes it easier in the long run."

"I hope so. I confess I also had an ulterior motive."

"The hope that one of them would give themselves away?"

"Or not, as the case may be." He perched on the edge of the writing desk. "Val was sick. Evie could scarcely bear to look at Honoria, though she forced herself to in the end. Quen stared at her for a good minute. What do you make of that?"

"Possibly no more than that Lord Quentin is the sort who likes to confront his demons head-on. He's always struck me as tougher than Lord Valentine, underneath the debauchery. Of course, he also made that comment about Miss Talbot being a heavy sleeper."

"So he did. One could argue that if he had inappropriate knowledge of her sleeping habits, he wouldn't have said anything of the sort. Or that he wasn't thinking clearly enough to make such a judgment and it was a revealing slip of the tongue."

Charles ran a finger over the pristine surface of a stack of writing paper. "One of the men here may have been the father of her baby and almost certainly bedded her last night. Val. Quen. Glenister." His mouth tightened for a moment. "Father. David and Simon, though I've never known either of them to so much as look at a woman. And me, of course. You know, I expect I could have slipped out of our bedroom without waking you."

Mélanie fingered a fold of her skirt. She'd exchanged last night's shirt and breeches for a cambric morning dress, scalloped and threaded through with peach silk ribbon. The ensemble of a decorous wife. "That depends. Your talent for moving quietly against my knack for waking at the smallest disturbance." She walked over to him and smoothed his disordered hair. "Dearest, you know I don't like to make assumptions. But I'd stake my life on it that you didn't murder Honoria Talbot."

"Bless you for that." He leaned in and brushed his lips across her forehead. "'Render me worthy of this noble wife.'"

"Charles, if it ever comes to the point where I have to stab myself in the leg to gain your confidence—"

"Don't worry, if I ever consider assassinating a would-be emperor, I'll be sure to confide in you."

He probably would, too. He just wouldn't turn to her for solace when the plan collapsed round his ears.

She hitched herself up on the edge of the writing desk beside him. "If Glenister's the one who got her pregnant, it would explain why she couldn't marry the baby's father."

Charles nodded, his gaze on the stack of writing paper.

Mélanie thought of the rooms they had found off the secret passage and the sort of games in which Glenister and Kenneth Fraser had indulged. "Well?" she said. "You've known him all your life."

"Would Glenister have seduced his niece and ward? Christ, Mel, Edgar and Gisèle and I saw little enough of our parents growing up, let alone their friends." He picked up a crystal paperweight and turned it over in his hand, watching the light bounce off the faceted glass. "When I was about six I overheard one of the housemaids tell another that she'd stumbled into the room occupied by the lady thought to be Father's mistress only to find her in bed with Glenister. It didn't cause any noticeable friction between Father and Glenister. The Glenister House set treats seduction as the ultimate game."

"'She's beautiful and therefore to be wooed,'" Mélanie quoted. "'She is a woman, therefore to be won.'"

"Quite." Charles returned the paperweight to the desk. "It's possible Glenister seduced Honoria. Or took her by force." His fingers whitened round the paperweight. "It's also possible Father bedded her before they were betrothed and then again last night."

"We're back to where we were last night. If your father was her lover, why didn't they make love in his room? If she and your father made love in the secret rooms we found, how did she end up in your father's bed?"

He drew a breath. "If she was pregnant by another man and went to Father's room so she could pass the baby off as his—Father can't abide anyone trying to make a fool of him."

"That would be a crime of passion," Mélanie said. "It doesn't explain the laudanum."

"She might have taken the laudanum herself."

"Perhaps if she simply meant to retire for the night, but I've never heard of anyone taking a sleeping draught before embarking on a seduction. Besides, if your father killed Miss Talbot, I'd think he'd prefer to have a Dogberry like Gilbert McKenzie investigate rather than you."

"Unless he's playing a very clever game. My father is one of the cleverest gamesters I know." Charles stared at the green and gold leather of the desktop between them. "I just wish I knew what the devil the game is that he's playing now."

"Lady Frances was right. Having you investigate is the only option."

He swung his gaze to her. "Mel, I'm almost thirty years old. From my earliest memories of banging my nursery spoon and riding a hobbyhorse to the moment we took our candles and went up to bed last night, Father's attitude toward me has swung between complete boredom and out-and-out contempt. Yet now he's willing—eager, even—to have me investigate his fiancée's murder, with all the bloody questioning and digging into the past that that's bound to involve. Which makes me wonder—"

"If he's using you, thinking he can manipulate you to get the result he wants."

"Father and Glenister, and perhaps even David, think they can control the investigation through me, for all my fine words to the contrary. Tidy away the messy bits. Avoid a prosecution, if that proves inconvenient. None of them want a family member in the Old Bailey."

She looked at him in the slanting sunlight. The bones of his face stood out, harsh and bleak, robbed of the humor and tenderness that usually lit his features. "Darling. Last night, you told your father that if Miss Talbot hadn't been dead when he came into the room, he should tell you now. What would you have done if he'd said yes?"

"I don't know," Charles said after a moment. "I'm not sure I want to know." He shifted his position, swinging his booted foot against the leg of the writing desk. "You haven't asked me yet."

"Haven't asked you what?"

"Why I didn't tell you Father had asked me to break the entail."

Pain lanced her chest, but she refused to admit it. "I confess I was curious, but I assumed you had your reasons."

"I think I was trying to sort out how I felt about it myself." He pushed himself to his feet, walked to the window embrasure, and stood looking out at the sea. "It's Father's house. He has a perfect right to leave it to whomever he wants."

Mélanie glanced at the age-darkened oak of the floorboards, the bits of fifteenth-century stone that still showed round the window, the plaster crest on the mantel. "But you love Dunmykel," she said.

"Unfortunately, yes. I probably shouldn't."

"You can't control what you love. Or whom."

"No. But it's hardly my first loss. Or my greatest." He turned from the window. "And God knows we have more important things to worry about."

She got to her feet and walked toward him, feeling as though she was picking her way through a wood set with mantraps. "Charles, I'm so sorry. I don't think I said that properly last night. I know she—was important to you." The words sounded inadequate, like a bare-bones synopsis of a complex love story.

She put her hand on his arm. He flinched as though she had touched a half-healed wound.

"I'm sorry," he said. "I—thank you." He moved to the door. "The next step is to look at Honoria's room."

Addison was standing guard outside Honoria Talbot's bed-chamber, shoulders straight, coat without a wrinkle, pale blond hair combed smooth. "No one's even tried to approach," he reported.

"Thank you," Charles said. "We've had a talk with the staff. I'll interview some of them privately later, but you might start doing some informal questioning of your own. They're more likely to talk to you than to me or Mélanie. In particular, we want to know if any of them is a likely candidate to have been hired or blackmailed by the Elsinore League."

Addison nodded. Charles had told him about the league before they left London. "Right, sir."

"One of the kitchen maids fainted at the news," Mélanie said. "A girl named Morag, with fair hair and freckles. I suspect it was more than shock. Ask Blanca to speak to her. She was there when the girl fainted."

"Thank you, Mrs. Fraser," Addison said in an impersonal voice that belied his far from impersonal interest in Mélanie's maid. "I'll see to it."

Charles turned the knob of the door to Miss Talbot's room and then looked back at Addison. "You might also investigate if it seems at all likely that one of the women on the staff spent any part of last night with my father."

Addison returned Charles's gaze for a moment, face at once neutral and sympathetic. "I'll keep that in mind, sir."

Charles opened the door of Miss Talbot's bedchamber. The curtains were still drawn, leaving the room in shadow. A faint scent of violet and jasmine lingered in the air, along with the chalky smell of face powder and the tang of lavender.

The bedchamber was scrupulously tidy. Fitton must have put things to rights before Miss Talbot sent her to bed. A dressing gown of ice-blue silk and Brussels lace lay across the foot of the bed in neat folds. The satin-banded coverlet was smooth, save for the corner where it was turned back to reveal the lace-edged sheet. Mélanie lifted the bedclothes carefully and pulled them to the foot of the bed. Unlike the bed in the chamber in the secret passage, this undersheet was pristine. "It looks as though Miss Talbot didn't even lie down in her own bed last night," she said. "And she quite definitely wasn't intimate with a man here."

Charles dipped his fingers in the water in the ewer on the satinwood nightstand and brought them to his lips. "No laudanum. I would think it would have had to be in something stronger to disguise the taste in any case."

Mélanie went to the table on the opposite side of the bed. A book lay beside the crystal Agrand lamp. Byron, *Don Juan*. Hardly surprising reading matter for a young woman. She opened the drawer in the table. A stack of handkerchiefs and something else that rattled. She reached into the back of the drawer and retrieved a small, three-quarters-empty glass bottle filled with a clear liquid. She unscrewed the top and sniffed for confirmation. "Laudanum. Most definitely. I wouldn't exactly say it was hidden, though it wasn't in plain view."

"So perhaps she did take too much laudanum on her own. Or perhaps she took a small amount on her own and the murderer drugged her with more."

"Or perhaps she didn't take it at all and the murderer planted this in her room."

Charles's gaze swept the room. The pink-flowered basin and ewer on the nightstand, the silk-draped dressing table, the painted beech wardrobe and writing desk. "You look at the dressing table. I'll take the wardrobe and writing desk."

The dressing table was a stark contrast to the tidiness of the rest of the room. A dressing case fitted with gilded mirrors spilled open. A thin film of face powder dusted the tabletop, a perfume atomizer lay on its side, a thin ivory-handled brush was smeared with lip rouge. Mélanie held the silver-backed hairbrush up to the light of the window. Several blonde hairs were caught in the bristles. "She seems to have tended to her appearance before she left the room. I remember she was wearing lip rouge when she—when I saw the body."

Charles nodded without looking up. He was lifting papers from Miss Talbot's writing case. "Nothing so far but letters to girlhood friends and a bill from her dressmaker."

Mélanie opened each of the silver boxes in the dressing case, but they contained no more than the ribbons and hairpins and jewelry that might be expected. She tugged open the dressing table drawer. Another stack of embroidered handkerchiefs, gloves of net and kid and silk in white, ecru, beige, lavender, lemon yellow. She lifted out the handkerchiefs and found nothing beneath them, then did the same with the gloves. A folded sheet of paper fluttered to the ground.

She caught the paper and spread it open. Pressed paper, cream-colored and heavy, covered in a strong black scrawl. She held it to the light of the window.

> *My darling—*
> *It's no good, I'm bloody awful at pretending I don't care. I love you—surely you know that? If I haven't said it, blame it on pride, not lack of feeling. Shall I swear it by the blessèd moon? I won't presume to swear by myself—I could scarcely hit upon a more profane object. Yet in this, believe me, love, I speak true. I can't believe you—of all women—would let fear of a society you laugh at stand in the way of our happiness—*

Mélanie turned the paper over. Nothing was written on the back. If there was a second page, it wasn't in the drawer.

"Charles. I've found something. A love letter."

He crossed to her side and stared down at the paper.

"Do you recognize the hand?" Mélanie asked.

He nodded. "It's Quen's."

Chapter 11

According to Alec, the footman on duty in the hall, Lord Quentin had gone outside half an hour since, accompanied by Miss Mortimer. Alec believed he'd heard them say something about walking to the lake.

Mélanie followed her husband's swift strides from the hall to the drawing room and through the French windows onto the granite terrace. The air had a chill bite, but there was no immediate promise of more rain. The sky was a smudge of slate and indigo. Below the terrace, greenery and stonework and well-cut granite steps tamed the cliff. At the base of the steps, the gardens stretched in a riot of color. And beyond them, the restless blue expanse of the sea.

Charles took the steps two at a time. Mélanie tried to match her pace to his, but her skirt, a fashionably narrow column, caught about her ankles.

Charles stopped. "Sorry. I didn't realize I was walking so fast. A craven attempt to run away." His gaze moved over the garden below, the knotted parterre in the shape of the griffin and dragon of the Fraser arms, the hedged walkways, the reflecting pool, the sunken sundial surrounded by a tumble of roses. "I taught Quen to hold a cricket bat on that bit of lawn by the parterre when I was ten and he was five. He managed to knock the ball into the center of the sundial. It was a capital hit."

Mélanie, focused on the thought of Lord Quentin as Honoria Talbot's lover, was brought up short by this image of him as a child.

Charles started back down the steps at a more temperate pace. "He was an engaging little boy. Restless, but not hard to entertain if you could find something that interested him."

"And Lord Valentine?" Mélanie asked.

"Val was determined to outshine his elder brother. When Quen was about eight he decided cricket was too tame and he tried to scale the Old Tower." Charles glanced over his shoulder at the thirteenth-century keep, which jutted out of the north wing. "Val followed him. Quen actually made it to the top. Val nearly did as well before he turned his ankle and got stuck. I had to go up after him."

Mélanie stared at the steep walls, with few handholds besides chinks in the mortar and an occasional arrow slit. "Somehow I doubt Lord Valentine thanked you."

"He gave me a bloody nose while I was bundling him onto the battlements. As soon as his ankle healed, he snuck out of the nursery at dawn and climbed the tower all over again. It's a wonder he and Quen survived to their majority without breaking their necks."

"What did Glenister think of the rivalry between his sons?"

"He encouraged it. Though he always tended to be harder on Quen and indulge Val more. Just as he prefers Val's more stylish brand of rakishness to Quen's out-and-out debauchery."

They reached the bottom of the steps and turned down a walk-way bordered by a yew hedge on one side and a line of purple holly-hocks on the other. The damp grass squelched beneath their feet. The air smelled of rain-drenched leaves and freshly turned earth.

Images ran through Mélanie's mind. Lord Quentin sick with drink at Miss Talbot's betrothal ball. Lord Quentin slumped in the corner of the drawing room last night. Lord Quentin staring down at Miss Talbot's body this morning, his face set with cold rage. "In the letter Lord Quentin accuses Miss Talbot of letting society's opinion stand in the way of their being together," she said. "But surely whatever his reputation, a marriage between them would have been seen as eligible. If she loved Lord Quentin and was carrying his child, why insist on marrying your father?"

"Why indeed? Of course Quen might not have been talking about marriage, though, it's hard to imagine he'd have believed she'd run off with him without it."

"Perhaps she was convinced he'd make an unreliable husband."

"And so she decided she'd rather marry my father?"

"It fits the facts as we know them."

"It doesn't fit Honoria."

"It doesn't fit the Honoria you thought you knew. But then, neither does the fact that she was pregnant."

Charles swung round to stare at her. "Damn it, Mel, don't. Not you of all people. Don't use the fact that she wasn't a virgin to drag her into the gutter."

"You know me better than that."

"Then what are you suggesting?"

"That Miss Talbot had secrets. You have to face the fact that she may not be the woman you thought she was."

"Just what is that supposed to mean?"

She stared at the raindrops glistening on the petals of the hollyhocks. "No one is truly who we think they are. Not exclusively, not entirely. There are always corners we don't see into. In most cases we'd be better off not knowing what lurks in those corners, but in this case you have to know. You have to pick through her past and uncover all the messy bits."

"And you think I'm afraid to do that?"

"I think it's hellishly difficult to dig into anyone's past, especially the past of someone you cared for, most especially someone you cared for and lost."

He drew a breath and released it. "I'd be a fool to claim I'm entirely objective when it comes to Honoria or Father or any of the people here. But you have to allow that I'm rational enough to tell a hawk from a handsaw, at least when the wind is southerly. Or I assume you'd have objected to the idea of my investigating Honoria's death in the first place." He resumed walking. "I'm not going to assume Honoria is guilty of every conceivable infamy simply because she happens to have been with child. I don't think you want to assume that, either."

"Of course not. But—"

His gaze moved over her face, slate dark and unyielding. "What?"

She looked back at him without blinking. "Miss Talbot struck me as a woman who liked to be in control—of situations, of people, of her own life. She knew exactly the right words to pick to drive her point across." Such as the point that she knew Charles far better than Mélanie did herself. "One doesn't present an image as flawless as hers without a great deal of thought and effort. And that thought and effort usually mean that flawless image masks something a great deal more complicated."

"You scarcely knew her."

"She called on me shortly before we left London. One can learn a lot in half an hour over a tea table. I doubt she so much as unbuttoned her gloves without thinking through the consequences of the action."

"You've spent too much time round diplomats and agents, Mel. Not everyone is a master schemer. For God's sake, you're usually so good at seeing beyond the obvious. Looking at the facts from every angle. Not judging people or jumping to conclusions."

"Damn it, Charles, I am looking at the facts. And before you go into your litany about knowing her better than I did—"

"Obviously I didn't know her as well as I thought. If I'd understood her better, I'd never have—I'd have known what to do or what to say to her and perhaps this wouldn't have happened."

She put a hand on his arm. "Charles. You couldn't have prevented this."

"You can't possibly know that."

"I know you. I know you're thinking you should have been able to protect her, the same way you wanted to protect me. But you can't always fix everything."

"Stop it." He jerked away from her with a force like the recoil of a gun. "Stop being so bloody sure you know what I'm thinking better than I do myself. Jesus, in some ways you don't know me at all."

Four and half years of marriage. Uncounted nights spent in his arms, uncounted meals eaten together, uncounted moments of shared danger. Uncounted chambers in his mind she knew she'd never glimpsed. "That's just the point."

"That you don't know me?"

"That you can't expect me to carry on this investigation without knowing all the facts you do about Miss Talbot."

His gaze cut against her own like the press of cold steel. "What are you asking? If I was her lover? You should know me well enough to know that I wouldn't—"

"Seduce a virgin?" She parried his glance like a rapier thrust. "I wouldn't think so. But I can't be certain of what you might do under every possible set of circumstances. As you just pointed out, in some ways I don't know you at all."

He continued to look at her in a silence heavy with words they'd never spoken to each other, pieces of their lives they'd left shrouded in mystery. "I wasn't her lover. Ever."

He turned on his heel and strode forward without waiting for her. For a moment Mélanie stood rooted to the damp ground, watching her husband retreat down the line of hollyhocks, each step tearing at the half-improvised, half-compromised bond between them.

When Francisco Soro sought them out in London, she'd been relieved at the call to adventure. Danger had always been the common ground in their marriage. But that was before she knew how close this particular danger cut to the most guarded recesses of her husband's mind and heart. Unraveling the truth about the Elsinore League and Honoria Talbot threatened to turn any common ground between them into a wasteland.

With a muttered curse that would have been more appropriate on the battlefield, she tugged up her narrow skirt, revealing an amount of calf and ankle that would have scandalized the patronesses of Almack's, and hurried after her husband.

She caught up with him on a rise of ground that overlooked Dunmykel's ornamental lake. A white marble folly gleamed beside the water, its columns artfully crumbled in imitation of a Roman ruin Charles's mother had sketched on her honeymoon. Charles didn't turn his head in her direction, but he slowed his stride to match hers as they descended the slope to the folly.

Lord Quentin and Miss Mortimer were sitting side by side on

the circular marble bench. Lord Quentin's arm was draped across Miss Mortimer's paisley shawl, and Miss Mortimer's hand rested on the rumpled superfine of his coat. They weren't talking, but they must have been lost in thought, for they both started at the approach of footsteps.

"I'm sorry." Charles stopped on the first of the marble steps. "I know the last thing you feel like doing is answering questions."

"On the contrary." Lord Quentin pushed himself to his feet. He still hadn't shaved, and if anything his cravat was more rumpled than before, as though he had bunched it in his fist. "If answering questions is the only way I can help—well, it's a damned sight better than doing nothing."

Miss Mortimer smoothed her hands over her sprigged muslin skirt. "We're going to feel beastly no matter what. We might as well be useful." She hesitated for a moment, looking out over the water. Her eyes were red-rimmed and her lashes spiky with tears. She was a bewitchingly pretty girl, with clean skin and vivid features, yet she must have been cast into the shade by Miss Talbot since childhood. "Honoria and I quarreled last night. She wanted to borrow my coral earrings for the next day, even though she has—had—twice as many pairs of earrings as I do, and she had a tiresome habit of losing the things she borrowed. I decided for once I'd put my foot down. Now it seems childish that I cared." She turned to Charles. "Were you looking for me or Quen or both of us?"

"For Quen, actually." Charles climbed to top of the steps. "But there's no hurry."

"No, I'd best go back to the house in any case. I should see how Uncle Frederick and Val are bearing up." Miss Mortimer squeezed Lord Quentin's hand. For an instant, as her gaze rested on his dark head, Mélanie caught a spark of tenderness in her eyes, sharper than cousinly affection. Poor girl. Mélanie wondered if she'd known about Lord Quentin and Miss Talbot. Bad enough to go through life in Miss Talbot's shadow. Worse to see her take the man one wanted for oneself.

Lord Quentin watched his cousin as she walked up the slope of the hill. "Typical Evie," he said, seemingly oblivious to the nuances in her gaze. "She thinks the family's her responsibility. I'm afraid she's got herself half convinced she should have known what was going to happen to Honoria and prevented it somehow." He put his hand over his eyes. His fingers shook. "I'm sorry. I still can't quite believe it happened."

"It's only been a matter of hours." Charles watched him for a moment. "There's no way to make this sound like anything but a platitude, but it does get easier. At least that's how it was for me when my mother died."

Lord Quentin returned Charles's gaze for a moment, his bleary eyes suddenly focused. "I don't remember my own mother's death— I was scarcely out of leading strings. Some of my school friends died in battle, but they were across an ocean. I've never—do you mind if we walk? It gives me the illusion that I'm doing something."

They descended the steps and set out along the gravel path that wound round the edge of the lake. "I keep remembering how I used to carry Honoria about on my shoulders when she first came to live with us," Lord Quentin said.

Charles glanced sideways at the younger man. Concern for the boy he'd taught to play cricket warred in his face with anger at the man who'd probably got Honoria pregnant. "I imagine you have more recent memories as well."

Lord Quentin scraped his uncombed hair back from his face. "I haven't seen much of Honoria lately. Evenings at Almack's and genteel drives in the park aren't exactly my style. And God knows Honoria would never be found in a gaming hell or—er"—he glanced at Mélanie—"any of my other usual haunts. When we did meet—Honoria gave up on me as a lost cause years ago. Probably when I brought a lady of uncertain virtue to her come-out ball. Or perhaps the night I burst into an inappropriate song at one of her musicales."

"She must have cared for you."

"We're a family. Evie would say that means we can't help but care for each other. In my more maudlin moments, I might almost agree with her. I might even confess to a passing affection for Val. But that doesn't mean there aren't times when we'd all cheerfully—"

He sucked in his breath. "I was going to say, 'wring each other's necks.' Which is either an appallingly tactless metaphor or a blunt statement of fact. Or perhaps both."

They walked in silence for a half-dozen steps. "We found your letter to Honoria," Charles said.

Lord Quentin stopped and stared at him. "You found my *what?*"

Charles took the letter from his coat and held it out.

Lord Quentin let out a shout of bitter laughter. "Oh, Christ."

"She was very lovely," Mélanie said. "It's understandable—"

The laughter faded from his face. "She was practically my sister."

"But she wasn't. And—"

"Honoria was the kind of a girl I run a mile from, Mrs. Fraser. My women have all been experienced and safely married. Starting with my godmother when I was just short of my sixteenth birthday."

"Do you deny this letter is in your hand?" Charles said.

"Oh, it's my hand all right. But—"

"We found it in her room."

"You—" Lord Quentin's eyes darkened. "The little devil."

Charles exchanged glances with Mélanie, then regarded Lord Quentin for a moment. "The lady to whom the letter is addressed is not Honoria?"

"Of course not."

"Who is the lady you were addressing?"

Lord Quentin drew a breath and started walking again. "I can't answer that."

Charles strode after him. "For God's sake, Quen. I'm trying to find out who strangled your cousin. I promise I won't reveal the lady's name unless it proves to have something to do with the murder."

"And if it does?" Lord Quentin spun round. "Her reputation would be ruined all the same. Don't think I haven't learned anything from my father. Whomever a gentleman may take to bed, it's distinctly bad manners to repeat her name in the morning."

Charles fixed him with a hard gaze. "I could show the letter to everyone in the house and ask for an explanation."

"Go ahead. Try it."

Mélanie caught up with the men. "I can't answer for the lady, Lord Quentin, but if that letter had been written to me, I'd like to think I wouldn't want my lover to protect my reputation at the cost of letting a murderer go free."

Lord Quentin swung his gaze to her. "You can't know—"

"If this lady cares for you as much as you care for her, surely she'd want to learn the truth of what happened to your cousin."

Lord Quentin started to speak, then bit back the words. He scanned her face as though searching for answers. "I don't know that most women would be so brave, Mrs. Fraser. But I expect you would. And—" He glanced over the water, then back at Mélanie. "I think she would as well."

"She?" Mélanie said.

Lord Quentin released his breath in a soft sigh. "Aspasia."

It was the last name Mélanie had expected to hear. "Aspasia Newland?" she said. "Chloe's governess?"

"And once governess to Honoria and Evie. Given my history, surely you don't think I'd cavil at debauching my cousins' governess."

The lake lapped softly beside them. The scent of roses and lilies drifted through the air. Charles was standing very still, leaving the scene in Mélanie's hands. Neither of them had ever let a quarrel interfere with the ebb and flow of an interrogation. Mélanie looked at Lord Quentin, dissolute, five-and-twenty, born to power and fortune, and thought of Miss Newland, self-possessed, the daughter of an Oxford tutor, close to forty. Then she thought of the hint of sensuality that Miss Newland's neat clothes and governess hairstyle could not quite obscure. She thought of Miss Newland's quick mind and Lord Quentin's angry intelligence. "You must have still been at Harrow when you met her."

Lord Quentin started walking again. "The part of my head that wasn't addled with drink was stuffed full of ideas. Aspasia could run rings round me with her Latin and Greek. We liked the same books. I don't think I've ever made such a thorough fool of myself."

"And then?"

"I went to Ireland for a month. Some damned riding party. I came back to find she'd left Father's employ and gone to work for Lady Frances."

"You went after her," Charles said.

"I very nearly burst into Lady Frances's house at an ungodly hour and created a scene, but I still had some vestiges of sense. I met Aspasia walking in the park with Chloe, who was scarcely more than a baby. One of those tiresome scenes ensued that occur when one hasn't the sense to let a love affair die a natural death."

He stared at the flickering shadows of the oak branches over-hanging the lake. "I thought I'd got over it. I had got over it."

"Until you came to the house party and saw her again?" Mélanie said.

"And realized my love burned stronger than ever?" His voice was as bitter as the stale dregs of burgundy. "It sounds like some-thing out of a bad novel, doesn't it? Val would say it's just pique because she turned me down. I daresay he'd be right. But whatever name you give to the feeling, it was still there."

"You called it love in the letter," Mélanie said.

"So I did. According to Father, telling a woman you love her is the ultimate card to play in the game of seduction."

"Is that what the letter was?" Mélanie said. "A gambit?"

"Isn't every step in a love affair, one way or another?" He ges-tured toward the letter, which Charles still held. "I wrote that in the drawing room last night. Then Evie called me over to turn the pages of her music. I tucked the letter under the ink blotter on the writing desk. When I went back it was gone. Honoria must have taken it."

"Did she know about your affair with Miss Newland?" Charles asked.

"Oh, yes." Lord Quentin continued walking, his gaze fixed straight ahead. "It was Honoria who forced Aspasia to leave Glenis-ter House."

Charles froze for a fraction of a second. "When did you discover that?"

"Only last month. Honoria was upbraiding me with my follies and she let fall a remark about my having debauched her governess. I asked her how the hell she knew and the whole truth came out. She'd learned or guessed about the affair five years ago. Instead of confronting me, she waited until I'd left for Ireland and then went to Aspasia with what she knew. She told her she couldn't in good con-science—Honoria's words, not mine—stand by while the affair went on, but that if Aspasia left and found a new position she wouldn't say anything to Father."

"You must have been furious," Charles said.

Lord Quentin gave a mirthless laugh. "I don't think I actually smashed anything, though I certainly felt like it. But it made me wonder—"

"If you could try again with Miss Newland?" Mélanie said.

"I should have known five years ago. I should have guessed. Honoria could be a damned interfering—"

He checked himself and looked from Charles to Mélanie. "A damned interfering bitch," he finished, flinging the words in their faces. "And now I suppose you're wondering if my display of grief has all been an act."

"Has it?" Charles said.

Lord Quentin tugged his ruined cravat loose and wadded it up in his hand. "I'm not that good an actor. I loved Honoria, because I'll never forget the orphaned child who was like a little sister to me. If I knew who murdered her, I'd kill the bastard with my bare hands. But I scarcely knew the woman Honoria had become in recent years. And what I did know, I didn't much like. If that makes me a suspect, so be it." He strode on, grinding the gravel underfoot.

"Why do you think she took the letter?" Charles said.

"God knows. For fear someone else would find it, perhaps. Honoria hated even a whiff of scandal. Once—years ago—I went to leave a birthday gift in her room and I found a whole stack of letters she'd apparently stolen from Val. Written by various ladies with whom he'd been rather closely acquainted. Some married, one or two not. I don't wonder at Honoria wanting to get them out of Val's hands, but if you ask me she'd have been wiser to return them to the ladies in question. I daresay she didn't want to admit she knew what was going on."

"You said she was interfering," Charles said. "Whom else did she interfere with?"

They were halfway round the lake. Lord Quentin turned and looked back at the folly. Rage and grief and regret did battle in his eyes. "Just about everyone she thought worth her notice. She liked to arrange people's lives for them. But people didn't always obligingly fall in with her plans. Last autumn one of her friends had the ill grace not to fall head over heels in love with the man Honoria had picked out for her. Instead she fancied herself in love with a journalist, of all things. And a friend of mine, to make matters worse. Honoria searched out the man's former mistress and paid her to confess all his nasty habits to the girl. Of course she probably saved my friend and the girl the disillusionment of falling out of love." He glanced at Charles. "I know, it's not the face Honoria showed to the world. It's not the face she showed to you. She always liked you twice as much as Val or me."

"What about Val?" Charles said. "How did he feel about Honoria?"

"Honoria drove Val mad, but not in the way you're implying. He called her Princess Icicle. Besides, Honoria wouldn't have gone beyond mild flirtation with anyone until she was married."

Charles's face didn't betray by so much as a flicker of an eyelid that they knew this not to be the truth. "Because she took her virtue too seriously?"

"Because she was too determined to remain in control." Lord Quentin's gaze moved over the mountains in the distance. "Father always indulged her in anything. Evie found it easier to play along with her. Val and I were off at school. I've sometimes wondered if I'd been there more—are we finished?"

"Just one more question," Charles said. "Were you alone last night?"

"Aside from a bottle of brandy. Pity. If I'd had the sense to take one of the housemaids to bed, I'd have an alibi." He turned to go. Then he looked back and fixed Charles with a hard stare. "Aspasia could lose her job. You won't—"

"Believe it or not, it's not my aim to ruin anyone's life. If for some reason this proves relevant to the investigation and the story gets out, I'll talk to Aunt Frances. She's not the sort to be put off by scandal and I know how she values Miss Newland. If worse comes to worst, I'll find Miss Newland a new position myself."

Lord Quentin gave a curt nod. "Thank you."

Charles watched him walk off, his own gaze as bleak as salt-scoured granite. Mélanie rubbed her arms. She was cold, and not because the sky was darkening. Her quarrel with her husband stirred between them, like the quickening buffets of wind that sent the clouds scuttering overhead.

"Charles, I like what I've seen of Miss Newland, and Chloe seems to adore her. But if Miss Talbot knew about Miss Newland's affair with Lord Quentin, Miss Newland has an excellent murder motive. Miss Talbot had the power to ruin her with a well-placed word."

"And Quen knew it." Charles started walking along the path toward the house. "Despite Quen's words, I suspect he'd do a great deal for Miss Newland."

Mélanie pulled her shawl about her shoulders. Nothing was to be gained from shying away from the hard questions. They had to play this out to the end game, even if that meant pressing against bruises and ripping the scabs from old wounds. "Lord Quentin said Miss Talbot wouldn't take a lover because she liked control. I think he was right in part. If she wanted to stay in control, she could only safely risk taking a lover who had more to lose from the affair becoming public than she did."

Charles started to speak, then bit back the words, his gaze going across the lawn. Blanca, Mélanie's maid, was hurrying toward them in a tumble of muslin and curly black hair come free of its pins.

"Mélanie. Sir." Blanca's urgent tone betrayed her excitement, as did her use of Mélanie's given name. "I hoped I'd find you."

"What is it?" Mélanie asked.

"It's not at all what I expected, but I suppose—*Dios,* I'd better start at the beginning. Addison would never forgive me for making a muddle of it. I spent a quarter-hour with Miss Talbot's maid, Mary Fitton. The poor girl is quite *desconsolada* about Miss Talbot's death, though I must say she sounds a much more exacting mistress than—"

"Blanca," Mélanie said.

"*Lo siento.* Mary had only been in the employ of Miss Talbot for two months. Miss Talbot dismissed her previous maid."

"Why?" Charles asked.

"I don't know, sir. I asked Mary three different ways. I'd swear she knows no more of the truth of it than I do. She doesn't seem to know a great deal else about Miss Talbot, beyond the type of face powder she wore and her favorite way of arranging her hair, which is actually quite—" Blanca drew a breath. "At all events, as Addison would say, I spoke then with Morag, the girl who fainted. You were right, Mél—Mrs. Fraser. She does know something. She was out walking last night with Joseph, one of the grooms. She's not supposed to be out after ten, so she was afraid to speak of it. I promised to keep it from Mrs. Johnstone," Blanca added, with a gaze that threatened defiance if her promise was countermanded.

"Naturally," Charles said. "Go on."

"Morag slipped back into the house through one of the library windows. It was just past one thirty this morning, as near as I could tell. She's sure she saw a panel by the fireplace ajar."

"That's hardly surprising," Mélanie said. "We know the intruder used the secret passage."

"Yes. But Morag also caught a glimpse of a man in the library. Not the intruder you spoke of. A man she recognized. The estate agent. Mr. Andrew Thirle."

Chapter 20

Mélanie's words of a few minutes before played through Charles's head with the clear precision of notes struck on a harpsichord. *If she wanted to stay in control, she could only safely risk taking a lover who had more to lose from the affair becoming public than she did.* And who would have had more to risk than Andrew, dependent on Honoria's fiancé for his employment and the house that was home not just to him but to his widowed mother? If Kenneth Fraser had so much as suspected Andrew was Honoria's lover, he'd have dismissed him without a reference.

Charles drew a breath. He felt as though he'd been punched in the stomach.

"It doesn't prove anything," Mélanie said.

"No. But we should talk to Andrew. Did Morag notice anything else, Blanca? Was Andrew alone? Did she notice anything out of place in the library?"

Blanca shook his head. "Mostly her worry was to get back to her room without being seen herself. She didn't put together the pieces until this morning when she heard about Miss Talbot."

"A quick-thinking young woman."

They started back for the house. Mélanie glanced at the watch pinned to her bodice. "I should go to the nursery," she said in a voice that was just a bit too brisk. "Jessica will be hungry. And I think you'll do better with Andrew on your own."

Charles nodded. He could see the embers of their quarrel in her eyes and taste the bitter ashes in his own mouth. He wanted to tell her he was sorry. He wanted to shake her and tell her that she couldn't understand events at Dunmykel the way she understood Continental politics. Above all, he was aware of a craven relief at escaping her relentless gaze.

Alec was still on duty in the hall. As a bright-eyed boy of ten, he had always known the doings of Dunmykel village and the other tenant families. At nineteen, two feet taller and garbed in green Fraser livery and a powdered wig, he was still an excellent source of information. Mr. Thirle, he said, had left the house half an hour since and gone to the gardener's bothy.

Charles descended the steps to the gardens once again, turned away from the formal gardens, and made his way along a primrose-bordered path to the stone bothy. As boys, he and Andrew had often gone to the bothy in search of Andrew's father, who had frequently conferred with the head gardener. It took a staff of twelve to look after Elizabeth Fraser's gardens, as well as the herb and kitchen gardens, the orchards, the orange and lemon houses, and the pinery.

The griffin-and-dragon crest was etched in the stone door of the bothy, along with the family motto. *Veritas est Alicubi.* It would have helped, Charles thought as he pushed open the door, if his ancestors could have been a bit more specific.

He stepped into a room filled with cool shadows and damp, loamy air. Andrew and Leith, the head gardener, were bent over a table spread with plans of the grounds. "Master Charles." Leith straightened up, hair a trifle whiter and face a trifle more lined than in Charles's boyhood memories. "We've heard about Miss Talbot. I'm so sorry."

"Thank you." Charles closed the door. "I'm afraid I need a word with Andrew."

"Stay here," Leith said. "I have to have to check on the lads in the orangery." He paused a moment, tugging at his rolled-up linen sleeves. "Your pardon, but I'm afraid work can't stop in the face of tragedy."

The door closed behind him. Andrew and Charles regarded each other across the stone room. The walls were painted blue to drive out the flies. Perhaps the color accounted for why Andrew's face looked so shadowed and drawn.

"Dear God, Charles," Andrew said. "I just heard an hour ago. Your father sent for me to discuss the funeral arrangements."

"They've decided about the funeral?"

"Tomorrow. David convinced Lord Glenister to have her buried here beside her father. At first he wanted to take her home, but David said there could be no question of leaving until—"

"We know who killed her," Charles said.

"Yes. Christ, I can't believe—have you discovered anything?"

"Nothing conclusive." Charles advanced into the room. Spades and trowels hung from wooden hooks all round. Hoes and rakes leaned against the walls. Harmless garden implements that were also tools of destruction. "Did you use the secret passage last night?"

"Did I what?" Andrew said.

"One of the housemaids caught a glimpse of you in the library."

Andrew let out a sigh. "Damnation."

"Did you use the secret passage?"

"Yes."

"Why?"

"You're not going to believe this."

"Try me."

"To get a book from the library."

Charles stared at the face of the man whose word he had relied on since they were children. "You're right. I don't believe you."

"It's not the first time I've done it. My parents had a decent enough collection of books, but nothing to compare to your father's library."

"You're at Dunmykel every day."

"You know what your father's like about his first editions."

"That never stopped you when we were boys."

"I've learned prudence."

Charles folded his arms. "For Christ's sake, Andrew, couldn't you come up with a more convincing story than this?"

Andrew aligned the blue-inked plans of the grounds on the table before him. "I daresay I could have done if it were a story."

Charles studied his friend's hands. "You always fidget when you're lying. That time your father caught us in the wine cellar, you tore a handkerchief to shreds before he got the truth out of us."

Andrew glanced down at the plans. The edges of the paper were frayed and smudged. "You've always been good at seeing into dark corners, Charles, but sometimes there's nothing in the shadows but shadows."

Charles rested his hands on the water-stained wood of the table. "Whatever it is, I'll do my damndest to keep it quiet. Better you tell me than that I stumble on it in some other way."

"I've told you."

"You weren't meeting with the smugglers by any chance, were you?"

"The *what?*"

"There are smuggled goods being stored in the cave at the end of the passage. You didn't know?"

"If I'd known there was smuggling on the estate, don't you think I'd have gone to your father?"

"No, I think you'd have done your best to turn a blind eye to the business. Especially given conditions since Father began the Clearances."

"But surely you don't think I'd have been working with them."

Charles surveyed his partner in fishing expeditions and cricket games, whisky drinking, exploring tide pools, and arguing the finer points of Adam Smith and David Hume. Andrew's blue eyes held scars that hadn't been there ten years ago. "I wouldn't have thought so."

"Besides, I wouldn't have gone to the library to meet smugglers who were using the cave."

"So what were you doing in the library?"

"Borrowing your father's copy of *The Wealth of Nations*." Andrew walked to the seed cabinet and pushed one of the metal drawers closed.

"You've read *The Wealth of Nations*."

"I wanted to read it again."

"Were you her lover?" Charles said.

Andrew's back stiffened. "Whose?"

"Honoria Talbot's."

Andrew turned slowly to face him. The light from the window set high in the wall spilled over his shoulder but didn't illumine his face. "What the devil have you heard?"

"What is there for me to hear?"

"Nothing. She joined me on my morning rides a couple of times. She stopped by my office once or twice to ask me to explain things about the estate. It's understandable. It was to be her home. For Christ's sake, Charles, do you really think a girl like Honoria Talbot would look twice at a steward? Especially her fiancé's steward?"

"She might if he was handsome and clever and rode like the devil."

"Very funny."

"If she rode with you and visited you in your office, she obviously looked more than twice at you."

"She was kind and remote and she saw me as one step removed from a servant."

"And you? How did you see her?"

"As a beautiful girl who was about to become the wife of my employer. Besides—"

"What?"

Andrew looked straight into Charles's eyes. "When we were young it was clear I wasn't the one she was interested in."

Charles decided to ignore this. Andrew knew too much of the past. "You haven't answered my question. Were you Miss Talbot's lover?"

"No, of course not."

"Damn it, Andrew, I could always tell when you were lying."

"You think I'd seduce an unmarried girl and risk ruining the pair of us? You have a poor opinion of my chivalry, not to mention my common sense."

But I can't be certain of what you might do under every possible set of circumstances. Mélanie's words echoed in his head. God knew Charles hadn't shared a fraction of his own life in the past ten years with Andrew. Or even of the events before he left Britain. "I didn't say you were lying about Honoria. But I'd swear you're lying about something."

For a moment, looking into Andrew's eyes, Charles thought he'd got through to him. Then Andrew walked back to the table and began to roll up the plans. "My dear Charles, even you are wrong upon occasion. I don't imagine any of us are thinking too clearly this morning."

That, at least, was true. Charles tried another tack. "Did you see or hear anything last night when you were in the library getting this book?"

"If I had, I'd have told you. You should know that."

"At the moment I can't afford to let myself think I know anything. Or anyone."

Andrew sucked in his breath, but he said nothing until Charles had turned to the door. "Charles?"

"Yes?" Charles looked back at his friend.

Andrew's face closed. He had the look of a man doing battle with physical pain. "Nothing. Just—I'm sorry you're in this mess."

"I'm sorry for us all."

Jessica pushed against Mélanie's breast with her small hands. Mélanie leaned back against the nursery window seat, cradling her daughter. She'd given Jessica's nurse a few moments to herself, and Miss Newland and Miss Dudley had taken the older children for a walk. Mélanie acknowledged a cowardly relief at this last. They would have to talk to Miss Newland about Lord Quentin's revelations, but she needed a moment to sort through her own thoughts.

In some ways you don't know me at all. Her husband's words hung in the air, pressed against the ash wood walls and mullioned windows, hovered over the well-worn carpet. She stroked her fingers over Jessica's golden-brown hair. She and Charles had knit themselves together in this small person in her arms. How odd that one could take a man into one's body and create a new life with him and yet wonder if one really knew him in the ways that mattered.

Unlike her first pregnancy, this one had been planned. She had told Charles she wanted another baby and she had longed for her second child with a fierceness even she could not explain. To bind Charles to her? To prove their marriage was born of more than impulse and necessity? To show her own commitment, a commitment that even now she could not put into words?

How ironic that she and Charles, in defiance of the custom for couples in the polite world, shared a bedchamber. It caused raised brows among those who were aware of the arrangement. A sign of intimacy. Or wantonness. The truth was, they had begun to do so out of necessity, because Charles's rooms in Lisbon hadn't allowed for more than one bedchamber. But neither of them had made any effort to alter the arrangement in Vienna or Brussels or Paris or now in Britain. And yet while that intimacy continued, the distance between them seemed greater than ever.

She had once thought that if she could only sort out her own loyalties, their oddly begun marriage had a chance of success. For all her supposed skill at reading people, she hadn't understood the depths of the problem. Charles had committed his trust, his honor, and his fortune to her with scarcely a second thought, but the innermost core of who he was remained locked in a code to which it seemed she would never have the key. She wasn't even sure she had the fight to search for it. Marriage was a shocking invasion of privacy.

"Mélanie?"

Simon's voice sounded from beyond the door panels. He turned the handle and stepped into the room. He didn't blink at the sight of her with her bodice unbuttoned and the child at her breast. "The perfect Madonna. If I was a painter like my father, I'd capture the image on canvas."

Mélanie glanced down at her unfastened gown and her happily suckling daughter. "If you captured *this* image on canvas, you'd cause quite a scandal."

Simon crossed the room, skirting a basket of toys, a wooden train, and a rocking horse with half the hair torn from its mane. "Causing scandal is my stock in trade." He dropped down beside her on the window seat. "I rather think, in another life, it might be yours."

Simon had a way of looking at her and seeing things that no one else did. Perhaps because, like her, he was an outsider in this world.

"I've caused more than enough talk already by the way I choose to bring up my children. Most people put it down to Continental eccentricity. I haven't bothered to say that feeding one's baby oneself would be considered just as eccentric among the first circles in France or Spain as it is here."

Simon leaned back and crossed his legs. "I understand you're setting quite a fashion. The most stylish young matrons are to be seen breast-feeding their children in Hyde Park or while they stop for an ice at Gunter's or even behind the potted palms at balls. But then most things you do set a fashion. I imagine it drove Honoria Talbot mad."

Jessica's head flopped back against Mélanie's arm. Mélanie lifted the baby to her flannel-draped shoulder and patted Jessica's back. "Rubbish. Honoria Talbot had no reason to be jealous of anyone, least of all me." Unless, of course, she had harbored feelings for Mélanie's husband.

"False modesty doesn't become you, Melly mine. Miss Talbot had beauty and polish, it's true. You have both, plus originality, which is ten times more rare. And ten times more valued by the *beau monde*."

"Until they grow tired and toss you aside like last year's gowns. Good girl," Mélanie added as Jessica gave a burp.

"But the more original you are, the longer you can fascinate. I shouldn't think you'll ever go out of fashion, my sweet. Miss Talbot would have been stepmother-in-law to the most intriguing woman in London. I can't imagine it's a prospect she relished."

Mélanie settled Jessica on her lap and tried to button her bodice one-handed. Simon held out his arms. "I'll take her."

Jessica leaned against him and looked up at him with a gurgle, a spit bubble forming on her lip. Simon coaxed her to grasp hold of his finger. "David would make a good father," he said, his gaze on the baby.

Mélanie did up the last button on the flap on her bodice. "So would you."

"Perhaps." He gave a crooked smile. "I'm not half as patient as David. As it hardly seems a likely prospect, in truth I've never considered it."

"Nor did I, until I found myself pregnant." Too late, Mélanie realized that this was not the best wording for a loving wife who was eager to give her husband children. Simon gave no sign that he had noticed, but she was sure he had. He was devastatingly accurate with language.

"Ma-ma," Jessica said. Unfortunately, she reached for the floor rather than for Mélanie as she said it.

Mélanie settled her daughter on the carpet with one of the window seat cushions at her back. She sat on the floor herself and Simon sat beside her, curling his long legs under him.

"How's Charles holding up?"

Mélanie's hands stilled for a moment, balancing Jessica against the cushion. Her gaze fastened on her wedding band. "He won't break, though he may wear himself ragged. He'd feel worse if he *wasn't* doing anything." She glanced at the white-painted table where Charles and Honoria Talbot had no doubt shared porridge and chocolate and jam tarts; at the sun-faded shelf of books beneath the window that Charles might have read to his young friend; at the golden-haired, china-headed doll that had probably been Gisèle's but conjured images of another little girl who might have played with it. "Miss Talbot was—important to him."

Simon didn't question her word choice, though again she could tell he had seen more than she'd voiced. "David's taken her death hard as well. He didn't know her all that well growing up—she lived with the Talbots more than with his family—but he takes his family responsibilities seriously. I sometimes think it would be easier if he'd seen more of her. As it is, he's inclined to view her as purer than snow and fairer than a lily."

Mélanie scanned Simon's frowning face. "Did you come to talk about Miss Talbot?"

"Yes, as a matter of fact." He looked down at Jessica, who was reaching for the shiny brass buttons on his coat. "I was hoping I'd never have to tell anyone this, because God knows it won't make David happy. But in the circumstances—it may be relevant."

"What?"

"The night we arrived at Dunmykel, I went to my room to find Honoria lying in my bed."

Mélanie stared at him, her image of Honoria Talbot once again fallen to bits in her mind.

"It's not the first time a woman's hidden in my bed," Simon said. "You'd be amazed at the lengths some actresses will go to for a part. And one or two women of fashion have thought I represented a unique challenge."

"Not to mention the fact that you're an indecently attractive man. But I would have thought—"

"That my devotion to David was protection enough? Does your devotion to Charles keep men from flirting with you?"

"No, but they aren't in the habit of hiding in my bedchamber."

Simon's face turned grim. "This is the first time it's happened with an unmarried girl. Not to mention one who was David's cousin. And in her fiancé's house. I didn't know her well. I'm not generally invited to family gatherings—to own the truth, I was a bit surprised to be included in this house party. I now suspect it may have been Honoria who convinced Kenneth Fraser to invite me. David insisted we get here as quickly as possible—he was worried about Honoria after the business in London. The night we arrived there was dancing, and Honoria contrived to waltz with me and—"

"Pressed closer against you than was necessary?"

"Yes. I thought it must have been an accident or a bit of girlish mischief. I don't shock easily, but I have to say I was shocked to find her in my bed later that night."

Mélanie looked at her daughter, wriggling on the brightly patterned nursery carpet in happy ignorance of the conversation taking place above her head. "What in God's name did Miss Talbot say when you walked into the room?"

"Nothing at first. The room was dark. I put down my candle and lit a lamp. There she was sitting up in my bed. She let the coverlet slither down about her. She wasn't wearing a nightdress. I think I was supposed to be overwhelmed at the sight and crush her to my manly bosom."

"What did you do instead?"

"I said, 'Dear me, I was under the impression that this was my room. Whom were you expecting?'"

"I don't imagine that went over very well."

"No. She looked quite cross. Then she opened those cerulean blue eyes very wide and said, 'Oh, please don't be angry.' I said I wasn't angry, but I was a bit old-fashioned and I thought she should leave. Her eyes filled with tears—it's a pity she couldn't have trained as an actress, I could have made something of her—and she said something along the lines of she'd loved me for years and soon she'd be married and this was her last chance. I said I was afraid it wasn't a chance at all and if she'd loved me for years she'd been damned quiet about it. That was when she jumped out of the bed and flung herself into my arms."

"Stark naked?"

"Stark naked. I started to worry that it was some sort of a setup and someone was going to burst into the room and catch us, only I couldn't imagine why she'd go along with such a plan. All the same, David was right next door and the last thing I wanted was for him to hear. I grabbed the coverlet and wrapped it round her and said thanks very much but it was time for her to go back to her room."

"Did she?"

"God, no. She twined her arms round my neck—she had a grip like a vise—and kissed me. I rather take exception to being kissed against my will. I caught her by the wrists and told her that even if I ever considered bedding someone of the female sex, she was the last woman on earth I'd choose. That got the point across."

"So I should think."

"She jerked out of my hold and slapped me. Raked her nails across my cheek, too. I'd never thought I'd see such rage on that porcelain face. It made her quite unattractive. I saw her dressing gown lying on the floor. I tossed it to her and suggested she go back to her own room and we could forget about the whole thing. She glared at me. And then—I couldn't hear very well, because she was wrapping the dressing gown round her—but she mumbled something about 'That's all very well for you to say, but what the devil am I going to tell him?'"

"*Him?*"

"That's what it sounded like. I can only assume someone put her up to it—that it was some sort of dare. But whatever was going on, she didn't mean to stop with a kiss. And no one learns how to use her tongue and teeth to that effect without practice. At the time I thought it was no business of mine if she'd slept with half of London. She was to be married in a couple of months and she and Kenneth Fraser seemed well suited. I saw no point in dragging David into a family imbroglio. But now that she's dead—" He looked at Mélanie, eyes gone serious. "I thought you and Charles should know. It's up to you what you do with the information."

Mélanie thought of her husband's tormented face when he refused to discuss Honoria Talbot. She could offer him the truth now, at least a version of it. She wondered if he'd ever forgive her. "Yes. Thank you, Simon."

Jessica stretched out a hand for Mélanie, lost her balance, and toppled to one side. Mélanie caught her just before she hit the floor and swung her up in the air. Jessica's cry of distress changed to a gurgle of delight. "Simon?" Mélanie said, helping Jessica to stand up on her lap. "This isn't a question I'd normally ask a friend, but did you and David sleep together last night?"

"Dear Lord, what we've come to, though I knew you were bound to ask sooner or later. Unfortunately, we both slept alone. David's a bit of a prude when he's under the same roof as his relatives." He reached out to tickle Jessica in the stomach. "If you have to tell David about Honoria's visit to my room, will you let me explain first?"

"Oh, yes. But it isn't David I need to talk to now."

Charles opened the door of the old drawing room, the oak-ceilinged chamber in the north wing that had always been reserved for private family gatherings. Oddly enough, this room with its canvaswork furniture and faded carpets had been one of his mother's favorite spots at Dunmykel. He walked to her Broadwood grand pianoforte and began to pick out a melody at random. He could still tell a hawk from a handsaw. Probably. But could he judge the veracity of his oldest friends? Could Honoria have been in love with Andrew? If so, why had she been so determined to marry Kenneth? Because Kenneth was the father of her baby? Or because Kenneth or Glenister knew who the father was and was using that knowledge to force her hand? It didn't fit Quen's version of an Honoria determined to be in control of any situation. It didn't fit the girl he had grown up with, the girl he remembered from Lisbon, the woman who had appealed to him for understanding on the terrace less than four-and-twenty hours ago.

He stared at his hands and realized, with a shock of surprise, what he was playing.

The door clicked and his wife slipped into the room. " 'Per pietà ben mio per dona,' " she said. "Perhaps more apt than you know." She closed the door behind her. "Charles, six years ago in Lisbon, did you find Honoria Talbot hiding naked in your bed?"

Chapter 21

Memories choked Charles's brain. The Spanish oak and the embroidered silk coverlet of the bed in his rooms in Lisbon. The erratic light of the candle that dangled from his nerveless fingers. Honoria, eyes blue-black and wide with pleading, lips parted, hair spilling over her naked breasts. His own breathing quickened, his thoughts a tumble of confusion, his body taut with unthinking response.

He looked across the familiar jumble of the old drawing room at his wife. At the sea-green eyes that could see things he could keep hidden from most people. So that sometimes his only hope of escape was to barricade himself against her. Perhaps he should have known she'd guess about Honoria. She'd always been able to piece things together quickly, but how the devil—

"She did the same thing to Simon the night he arrived at Dunmykel," Mélanie said.

His fingers thudded against the keys of the pianoforte. "*What?*"

She crossed the room to him. "Listen, Charles, I don't know how this fits with the Elsinore League, but I think I understand at least some of what's been going on." She scanned his face, the way she did with the children when she was forced to break disappointing news. "I know this is difficult, darling. I know it flies in the face of everything you believe about her. But at least hear me out."

He got to his feet. He felt as though he'd been pushed off the cliffs on Dunmykel Bay. "When have I ever failed to hear you out?"

"I know. It's one of the things I lo—it's one of the wonderful things about you." She seized his hands in a firm grip. Her eyes were like polished agate at the bottom of a deep, still pool. "I think Miss Talbot was in your bed three nights ago for the same reason she was in Simon's three nights ago. Because of a dare."

He bit back an incredulous laugh. "Mélanie—"

Her grip on his hands tightened. "She made every effort to get Simon to take her to bed. When he turned her down flat, she muttered something about 'How am I going to explain it to him.'"

But I love you, Charles. A beseeching voice. A tremulous voice. A voice that shook with sincerity. "You think a man dared Honoria to seduce me and now Simon." It sounded even more ridiculous when he said it aloud.

"A particular man. The man who gave Miss Talbot his love letters from other women as proof of the success of his seductions."

"Val?"

"It explains why Lord Quentin saw letters from his brother's mistresses among Miss Talbot's things. It explains what she was doing in your bed and later in Simon's."

He jerked his hands from her grip. "It fits some of the facts without making any sense at all. You can argue that I didn't know Honoria, but what has everyone kept saying about her? That she wanted to be in control. And you're suggesting that she risked everything for—not even for love but for—"

"Power. Control."

"How the hell would risking her reputation give her control?"

"As an unmarried virgin, she was in a powerless position. A pawn. The most she could do was defend her virtue. This let her be a player in the game."

"The game?"

"The oldest game of all, darling. The game of the Glenister House set. The game your father and Miss Talbot's uncle excel at."

"But you can't assume Honoria would have cared—"

"She must have lived and breathed it growing up in Glenister House. She'd have watched her uncle conduct his intrigues and then Lord Quentin and Lord Valentine."

"You think I don't know? I grew up in that world, too."

"And you walked away from the intrigues. But you can't assume Miss Talbot felt the same. Besides, she couldn't run off to Lisbon."

He saw Honoria as a little girl in a white frock twisting the adults round her finger when she, Evie, and Gisèle got up to some mischief or other. And then for a moment he saw her as she'd been last night on the terrace. *You don't have the right to demand anything of me anymore.* "It's a reach."

"Think, darling. Forget your need to defend her memory. Forget the girl you thought you knew. Forget the girl you loved."

"I didn't—"

"You did love her, Charles, one way or another. No sense pretending now. But look at the facts. Why else would she have tried to seduce Simon? He's by far the greatest challenge at the house party. If she'd succeeded, she could have been sure he wouldn't have told anyone, and even if he had, who would have taken Simon's word over hers? Having failed with him, I expect she'd have turned her attention to someone like Andrew Thirle—"

"She did. I mean, she—dear God." Andrew's account of Honoria's rides with him echoed in Charles's head. He closed his eyes for a moment while the sense of having been a fool washed over him.

He opened to eyes to find Mélanie's gaze slashing into his own, pinning him where he stood, forcing him to confront the truth. He drew his tattered defenses about him and said the few words that needed to be said.

"We have to talk to Val."

Charles pulled the gig (the carriage the Dunmkyel grooms had been able to ready most quickly) up in front of the lime-washed façade of the Griffin & Dragon, tossed the reins to a stable boy, and helped Mélanie down from the carriage. Val had left for the village just after the gathering in the Gold Saloon. Charles would lay a monkey he was to be found in the inn.

The varnish on the front door was peeling and a couple of the windows had cracks he didn't remember, but the primroses spilling out of the window boxes were as plentiful as ever. The familiar smells of local brewed ale and cider greeted him when he opened the door, as though they had leached into the wood and stone. Instead of escorting Mélanie to the coffee room, where under normal circumstances they would have refreshed themselves, he steered her down a twisting, low-ceilinged slate-flagged passage to the common room with its rough stone walls and high-backed benches and gleaming dark bar. The buzz of conversation, audible from the passage, came to an abrupt halt at their entrance. Someone clunked a tankard down on a deal tabletop. Someone else hastily extinguished a pipe. A score of curious gazes turned their way, much as when he'd taken Mélanie to one of the Regent's receptions at Carlton House a month since.

Bits and pieces of his own past shone back at him from the startled eyes and wind-chapped faces. Men with whom he had played village cricket, men who had given him rides on cart horses and handed him peppermints over shop counters. Men to whom he was now a stranger, returned from an alien world, seemingly heir to the man whose policies had threatened their livelihood and sent much of their kin off to seek work in factories in the south.

A slosh and a clatter broke the silence. A towheaded boy, who probably had not been born when Charles left Britain, had dropped the ale pot he carried.

"Mind what you're doing, Dugal." Stephen Drummond, whose father owned the Griffin & Dragon, cast a glance at the boy and then walked toward Charles and Mélanie. "Ch—Mr. Fraser." His grin of greeting changed to a cautious nod.

"Hullo, Stephen." Charles checked his impatience to find Val and smiled at his boyhood friend. Stephen had smuggled ale out of the tavern on more than one occasion to share with Charles and Andrew on fishing expeditions. "How's your father keeping?"

Stephen's blue eyes closed a shade further. "He died last winter."

"I'm sorry to hear it," Charles said, aware as he spoke how inadequate the words sounded.

Stephen nodded again. Charles introduced Mélanie, who was continuing to draw a number of surprised looks. But then Mélanie always attracted attention, one way or another.

"Mrs. Fraser." Stephen inclined his head and then nodded toward the towheaded boy, who was now mopping up the spilled ale. "Dugal, my eldest." He looked back at Charles. "I married Alice Ellon the year after you left for the Continent."

The name conjured up a memory of a girl with coppery plaits and a smattering of freckles who had played with Andrew's twin sister. "He's a fine lad. I didn't realize about you and Alice."

"No reason you should." Stephen shifted his weight from one foot to the other, creaking the leather of his boots. "Mrs. Fraser might be more comfortable in the coffee room. I can have coffee sent in. Or tea. Was there something in particular you wanted, sir?"

"We're looking for Lord Valentine," Charles said. "Is he here?"

Stephen's gaze moved toward the slate fireplace. "Y—er—no, he left some time ago."

"Damn it, Stephen." Charles nearly grabbed his old friend by the collar of his coat. "I don't care how many doxies he's with. I need to see him."

Someone let out a coarse laugh, quickly smothered. Stephen flicked a surprised gaze at Mélanie, then jerked his head toward the stairs. "First room on the right. But—"

"Thank you."

"Charles," Stephen said as they turned to go.

Charles looked back at him, one hand on the doorframe.

"We heard the news about Miss Talbot. I'm sorry."

Charles had an image of Stephen helping a ringleted, muslin-skirted five-year-old Honoria over the rocky cliffs down to Dunmykel Bay. He nodded, not sure he trusted himself to say more, not sure what more there was to say. Then he strode up the spiral stairs, Mélanie at his heels, and pushed open the first door on the right.

Grunts and the smell of brandy greeted them. Val had a fair-haired young woman pushed up against one of the spooled bedposts, her bodice unbuttoned, his mouth against her breasts, one hand fisted in her hair, the other gripping her bottom.

Charles crossed the room in three steps, seized Val by the back of his shirt, and hurled him against the scarred deal wall.

He turned to the woman, who was pulling the flaps of her bodice closed over her red-marked skin. "My apologies for the intrusion, madam. I trust Lord Valentine will make it up to you later."

Val pushed himself upright. "You bloody, interfering—"

"There are ladies present, Val." Charles held the door open for Val's fair-haired friend. The young woman did up the last button on her bodice, cast a glance at Val, and swept from the room, head held high.

Charles slammed the door shut behind her. The heavy brass knocker rattled in its oak frame. "How long have you and Honoria been playing at *Les Liaisons Dangereuses*?"

"What?" Val was trying to do up the buttons on his trousers.

"Don't tell me you haven't read it. You and Honoria may not have reached Valmont and Merteuil's level, but you came close. You dared each other to seductions and collected trophies as proof of your success."

"That's ridiculous."

Charles grabbed Val by the throat and pushed him up against the wall. A pewter candlestick thudded to the floor. "I'd like nothing better than an excuse to thrash you within an inch of your sorry life. Now unless you want us to tell your father, you'll answer all our questions truthfully. Then there's a chance I won't break every bone in your body."

Val's fair skin drained of color. The smell of sweat and fear radiated from his body. "What do you know?"

Charles took a step back and glanced at his wife. "Mel?"

"You gave your mistresses' letters to Miss Talbot," Mélanie said, "presumably as proof of your success. You challenged Miss Talbot to seduce Simon Tanner and she failed. Miss Talbot went to your room last night and you bedded her yourself. The only thing I'm not sure of is whether or not you killed her afterward."

Val slumped against the wall, eyes wide and glazed. "How—"

"Logic and deduction," Mélanie said, her voice as cool as a steel blade. "Well? Are you going to fill in the rest of the details?"

Val put his hand to his throat where Charles had grabbed him. "It's not the way you make it sound. Not exactly. The first time we— I didn't force her. I've never forced a woman in my life."

"Commendable." Charles barely restrained the impulse to throttle him again.

"She wanted it as much as I did. At least she did before I bedded her. Afterward she threw a tantrum."

"How old were you?" Charles asked.

"I was sixteen, she was fifteen. She wasn't my first."

"But you were hers?"

"What? Oh, yes. Of course." Val pushed his sweat-drenched hair back from his forehead. "She got angry afterward, the way girls do. But Honoria isn't—wasn't—like other girls. Everyone thought she followed the rules, but actually she made her own. After her first fit of playing the wounded virgin, she said that if she told Father what had happened, he was sure to believe her side of the story. I'd have to marry her and she'd see to it her money was tied up so I couldn't touch a penny of it. She said she wasn't in any more of a hurry to get married than I was. Instead we'd keep each other's secrets."

"And so your game began," Charles said.

"If you want to call it that."

"You dared each other to further conquests."

"Not exactly, not at the beginning." Val smoothed the rumpled superfine of his riding coat. "When I brought a school friend home for the holidays, Honoria made me help contrive things so she could seduce him. That was all her idea."

"You weren't jealous?"

"No. Well, yes, a bit, but I was pursuing the wife of one of our neighbors at the same time. We—er—compared notes."

"Quite an erotic game in itself," Mélanie said.

Val's gaze flickered toward her, wide with surprise.

Mélanie returned his gaze without blinking. "That was when you began daring each other?"

Val nodded.

"And then you went to Lisbon with David and his father," Charles said. "And you dared Honoria to seduce me."

"That was Honoria's idea. I warned her you'd insist on marrying her. She said she might rather like to be married to you. I don't think she ever quite got over her pique at not succeeding with you. She had more than half a mind to try with you again now you were back in England. I told her you were a lot safer now you were married."

Charles drew a breath. The smell of sweat and brandy in the room was not as foul as the rank stench in his mind. "I can see you ignoring the risks, but didn't Honoria know she was playing with fire? Getting caught would have been awkward for you. It would have meant ruin for her."

"She only took men who had more to lose than she did if the truth got out. She used to complain because she had to pretend to be Miss Prim and Proper and I could flaunt my reputation. But she liked the risk. It was—"

"An aphrodisiac," Charles said.

Val's brows lifted. "Yes."

"Suppose she'd found herself pregnant?"

"She was careful about the times. And she—" Val broke off. For all he'd already admitted, this last seemed to make him too uncomfortable to voice.

"I expect she used sponges," Mélanie said.

Val stared at her as though she had stumbled through a portal from another world. "It worked very well until—"

"We know she was with child," Charles said.

Val's eyes darkened to cobalt. "Yes, damn it, and it was my baby. She had no right to go off and marry someone else."

"Are you saying you wanted to marry her yourself?"

"I suppose so. Eventually. I'd always assumed—but I'd have married her straight off because of the baby. Only she had to go and promise herself to your father."

"Why?" Charles asked.

"She said he could give her what she wanted."

"What did she want?"

"God knows what women ever want."

"Power?" Mélanie said.

Val stared at the cracked looking glass above the chest of drawers for a moment. "Perhaps." He shook his head. "We had a terrific row when I found out about the engagement. I went to Father, because I was sure he'd see sense—"

"You told your father Honoria was carrying your child?" Charles said.

"I was sure he'd insist she had to marry me. It's not very sporting to foist your son's bastard off on your best friend. But Father told me if I ever breathed a word of it, he'd strip me of my allowance and send me to the plantation in Jamaica." Val sucked in his breath, as though realizing he'd done precisely what his father had ordered him not to.

"But her betrothal didn't end your game?"

"Honoria said it didn't have to. She seemed to think it would add an extra thrill. What could be more of a challenge than to deceive her betrothed under his own roof while he thought she was a spotless virgin? And I thought—"

"That this would be a way to hold her," Mélanie said.

"No. That is—oh, what does it matter. The point is, that was when I challenged her with Simon Tanner. I said it would be her greatest coup if she could pull it off. And he'd never talk—I mean, how could he risk David knowing he'd been unfaithful with David's own precious cousin? Besides, no one would take the word of an upstart playwright over Honoria's. I actually thought she'd pull it off, too. If any woman could tempt him, Honoria could."

"If any man could tempt another man, I'd think Simon could," Mélanie said. "Could he tempt you?"

"What? No, of course not. But it's not the same thing at all."

"Isn't it?"

Val snatched up the open brandy that stood atop the chest of drawers and took a swig. "Anyway, she had to admit she failed with Simon. She was quite cross about it. So I said what about Thirle, your father's steward."

Charles's throat closed. "Go on."

"Well, Honoria was keen to try. Thirle has a strength about him, this unshakable air of doing what's right—"

Charles felt his mouth tighten. "Andrew's a good man. We forgive you the praise."

"Honoria had already gone riding with him a few times before the business with Tanner. Thirle seemed intrigued, but not too intrigued. So it was still a challenge. Then last night Honoria came to my room and told me Thirle wouldn't work."

"Why?" Charles asked.

"She wouldn't say. She snapped at me when I pressed her."

"And?" Charles said.

"She left. That was all."

"All?"

"Well, we—er—spent some time together."

"You had intercourse." Charles saw no reason to use a prettier term for it.

"She was already pregnant. We didn't need to worry—"

"Didn't you wonder how she meant to pass the child off as Kenneth Fraser's?" Mélanie asked. "The wedding was two months away."

"She said she'd have to slip into his bed before too much longer. She didn't seem very worried about it."

"And you?" Charles said. "Surely you hadn't got over your anger at the thought of your child being passed off as another man's."

"Between them, Honoria and Father had made it clear there wasn't much I could do about it."

"Not even argue with her? If the woman I loved was lying in my arms, I'd certainly avail myself of the opportunity to try to win her back."

Val clunked the brandy bottle down on the dresser. "Damn it, how do you do it? It's like witchcraft. Yes, all right, last night I tried to talk her into breaking with your father and marrying me. We had a rip-roaring quarrel, not for the first time. But I didn't kill her, if that's what you're thinking."

"What time did she leave your room?"

"A little past one."

"Did she eat or drink anything while she was with you?"

"We had a drink. Before the quarrel."

"What sort of a drink?"

"I had whisky. I keep a bottle in my room. Never know when you'll need it at family affairs. Honoria doesn't like whisky. She had brandy."

"Which you also kept in your room?"

"No, she brought it with her."

"Where's the bottle now?" Charles asked.

"In my wardrobe. She left it when she flounced out after the fight."

"Did you and Honoria experiment with opiates?"

"Er—I did once get some stuff from a fellow at my club. It was supposed to heighten—" Val looked at Mélanie and glanced away. "Honoria quite liked it. But if she was doctoring her brandy, she didn't tell me about it. Mind you, if she was going to slip into your father's bed last night, she might have wanted double Dutch courage."

"Where did she keep the brandy?" Charles asked.

"In her dressing case."

"Who else knew it was there?"

"How the devil should I know? Honoria didn't flaunt it, but she didn't go to great lengths to hide it, either. Anyone who made a cursory inspection of her room would have found it."

"What did you do after Honoria left you last night?"

"Went to bed."

"Did you know she'd gone to my father's room?"

"Not for a certainty, though I knew she meant to do so soon. But what could I do? I've already told you what my father threatened if I let slip the truth." Val shifted his weight from one foot to the other. "See here, Fraser—"

"I'll have to question your father about Honoria's pregnancy. There's no way round that."

"But—"

"The woman you claim you wanted to marry is dead, Val, along with your unborn child. I wouldn't think much else would matter to you besides finding the killer."

To Charles's surprise, Val met his gaze and gave a slow nod. He was pale, but his eyes hardened with determination.

"One more thing," Charles said. "My sister."

"You mean what are my intentions?" Val's mouth curled. "Don't worry, Charles. I was more apt to run risks when I was younger. I know to avoid seducing well-born virgins now. Gisèle's a tempting morsel, I'll grant you. I've begun to wonder—a fellow has to get leg-shackled at some point."

"You so much as dance with my sister and I'll make sure not only your father but my father and Aunt Frances know every word you've told me. After I've torn you limb from limb. Are we clear?"

"Steady on, Fraser. I told you I wouldn't—"

"Are we clear?"

Val swallowed. "Yes."

Chapter 22

Charles said nothing until he and Mélanie were seated in the gig and he had given the horse its office. Bits of granite and lime-wash and slate and thatched roofs flashed by like fragments of memory as he navigated the village's main street.

He could feel the concerned pressure of his wife's gaze. Like a warm, smothering blanket. He wanted to pull up the carriage, give her the reins, and stride across the fields, away from her all-knowing expression. But he had to try to explain. He owed it to her, and perhaps to himself.

"That night I found her—Honoria—in my bed in Lisbon. I told her I was flattered—honored—but I couldn't possibly—" His throat felt as if it was stuffed with cotton wool. "I told her I'd make her a damnable husband. Which was true."

"You told me the same thing. About thirty seconds after you asked me to marry you."

He felt a bleak smile twist his lips. "That was me trying to be fair and let you know what you were getting yourself in for."

"And I was alone and pregnant and needed a husband. Miss Talbot didn't."

Need. Want. Desire. Love. They twisted and turned until one couldn't tell where one left off and the other began. "There was no question of my marrying Honoria. Christ, she was little more than a child. But I felt as if I'd hurt her. It's a frightening thing to make oneself vulnerable to another person." The words thickened like condensation in the air. He wasn't sure if he was talking about Honoria or himself. "It seemed the least I could do in recompense was not to parade her vulnerability before the rest of the world."

"That makes sense."

He glanced sideways at her. "Except that once she was killed I should have told you. I told myself it couldn't have anything to do with her death, so I was justified in keeping quiet about it. As it turns out, I was wrong." He owed her more of an explanation, but he couldn't be sure enough of his own feelings to offer one. He was afraid that if he spoke at all, he'd strip himself raw and never heal. Instead he fell back on the practicalities of the investigation. "Do you believe Val?"

Mélanie looked at him for a moment, then sank back against the squabs. "I'm inclined to. Do you?"

"I'm afraid so. I doubt he could have made it up." His fingers tightened on the reins. "The bastard. The sick, scheming, immoral—"

"Charles—"

"Yes, all right. But why in God's name—"

"Was he so successful? The eternal lure of Don Juan. Women like to think he's looking for his one true love and that they'll be the one to tame him. And all the time all he wants is another name to add to his infernal list. *Il catalogo è questo*."

"If Father discovered even a quarter of what Honoria and Val were up to—"

"He might have killed her," Mélanie said. "But we have no reason to believe he did find out. Lord Valentine could have killed her. He obviously cared more about losing her than he was willing to admit. Lord Quentin was furious with Miss Talbot for breaking up his affair with Miss Newland. Miss Newland knew Miss Talbot could ruin her."

"And Gisèle would have been consumed with jealousy if she'd learned about Honoria and Val," Charles said, in a flat voice that held all his fears for his sister at bay.

Mélanie tugged at one of her gloves. "Why do you think Miss Talbot gave up on Andrew Thirle? Do you think it went farther than she admitted and he turned her down?"

"If that was the case, why not admit it to Val? She admitted she failed with Simon." Charles considered Andrew with what detachment he could muster. "Andrew's never been one to fall quickly for a pretty face. He fancied himself in love with an attractive widow for a month or so when he was at university, but other than that I've never known his heart to be seriously engaged."

"Do you think he's in love with Miss Talbot?"

"Perhaps. I can't read him as well as I once could. I'm quite sure he was lying about what he was doing in the house last night." Charles drummed his fingers on the leather of the carriage seat. "If Val's right, Honoria wasn't unduly troubled by her pregnancy. And yet I'd swear she was frightened of something last night." He again felt the pull of her unvoiced plea. "So what the devil was it?"

"And what drove Glenister to insist on the marriage."

"Quite. I'd have thought Glenister would have preferred to see Honoria married to Val and keep her money in the family."

Mélanie looked at him for a moment. "Charles—" she said in a gentle voice that cut into him like a knife slicing into raw flesh.

" 'Charles' what? Do I feel like a fool because for all these years I thought Honoria had a schoolgirl infatuation with me and she was playing a game with me the whole time? Of course I do. Do I feel betrayed because my childhood friend wasn't who I thought she was? Yes to that as well. Does this change my determination to find out who killed her? Of course not. Can I make sense of any of this? Not remotely. So the only thing to do is try to discover more of the facts."

Mélanie continued to look at him. He had the strangest sense that he was bleeding inwardly.

Her hand lay on the carriage seat between them. The top button of her glove was undone. He stared at the pale, exposed skin and had an image of himself tugging at her laces, pushing her gown from her shoulders, tasting the warmth of her flesh. Then he saw Val pawing and sucking the naked skin of the girl in the inn. And the paintings of Shakespearean characters disporting in his father's secret love nest. "I owe you an apology for last night."

"Charles, I'm not sure what you're talking about, but you can scarcely be held responsible for anything you did or said after we found Miss Talbot's body—"

"Not after we found Honoria. Before."

She was silent for a moment, but he knew at once that she understood what he referred to. "Darling, we've been married more than four years. However much well we do or don't know each other, surely you can't have any doubt that I enjoyed that part of the evening."

"I wasn't—it shouldn't ever be like that between us. Without thought."

"As I recall, I was the one who didn't want to think. Besides, legally you can take whatever you want from me."

"That's barbaric."

"That's marriage."

"Not our marriage." He drew a long, uneven breath. "I hate to think that what passes between us has anything to do with—"

"Lord Valentine and the girl at the inn? Lord Valentine and Miss Talbot? But on the crudest level it does. Lovemaking doesn't always have to mean more than an exchange of pleasure. Surely there's no harm if the pleasure is mutual."

"That reduces us to rutting animals."

"Perhaps animals have the right idea. They don't try to think about everything so much."

"It cheapens what we have."

They were driving down a lane overhung with yew trees. The face Mélanie turned to him was laced with shadows. "Nothing honest can cheapen what we have. Perhaps the question is, what do we have?"

A question they had never confronted in a marriage born of circumstance and exigency. A question to which even now he could not give an answer.

Dunmykel's pale walls flashed into view. Charles turned the gig over to a groom and they went upstairs to Val's bedchamber without further speech. He opened the mahogany wardrobe while Mélanie held a lamp. Behind the rows of Hessians, topboots, and silver-buckled shoes stood a green glass bottle. Charles uncorked it. The smooth, supple, seemingly undiluted aroma of good cognac. He took a sip and swirled it in his mouth. Rich, mellow, velvety. And something else, a faint, sickly sweet undertaste that probably would have been undetectable if one hadn't been looking for it.

He handed the bottle back to Mélanie. She took a sip and nodded. "Laudanum."

Charles recorked the bottle. "Lord knows Val's capable of idiocy, but if he doctored Honoria's brandy, I doubt he'd be fool enough to leave the bottle in his wardrobe and tell us where it is."

"So Miss Talbot drugged it herself—which I still find hard to believe if she was planning to go to your father's room—or someone else doctored the bottle while it was in her room."

Charles nodded. "Glenister's the next one to talk to."

"And I should talk to Miss Newland about her affair with Lord Quentin and what Miss Talbot knew about it." Mélanie moved to the door. She turned back for a moment as though she meant to say more, scanned his face, and then swept from the room with a rustle of Parisian-stitched skirts.

"Come in, Charles."

His father and Glenister were seated side by side on the high-backed needlepoint chairs that flanked the fireplace in the study. Difficult to believe these were the same two men who had come to blows last night in Kenneth's dressing room. Kenneth's face was gray and the lines in his skin stood out more sharply than usual, but his features were under iron control. Glenister had shed his anguished bewilderment as a snake sheds its skin. They looked like generals ranged together against a common enemy, his father and his father's closest friend, the one determined to marry the other's ward, the other equally determined to enforce the marriage, despite the fact that the ward was pregnant with his son's child.

"You've learned something?" Kenneth asked.

"Yes, as it happens." Charles seated himself on a cushioned bench and leaned back, holding both men with his gaze. "Honoria was with child."

The words lingered in the air like smoke from a pistol shot. The blood drained from Kenneth's face. "If this is your idea of some sort of game, Charles—"

"It's no game, as I think your friend can tell you."

Kenneth swung round in his chair. Glenister was staring straight ahead. He looked as though he had swallowed poison but was not surprised to have found it in his glass.

Kenneth's gaze turned molten. "Frederick—"

"Don't be ridiculous, Kenneth. How could I—"

"Mélanie guessed and I bullied Val into a confession," Charles said. "Why were you determined to pass off your own grandchild as my father's son or daughter, sir?"

Glenister pushed himself to his feet. "Just because we agreed to allow you to investigate doesn't mean I have to sit here and listen to your impertinence, Charles."

"Would you rather I brought Val in and let you listen to his?"

Glenister's mouth thinned. "By God—"

"Val says Honoria was carrying his child and that he informed you of this fact shortly after her betrothal to my father was announced. He said you threatened to pack him off to Jamaica if he didn't keep quiet about the pregnancy."

"Why the devil would I—"

"That's what I'm asking, sir."

Glenister spun away and strode to the fireplace.

"Frederick?" Kenneth said in a quiet voice that was as dangerous as a lit fuse.

"You're taking Charles's word over mine?"

"Yes. But if you prefer, we can ask Val for the story."

Glenister's hands tightened on the gray marble of the mantel. "Val had been—apparently the affair had gone on for some time. Since Honoria was fifteen. That should give you a sense of the sort of man my younger son is. Would you want him married to your daughter?"

"No." Kenneth was on his feet, gaze trained on Glenister. "But he isn't my son."

"And God help me, he's mine." Glenister looked at his old friend, head held high. "I had no notion of what was going on between him and Honoria until he came to me the day after your betrothal was announced and claimed Honoria was pregnant with his child. You must believe that."

Kenneth continued to stare at him. Charles remembered that look from childhood. It could cut one to ribbons more effectively than the slice of a birch rod.

"The boys were little more than babies when my wife died," Glenister said. "I indulged them. I indulged Honoria. Perhaps Evelyn was lucky that she was older when she came to our household." He cleared his throat. "I knew about Quen's and Val's escapades. They seemed harmless enough, if a bit crude. The sort of thing—"

"You got up to yourself," Charles said.

"If you like." Glenister risked a brief glance at Kenneth's icy face, then stared at the wainscoted wall opposite. "Quen seemed the most likely to step over the line. I confess I was proud of Val."

"Until you learned he'd seduced Honoria," Kenneth said.

"Damn it, a gentleman doesn't—I thought he knew."

"Perhaps someone needs to write up a manual of gentlemanly conduct," Charles murmured. "They could be awarded when one leaves Harrow or Eton or when one receives membership at Brooks's or White's."

"This is no time for your radical nonsense, Charles. God knows I wouldn't want my sons to be monks, but certain women are off limits."

"Difficult for the women who fall on the other side of the dividing line."

"Those sort of women know how the game is played. And if they don't—"

"Worse luck for them?"

Glenister grimaced but made no comment. "I was horrified by Val's revelations. But much as it grieves me as a parent to say so, the thought of Honoria married to Val seemed even more horrific. I thought the best thing for Honoria was a stable marriage. To a man I trusted." He turned to Kenneth. Kenneth looked back at him with a gaze that could cut diamonds.

"Because it had worked so well for my mother?" Charles said.

"Your mother and Honoria were very different women." Glenister looked Kenneth straight in the eye. "I'm sorry, Kenneth. But I was thinking of Honoria. With you she would have had stability, a household of her own, protection."

Kenneth's gaze offered no break in his defenses. "It didn't occur to you to tell me, I suppose?"

"Would you have married her if you'd known?"

Kenneth made no answer.

"So I thought," Glenister said. "And damn it, it isn't as though the baby would have been your heir. You already have a firstborn son."

Kenneth cast a brief glance at Charles. "So I do." He turned his gaze back to Glenister. "Of course, if I'd gone ahead with breaking the entail, Honoria's child by your son might have inherited this estate."

Glenister looked away. "I know. I'm sorry. But I had to do what was best for her." His voice cracked, like wood smashed by a boot heel. "I may have failed as a father, but I owed her that much."

Kenneth folded his arms across his chest and stared at his friend for a long, fraught moment. "It's a good story, Frederick. You play the grieving father and guardian very well. But we both know damn well that isn't how it happened. Now I think you'd better tell us the truth."

Chapter 23

Aspasia Newland regarded Mélanie with a level blue gaze. "I should have expected this. Why is it that the secrets one most wishes to keep are always the quickest to be discovered?"

Mélanie studied the woman who had been Honoria Talbot's governess. A heart-shaped face, which could not quite be rendered severe by the way her brown hair was scraped into a tight knot. A full-lipped mouth drawn into firm lines of self-restraint. Delicate features set with a wariness as closed as one of Portia's caskets. "My husband and I have no wish to share the information with others."

"That's kind of you, Mrs. Fraser. But the trouble with such secrets is that once they get about they're fiendishly difficult to control. It wouldn't be very good for my charges if their governess was known to have such a reputation."

She glanced at the reflecting pool. Chloe and Colin were sitting on the stone rim sailing a boat back and forth between them, while Jessica's nurse and Miss Dudley, Colin's governess, sat nearby and watched Jessica in her baby carriage. Berowne, Mélanie and Charles's cat, was curled up in a patch of sun on the lawn. Mélanie had told Colin and Chloe about Miss Talbot's death. Colin had turned solemn and Chloe had asked a number of questions, but now they both seemed to have taken the news in stride. Neither had known Honoria Talbot well.

"Chloe already has her mother's reputation to contend with," Mélanie said. "And her mother's birth and fortune to help her do so."

"You're a generous woman, Mrs. Fraser. But you're a stranger to this world. People are freer on the Continent. I wonder if you realize just how rigid the British can be about the morality of such matters." Miss Newland ran a finger round the stiff lace that edged her high-standing collar. "I don't suppose you'd believe I've been debating with myself whether or not to make a confession to you about my involvement with Lord Quentin."

"You'd have had no reason to think the affair had anything to do with Miss Talbot's death." Mélanie scanned Miss Newland's face. "Unless you knew something more. Perhaps concerning Miss Talbot and Lord Valentine?"

Miss Newland's brows lifted.

"We've discovered that Miss Talbot had had a liaison with Lord Valentine for some time," Mélanie said, in the tone she'd have used to say they'd discovered Honoria was fond of painting watercolors.

"I see." Miss Newland smoothed her hands over the dove-gray bombazine of her skirt. "I begin to see why your husband was given the task of investigating Miss Talbot's murder. He's obviously quick to discover information. As you are yourself."

"You knew about Miss Talbot and Lord Valentine?"

Miss Newland looked out across the garden, as elegant and whimsical as a spun-sugar confection from Gunter's, set between the untamed wildness of the cliffs and the sea. "My father was a classical scholar—an Oxford don until he married my mother and was forced to resign his position. After that he eked out a living doing private tutoring. I grew up on the stories of the Greeks and Romans. The Oresteia. Jason and Medea. Paris, Cassandra, Hector, Troilus, and the rest of Priam and Hecuba's brood. When I was a girl, I thought of those stories as fairy tales. But the longer I've lived in the world of the *beau monde,* the less fanciful they seem."

"Glenister House strikes me as a difficult place in which to be employed."

Miss Newland broke off a leaf from the birch tree beside them and twirled it between her fingers. "One has an odd view of a household as a governess. One sees bits of everything and the whole of nothing. I knew Lord Glenister's reputation, of course. But like most men in his position, he was careful to keep his amorous escapades well away from the sphere Honoria and Evelyn inhabited. It was my job to shelter them from their uncle's world. In that sense, you might say my days at Glenister House were my most egregious failure as a governess."

"How old were the girls when you went to Glenister House?"

"Honoria was fourteen and Evie thirteen. Honoria had joined the household at three when her father died. She was used to having her own way in everything. Evie had only been at Glenister House for three years. Her mother eloped with a half-pay officer and gave birth to eight children in quick succession. Lord Glenister took Evie in as a kindness to his sister. Evie missed her own family dreadfully, though she was fiercely loyal to her uncle and cousins. In some ways she was far better at managing things and people than Honoria was herself. Even at thirteen she was beginning to run the household."

"And Lord Quentin and Lord Valentine?"

Miss Newland lifted a brow with all the coolness of the most regal dowager dampening pretensions. "They were away at school. My involvement with Lord Quentin didn't begin until some years later." She did not elaborate. But then, as Mélanie well knew, it was one thing to be honest about the facts. It was quite another to be honest about the feelings that lay beneath.

"When did you first suspect something between Miss Talbot and Lord Valentine?"

Miss Newland frowned down at the leaf clutched between her fingers. "Looking back, I think I suspected the liaison for some time before I'd even admit it to myself. I didn't want to believe it. Lord Valentine needled Honoria in a way that seemed wholly unromantic, and I couldn't imagine a girl like Honoria running such a risk. I misjudged her."

"In what way?"

Miss Newland smoothed the crumpled leaf. "I didn't realize that her concern for the rules of society was a sham. She wanted to succeed at the social game, but not because she took it seriously. Because it was an avenue to power. She liked to be in control—of situations, of her environment, of the people about her."

It was a cold analysis of a girl who had been little more than a child when she was in Miss Newland's charge. Miss Newland must have realized it, for she gave Mélanie a bitter smile. "You think I might betray more maternal warmth? Given what you've already learned about my past, I think we're beyond appearances, Mrs. Fraser."

Mélanie made no comment. She wasn't at all sure they had got to the truth of Miss Newland's relationship to the Glenister House family. "What convinced you of Miss Talbot's affair with her cousin?"

"The crudest of evidence. I walked into the library at an inopportune moment to find them engaged in an activity that had nothing to do with books." Miss Newland dropped the birch leaf on the ground and clasped her doeskin-gloved hands together. "They didn't appear particularly embarrassed. Honoria asked me to wait for her in her sitting room. She joined me there a quarter-hour later and told me if I breathed a word of what I'd seen she'd reveal my liaison with Lord Quentin. I knew she was a strong-minded young woman, but I don't think it was until then that I realized what nerves of steel she possessed."

"She put you in a difficult position."

"Yes. Whatever I may think of the strictures placed upon unmarried women, there's no escaping the fact that Honoria risked ruin." Miss Newland's gaze moved to her current charge, Chloe, trailing her blue satin sash in the water as she stretched out an arm to retrieve the toy boat. "I could not in good conscience collude in her love affair with her cousin. Dear me, what a shocking hypocrite I sound talking about conscience. Chloe, dear," she called out, her voice raised, "be careful."

Chloe sat up, the boat clutched in one hand, and waved to her governess. Miss Newland waved back. "On the other hand, if I exposed Honoria's love affair to her guardians, I would bring censure upon Honoria and disgrace upon myself. Honoria would probably have been forced to marry Lord Valentine, which did not seem to me to be a solution that would ensure happiness for either of them. I would have been turned off without a reference." She turned her gaze to Mélanie. "I confess I also felt a certain fellow feeling for Honoria. It's difficult for a woman, particularly an unmarried woman, to take control of her life."

Memories clustered behind Mélanie's eyes, threatening to turn her thoughts from the matter at hand. "So your only solution was to leave."

"Yes."

"It must have been difficult to leave Lord Quentin."

Miss Newland touched the locket she wore on a black velvet ribbon round her throat. "Difficult enough that I knew I had allowed the affair to continue far too long." Her gaze lingered on a statue on the edge of the lawn, an Italian marble water nymph, her legs and arms bent in sensuous curves, an open shell clutched in one hand with blatant suggestion. "A sensible woman in my position learns to live without pleasure, Mrs. Fraser. I'm afraid I'm not that sensible. But I have learned one can't afford to take pleasure too seriously or to let any one person become vital to one's happiness."

The words might have come out of Mélanie's own mouth five years ago. The problem, of course, was that a person could become vital to one's happiness without one realizing what was happening until far too late.

"You didn't tell Lord Quentin about his brother and Miss Talbot?" Mélanie said over the cottony taste in her mouth.

"No. It would have put him in an intolerable position with Honoria and Lord Valentine, and he has enough trauma in his family as it is." She turned to look at Mélanie, her face shadowed by the overhanging branches of the birch tree. "Honoria still had the power to ruin me, of course. Which I suppose gives me an excellent motive to have killed her."

Glenister stared at Charles's father across the gilt and leather of the study. "I don't know what you're talking about, Kenneth."

"You can spare us the protestations, Frederick. You aren't a good enough actor to pull them off." Kenneth turned to Charles. "I never particularly wanted you to hear the truth of this, but I don't see another option."

Charles sat back on the bench, feeling as though he had stumbled into an alternate version of reality. His father, who had never in his life confided in him, was volunteering information without prompting. Signal fires of alarm went up in his head.

"Will you tell the story," Kenneth said to Glenister, "or shall I?"

"I don't see what story there is to tell."

"As you wish. Correct me if you disagree with my version of events." Kenneth turned back to Charles, though every word he spoke seemed to be a dart aimed at Glenister. "Some years ago—you and Edgar would have been scarcely out of leading strings and it was before Quen and Val were born—Glenister and I were comparing notes on our latest amorous adventures. Which after a time do have a certain sameness, I confess. I don't remember the names of the ladies in question, but as I recall, Glenister professed a preference for married ladies of quality over courtesans—is that how it was, Frederick?"

"I don't remember," Glenister said in a tight voice.

"Sad what age does to the memory. In any event, Glenister remarked that while married ladies who had already produced an heir were fair game, no gentleman could or would foist a bastard heir on another gentleman. I took his words as something of a challenge. I've always enjoyed challenges. I wagered him—what were the stakes, Glenister? A racehorse? A yacht? Ah, yes, my new curricle team against a bronze of his I'd always coveted. The terms of the wager were that I could seduce a married lady who had not yet given her husband an heir. Glenister said he thought I'd finally set myself up for a failure. Those were your words, weren't they, Frederick? I swear I remember correctly."

"Damn you to hell," Glenister said, his face white.

"I've already seen to that on my own. I'm sure we shall meet there and find the company a great deal more convivial than in heaven." Kenneth looked back at Charles. "You've probably guessed what transpired next. Frederick went off to the Continent for four months. The childless married lady to whom I chose to lay siege was Frederick's lovely young bride."

Glenister was staring at Kenneth as though he'd wrest him limb from limb. Charles looked into the cool mockery of his father's gaze. "Quen."

"Precisely. By the time Frederick returned to Britain, his wife was more than a month gone with child. Quen is most probably my son. Unless of course she was playing her husband false with another gentleman as well."

Glenister jerked forward as though to strike Kenneth, then held himself back. "You bastard. Even now you show no remorse."

"What would be the point? And really, Frederick, you should have known what you were setting yourself up for when you went away for four months directly after leaving me such a challenge. Very careless."

Glenister snatched a Limoges casket from the console table and hurled it to the floor.

"My God," Kenneth said, "that was fourteenth-century."

"We've both got good at smashing things."

"Does Quen know?" Charles asked.

"No." Glenister strode through the ruined casket, grinding shards of porcelain beneath his boot heels. "No one does. Nothing would have pleased me more than to call Kenneth to account, but I couldn't do so without—"

"Making it obvious that you had horns on your head," Kenneth finished for him.

"And so we continued to go on as we had before. Though I need hardly say our friendship was never the same."

"Until you saw a way to take your revenge." Kenneth's gaze turned to ice. "What I want to know is, did you deliberately arrange for Honoria to be pregnant with your son's child when I became betrothed to her or did you simply take advantage of a fortunate accident?"

"I'd never—" Glenister's eyes went wide with outrage. "Good God, she was my ward."

"Whom you allowed your son to seduce."

"If I'd had an inkling of what was going on do you think I'd have allowed Val within a foot of her?" Glenister wiped his hand across his brow. "I wasn't happy when Honoria told me she wanted to marry you, but I could scarcely refuse without telling her the truth about Quen."

"It didn't occur to you to do so?" Charles asked.

"I—" Glenister strode to the far end of the room. "Honoria insisted it was what she wanted. Then, after the betrothal was announced, Val came to me and told me Honoria was pregnant with his child, that they'd been lovers for years—"

"And you saw your way to revenge," Kenneth said.

"All right, yes." Glenister spun round to face him. "Damn you, it was no more than you deserved."

"Dear Christ." Charles pushed himself to his feet. "She was little more than an object to either of you, was she? To be preserved like one of your paintings or statues and then used to make a point when you decided she was tainted."

His father's cold gaze raked his face. "What was she to you?"

"A friend. But I don't expect you to understand."

"She had to marry someone," Glenister said in the sort of tenacious voice used by the inebriated. "Whatever I think of Kenneth, she had a better chance of happiness with him than with Val."

"When were you planning to break the news to me?" Kenneth asked.

"I wasn't. I wouldn't have done that to Honoria. It would have been enough that I knew."

"And if I had found out?"

"There was no reason—" Glenister's gaze jerked to Kenneth's face. "Oh, my God. Did you? Is that why she died?"

Kenneth looked at him down the length of the study. "I gave you my word I didn't kill her."

"And I have cause to know just how reliable your word is, don't I?" Glenister glanced out the mullioned window. "For years—those damnable years of pretending we were still friends—I wondered why you'd done it. And then I realized you'd always hated me. You never got over the fact that I was the future marquis and you were the poor orphan who was sent to Harrow on your godfather's charity. You couldn't bear it, could you? Those months of making the Grand Tour and picking out the finest treasures only to see me buy them."

Kenneth's gaze flickered for a moment, then went still. "Your timing's a bit off, Frederick. By the time of my liaison with your wife I was quite comfortably situated."

"Thanks to a lucky legacy and an even luckier marriage. But it couldn't equal a marquisate. I have a position you'll never have and you couldn't bear it because you thought you were so much cleverer than I was. So you went out and proved it."

Kenneth's gaze remained steady, though Charles noticed his lips whiten slightly. "You overrate yourself, Frederick. You've never been that central to my thinking."

"That's why you wanted Honoria, isn't it?" Glenister said, as though the thought had only just occurred to him. "She was one more treasure you could take from me."

"My dear Glenister. Once again you've got it all backward."

"Not this time. I know you, Kenneth. Far too well." Glenister looked at his former friend as though he'd like to rip the truth from his throat. "The only thing I'm not sure of is if you smashed her the way I just smashed your precious casket."

Miss Newland regarded Mélanie without flinching. "I wish I could say that I would have come to you with all this information if you hadn't learned of my prior relationship to Lord Quentin. But in truth I can't tell you what I would have done. Self-preservation is a strong instinct."

And Honoria Talbot had had the power to threaten Aspasia Newland's security indefinitely.

"Mama." The exclamation from Chloe cut across the lawn. Lady Frances was sweeping down the stairs from the terrace in a swirl of lavender lustring. She paused to admire the toy boat, then crossed the lawn to join Mélanie and Miss Newland.

"Mélanie. I should have known I'd find you being a devoted mother. Miss Newland, will you excuse us for a moment?"

"Of course." Miss Newland smiled with no hint of the revelations of a few moments before and went to join the children.

"Admirable woman," Lady Frances murmured, looking after the governess's straight-backed figure. "I don't know how she does it, tending other people's children year after year. I barely manage with my own, though I think I'm doing rather better with Chloe than I did with the others. Mélanie, I need to talk to you." She spun round and laid a hand on Mélanie's arm. "I don't suppose Kenneth's given any further explanation of his whereabouts last night?"

"Only that he was in the library."

Lady Frances snorted. "How idiotic. And Charles is afraid his father killed Honoria. No, don't argue the point, one could see it in his face last night."

"He could hardly fail to at least wonder," Mélanie said.

"In the circumstances, I suppose you're right." Lady Frances removed her hand from Mélanie's arm. "But Kenneth couldn't have killed Honoria. You can take my word for it."

Mélanie studied Charles's mother's sister. "How can you be sure?"

Lady Frances lifted a well-groomed brow. "My dear, isn't it obvious? Because Kenneth spent last night with me."

Chapter 24

Charles left the study with more questions than he'd had when he went in search of his father and Glenister. He paused at the bend in the corridor between the north wing and the central block and rubbed his hand over his eyes. If their story was to be believed, Quen was his brother. Probably. At the moment, he couldn't afford to consider the fact except as it might impact who had killed Honoria.

"Charles." His sister's voice came from the hall. From the note of insistence, he suspected it was not the first time Gisèle had called his name. "I need to talk to you." She came running toward him, muslin skirts rustling, kid slippers thudding against the marble tiles.

"Gelly." Charles forced his mind from the revelations in the study to the earlier revelations that involved the man his sister loved.

Gisèle clutched his arm. "Is it true? I know you talked to him."

Oh, Christ. Had Val gone to Gisèle and tried to make excuses for himself? Charles looked down at his sister, subduing the impulse to smooth her hair as he would have done when she was a girl. "Yes, I talked to him. Gelly, I don't know what you've heard—"

"You have to listen to me, Charles. I know you think you understand, but you've got it all twisted round backward." Gisèle glanced toward the hall, where Alec was still on duty, then dragged him through the nearest door into the old drawing room.

Charles looked at his sister's flushed face and determined eyes. Even before Val's revelations about Honoria, he'd hated the thought of Gisèle spending the rest of her life with Valentine Talbot. But he hated, too, the thought of wounding the vulnerability that lay behind her fierce defense of the man she thought she loved.

Gisèle's eyes went dark with loathing. "Oh, God, you're doing it, too."

"What?"

"Looking at me like that."

"Like what?"

"Like you think I'm going to put a pistol to my head. It's what everyone does whenever I lose my temper. The legacy of being Elizabeth Fraser's daughter."

Charles flinched. Her words cut close to his fears both for her and for himself. He stared at the canvaswork chairs grouped round the rosewood table in the center of the room. He could picture his mother sitting there reading them a story during one of her fleeting visits to Dunmykel, her quicksilver voice weaving a magical tapestry. His gaze shifted to the Sèvres vases on the mantel. One of the set was missing. He could still hear the crash when their mother had thrown it against the linenfold door.

"Mother didn't leave any of us an easy legacy," he said. "But I know you aren't her any more than I am."

"I sometimes wonder if you know me at all, Charles. No, don't." She put out a hand to stop him from speaking. "I shouldn't have said anything. The important thing is that you don't understand what happened last night. You have to—" She stopped as though the words had got caught in her throat and picked at the basket-weave embroidery on one of the chair backs.

Charles felt his way carefully, not sure how much Val had told her. "Gelly, I know you care for him—"

"You can't believe—" Gisèle looked up at him. "How on earth do you know I care for him?"

"You haven't exactly made a secret of it."

"I know you're quick at things, Charles, but I didn't think you paid that much attention to me."

"Of course I pay attention to you. You're my sister."

"That didn't stop you from—oh, poison, I'm doing it again. Look, I don't know exactly what you believe—"

"I don't know what exactly he's told you."

Gisèle blinked. "He hasn't told me anything. He's the last man on earth who'd come running to me because he needed help. You should know that. He's your friend."

"Val and I were never friends."

"You always—" She stared at him as he though he'd started quoting from the wrong play. "Val?"

"Val. Lord Valentine Talbot. The man you've been flirting madly with for the past two months."

"Oh, for God's sake, Charles. You didn't think I was actually in love with *Val,* did you?"

"*Actually* in love? No. But I thought you'd convinced yourself you loved him." He studied his sister's face, the brilliant scorn in her eyes, the twisted mockery in the curve of her mouth. "It seems I was wrong."

"That's really what you think of me? A silly little chit whose head could be turned by a man like that?"

"When it comes to infatuation, sense often has very little to do with it."

"I know we don't know each other well, but somehow I thought you had more faith in me."

"Gelly—"

"It doesn't matter now, Charles." She straightened her slender shoulders. In that moment she reminded him keenly of their mother, not her instability, but her air of command. "Marjorie, my maid, is second cousin to Morag, who works in the kitchens. Morag told Marjorie that she slipped back into the library late last night and saw—"

"Andrew." The puzzle pieces locked into place in Charles's mind. "You're concerned about Andrew."

Gisèle took a step toward him, eyes emerald green with urgency. "I know how it must look, Charles, but it—why he was in the house last night—it doesn't have anything to do with Honoria's death."

"How can you be sure?"

"Because I know why he used the passage. He was seeing me back to my room."

"*What?*"

"No, not like that. Not that I didn't—" She turned on her heel and fiddled with the vase of roses that stood on the pianoforte. "Last Christmas—before you came back from Paris—we came to Dunmykel for the holidays—Aunt Frances and Chloe and me. Father joined us just before Christmas. It was years since I'd been here— Aunt Frances isn't fond of the house. I think it was the first time Andrew had thought of me as grown up. At least I thought he thought of me as grown up." She snapped off a rose that was drooping and jabbed the shortened stem into the water.

Wounded pride and an injured heart radiated from the curve of her shoulders and the sting in her voice. "'Grown up' is a relative term," Charles said in the gentlest voice he could.

"I'm the same age Mélanie was when you married her."

The truth of this statement was like the shock of a cloudburst. "Very true," Charles said. He couldn't explain the experiences that had made the nineteen-year-old Mélanie old beyond her years, so instead he said, "But I was younger myself. Andrew's more than ten years older than you."

"Father was more than thirty years older than Honoria, though perhaps that's not the best parallel." She pushed her fringe of curls back from her forehead. "Anyway, Andrew thought I was grown up enough to kiss. Well, I suppose to be fair, I kissed him, but he definitely kissed me back." She looked at Charles over her shoulder with a gaze that dared him to exclaim with shock at the image of his baby sister locked in his friend's arms.

Charles suppressed the impulse to do so. "And then?"

Gisèle looked away. "The details don't matter. The point is Andrew told me it couldn't go any further."

"Further than what?" Charles said, leashing the alarm in his voice.

"I told you he—I—we kissed. Once. I thought it meant more than it did. To him it must have been holiday cheer or loneliness or something."

"It's not easy, caring for someone more than they care for you," Charles said, and then wondered what the devil he was doing giving romantic advice. His experience was decidedly limited.

Gisèle spared him another brief glance. "I was furious and hurt.

That's why I struck up the flirtation with Val this spring and why I didn't want to come to the house party. Then I decided I had to see Andrew again and try to make him understand." She swallowed. "I know, I should have accepted how he felt, but—"

"It's difficult to make the feelings go away."

"Yes." She started to look away, then seemed to force herself to keep her gaze on his. "Last night, I went through the secret passage and slipped into Andrew's room."

Charles had visions of Honoria in his rooms in Lisbon. "Gelly—"

"Don't worry, Andrew was horrified. He was very kind, but he said I had to understand there could be nothing between us. He doesn't love me."

Renewed fear tightened Charles's throat. "Do you think he might be in love with someone else?"

"How on earth should I know?" Gisèle said with a swiftness that betrayed more clearly than any words that she, too, feared Andrew had been in love with Honoria.

"What time was it when you got back to your room?"

Gisèle's fingers curled round the broken rose stem. "Charles—"

"What time, Gelly?"

Her eyes were wide and as fragile as porcelain. "One-thirty."

Which meant Andrew had still had time to have gone to Kenneth's room and killed Honoria.

Lady Frances regarded Mélanie as though she were gaping, which, Mélanie realized, she very likely was. "I know. You thought Kenneth and I detested each other. We do. We have since he married my sister, if not before. My dear, surely you're old enough to realize that liking has very little to do with it."

"No, of course not." For a moment Mélanie could feel Charles's hands on her skin and his lips against her throat. And then the memory of other hands, other kisses, other moments of oblivion. "That is—"

Lady Frances let her gaze drift round the garden and linger on her daughter for a moment. "It's odd. After watching the early days of my sister's marriage, I was determined not to marry someone as cold and remote as Kenneth. So I chose George Dacre-Hammond, who was darkly handsome and looked very dashing in his military uniform. We were married nearly a year before I realized how dull he was. I disliked Kenneth, I thought he was horrible for my sister, but he challenged me in a way my husband never did."

Lady Frances's acid-tongued exchanges with Kenneth Fraser echoed in Mélanie's head. "When—"

"An alcove during a Christmas house party." Lady Frances tucked a strand of golden hair beneath her satin-straw hat. "Here, as it happens, which perhaps accounts for my somewhat conflicted feelings about the place." She glanced up at the house, a turreted mass against the blue sky, washed white by the sunlight. The thirteenth-century tower, the fifteenth-century north wing, the seventeenth-century central block and south wing, all overlaid by the embellishments and improvements of the eighteenth century. A jumble of eras, layered one on top of the other, like a tangle of memories. "Afterward I was half disgusted, half intrigued. I felt guilty at deceiving my sister, though Kenneth said Elizabeth couldn't care less and he was probably right."

"Did she know?" Mélanie asked. Charles's mother still remained a cipher to her.

"I'm quite sure she suspected. I never told her, perhaps out of guilt, perhaps because the secrecy gave spice to the liaison."

Mélanie fingered the coquelicot border of her Lyons scarf. On the drive back from the village, she'd told Charles that at its crudest level lovemaking came down to the same thing. And yet she wasn't entirely sure that was true anymore. Four and a half years of marriage had shaped what she and Charles gave and took from each other, in bed and out of it. With the weight of so much between them, it was impossible for pleasure to be merely casual or for a caress to hold no meaning beyond momentary delight.

"The affair continued all these years?" she asked Lady Frances.

"Off and on," Lady Frances said in the tone she might have used to discuss whist partners. "It was never anything like exclusive. But oddly enough for two people who quickly tired of lovers, we didn't get bored with each other. I kept thinking just one more time and I could make sense of Kenneth. Kenneth likes to master women and he could never succeed in mastering me, which made me a continual challenge."

On the sunny patch of lawn some twenty feet away, Lady Frances's daughter and Mélanie's son were now building a block tower while the cat raced in circles round them. Their shrieks of excitement carried on the breeze. Was it a fool's errand, Mélanie wondered, to even try to shield one's children from the reality of the world? "And Mr. Fraser's betrothal?" she said. "Did that change things?"

"My dear Mélanie, in our world marriage rarely changes these things." Lady Frances stared into the cool shadows by the granite steps. "But as it happens, I told Kenneth it had to end now that he was marrying again. Honoria didn't necessarily play the game by the same rules as he and I and Elizabeth."

"So last night was a farewell?"

A whisper of something too intense to be shared drifted through Lady Frances's gaze. "In a manner of speaking."

"Did you go to the rooms off the secret passage?"

Lady Frances's penciled brows rose. "You know about them?"

"Charles and I found them last night. It was clear a couple had been there."

Lady Frances did not flush. "Yes. Kenneth and I were there last night. We went downstairs shortly after midnight. We returned to our own rooms just before three. Kenneth went upstairs first, just in case anyone was up and about. I lingered downstairs, which is why I didn't hear him scream. He must have gone straight to his room and found Honoria."

"You didn't see anyone else downstairs?"

"No. The passage and the library were empty when we came through. The intruder Charles saw in the library must have come just after."

"Had you been in Mr. Fraser's secret rooms before?"

"Occasionally. They're a bit cold, but they have their charms."

"They seem designed for more than merely one couple."

"Very tactfully put. The correct term, I believe, is orgy. More appealing in theory than in fact, if you ask me, though it has a certain piquancy every now and again. The rooms off the caves were designed for house parties at which the women present weren't ladies. I had heard rumors for years."

"What sort of rumors?"

"The titillating sort involving various acts of debauchery. I teased Kenneth to invite me, but he never did. So I—" Her gaze clouded. "I suppose in a roundabout way it might have to do with Honoria."

"What might?"

Lady Frances took a step away, into the shadows of the over-hanging birch. "It was years ago. The autumn of 1797. My second son, Christopher, was cutting his baby teeth. I was staying at my father's in Alford with the children. Elizabeth was there as well with Charles and Edgar, and my friend Lousia Mitford with her brood. Then Cyril Talbot stopped by and left Honoria with us while he went off to Dunmykel. Kenneth and Glenister and some of their other friends were having a shooting party, though I suspected the majority of their games didn't involve guns. I was longing for some excitement, cooped up in the Highlands with a houseful of children. Elizabeth said she already knew more than she wanted to about how Kenneth spent his leisure hours, but Louisa and I decided to pay the gentlemen a surprise visit at Dunmykel."

"And?"

"I don't think I've ever received such an ungracious greeting from a group of gentlemen. I expected to find a party of doxies installed, but if so, they whisked them out of the way when we arrived."

"Was this when—?" Mélanie did sums in her head. "Charles told me Miss Talbot's father died in a shooting accident at Dunmykel."

"So he did, in a manner of speaking." Lady Frances turned to Mélanie. Through the shadows, Mélanie could see the dark line of the other woman's drawn brows. "No one was in much mood for carousing. Louisa and I took ourselves off to bed after dinner." She fell silent for a moment. A gold crest fluttered its wings overhead. "Perhaps it would have been better if there had been doxies present or if Louisa and I had stayed awake. The gentlemen apparently got up to shooting games after broaching several bottles of brandy. Cyril shot himself in the chest."

"Dear God."

"To do Glenister justice, I think he blamed himself. He was a broken man, much as he was last night when he saw Honoria."

"Did you see Lord Cyril's body the next morning?"

Lady Frances lifted her brows. "No, they had him decently put in a coffin, thank God. The funeral was the next day. Louisa and I stayed for it and then returned to my father's."

"Do you remember who else was at the shooting party?"

Lady Frances frowned. "Sir William Cathcart. Billy Gordon. And several men I've never seen before or since. A couple of them gave innocuous English-sounding names, but I'd swear they were really French. Probably friends of Kenneth's from the Grand Tour. I suspect they were visiting Britain incognito, as we were at war with France at the time, and everyone kept worrying about an invasion. And there was an Irishman whose name I can't recall at the moment. He had the coldest eyes I've ever seen. As if Scotland isn't chilly enough."

Mélanie watched as the gold crest flew from the tree branches overhead to the hedge opposite. "Are you sure they were playing shooting games?"

She felt the sudden sharpness of Lady Frances's gaze like the rake of nails on her skin. "Are you asking if Cyril could have died differently?"

"Do you think he might have?"

Colin let out a cry of delight on the lawn. Miss Newland's murmuring voice carried on the wind, the words indistinguishable. "Did I think it at the time?" Lady Frances said. "No. But if you're asking me if it's possible—" A host of possibilities hovered in the air as she drew in her breath. "I suppose—yes. It's possible."

"Do you still think the purpose of the house party was debauchery?"

Lady Frances was silent for a long moment. "That's the purpose of most activities the Glenister House set engages in. And yet when we failed to find any women present, I did wonder—"

"If there was another reason for the gathering?"

"No." Lady Frances adjusted the brim of her hat. "If perhaps this particular debauchery didn't involve females at all."

Gisèle stood at the window of the old drawing room after Charles had left, willing her heart to slow and her breathing to return to normal. She had done it. She had lied to her clever brother. And he seemed to have believed her.

She rubbed her arms. Triumph surged through her, but there was a bitter taste like burnt toast on her tongue.

She spun away from the window. Her gaze went to the hearthrug where Charles had built block castles for her dolls, to the pianoforte where he'd helped her master the *Waldstein* Sonata, to the window seat where he'd held her horn primer and helped her learn her letters. She tugged her shawl up about her shoulders. She had long since ceased to be the ringleted little girl who thought her brother's tall shoulders could shield her from all harm. And that brother was gone in any case, replaced by a cool-eyed stranger who probed relentlessly at truths she couldn't allow to come to light. She had no room for guilt. She had done what had to be done. Now she had to continue to do it and see this business through to the end.

She should be able to do so. After all, she was Elizabeth Fraser's daughter.

Chapter 25

Charles found his wife sitting on a granite bench in a quiet bit of garden, her gaze fixed on the hedge opposite. He paused along the walkway, allowing himself the luxury of a moment to appreciate the way the curve of her bonnet shadowed her cheekbones and her eyes caught the sparkle of the early evening sun. His throat tightened with the ache of something he could imagine but would never really know.

As usual, she glanced up, quickly aware of his regard.

"You've learned something," he said.

"Yes." She scanned his face. "From the look of it, so have you."

He nodded and sat beside her.

"You first," Mélanie said.

His own gaze went to the intricately interwoven leaves and branches of the hedge. Impossible to tell what lay at the heart of that thicket. "A number of things. The most significant of which is that Quen seems to be my father's son."

Mélanie drew a breath that was like the slice of a knife. "Start at the beginning, Charles."

He managed to give a reasonably coherent account of his scene with his father and Glenister. Mélanie heard him out in silence. She didn't offer sympathy or ask him how he felt about the revelations, which was a good thing because he didn't think he could have borne it. She watched him for a moment when he finished speaking. He could feel the press of everything they had and hadn't said to each other in the course of the day. "I suppose the first question is the one we keep asking," she said. "Do you believe them?"

He stared at the toes of his boots against the damp grass. "Father might have been able to stage the scene in the study, but I don't think Glenister's a good enough actor. So I'm inclined to believe them about the wager and Glenister's wife. And Quen." He brushed a fallen leaf from the bench. "But I think it's possible Father was playacting when he claimed to be shocked that Honoria was pregnant."

"Did he seem to be acting?"

"No, but when Father's at his best he seems utterly genuine." Charles shifted his position on the hard granite. "We're back to the likeliest scenario. Honoria slipped into his room, he realized she was pregnant, he jumped to the conclusion that Glenister had connived at revenge—"

"Charles, your father couldn't have killed Miss Talbot."

"Mel, we keep going round in circles on this, but you can't deny it's possible—"

"Yes, I can. Now. Your father couldn't have killed Miss Talbot because he has an alibi. Your aunt Frances."

"What the devil would Father have been doing with Aunt Frances in the middle of the—oh." He stared into his wife's open gaze. "Good God."

Mélanie smoothed her hands over the sheer fabric of her skirt, as though determined to press out every wrinkle, and told him about her talk with Lady Frances.

Countless verbal duels between his father and aunt ran through Charles's head. He rubbed his hand over his eyes. "I always thought they despised each other."

"Respect and liking don't necessarily have anything to do with it, as Lady Frances pointed out to me."

Charles looked at his lover and wife, thought of holding her in his arms, touching her, taking solace from her warm flesh. How poorly demarcated was the line between want and need, between lust and tenderness, between giving a lover pleasure and using her for it. When did desire become manipulation and honesty give way to deceit? Was what Romeo felt when he took Juliet in his arms so different from what Edmund felt when he kissed Goneril or Regan?

"I suppose . . . I always credited Aunt Frances with better taste."

"For what it's worth, I think she's rather shocked by her own response to your father. But, darling, whatever else it means, it means your father can't have killed Miss Talbot."

"Unless Aunt Frances is lying."

"You think she's telling the truth about having an affair with your father but lying about the times?"

"It doesn't seem likely, but it's a possibility."

"A remote one."

"Yes." He drew a breath. The air seemed lighter. Which was absurd, because any relief at his father's innocence was tempered by the fact that someone else, very likely someone who mattered more to him than his father did, was undoubtedly guilty.

He focused on another piece of information from her account of her talk with Lady Frances. "Interesting that Cyril Talbot's death wasn't the simple hunting accident we'd been led to believe."

"And that Lady Frances suspected some of the men present were Frenchmen incognito. Of course if they were friends of your father's from before the war, they might have simply been using assumed names to spend a fortnight indulging themselves with old friends."

"Or they could have been members of the Elsinore League using the house party as a cover to meet with Cyril Talbot, who may have been Le Faucon de Maulévrier."

"Or one of the mysterious Frenchmen or the Irishman with the cold eyes could have been Le Faucon and Lord Cyril could have been a member of the league. Either way, I continue to wonder how accidental his death was."

"Or if he really died at all? I still find it hard to believe he's alive somewhere, but then Cyril's death is a truth I grew up with. If Father and Glenister were helping members of the Elsinore

League stage Cyril's death and disappearance, one can see why they'd have been so ungracious about Aunt Frances and Louisa Mitford's arrival. On the other hand, Aunt Frances's theory that Father and Glenister and Cyril and the others were in the midst of some sort of all-male orgy would explain it as well." Charles ran a finger over the granite of the bench, pockmarked by time and salt air. "I never thought of Father and Glenister as lovers, but I suppose it makes a sort of odd sense of the way they've competed and tried to take each other's women and stayed friends of a sort despite all the betrayals."

"Charles," Mélanie said, with that intent, breathless note she got in her voice when she was piecing things together, "suppose both theories are true. Suppose it was an all-male orgy and suppose Cyril Talbot and some of the others were members of the Elsinore League. Suppose one of the incognito Frenchmen was Colonel Coroux. Then perhaps he wasn't trying to blackmail Le Faucon or another member of the Elsinore League to help him escape France. Perhaps he was blackmailing your father and Lord Glenister about their relationship or about Cyril Talbot's past. The coded letter Francisco gave us that threatens to reveal the truth could have been written to your father and Lord Glenister, and they could be the ones who 'fear for Honoria.' Fear her learning the truth of her father's past or the truth that they were lovers. Or both."

"And if Tommy's right that Le Faucon plans to assassinate someone to cover up his past, the target could be Father or Glenister. Or both of them."

"Yes. Unless we were right last night to suspect that target was Miss Talbot herself."

"I still don't see what Honoria could be expected to remember about events that happened when she was little more than a baby. Or why she'd suddenly be a threat now."

"We could confront your father and Lord Glenister, but assuming it's true they'd probably deny the whole emphatically."

"Quite. Better to wait and see if Tommy can shed some light on the matter tonight. I'd rather have as much ammunition as possible before we spring this on Father and Glenister. It's still entirely possible Honoria's death had nothing to do with the Elsinore League."

Charles drew a breath. "I also had a talk with my sister." He told her about Gisèle and Andrew. "Which explains what Andrew was doing in the house. But Gisèle obviously suspects he was in love with Honoria, and if she's right it gives him a motive. Andrew isn't in the estate office. I just walked over to the lodge and his mother says he hasn't been home. I'm not sure—"

Footsteps thudded on the grass. "Charles." David strode up to them, face ashen. "I'm sorry, I know you shouldn't talk to me about any of this, but I need to know. Simon told me—about Honoria— about her coming to his room. I didn't want to believe him at first. Christ, I actually accused him of lying to me. It's the first time I've ever done that. I still can't—in God's name, why? Do you have any idea?"

Charles got to his feet and faced his friend. "Why she went to Simon's room? Yes. Why she was killed? A number of ideas, but no answers. Yet." He glanced at Mélanie. "I think it's time for another council of war. But we should include Simon as well."

"Are you sure you want to tell us anything?" David said. "Technically we're both suspects—"

"Technically. But—"

"I know, you can't imagine either of us having killed her. But I can't imagine anyone in the house having killed her."

Charles smiled and clapped his friend on the shoulder. "Actually, I was going to say that even in the event you or Simon killed her, I think we still have more to gain than to lose from hearing your reactions to what we've discovered."

David looked at him for a moment, then gave an answering smile. As they started for the house, Charles wondered if his friend had the faintest idea how very much in earnest his words were.

A buffet supper had been laid out in the dining room, sparing the guests the awkwardness of a formal dinner. Charles, Mélanie, David, and Simon carried plates into the old drawing room and picked at the food while Charles recounted nearly all of what he and Mélanie had discovered in the course of the day. He omitted Gisèle's revelations about her feelings for Andrew.

Mélanie watched David and Simon as they heard her husband out. David became progressively paler. Simon frowned, but didn't appear surprised.

"I was there," David said when Charles finished speaking. "In Lisbon. And you never told me—"

"What good would it have done?" Charles was leaning against the pianoforte, hands locked behind him. "I thought it was a schoolgirl infatuation. I thought she'd grow out of it."

"But she didn't. I mean—" David swallowed, as if he still couldn't believe it. "She didn't grow out of whatever it was. If you'd told me—"

"If I'd told you, then what?"

"I'd probably have suggested you marry her."

"Yes, I expect you would have done. Hardly the wisest course of action for any of us."

Echoes of what might have been reverberated between the two men. "You could have—"

"Protected her? Honoria didn't want to be protected."

"She cared about you. I'd swear to that." David regarded his friend for a moment. "I think she loved you."

"I'm not sure Honoria knew what love was. But even if she had cared for me, love is notoriously unreliable as a guarantee of happiness."

Mélanie stared at the blood-red claret in her wineglass, willing her inward flinch not to show in her eyes.

"How could she?" David took a turn about the room. "How could she degrade herself like—"

"Like Glenister, Quen, and Val?" Simon said in a voice as dry as the best *fino*.

"No. Yes. Damn it, you know it's different with girls."

"Because we don't want to do those sorts of things?" Mélanie looked up from the glass. "Or because we're not supposed to?"

David drew a breath and ran a hand over his hair. "You're kind to defend her, Mélanie. But you know you'd never do such things yourself."

Mélanie took a sip of wine, gaze fixed on the gilt-edged rim of her plate. She could feel Simon watching her.

"Can you be sure?" David said to Charles. "Of the whole story?

We only know bits and pieces and we only have Val's word for it. Suppose he's making it up about Honoria and him playing these games—"

"And some other man dared Honoria to slip into my bed?" Simon said.

David rounded on his lover. "You haven't been any help, either. If you and Charles had both been honest with me at the time—"

"You'd have suggested Honoria marry me? That would have created some interesting family gatherings."

"If you're going to talk like one of your damn plays, then shut the hell up."

"Only trying to be honest, old boy."

"I don't know where to begin to look for honesty. Honoria's whole life was a lie."

"She wasn't what you thought she was," Simon said. "Which of us would be, put under a microscope? Christ, you and I live a secret every day of our lives—"

"If you're going to put my loving you on a par with conducting love affairs for sport—"

Simon brushed his fingers against his lover's cheek. "No. Fair enough."

"She was surrounded by romantic intrigue and yet expected to remain under glass," Mélanie said. "Like Ophelia at Elsinore. 'The chariest maid is prodigal enough if she unmask her beauty to the moon.' I'm quite sure Lord Glenister and Mr. Fraser would have been quick to second Laertes's opinion." She thought of the Fragonard paintings that were littered about the house. Young lovers in a rose-strewn garden, watched over by Venus and Cupid. A world of sugar-coated romance with carnality pulsing just beneath the surface. "Miss Talbot had an enviable position in life—far more so than most women. She had an old family name and a fortune and all the pin money she could spend. But there wasn't much she was allowed to do with her life beyond looking decorous until she married. I don't think much of how she tried to use Simon. And Charles. But I think I'm coming to understand her. She wanted to be more than a pretty ornament."

She could feel Charles's gaze upon her as she spoke, but he said nothing. David pushed aside his untouched plate. "Women don't have many choices in life. I'm not—I do understand that. But she could have written or painted or composed music—"

"She grew up in the Glenister House set," Charles said. "Sexual intrigue was the currency of power."

"It's a pity she couldn't have gone into the army or politics," Mélanie said. "She'd have made an admirable general, and I imagine she'd have been quite lethal at steering a bill through the House."

David shook his head. "It seems so—joyless."

Simon took a sip of wine. "Joy comes in many different forms. As I'm sure Lady Frances would say."

"Oh, God, Lady Frances," David said. "I still can't believe—"

"That she was Father's lover?" Charles said. "Surprising, I'll grant you. More surprising, perhaps, than the thought of Father and Glenister as lovers."

A look of revulsion crossed David's face, as though he couldn't bear the thought that Kenneth's and Glenister's amorous intrigues were remotely similar to his own love life. "Surely if they were lovers—"

"They'd have behaved more like you and Simon?" Mélanie said. "Not necessarily. Mr. Fraser and Lady Frances didn't behave a bit like Charles and me."

A rap sounded at the door. Addison and Blanca stepped into the room. "Sorry to interrupt," Addison said, "but I thought you'd like a report on our questioning of the staff."

"Very much so," Charles said. "Come in. Have you eaten?"

Blanca wrinkled her nose and cast a glance at the scarcely touched plates that littered the room. "They had food set out in the servants' hall like they do abovestairs. None of us were very hungry, either."

Blanca and Addison sat side by side on one of the cream silk sofas, a very correct three feet apart. The affection between them was obvious to one trained at observing, but Mélanie could only guess at the exact state of their relationship. If it was up to Blanca, she suspected the two would have been lovers years ago, but Addison took the gentleman's code every bit as seriously as Charles and was every bit as guarded about his feelings.

"We've talked to all of them, at least a bit," Blanca said, smoothing her skirt. "Some of the maids were inclined to look down their noses at me because I'm a foreigner—either that or they were jealous because I know all the latest styles from Paris—but I did very well with the footmen."

"Hardly surprising on either score," Mélanie said.

"Except for Miss Talbot's maid, most of the staff and the visiting servants have been at their posts for some years," Addison said. "That doesn't, of course, preclude their having been employed by the Elsinore League, but it does make it less likely."

"And with all the visiting valets and ladies' maids, most of them are sleeping three and four to a room," Blanca added. "It is not an easy thing to slip from one's bed or do anything remotely interesting at night when conditions are so crowded." She cast a sidelong glance at Addison.

"Quite." Addison kept his gaze fixed straight ahead. "The one young lady Blanca spoke with, Morag, who had slipped out to meet her young man, had sworn the other three maids who shared her chamber to secrecy."

"One of them, Marjorie—Miss Fraser's maid—seemed very nervous about the whole thing," Blanca said. "But all I could get her to admit was that she was afraid of getting Morag in trouble."

"It was difficult to get any of them to admit to anything," Addison said. "But then discretion is a vital attribute when one is in service."

"As we have cause to be extraordinarily grateful for in your case," Charles said.

Addison gave a brief, warm smile that made him look quite five years younger. "Your father's and Lord Glenister's valets were particularly reluctant to say anything about their masters. But I did gather that Mr. Fraser and Lord Glenister and their friends have had many gatherings here through the years. Shooting parties, I understand. Not the sort of parties at which—"

"Women were present," Charles finished for him. "At least not wellborn ladies."

Addison nodded. "Lord Cyril Talbot met his death at one of those shooting parties. An accident with a gun, apparently. A few of the current staff were present on that occasion—Hopetoun was a footman at the time and Mrs. Johnstone was an upstairs maid—but it was a bit difficult to get the exact sequence of events straight. Apparently none of the staff were allowed in the room after Lord Cyril shot himself."

Charles leaned forward. "Are you saying my father deliberately kept them out?"

"No one put it in so many words, but that was the impression I received," Addison said. "Also—"

"Lord Cyril didn't die immediately, but they didn't send for a doctor," Blanca said.

Addison swung his gaze to her. "We don't know that for a fact."

"No, but we can jolly well put the pieces together, as you're always saying. Mrs. Johnstone was sure she heard Lord Cyril's voice inside the library after he was injured. And no one remembers anyone sending for a doctor."

"Do any of them remember seeing Lord Cyril's body?" Mélanie asked.

Addison met her gaze for a moment. "No. Hopetoun doesn't remember any of the footmen being called upon to transport the body to the chapel or to arrange for the coffin. Mr. Fraser and Lord Glenister and their friends must have done it themselves."

Evie cracked open the door to the Blue Saloon. She wasn't sure why she had thought she might find him here, save that Honoria had once said it was her favorite room at Dunmykel. The room was in shadow, lit only by the glow from the windows. The sun was just beginning to set. The rays of light slanting through the windowpanes picked out his golden hair, so like Honoria's. He was hunched on a settee by the fireplace, back to the door, shoulders shaking.

Evie slipped into the room and pulled the door to behind her. "It's all right to cry. She was your cousin. Not to mention that she was carrying your child."

Val went completely still, then looked round to stare at her through the shadows.

"Oh, for God's sake, Val, I'm not blind. Or deaf. Surely you don't think I could have lived in Glenister House all these years and not known?"

"You never—"

"What on earth was I supposed to do?" Evie crossed to the lapis lazuli–inlaid writing table behind the settee, found a flint in one of the drawers, and lit a pair of tapers in Sèvres candlesticks. "Tell you and Honoria that what you were doing was deplorable and dishonorable and likely to get all sorts of people hurt? It was, you know, but neither of you has ever listened to a word I've said. I tried to get Honoria to talk when I suspected about the baby, but she wouldn't discuss it with me. I couldn't even get her to return my earrings. How the devil was I supposed to control her in this?"

Val continued to stare at her over the back of the settee. The candlelight glistened off streaks of damp on his cheeks. "How can you talk about it so calmly—"

"Why not?" Evie put the flint away and pushed the drawer shut with a snap. "You can."

"Yes, but—"

"Oh, I see, you don't usually discuss this sort of thing with virgins. Unless they're the virgins you take to bed?"

He flushed claret-red. "Evie—"

"I know, the rules are different when it comes to girls who might be your sisters. Only with Honoria they weren't."

"For God's sake, you shouldn't even know—"

She walked round the settee and dropped down beside him. "It's a little late, Val. I grew up in Glenister House."

Fear flashed in his eyes like a signal fire. "Oh, Lord, you haven't—"

"No, I'm still distressingly pure. I'm not quite sure why, except I have these absurd delusions that I'm supposed to wait for love and marriage."

"You are," Val said, with an earnestness that under other circumstances might have been funny. "I mean—"

The pain of the past four-and-twenty hours bubbled up inside her. She laid her hand over Val's on the silk damask of the settee. Cerulean blue. Honoria's favorite color. "It's all right, Val. There's no sense in recriminations now. I didn't understand her. God knows, at times I hated her."

His gaze swung to her face, wide with surprise.

"Don't look at me like that. You know how maddening Honoria could be. I wouldn't be human if I hadn't hated her on occasion. I suppose that gives me a motive, but then everyone else seems to have one."

Val grimaced. Evie squeezed his hand. She hadn't come here to talk about motives. "But I do miss her. As you must."

He opened his mouth as though to speak, swallowed, and nodded.

She laced her fingers through his own. "Tonight I keep remembering the good things. The way she'd slip into my room and hold my hand when I first came to Glenister House and I'd wake crying for home. Those wonderfully silly theatricals she organized the summer we were in Argyllshire and it rained a fortnight straight. The Christmas she decided to knit us all presents and gave us those horribly lopsided scarves. It was rather endearing that there was something Honoria wasn't good at."

Val gave a choked laugh and tightened his fingers round her own.

They sat in silence, surrounded by the glow from the two candles. They'd sat like this on the schoolroom hearthrug, in the long-ago days when she'd first come to Glenister House and had thought her cousins could do no wrong. Before she'd understood the darkness that lurked in all of them.

Even her.

If London had stirred unwelcome memories, Scotland chilled him to his very bones. The heavy damp in the air was worse than London's soot and grime. The tiny hold of the boat that had brought him up the coast made the fishing boat that had ferried him across the Channel seem as spacious as a yacht. His drafty room in the London lodging house had been exquisite luxury compared to this granite hut with cobwebs in every corner and the smell of peat soaked into the stones and rafters.

Still, he'd known worse. Mud huts in Spain. Caves in the Pyrenees. A burned-out farmhouse in Russia with ice crusting the roof and snow falling through the charred ceiling.

But he hadn't felt such a fool in any of those locations. His failure in London lingered at the back of his throat, like the taste of rancid meat. He shouldn't have allowed Soro's mistress to escape him.

Even then, he might have been able to put things right had not this abrupt journey to Scotland prevented him from searching for her. He wouldn't make the same mistakes here. He tugged open the string on his powder bag and began to load his pistol for the night's work ahead.

Chapter 26

Even at a quarter to midnight, a faint glow lingered in the sky. It seemed as though it must be too early for their rendezvous with Tommy. Mélanie kept pace beside Charles as they made their way across the grounds to the chapel. She could not accustom herself to the long Highland summer days.

Charles was silent and purposeful beside her. She matched her stride to his. She was wearing her breeches and shirt again, with a wool coat buttoned close to her throat for warmth and her hair bundled up into a cap. It was a relief to be moving again, to have a clear purpose in mind. Their council with Simon and David had gone round in circles, possibility after possibility discussed and debated, none of them provable, none explaining the whole story.

And yet for all the talk, a great deal remained unvoiced. Such as how Charles felt about the possibility that Lord Quentin was his brother.

The colorless light flattened out the dips and rises in the ground and blurred the line between shape and shadow. The rumble of the sea sounded to the right, an ever-present pull. A salt tang drifted on the air. The rustling of birds and the stir of wind warned of the birch coppice to the left. They were back in the world of darkness and shadows, the world in which she and Charles and Tommy Belmont and Francisco Soro had lived for so long. A world into which Honoria Talbot had somehow stumbled.

Here, as in the London streets the night they'd gone to meet Francisco, her senses were keyed to danger. Even so, it was a moment before she caught the break in the pattern. She seized Charles's arm. He went still, and she knew he'd heard it as well. Footsteps off to the left, faint but distinct.

"I'll go," she whispered.

He caught her hand in a hard grip.

"Don't be silly, Charles. Whatever Tommy knows, he's much more likely to confide in you than in me. We can't afford to be late and we can't afford not to find out who else is traipsing about the grounds at midnight."

"It might—"

"Be dangerous." She disengaged her hand from his own. "Hardly a novelty. I have a pistol. I'll meet you at the chapel. If you aren't there, I'll go back to the house. Just take care you don't murder Tommy. Or let him murder you."

He pulled her to him, pressed his lips to her hair, and released her.

She slipped through the ghostly white of the birch trees, following the telltale creaks of her quarry. The echo of footfalls on the fallen twigs and leaves told her she was gaining ground. As she emerged from the coppice she caught a flash of white. A skirt. The person she was following was a woman. Or dressed like one.

She dodged to the side, round two close-set trees. A dry branch cracked beneath her foot.

Her quarry spun round. He or she had sharp ears.

"Who's there?" said a voice that belonged unmistakably to Gisèle Fraser.

The chapel was a gray smudge, the holly branches creating a darker tracery against its granite walls, the oak door and the stained-glass window above only faint blurs. Charles climbed the steps, by instinct and memory as much as sight, found the age-worn iron handle, and pushed open the door.

The interior was cloaked in darkness. He paused, letting his senses adjust, letting the smell of damp and dust and the lingering spice of scented candles wash over him.

A hand shot out of the darkness, grabbed him, and flung him against the wall. His head slammed into the granite. His senses swam for a moment.

"Is it true?" The voice was a harsh rasp in his ear. Wild eyes glittered at him in the darkness.

Charles struggled to draw a breath past the hand that was squeezing the life out of his throat.

"Is it?"

He caught a note of familiarity beneath the raw desperation in the voice. "Tommy—for God's sake."

The hold on his throat slackened. "Tell me."

Blessed air rushed into his lungs. "If you mean was Honoria killed last night, yes, she was."

A gasp echoed off the yew rafters. Tommy dropped his hand from Charles's throat as though the confirmation had drained him of the will to fight. "In God's name, who?"

"That's what I'm endeavoring to learn." Charles dug a flint out of his pocket. He could see enough now to make out the candles, stuck in tall iron holders at the end of each pew. He lit the two nearest. In the flare of light, Tommy's face was gray and drawn, marked with the ravages of a day spent alternating between fear and despair and probably downing a bottle or so of whisky.

Tommy turned his head away from the light. "I was trying to learn what had become of McGann. The villagers were talking about it. About Honoria. I couldn't believe—who the devil—"

"Were you in the house last night?"

"What house? Dunmykel? No, of course not. What the hell would I have been—"

"You didn't use the secret passage?"

"What secret passage? Charles, in God's name, what happened to her?"

Charles stared into Tommy's blue eyes. He'd never thought they could contain such heat. "When did you last see her?"

"In Lisbon." Tommy ran a hand over his hair. A little of the habitual sangfroid returned to his features. "You know that."

"Not yesterday?"

Tommy gathered his forces for a denial, then gave it up, like a swordsman letting his weapon clatter to the ground. "Christ, Charles, are you sure one of your grandmothers wasn't a witch?"

"In my family, I'm not sure of anything. How the hell did Honoria know you were here?"

Tommy tugged at his carelessly tied cravat. "She didn't. I sent word to her."

"Why?"

"I wanted to know what the devil she was doing throwing herself away on your father."

Charles held his gaze in the candlelight. "You were lovers in Lisbon."

"Don't be ridiculous."

"Tommy, this is no time for chivalry."

"I'm not—"

"You don't have to worry about protecting Honoria's reputation. Not with me."

"She—"

"She's dead. I want to find out who did it. I think you do, too."

Tommy stared at the small circle of candlelight on the flagstone floor. "I'd have had to be blind not to notice she was beautiful, but I never expected—to own the truth, I thought she was in love with you."

"You're an observant man, Belmont, but you're not infallible."

"No?" Tommy's gaze moved to Charles's face, black and hard as onyx. "Do you remember that picnic we all went on when Honoria and Val and David were in Lisbon with Lord Carfax? We visited some ruined castle or other. I thought she was trying to make you jealous. I *still* think she was trying to make you jealous."

The memory flashed in Charles's mind. Three days after the night he'd found Honoria in his bedchamber. Blankets spread on green sloping ground, hampers of cheese and bread and cold chicken and red wine. Honoria leaning close to Tommy, laughing up at him from beneath the brim of a pale straw bonnet with apricot ribbons. He'd done his best to ignore her behavior because that seemed the most prudent course of action. Just as he'd done his best to ignore a flash of jealousy he'd had no right to feel.

"You went back to Lisbon early for some meeting or other," Tommy said. "There was a rainstorm and Honoria and I got separated from the others and took refuge in an abandoned farm house. We'd drunk a fair amount of wine at the picnic and I opened another bottle to warm us up and—"

"One thing led to another," Charles said.

"Go ahead, say it. I was a cad, a blackguard, call it what you will." Tommy strode down the darkened length of the chapel. "I stay away from virgins as a rule. Far too much risk of being caught and not very sporting to take advantage of them when they don't know the rules of the game. Though as it happens—" He swallowed whatever he'd been about to say.

"Honoria wasn't a virgin."

"How—no, I think I'd rather not know how the hell you knew that."

"Not in the way you'd be pardoned for suspecting."

"I asked her to marry me." Tommy turned round and looked at Charles through the shadows. "The shock on your face speaks wonders for your opinion of my character, Fraser. What, I wasn't supposed to worry about the consequences of what we'd done because she'd done it with someone else first? I don't know when the devil she lost her virginity or to whom, but that didn't change the fact that if word of our tryst got out she'd be ruined. Say what you will about me, I don't turn tail and run from the consequences of my actions."

"No, you don't." Charles regarded his former colleague for a moment. "Honoria turned you down?"

"She was refreshingly honest. She said she didn't have any more desire to get married at that point than I did, and there was no reason anyone should know what had transpired between us." Tommy scraped a hand through his hair. "I've always wondered if I believed her protestations too readily because I didn't want to get married myself. Of course, I think I'd have pressed her harder if I'd thought she really cared for me. If I hadn't suspected the whole thing had been a ploy to make you jealous."

"If Honoria wanted to make me jealous, it was out of pique, not love."

"Are you sure you know the difference? Jesus, are you sure there is a difference? Pique, love—in the end it all comes down to the same thing. Honoria wanted you. And you wanted her."

"I didn't—"

"Oh, for God's sake, man, admit that much. You wouldn't be human if you hadn't."

The pull of a pair of blue eyes. The gleam of pale skin. The grip of desire that for a moment threatened to overwhelm reason. "Wanting isn't the same as—"

"Loving? Christ, you haven't gone and turned into a romantic, have you?" Tommy dropped down on one of the pews. "You think what you feel when you reach for Mélanie in the dark is somehow different, better, purer? That you've never buried yourself in her to blot out the horrors you've seen or to work off your frustration at the latest ambassadorial directive? Don't tell me there aren't moments when any warm body would do and she just happens to be the one nearest at hand."

Images of the previous night flashed before Charles's eyes. "If you value your life, Belmont, you'll leave my wife out of this."

"That's the problem with you, Fraser, always trying to make things mean some bloody thing or other. It's the war all over again."

"The war?" Charles was still trying to recover from the bone-deep cut of Tommy's words about Honoria and Mélanie.

"You were always looking for truth and justice in the war, always trying to do what was right. You questioned everything to the point of not being sure which bloody side you were on. If you could have just faced the fact that our only goal was to make sure our side won and that it wasn't going to be pretty doing so, you could have spared yourself and the rest of us a lot of tiresome, tormented brooding." Tommy shook his head. "At least you used to have the guts to admit you didn't believe in love."

"I never said I didn't believe in it. I said—"

"That you didn't think you were capable of it, whatever that means, and that even if you were, you doubted it would last. Which was a fancy Charles Fraser way of admitting that love's no more than a thing of airy nothings. You were honest in those days. Now you're trying to cloak desire in fancy dress instead of accepting it for what it is. What it will always be, regardless of marriage lines and droning clergymen and gold rings. What I felt for Honoria—what you felt for Honoria but were too high-minded to act on—is the same as what you feel for your precious Mélanie. At heart, it's the same animal urge that drives all of us."

"The same animal urge that made you want to stop Honoria from marrying my father?"

Tommy rubbed his hand over his eyes. "Fraser, I wouldn't recognize love if it slapped me in the face and challenged me to pistols at forty paces. But I never forgot Honoria. Jesus, they said she was strangled—"

"She was drugged with laudanum. She wouldn't have felt anything. Just what were you planning when you saw Honoria yesterday?"

"I wanted to make sure she was happy. I couldn't imagine the girl I knew spending her life with Kenneth Fraser. I sent her a message—yes, I know Castlereagh would skin me alive if he knew—and asked her to meet me in the churchyard."

"What did she say?"

"That she knew her own mind. She seemed—" Tommy paused. Charles couldn't see his face in the shadows, but he could hear the frown in his voice. "She seemed harder than I remembered."

"It's been six years. I expect we're all harder."

"She didn't want to talk about her betrothal at all. She said—" Tommy glanced about. "Speaking of marriage, where's Mélanie?"

"Following someone. What did Honoria want yesterday?"

"To know what I was doing here." A note of surprise reverberated in Tommy's voice. "She guessed Castlereagh had sent me."

"Did she guess why?"

"Not exactly. She wanted to know what it had to do with your father. And Glenister."

"And you told her—"

"Charles, I told you yesterday—"

"I know what you told me yesterday. Does what brought you here have anything to do with my father and Glenister?"

Tommy drew a breath. "It might. They may have known Le Faucon de Maulévrier. Years ago. Before the Revolution. That's all Castlereagh told me. That, and that he didn't want you to know."

"He obviously thought my filial scruples were stronger than they are. What did you tell Honoria?"

"I said it was possible your father and her uncle had been involved in something dangerous. That I couldn't tell her more now, but if she had the least doubt she shouldn't marry Kenneth Fraser."

"And she said?"

Tommy gripped the back of the pew. "She asked what *her* father had to do with it."

"What does Cyril Talbot have to do with it?"

"Nothing, as far I know. Castlereagh never mentioned him. He died years ago, didn't he?"

"In 1797. What else did Honoria say to you?"

"We ended up talking at cross-purposes. She was trying to get me to explain something I didn't understand and I was trying to get her to explain why she was marrying Kenneth Fraser. My God, is that why she was killed?"

"I'm not sure." Charles watched a rivulet of white wax hiss into the iron candlestick. "What happened then?"

"She left."

"Just like that?"

"All right, I made a fool of myself and tried to kiss her. Did kiss her. God knows why. To see if there was anything left? Because I thought it was my last chance?"

"Did she kiss you back?"

"Ah—yes, actually." Tommy coughed. "I asked her to marry me. I meant it. More than I did six years ago, though God knows what sort of a mull I'd have made of it if she'd actually said yes. Our work doesn't exactly fit us for marriage, as you used to say in the old days—" He looked up at Charles. "I suppose four and a half years of wedlock has changed your mind about that as well."

Charles wiped the dripping wax from the candle. It stung his finger.

"Shoe's on the other foot, is it?" Tommy said. "Can't say I'm surprised. Mélanie's a remarkable woman, but it can't be easy—"

"We were talking about Honoria."

"So we were. Say what you will, if she'd taken me, perhaps she wouldn't—Charles, so help me, did your father—"

"He seems to have an alibi. Was that the last time you saw Honoria?"

"Of course. Christ, are you asking me—"

"The same question I've asked of just about everyone."

The pew scraped against the flagstones as Tommy pushed himself to his feet. "You think I broke into the house, broke into your father's room, and strangled Honoria?"

"How do you know she was in my father's room?"

"Gossip travels fast. Charles, after Honoria left me yesterday, I asked some questions round the village, I went back to my camp, and I went to sleep. You have my word on it. I know that means absolutely nothing to you—"

"Not nothing." Charles glanced at the stained-glass window over the door, the blues and reds lit faintly by candlelight. What kind of religion venerated a virginal mother? "Just not a guarantee."

Mélanie hesitated in the shadows of the birch coppice. If she stayed still, Gisèle might decide the sound had been a deer or a badger. On the other hand, she might decide to return to the house instead of continuing on whatever errand she was in the midst of. Or she might already be on her way back to the house, in which case Mélanie would learn nothing by following her. While if she spoke, she might be able to persuade her young sister-in-law to talk.

Mélanie stepped out of the shadows. "Gisèle? Don't be alarmed. I'm sorry to have startled you."

"What—*Mélanie?*"

Mélanie crossed the open ground. "It's a little late for an evening stroll."

"I couldn't sleep. I often walk late at night in the summer. I like the Highland evenings." Gisèle's gaze swept over her. "What are you doing out? Good God, Mélanie, what are you doing in those clothes?"

"I think skulking's the term. Breeches are handier than a frock for clambering over rocks. I suggest trying it if you do this sort of thing often."

"I don't. I mean, I often walk, but I don't—"

"Do whatever else it is you're doing?" Mélanie studied Charles's sister in the meager light. Gisèle's pearl earrings and ringleted hair might seem out of place, but beneath the girlish softness was a strength Mélanie hadn't noticed before. "Look, Gisèle, I realize you don't know me very well, but I think you might be surprised at how helpful I can be."

"You don't—"

"Understand?" An image of speaking to her daughter in twenty years' time flashed into Mélanie's mind. "Try me."

Gisèle's gaze darted over Mélanie's face.

"I know I'm not Charles," Mélanie said.

"No, you aren't Charles." Gisèle gave a brief, hard laugh. "It's not really my secret to tell. It could put people in danger—"

Mélanie caught the sound of rustling in the underbrush. She seized Gisèle's wrist a half-second before three men rushed at them out of the trees.

"Run," Mélanie hissed, pushing her sister-in-law away from her.

"But—"

"Charles is in the chapel. *Go.*"

Gisèle stumbled off just as rough hands caught Mélanie from behind.

Chapter 27

Tommy strode down the length of the chapel, boot heels slamming into the granite like hammer blows. "Why the devil would I hurt Honoria? Because I was playing the spurned lover? Look, old man, I cared about her. I thought I'd make her a damned sight better husband than your father. But to be brutally honest, my feelings don't run that deep for anyone."

"That, I suppose, is why you nearly dashed my brains out against the chapel wall a quarter-hour ago."

"That was—" Tommy's hand closed on the back of a pew. "I could scarcely think straight. I couldn't believe she was dead. I kept worrying that something I'd done or not done had contributed to it."

The lash of self-hatred in Tommy's voice flicked against a raw wound in Charles's own mind. "Honoria played dangerous games. You've never been one to overindulge in guilt, Tommy. Don't start now."

Tommy looked at him, the usual reckless glint back in his gaze. "Unless of course I killed her."

"Quite."

Tommy lifted his hand from the pew back. "What sort of games?"

Before Charles could answer, the chapel door thudded open. "Charles." Gisèle stumbled into the chapel. "Thank God."

Charles caught his sister by the arms. She was breathing so hard she could scarcely stand. Her hair fell about her face in a tangle, and the flounce was torn half off her gown.

Gisèle gripped his shoulder. "They've got Mélanie."

Fear bit Charles in the throat. "Who does?"

"Men. They jumped out of the trees at us. I think they might be smugglers."

"Where?" Tommy joined them. "Where were you when they grabbed you?"

"The edge of the birch coppice. I think they think—" Gisèle pushed her tangled hair out of her eyes. "Who are you?"

"Thomas Belmont," Charles said. "My sister, Gisèle."

"Enchanted," Tommy murmured.

Gisèle tugged a yew leaf out of her hair. "You went to Harrow with Charles, didn't you? Aren't you stationed in Paris?"

"Theoretically that's where I am now. Do these men know who Mélanie is?"

"No, that's just it. I think they think she's a boy, because of the way she's dressed."

"Ah, yes, Mélanie's adventuring clothes. How could I forget, particularly when they show off her legs so well. Stop glowering, Fraser, surely when she tells them she's your wife, they'll let her go."

"If she tells them," Charles said.

"Why wouldn't she?"

"Because she'll think she can get more information out of them by playing along with the charade. The only problem is, this particular charade includes knives and guns." Charles shut his mind to a number of unpleasant possibilities. He was used to doing so where Mélanie was concerned.

Concern flickered in Tommy's eyes. "It's been too long since we've done this. I keep forgetting she's as mad as you are. Now would be a good time for one of your irritatingly brilliant plans, Fraser. For Mélanie's sake, I even promise not to raise objections."

Charles scowled, feeling anything but brilliant. "The smugglers have been using the cave at the end of the secret passage."

"Yes," Gisèle said, "they have, but that's not where they'll have taken her tonight."

"How can you—" Charles stared at his sister. Her face held fear and urgency, but no hint of surprise at the events of the night. "Gelly—"

"Don't look at me like that, Charles." Gisèle straightened her shoulders. The candlelight bounced off her cheekbones and hollowed out the girlish softness of her face. She seemed to have grown a couple of inches taller in the last five minutes. "For heaven's sake, you didn't really think that all I was doing last night was throwing myself at Andrew like a lovesick schoolgirl, did you?"

The grip on Mélanie's arms felt tight enough to dislocate her shoulders. Hot breath that smelled of garlic and sausages wafted over her. "Search his pockets," her captor said.

Another of the men moved to comply. Mélanie kicked him in the stomach as he bent over her. The man grunted in pain, staggered, and slapped her across the face. The blow sliced through her jaw and sent a wave of nausea into her throat. She decided she'd put on enough of a show of a struggle. She didn't want to do so much that they actually released her, for the same reason she hadn't pulled out her pistol in the few seconds before they'd reached her and Gisèle, for the same reason she didn't try announcing she was really Mrs. Charles Fraser. She didn't want them to let her go. She wanted to find out what they were up to.

"Hah." The man who was searching her pulled her pistol from her coat pocket. "Running about with a gun. Fancy silver thing, too. That just about proves you're him. Where's your friend?"

"Don't know," Mélanie muttered. She'd never actually attempted a Perthshire accent, but her effort was apparently believable enough not to undeceive her captors.

"Not bloody likely. You know. Probably sent your sweetheart off to warn him." The searcher drew back his arm to hit her again.

"There's no time, Bill." The third man, who had been hanging back, grabbed his arm. "We're late as it is. We'll have to take the boy with us. Here, tie him up."

The man holding Mélanie lashed her arms together with what felt like a piece of twine and pressed the cold metal of a pistol against her side. "Not a word out of you, mind. March."

Jaw still tender, Mélanie nodded.

They pushed and dragged her over the uneven ground. Her head was spinning, but the sound of the waves and the whiff of salt told her they were moving toward the coast. She slouched her shoulders and shifted her center of gravity low in her pelvis. Posture was more than half the work of masquerading as the opposite sex. Her captors said nothing as they walked, save to mutter once or twice about being late and "Mr. Wheaton" being angry.

The path snaked downhill. At last they came to a halt in front of a thatch-roofed stone cottage on an open bit of ground, exposed to the buffeting of the wind off the sea. A chink or two of light showed behind burlap nailed up over the cottage's windows. One of the men rapped at the door. A moment later it was jerked open by a thin man with straw-colored hair. He scanned the three men and Mélanie. "You're late."

"Bit of a disturbance," the one called Bill said. "We found one of them."

The thin man raked Mélanie with his gaze for a moment, then gave a brisk nod. Her captor pushed her into the cottage.

The air in the single room was clotted with smoke and the smell of close-pressed bodies, sour beer, and tallow candles. The greasy yellow light flickered over smoke-stained whitewashed walls, rough plank furniture, and a jumbled crowd of men. About a dozen of them, she decided, willing her vision to clear. The crowd went silent when they entered the room, and she felt the press of a multitude of gazes upon her. She was accustomed to making entrances, but not quite of this sort.

More than one face looked familiar from their visit to the Griffin & Dragon, but she saw no spark of recognition in the gazes turned her way. A stout gray-haired man in an old-fashioned claret-colored frock coat sat in an armchair covered in stained blue canvaswork. A broad-shouldered man with close-set eyes and a pistol stuck in his belt stood on one side of the chair, a dark-haired man in a black coat holding a ledger on the other. The other men present appeared to be Dunmykel tenants, but the three in the center of the room had the mark of outsiders—something about the way they stood, the cut of their coats, the careful distance between them and the others.

Mélanie's captor addressed the man in the armchair. "Sorry to be late, Mr. Wheaton. We've found one of the rascals." He jerked Mélanie forward. "Had a pistol on him. There was a girl with him, but she ran off before we could catch her. Wouldn't tell us where his friend is, but I fancy you can make him talk."

"So you're one of the lads who chose to defy me." Wheaton's gaze swept over Mélanie. His accent didn't sound Scottish. London, with a lingering trace of the North Country. The claret-colored coat might be old-fashioned, but the cut and fabric were expensive, as was the buff-colored satin of the waistcoat beneath. Underneath the bushy gray hair, his face was surprisingly youthful. His blue eyes were sharp and appraising but didn't seem to see beyond her disguise. Thank God for the dim light.

Wheaton leaned back in his chair. "I don't know whether to admire your pluck or pity your stupidity. Or both." He fixed her with a gaze as hard as the pistol barrel still pressed against her ribs. "Where's your friend?"

"Where you won't find him," Mélanie said in the lowest, roughest voice she could manage.

"See here, lad, I don't have time to waste dancing about the question. I don't doubt you had your reasons for what you did. I'm not much interested in them at the moment. I run a business. You and your friend interfered with that business. To such an extent that I was forced to leave the convivial comforts of London and pay a visit to this"—he glanced round, his gaze lingering on the dirt floor and the traces of damp on the walls—"place." His inflection managed to make the word "place" seem several degrees lower than a backwater. "We've lost—how much is it in the last quarter, Mr. Pryce?"

The man in the black coat flipped open the ledger and peered down at the pages. "Sixty-five pounds, eight shillings, nine pence."

"Sixty-five pounds, eight shillings, nine pence." Wheaton stared hard at her as he repeated the words, each number like an accusation of a capital crime. "I'd be a poor businessman if I didn't do what it took to stop you from interfering again. Is that clear?"

"Crystal," Mélanie muttered, and then decided that had probably been a poor word choice.

Wheaton's gaze lingered on her. She understood the hard gleam in the depths of his eyes. Not evil, which she had long since ceased to believe existed, at least in its pure form, much as she had ceased to believe in absolute good. This was something that could be just as deadly—a willingness to do whatever it took to achieve a desired objective. "So where's your friend?" he demanded.

"I don't know."

His hands closed on the arms of the chair. A piece of wood gave way with a crack. "You're not in a position to play games, boy. And your insolence grows tiresome." He jerked his head at the man with the close-set eyes, whose broad shoulders and crooked jaw indicated that he might have been a prizefighter. She had ten seconds to brace herself. This time the blow caught her in the stomach. She doubled over, gasping.

"See here, Mr. Wheaton," said a deep voice. Mélanie was bent over concentrating on not being sick, but the voice sounded like Stephen Drummond, proprietor of the Griffin & Dragon. "He's only a boy."

"When boys start interfering in men's affairs, they have to take a man's punishment."

"Who the devil is the lad?" said another Scots voice. "I've never seen him before."

"I'm from Inverurie." She didn't have to work to make her voice sound thick. "Don't know anything about the rest of it. What you're talking about."

The prizefighter grabbed her by the shoulders, jerked her upright, and struck her a blow that sent her careering back against the wall.

The door burst open. "For God's sake, have you gone mad, meeting tonight of all nights?"

It sounded like Andrew Thirle. It was Andrew, Mélanie saw, lifting her head and blinking through blurred vision. She turned her face to the shadows.

Andrew's gaze swept the room. "You could have been followed

here," he said to the group in general. "Everyone's asking questions just now. If someone found you were meeting—" His gaze moved past Mélanie. Then he broke off, swung his gaze back to her, and stared. "Good God, you blithering idiots—"

He got no further. The man behind him brought a cudgel down on his head. He collapsed on the dirt floor, unconscious.

"What the hell did you do that for?" Stephen Drummond said. "It's Andrew Thirle."

"Yes, it's Mr. Thirle." The man who'd struck the blow set down his cudgel. "He's not on our side anymore, in case you'd forgotten. Now there's a chance he won't remember everyone he's seen here."

"Too risky," Bill muttered. "No telling what he might remember."

Wheaton glanced at Andrew as though he were a troublesome piece on the opponent's side of the chessboard. "Thirle always had an annoying habit of blundering into the wrong places. It doesn't look as though ten years have improved him. What's his price these days?"

"Doesn't have one," Bill said. "Pure as the driven snow since he took over running the estate."

"Unless his price is Mr. Fraser's daughter," Mélanie's captor suggested with a rough laugh. "Or his fiancée."

"Or his own past," Stephen muttered.

"Won't do," Bill said. "Thirle's turned into the sort of idiot who risks his neck for his principles. The only way to be sure he's silent is to throw him down a well. Make it look like he took a tumble in his cups. No one'd know the difference. Leastways, they couldn't prove it."

Jaw smarting, bile in her throat, Mélanie began to wonder if she'd made a serious miscalculation. Even if she revealed who she was, they might decide that having abused Mrs. Charles Fraser so badly, their only hope was to get rid of her. She ought to be able to fight her way out, but she couldn't do so and get Andrew out with her.

"What does Thirle know about the current operation?" Wheaton asked.

"Nothing," Stephen said. "He hasn't had anything to do with it since he went off to Edinburgh. The lads knew to keep him out of it when he came back to Dunmykel."

"That's to say, we knew enough to *try* to keep him out of it." Bill rubbed his jaw. "Someone helped the wounded lad last night. He ran into the passage but we never found hide nor hair of him. The lodge opens onto the passage. Couldn't help but wonder—"

Wheaton swung his gaze to Mélanie. "Did Thirle help your friend last night? Is that how he knew about our meeting tonight?"

"No!" Mélanie's voice squeaked without any effort on her part. "Why would Mr. Thirle help me?"

"A tender heart, perhaps? This sense of fair play we've been hearing about? Atoning for the sins of his own past?"

Mélanie shifted her tack. "You think I've been smuggling. Me and this friend you keep talking about. Interfering with your trade."

"You know damn well you have. Making your own trips to the south, bringing back goods, selling them at a lower rate."

"A clever plan. But not mine. Look, it's bad enough with the laird's lady being found dead this morning—"

Another blow caught her across the mouth. She tasted blood. "What do you know about the girl's death?" Wheaton asked.

"Nothing." The words came out thick, thanks to the cut to her lip. "Save that it's no time to be making trouble."

"Which is why you should tell us the truth."

"I would if—"

As she sought for words to cover her appalling lack of invention, the door thudded open yet again. Through eyes glazed with pain, Mélanie saw her husband stride into the cottage, followed by Gisèle and Tommy Belmont. She would have let out a gasp of relief, save that deep breathing of any sort hurt too much.

Charles's gaze settled on her for the briefest instant, then swept the company. "Sorry to interrupt. Just in case you're thinking of overpowering us, Mr. Belmont and I are both armed. Hullo, Stephen. I didn't expect to see you again so quickly."

"Charles." Stephen Drummond flushed, but did not avoid Charles's gaze.

"Quite a gathering of old friends. But I don't believe I know you, sir." Charles turned to Wheaton. "I'm Charles Fraser. My sister, Gisèle, and the Honorable Thomas Belmont."

Gisèle gave a cry and dropped down beside Andrew. "Murderers! What have you done to him?"

Wheaton bowed in the manner of a banker to a lady of fashion who has been shown into his office. "I assure you, Miss Fraser, the poor gentleman is merely stunned."

Gisèle smoothed Andrew's hair back from his forehead. "How?"

"An unfortunate accident. I'm afraid Mr. Thirle suffered a fall in the road and hit his head. One too many pints in the village, perhaps. A couple of the men carried him in here to recover." He looked at Charles and Tommy, who were standing on either side of the door, pistols drawn. "There seems to be some misunderstanding about our purpose here this evening. My name is Wheaton. I'm up from London on a fishing trip and looked up some cousins I'd never met before. They were kind enough to arrange a little party. We were just debating the best way of getting Mr. Thirle home. He's a friend of yours? Perhaps you could see him to his house?"

"It's a bit more complicated, I'm afraid," Charles said. His gaze drifted over the crowd and fastened on Mélanie. "You'll have to permit me to see my wife home as well. My dear, what sort of deception have you been practicing on these gentlemen?"

Mélanie straightened her shoulders and lifted her head as though she wore a trained court gown and a diamond tiara. "Really, darling, I was about to tell them when you burst in so unceremoniously. There was no need to bring guns into it."

Chapter 28

Mélanie crossed the uneven floor to her husband. She was quite proud of her ability to keep her gait steady, but as she moved into the light, Charles's gaze went to her jaw, where a bruise must be rising.

"A misunderstanding," she said.

"Quite." He put out a hand, turned her face toward him, and brushed his fingers against her cheek. His eyes turned the color of a frozen stream. "Who did this?"

"Charles," Mélanie said, "in fairness, they thought I was—"

"A boy." He undid the twine that bound her hands. She felt his gaze linger on her chafed wrists. She'd rubbed them raw loosening the twine. He clenched the twine in his fist and looked at the company of men. "Do you enjoy beating up children?"

"He didn't look like a boy," her former captor muttered. "He—"

"Shut up." One of his friends kicked him.

The full realization of what they had done settled over the company. They had tied up, beaten, and held at gunpoint the wife of the heir to Dunmykel. The disbelief, shock, and horror sinking into their eyes might have been darkly comic if she hadn't still been nauseated.

"My God," Stephen Drummond said. "It was bad enough when we thought—"

"My profoundest apologies, Mrs. Fraser." Wheaton had gone pale beneath his ruddy complexion, but his gaze was steady as he turned to Mélanie. "I need hardly say—"

Charles spun round, pushed Wheaton into his chair, and pressed his pistol into the buff-colored satin of Wheaton's waistcoat. "Do you imagine an apology can settle this?"

The prizefighter took a step toward his employer.

"I wouldn't if I were you," Tommy said, pistol drawn. "Fraser's a crack shot and he has an inconvenient temper."

Charles hadn't taken his gaze off Wheaton. "Do you think I'm the sort of man who stands idly by when his wife's been assaulted? You have a poor opinion of my sense of honor, Mr. Wheaton."

Mélanie bit back an interjection. It was unlike Charles to go on about honor when they should be focused on getting everyone safely out of the cottage.

"It was naturally a horrible accident," Wheaton said, "but I assure you we meant no—"

Charles grabbed Wheaton's arm and jerked it behind his back. "What you meant doesn't have a damn thing to do with it. You may be in the habit of not retaliating when your women are harmed, but I assure you I am not."

That settled it. Charles was definitely playacting. If only her head would stop spinning, perhaps she could figure out his game and play along better.

The cottage had gone silent, all attention focused on Charles and Wheaton. Qualms of conscience aside, while killing Andrew and possibly Mélanie herself had been feasible, the smugglers must realize they could never get away with killing Charles, Gisèle, and Tommy as well. A quick glance over her shoulder showed Mélanie that Tommy stood with the door at his back, his pistol trained on the prizefighter. Gisèle had pulled Andrew into her lap.

Charles released Wheaton and took a step back. Wheaton surveyed Charles with as steady a gaze as if he were facing him over a decanter of port instead of the barrel of a gun. "Naturally I don't know the charming Mrs. Fraser's reasons for wandering about the estate at midnight dressed as a boy. I hesitate to speculate on so delicate a matter. But I imagine it is something neither Mrs. Fraser nor you, sir, would wish discussed."

Charles smashed his fist into Wheaton's jaw. "There's one thing that can save you, Wheaton."

"What?" Wheaton's voice was hoarse.

Charles leaned in and grasped Wheaton by his neckcloth. "Information."

"Of what sort?"

"A woman was murdered last night."

The room went so still that the scrape of wind against the chinks in the mortar echoed in the air.

"I don't know anything about that," Wheaton said.

"But you may know about prior events that are linked to her death."

"What events?"

"Concerning your work here on this estate and your connections in France. Do you want me to say more?"

Wheaton jerked away from Charles's hold. "Talking can get a man killed, Mr. Fraser."

"So can not talking, Mr. Wheaton."

Wheaton held Charles's gaze for a long moment. The tallow light gleamed steadily on the pistol in Charles's hand.

Wheaton gave a crisp nod and looked at the men. "Out. All of you."

The men filed out of the cottage, including the man with the ledger. The prizefighter hesitated for a moment, but at a curt nod from Wheaton he, too, followed. Tommy remained by the door, pistol in his hand, keeping a wary eye on them as they left.

"Perhaps I could have my pistol back," Mélanie said as her former captors moved to the door.

"Oh—er—of course. Ma'am. Madam." The man who had searched her pockets pulled the pistol from his own pocket, handed it to her, stared at her for a moment, and then gave an awkward half-bow before hurrying after his companions.

Stephen Drummond paused by the door and turned back to look at her. "I should have stopped it, Mrs. Fraser. No matter who you were."

"You might have got your own neck broken," Mélanie said.

"That sounds rather poor as excuses go." Stephen shifted his gaze to Charles. The two men regarded each other for a long moment, heavy with memory and guilt on both sides. Charles inclined his head. Stephen gave a crisp nod and followed the others from the cottage.

Charles glanced at his sister, who was sitting on the floor, Andrew's head cradled in her lap. "Keep Andrew still, Gelly. We don't want to risk moving him with a head injury. Is his breathing regular?"

Face set in determined lines, Gisèle nodded.

"Good." Charles gave her a brief, warming smile.

An answering spark kindled in Gisèle's eyes.

Wheaton pushed himself to his feet and gestured to the armchair. "Mrs. Fraser? Won't you sit down?"

Mélanie sank into the chair. The feel of solid support at her back was more of a relief than she would have admitted. She reached out to smooth her skirt and then remembered she wasn't wearing one.

Charles glanced round the room. "You must have some whisky or brandy about here somewhere."

"Both," Wheaton said. "Which do you prefer?"

"Anything as long as it has alcohol."

Wheaton produced a bottle from a dresser in the corner.

Charles opened the bottle, releasing the smoky aroma of Islay malt, splashed a third of the contents onto his handkerchief, and pressed the handkerchief against the corner of Mélanie's mouth. The whisky burned like acid against her skin, but she couldn't very well complain. It was the sort of thing she was always doing to him, and it would be very inconvenient to come down with an infection just now.

Charles smoothed her hair back from her face and let his fingers linger against her cheek for a moment. Then he perched on the arm of her chair, one hand on her shoulder, and looked at Wheaton, who was leaning against the dresser. "You've been storing goods in the cave at the end of the secret passage."

Wheaton jammed his hands into the pockets of his coat. "I run a large operation in the south, Mr. Fraser. I send shipments up the coast to a number of locations, including Dunmykel Bay. The men on the estate in my employ sell to most of the local gentry. Blockades and excise taxes don't dim gentlemen's taste for brandy and champagne."

"But your operation here became more complicated." Charles's tone made it a statement rather than a question.

"Upon occasion."

"In what way?"

Wheaton paced across the room. "I assume you know your father has a fondness for collecting things."

Face neutral, Charles nodded.

"A number of his friends like to collect as well. Picked up a taste for it on the Grand Tour, I don't wonder. But what with armies marching to and fro across the Continent, it hasn't been so easy to get Italian marbles and French paintings and Spanish sculptures and the like."

"You've been smuggling works of art out of the Continent for my father and his friends?"

Wheaton turned to face Charles across the room. "Men in my employ on the Continent have undertaken such jobs from time to time."

"And the parcels came here?"

"Sometimes. Or to other spots in England and Scotland. Even to the east coast of Ireland once. I didn't always see the parcels for myself, but on occasion I was asked to oversee the shipments personally. For a considerable fee, of course. On one of those occasions, the wrapping came loose on a sketch. A Da Vinci. Exquisite thing. I must say, until then I'd never understood how a man could pay so much for a bit of ink and paper." Wheaton shook his head as though he could not reconcile the beauty of the sketch with the world of shipments and ledgers, crates of brandy and tins of tea.

Charles reached into his pocket and drew out Mélanie's now much-creased drawing of the Elsinore League seal. "Do you recognize this?"

Wheaton crossed the room, a wary eye on Charles's pistol, took the sketch, and held it to the light of the tallow candle that stood on a three-legged table beside the armchair. "It's a seal," he said. "Your father and some of his friends use it on orders involving a special delivery."

Tommy's head jerked up. "*Kenneth Fraser* uses that seal?"

"Which friends?" Charles said.

"Lord Glenister. Sir William Cathcart. A Mr. Gordon."

"What about Lord Cyril Talbot?"

"Glenister's younger brother? I'd nearly forgotten about him. Yes, I delivered packages to him once or twice."

"Do you think these men were part of some sort of organization?"

Wheaton gave a coarse laugh. "Do drinking and whoring and orgies constitute an organization?"

"Have you ever heard of something called the Elsinore League?"

"Elsinore?" Wheaton frowned, then gave an unexpected laugh. "By God, that's rich. I once took a parcel—a statue, I think—to Mr. Gordon personally and I heard him mutter something that sounded like 'Elsie's snore.' Lord Glenister was there, too. He shut him up. Seemed quite perturbed. I couldn't make sense of it. Thought Elsie must be a lady with a jealous husband."

Charles swung his booted foot against the side of the chair. "Did you ever transport a person rather than a parcel?"

Wheaton dropped the sketch on the table. "Good God. How did you know?"

"Clever deduction. Or lucky guess. Did you bring a passenger with you on your recent journey to Dunmkyel?"

"This trip was to plug the leaks in my own operation."

"That wouldn't have stopped you from taking on a passenger."

"But as it happens, I didn't."

"But on previous trips?"

"Mr. Fraser—"

"This prevarication grows tiresome, Mr. Wheaton."

Wheaton walked back to the dresser and drummed his fingers on its scarred top. "Recently your father wanted us to pick up a gentleman on the French coast near Calais and bring him to England."

"And then to Dunmykel?"

"Not directly. We let him off in London. A few days later I got word that we were to bring him up the coast to Dunmykel."

'When was this?"

"A bit over a fortnight since."

Mélanie could feel the quickening interest radiating off Tommy.

Gisèle was stroking Andrew's hair, but her gaze said that she missed nothing of the conversation.

"Who?" Charles said.

"Your father didn't give us a name. Neither did the gentleman."

"You met him?"

Wheaton took a glass from the dresser and filled it with whisky. "I went on the run over to France. I don't as a rule, but in this case your father requested it."

"Was the gentleman you transported a Frenchman?"

Wheaton took a meditative sip of whisky. "I assumed so at first. He spoke English with a French accent."

"But?"

Wheaton stared into his glass. "I meet a lot of Frenchmen in my line of work. After a bit, I realized there was something a bit off about his accent. Almost as though he was trying too hard to maintain it."

"You think he was British?"

"I suspected as much. Though he could have been German or Russian or Swedish or Dutch-Belgian or God knows what."

"What did he look like?" Tommy said.

"About Kenneth Fraser's years. Middling height, didn't run to fat. Graying hair. It looked as though he'd once been fair-haired, but it was difficult to tell and I only saw him at night. Blue eyes, I think. Cold blue eyes."

"What did he talk about?" Charles asked.

"Very little. Sat in the cabin, kept himself to himself."

Charles leaned forward. His anger had been replaced by the quiet intensity he used to draw confidences from people. "Surely in all the hours of a Channel crossing he said something memorable."

Wheaton took another sip of whisky. "He did say one odd thing. It was just before we docked in England. He'd come up on deck and I went over to him at the rail to tell him we'd reach land soon. He kept looking out over the water and he said, 'Neither a borrower nor a lender be.' Then he looked me full in the face and added, 'I'm not sure that's the best advice, Mr. Wheaton. I've found old debts can come in remarkably handy.'"

"What do you think he meant by that?"

"I haven't the least idea. But I can tell you, I was glad to put him ashore in England and glad I didn't have to travel up the coast with him. I'm not a fanciful man, Mr. Fraser, but he gave me the chills."

"Why?"

Wheaton seemed taken aback by the question. He thought for a moment, twisting the glass in his hand so the candlelight bounced off a chip near the rim. "He was perfectly polite. Thanked me, even. But I had the sense he could have cut my throat and barely stopped to draw a breath."

Charles leaned back against the chair. His fingers were cool and steady on Mélanie's neck. "Was Giles McGann involved in transporting this man?"

Wheaton banged his whisky glass on the dresser. "Good Christ, it's a wonder you need me for information at all."

"You'll get used to it," Tommy muttered.

"I take it that's a yes?" Charles said.

Wheaton blotted a spattered drop of whisky with his finger. "McGann came down from Scotland and escorted the gentleman to Dunmykel. On your father's orders."

Mélanie felt the chill that ran through her husband. "Where's McGann now?" Charles said, without a change of inflection in his voice.

"I don't know. The lads say no one's seen him since he and the passenger disembarked a week since."

"Wheaton—"

"That's the God's honest truth, Mr. Fraser." Wheaton tossed off the last of the whisky. "At least as far as I know it."

"Have you ever heard of Le Faucon de Maulévrier?"

"Le who?"

"Or seen this?" Tommy pulled a drawing of Le Faucon's seal from his pocket.

Wheaton shook his head. "The only seal I ever saw was the other one, with the castle."

"Did—"

A stir of movement came from the corner of the room. "What—" Andrew struggled to sit up.

"Shh." Gisèle gripped his shoulders. "Don't try to move. You hit your head."

He caught her hand and pulled it to his cheek. "Gelly? What are you—"

"It's all right. Everyone's safe. Charles is questioning Mr. Wheaton."

"What the devil is Charles—Mrs. Fraser." Andrew searched the room with an anxious gaze.

"I'm quite all right, Mr. Thirle," Mélanie said. "And under the circumstances, don't you think it's past time you started to call me Mélanie?"

He gave a shaky smile, tried to sit up, and fell back in Gisèle's arms.

"Be careful." Gisèle stroked his hair, her face bathed in tenderness. Andrew looked up at her, the tenderness mirrored on his own face. For a moment, Mélanie doubted either of them was aware of their surroundings or of any of the other people present.

Charles sent them an appraising glance but merely said, "Don't try to move too quickly, Andrew. You had a bad blow to the head. We'll get you home in a bit." He got to his feet and faced Wheaton. "I'm aware that conditions on the estate are difficult. I have no sympathy with my father's Clearances. I can understand the attraction smuggling holds for the tenants. I hate to see them risking arrest and giving a cut of any profits they make to you, but if that's the only way they can make ends meet I certainly won't condemn them. But if anyone lays a hand on anyone on this estate, whether it's my wife or one of the tenant lads, I'll take it as a personal attack." He glanced at the pistol in his hand, then back at Wheaton. "Are we clear?"

"Crystal, Mr. Fraser."

"Good. Wait in the cottage for a quarter-hour after we leave. After that I don't care where you go, so long as—"

"Don't worry, I'll be gone at first tide."

"On the contrary. I insist that you stay in the vicinity until the matter of Miss Talbot's death is resolved. We may have need of your evidence. Do I have your word?"

"Does my word mean anything?"

Tommy gave a derisive snort, but Charles merely said, "You're a businessman, Wheaton. I assume you know the dangers of reneging on a bargain. Do I have your word?"

"For what it's worth, yes. You can reach me through your friend Drummond at the Griffin & Dragon."

Charles nodded and turned to the corner of the room. "Andrew? Do you think you can walk?"

"Of course." Andrew lurched to his feet, staggered, and would have fallen if Gisèle hadn't caught him about the waist.

"Here." Tommy took Andrew's weight on his shoulder. "Let me, Miss Fraser. I'm a bit taller than you."

"I'm stronger than I look," Gisèle said, draping Andrew's other arm round her shoulders.

Tommy and Gisèle helped Andrew from the cottage. Charles handed Mélanie to her feet and they followed. The five of them stood still for a moment after Charles closed the door to the cottage. The events inside the cottage reverberated in Mélanie's mind like the click of the latch. The moon was cool and ghostly in the smudged gray of the sky. The air outside seemed to have grown colder in the past—what had it been—an hour? She could feel it pressing against all the sore places in her body.

Andrew detached himself from Tommy and Gisèle, drew a deep breath, and then looked at Tommy as though realizing for the first time that he didn't know him.

"His name's Tommy Belmont," Gisèle said. "Officially he's in Paris right now, but he's here doing something mysterious."

Andrew accepted this with a celerity that indicated both a keen knowledge of the workings of Gisèle's mind and a clearing brain. He shook Tommy's hand. "My thanks for your help. But what the devil—"

"We should talk," Charles said. "But not here. The lodge?"

Andrew nodded.

"You can't walk all the way to the lodge," Gisèle said.

"Of course I can. I've suffered worse taking a tumble from my horse." He touched Gisèle's arm, bare below the puffed muslin sleeve of her frock. "Good God, Gelly, you're shaking like a leaf."

"I lost my shawl."

"Here." He struggled out of his coat.

"Andrew—"

"I had a blow to the head, I'm not coming down with pneumonia. Don't fuss. I have sleeves. You don't." He put the coat round her.

Gisèle let him do so and took his arm, which seemed to satisfy her as to ensuring he could walk. Tommy glanced at Charles and then followed close behind the couple, conveniently close should Andrew stumble, pistol drawn in case of further disturbance.

"What about you?" Charles said to Mélanie. "Can you walk?"

"Of course I can walk." Not entirely steadily, but that would improve with fresh air and exercise.

"You're almost as bad a liar as Andrew. Put your arm round me."

She did and winced, which earned her a sharp look from her husband. But he merely adjusted his hold to a more comfortable position and helped her along the path after the others.

"I must say that was a very impressive performance in the cottage, Charles," Mélanie said when they had climbed to the top of the cliffs. "If I didn't know you so well I'd have thought you really were furious."

Charles stopped walking, spun to face her, and seized her by the shoulders. "What the hell did you think you were doing?" he said, his level voice gone as sharp as the wind.

Mélanie looked up at her husband. The moonlight fell over his face, sharpening his nose and cheekbones, accentuating the angry line of his mouth, deepening his eyes to blue-black. "Wasn't it obvious what I was doing? Obtaining information."

"A little more information and a few less bruises would speak better for your sense."

"If I hadn't been bruised, Mr. Wheaton wouldn't have talked to you."

"Even you couldn't have foreseen how that would play out, Mel."

"Not exactly. But I knew playing along was our best chance of getting information. For God's sake, Charles, I wasn't in any real danger. You know me, I never let myself get trapped. I had the bonds on my wrists loosened and I knew exactly where the windows were. I could always have run."

"And taken Andrew with you?"

"Andrew did complicate things, but—"

"But what?" His gaze sliced into her own. "Even if you'd told them who you were, they might have decided it had gone too far and they were better off killing you."

"It wouldn't have—"

"Come to that? You can't possibly know that." His grip on her tightened. Something had broken in the depths of his eyes, releasing a molten torrent from a part of him she rarely glimpsed. "Jesus, Mel, you might remember that you have children."

"I never forget that I have children."

"No? Then you've got to stop thinking you can heap any abuse on yourself without fear of the consequences."

"I'll stop whenever you do."

"What the devil's that supposed to mean?"

"Oh, for God's sake, Charles. You got shot the night we met Francisco, you nearly got knifed in Covent Garden, and then you were shot at again last night. And that's just the past fortnight."

"Are you suggesting we should have ignored Manon's message?"

"No. I'm saying you didn't have any choice. Just as I didn't have a choice tonight."

"There's always a choice."

"Not one I'd ever have made. I'm not Honoria Talbot. I never will be."

"Don't bring Honoria into this."

"She's already in the middle of it. One way or another she's been at the heart of everything that's happened for the past fortnight, and you wouldn't be human if you weren't thinking about the life you might have had with her—"

"Damn it, Mélanie, don't try to change the subject. I never wanted a life with Honoria."

"I know, you never wanted to be married at all or you never thought you deserved to be—"

"As you pointed out, I haven't exactly been a model husband."

"Charles—"

He released his grip on her. "Tommy's a bloody impertinent bastard," he said in a low, harsh voice. "But sometimes he sees too damned much."

"Too much of what?"

"The truth."

"About?"

"It doesn't matter." He glanced away and drew a long breath.

"We make choices. We have to live with them." He turned, wrapped his arm round her again, and drew her after the others.

She made no reply, because to Charles's words there was really nothing to be said. That, after all, was what their marriage had been about from the first. Learning to live with choices. Or trying to do so.

They followed Andrew, Gisèle, and Tommy along winding paths past the birch coppice to the lodge. Andrew fished a set of keys out of his pocket and unlocked a side door onto a vaulted kitchen filled with cool shadows and the smell of peat and lemon oil. He lit a lamp on the deal table in the center of the room, went to light another, gripped the edge of the table, and dropped down heavily into one of the straight-backed chairs.

"Sorry. 'Fraid I'd better sit down. Charles, there's some whisky on the sideboard."

Gisèle felt his forehead. "I'm not sure a drink would be good for you after that blow to the head."

"Fine, I won't drink. Offer some to everyone else."

"I'll make tea. We're all chilled." Gisèle shrugged out of Andrew's coat, draped it over a chair back, and went to the range. The iron doors squeaked and the embers hissed to life as she stirred them with the poker.

Charles pressed Mélanie into a chair and finished lighting the lamps. Tommy added some peats from a basket beneath the stove to the fire in the range.

Andrew stared across the table at Mélanie, his gaze moving over her wool coat and linen shirt and cloth cap. "You *are* dressed like a boy. I thought it was just the blow to the head playing tricks on me. What in God's name were you doing?"

"Trying to find out what the smugglers were up to." Mélanie tugged off her cap and shook out her matted hair. She looked from Andrew, sitting statue-still at the end of the table, to Gisèle, slender and straight-backed, her muddy white dress outlined against the black iron of the range as she filled the kettle. "I think I have it sorted out. Wheaton has a smuggling operation in the south. His men ferry goods up here, goods that men on the estate have been hiding in the caves and then distributing. But a couple of Dunmykel men started their own operation bringing contraband from the south. It got bad enough that Wheaton came up here to investigate.

Last night the rogue smugglers had a run-in with his men. One of them was shot. He and his confederate—who they thought I was— got away and are hiding somewhere on the estate." She paused a moment. "The smugglers thought the two men must have had help last night."

Andrew regarded her with a steady blue gaze over the lemon-scoured deal of the table.

Gisèle turned from the range, a blue enamel tin of tea in her hand. "His name's Ian. He's Marjorie—my maid's—younger brother."

"Marjorie told you he was in trouble?" Charles struck a spark to the last of the lamps.

Gisèle set down the tin and reached for the teapot. The brown glaze gleamed in the lamplight. "Marjorie woke me last night in a panic. She said Ian had been shot and he was hiding in the secret passage. I woke Andrew. Ian couldn't be moved far, but we had to get him somewhere where he could be warm and dry and out of sight for a few days."

"The Old Tower," Charles guessed.

Gisèle's eyes widened in acknowledgment. "Yes."

"How badly hurt is he? We saw blood in the passage."

"It's only a flesh wound, but it's in his leg, so it's difficult for him to walk. We bandaged the wound and took him some blankets and food. Then Andrew saw me back to the house. That part of the story I told you was true."

Andrew looked up at her. "What story?"

Gisèle began to spoon tea into the teapot. "Charles found out you used the secret passage last night. He was suspecting all sorts of things and probably ignoring other things that might actually have to do with who killed Honoria, so I had to give him an explanation. I told him you were in the passage last night because you were seeing me back to my room because I'd gone to your room because I wanted to get your attention which of course I did—want to get your attention, that is, at least I used to—but even at my silliest, I'd never—"

Andrew's fingers clenched on the edge of the table. "Gelly, you didn't have to—"

Gisèle measured another precise spoonful of tea. "I know it sounds absurd, but I had to tell him something, and Charles actually believed me." She cast a sidelong glance at her brother. "You see why I had to wake Andrew last night, Charles. I knew I'd need help with Ian and I didn't have anyone else to turn to."

Charles leaned against the table, arms folded across his chest. "Some sisters would turn to their brothers."

Gisèle snapped the lid of the tea tin shut. "I knew Andrew would be sympathetic to Ian. He's always worrying about the tenants and he knows how difficult Father's Clearances have been for everyone—"

"And you thought I wouldn't be sympathetic?"

The kettle began to whistle. Gisèle picked it up and poured water into the teapot. Her hand jerked, sending a cloud of steam and droplets of scalding water into the air. "I don't know what you think about much of anything, Charles. You know me so little you believed I'd fling myself at the head of a man who's made it clear he doesn't want me." She dropped the lid onto the teapot with a clang. "After nine years the normal rules for siblings don't apply to us anymore."

"Point taken," Charles said. "You and Andrew were meeting tonight?"

Andrew, who'd been staring at Gisèle like a man who'd had his soul ripped out, jerked his gaze to Charles. "No, we weren't meeting. I took a parcel of food to Ian's confederate Jamie, who's hiding in an abandoned cottage. I arrived to find Gisèle had already been there." He cast a grim glance at Charles's sister. "Though we'd agreed I'd take care of visiting Jamie and she had no business running round the estate in the middle of the night with a murderer lurking about."

"Oh, for heaven's sake," Gisèle said. "Honoria was murdered in the house. I was probably safer outside."

"You could have been—"

Gisèle grabbed a tin of sugar off the shelf above the range and plunked it down on the table. "You don't have any right to tell me what to do, Andrew."

"No." Andrew drew a long, hard breath. "Fair enough. In any case, I was on my way home when I saw a light by the smugglers' cottage. I thought the men were mad to be meeting so close to the house, especially with you—"

"Snooping about," Charles finished for him.

"To put it bluntly. I went to warn them and—you know the rest."

"Did either of you see anyone else in the secret passage last night?"

They shook their heads without hesitation.

Gisèle picked up the teapot and poured tea into black lustre mugs. Tommy passed them round.

"Did the smugglers say anything else before we got to the cottage?" Charles asked Mélanie.

Mélanie reached for the milk jug. "Nothing of substance."

She carefully avoided looking at Andrew, but she felt his gaze on her. "You're a generous woman, Mrs. Fr—Mélanie. But I'm quite sure they must have said more after they knocked me unconscious."

Mélanie added a dollop of milk to her tea. "If there's more to be said, I think it's your story to tell, Andrew."

Andrew curved his hands round the mug Tommy had given him. "Knowing Wheaton, I imagine he made some comment about my predilection for untimely entrances."

Charles watched his friend without speaking. Gisèle gave a soft gasp. Andrew looked briefly at her. "Oh, yes. There was a time when I knew Wheaton rather well." He blew on the steam from the tea, dispersing it like a cloud of memories. "With the Clearances more of the Dunmykel men have become involved—men like Stephen Drummond, who only got pulled in recently. But the smuggling operation has gone on for years. I suspect my father deliberately turned a blind eye to it. My father was—a good man."

"So he was." Charles dropped into a chair. "I can't tell you how often I envied you your fortune in parentage. It was only later that I realized having a saint for a father can have its own drawbacks."

Andrew hunched his shoulders. "I never could seem to be what he wanted. Or perhaps I didn't try hard enough. Perhaps I didn't want to try." He glanced sideways at Charles. "Remember how I used to say that it was all very well for you to love Dunmykel, when you spent two-thirds of the year at Harrow? It was different to be marooned here all the time." He lifted the mug and took a deep swallow that must have burned his throat. "I started working with Wheaton's gang when I was sixteen."

Charles twisted his own mug on the table before him. "I'd have been fourteen . . . so you were working with them when I was home from Harrow for the holidays?"

"You weren't much more than a child, Charles. I at least had enough sense to know it was nothing I could involve you in. But I did boast about it to Donald Fyfe one night when we'd filched some of Father's whisky. Donald insisted I introduce him to Wheaton."

"Donald?" Gisèle said. "He was the Fyfes' eldest son, wasn't he? The one who—" Her eyes filled with the knowledge even as the words died on her lips.

"Who died in a fishing accident," Andrew supplied in a flat voice. "Only he wasn't fishing, he was sailing back down the coast with me after delivering a load of contraband to Arbroath. And it wasn't an accident."

"What happened?" Gisèle said in a small, intent voice.

Andrew studied the condensation on the lip of his mug. "The excisemen were swarming about that summer. We should have known—" He bit back the words with the self-recrimination Mélanie knew all too well from the aftermath of a failed mission. "They surprised us on the beach after we made our delivery. We managed to get the boat out to sea, but they shot at us from the mainland. Donald fell overboard."

Gisèle sat very still, her eyes round and dark.

"And then?" Charles said in a soft voice.

"I jumped in after him, but I couldn't—I couldn't even get his body back onto the boat. I managed to sail home. The excisemen were hovering round Dunmykel, too. I got to Giles McGann's cottage. He hid me."

"McGann?" Tommy leaned forward with sudden interest. "Do you know where he is now?"

"No. I wish I did. I hope to God he hasn't—he kept me from falling to pieces when Donald died. I wanted to unburden my soul and confess to everyone. McGann pointed out that it would be scant comfort to my parents if I was hauled off to prison and that it would be kinder to Donald's family to let them believe he died in a fishing accident. I stuck by the story, but I think my father guessed the truth. When the excisemen came about asking questions, he lied and said

I'd been at home, as though he knew my whereabouts that night wouldn't hold up under scrutiny. He never confronted me with what had happened, but I don't think he ever forgave me."

"Oh, Andrew," Gisèle said.

"I'm sorry, Gelly. I told you once I wasn't the man you thought I was. Perhaps I should have made it clear just how true that was."

"Was that when you stopped working for Wheaton?" Charles asked.

Andrew nodded. "The smugglers were forced to cut back their operation for a bit. I went off to university in Edinburgh."

"And your visits to Dunmykel became scarce," Charles said. "I thought it was the lure of university life. But when we were both at Dunmykel for holidays I never guessed—"

"I'm better at dissembling than you give me credit for." Andrew gave a smile that didn't touch the ghosts in his eyes. "Besides, when I was with you I could pretend it had never happened. I couldn't do that when I had to look Donald's family in the eye. Or see the unspoken censure in my father's gaze. I took to spending as much time as I could in Edinburgh. Then Father became ill and I realized I couldn't keep—"

"Running away?" Charles said.

Andrew met his gaze in a moment of unspoken understanding. "Yes. So I took over managing the estate and found myself turning a blind eye to the smuggling, just as my father had once done. One's conscience can't be troubled by what one doesn't know about. Or so I thought."

Gisèle tore her gaze from Andrew and looked at her brother. "What does all this have to do with whatever the Elsinore League is and why is Father smuggling people out of France?"

Tommy took a sip of tea. "Those would seem to be the pertinent questions."

"I know you aren't supposed to tell us things," Gisèle said, "but honestly, Charles, I think we can be more help to you if we understand what's going on."

Charles glanced at Tommy. "She has a point," Tommy said. "They've overheard enough at this point that they might as well hear the rest of it."

Charles nodded and gave his sister and Andrew a brief outline of what they knew about Le Faucon de Maulévrier and the Elsinore League.

Gisèle frowned into her tea. "Charles, you aren't trying to tell me Father was secretly a revolutionary, are you?"

"I seriously doubt it," Charles said. "For any number of reasons."

"So why was Mr. Fraser helping these people?" Andrew asked.

"I'd like to know that myself," Tommy muttered.

Mélanie turned her mug between her hands. "Suppose we've got the information twisted about? Suppose the Elsinore League wasn't Le Faucon's organization? Suppose they were some sort of club to which Mr. Fraser and Lord Glenister and their friends belonged?"

"You mean like the Hellfire Club?" Gisèle said. "Drinking and carousing and unspeakable orgies?"

"Aunt Frances hasn't neglected your education, has she?" Charles said. "Yes, I think that's the sort of thing Mélanie means. It's true that the ancient Greek masking a relatively simple code seems more like something that might have been invented by a bunch of clever undergraduates than the work of seasoned agents."

"That's all very well," Tommy said, "but Castlereagh told me Le Faucon began the Elsinore League—"

"Le Faucon, whoever he is, may have been one of the founding members," Mélanie said. "But not for the purposes of intelligence gathering."

"You think Le Faucon was a drinking and wenching companion of Kenneth Fraser and Lord Glenister?"

"Why not? They traveled on the Continent. They had a number of foreign-born friends. And as you yourself pointed out, Le Faucon might have been English."

"But what would that have to do with Father smuggling people out of France now?" Gisèle asked.

"Because your father may well have had French friends who wound up on the opposite side in the war," Mélanie said. "And those friends are now blackmailing their former companions into helping them escape France, using the seal of the Elsinore League for their documents."

"Blackmailing them over what?" Andrew said.

Charles flicked a glance at Mélanie. "Their own past. Or possibly that Cyril Talbot actually was involved with Le Faucon."

"Lady Frances described a man—supposedly Irish—who was present when Lord Cyril died who seems to resemble the man Wheaton brought to Britain," Mélanie said.

"So you think this man with the cold eyes was Le Faucon?" Andrew asked.

"Very likely," Charles said. "Unless Cyril Talbot was Le Faucon himself."

"Good Christ," Tommy said.

"Sorry, old man," Charles said. "We hadn't had time to share that theory."

Gisèle spooned more sugar into her tea and stirred it without seeming to see what she was doing. "You think Father and Glenister were being threatened with Honoria learning the truth about all of this?"

"That would fit what Francisco said and what Manon told us."

"It might fit with something else I remember." Gisèle folded her hands in her lap. "It was after Mama died. More than a year later. A few weeks after my tenth birthday."

"Just after I left for the Continent," Charles said.

"Yes." She took a sip of tea and made a face, perhaps because it was too sweet. "I was living with Aunt Frances, but she'd gone to a house party and I was spending a fortnight at Dunmykel. For once Father was in residence. Lord Glenister came to see him, which cheered me up because he brought Honoria and Evie. One night we all snuck downstairs. We were hanging about on the terrace outside the windows of the billiard room. Father and Glenister were playing billiards and arguing. Glenister said something like 'We never should have involved the members in something so personal.'"

"'The members'?" Charles said.

"Yes, it stuck in my mind because I never could work out what they were members of. I thought he must be talking about Brooks's or the Jockey Club or something. And then Father said, 'It was your mess, Glenister, I just helped you tidy away the pieces.'"

"What did Father say?" Charles asked, gaze trained on his sister.

"'We did what had to be done. We made use of the best resources at hand.' And then something about 'If we're lucky, they'll all die in the war.'"

"They?" Tommy asked.

"I couldn't work out who he meant from what I heard."

"What happened then?" Mélanie asked.

"It was getting cold on the terrace and Father and Glenister were mumbling, so it was hard to hear any more, but Honoria didn't want to leave. Evie and I had to drag her back upstairs."

"Did you talk about it afterward?" Charles asked.

"Of course. I thought Lord Glenister had broken a Sèvres vase or something and Father'd helped him tidy away the pieces. I asked Honoria what her uncle had broken and she just gave me one of those odious superior looks of hers." Gisèle sucked in her breath. "Oh, poison, I keep forgetting she's dead. But it was odious. Evie tried to distract me by offering to play lottery tickets, but I asked Honoria what the conversation really meant. She said, 'I don't know. Yet.'"

Tommy released his breath. "Judging by her talk with me yesterday, she was trying to find out up until her death."

"Unless she did finally find out and that's why she died," Charles said. "And why Colonel Coroux met his death in the Conciergerie."

"Something to do with Cyril Talbot's death?" Tommy asked. "Or his supposed death?"

Possibilities hung in the air like the smell of peat from the fire in the range. Tommy stared straight ahead, face unreadable. Andrew's mouth hardened. Gisèle shivered.

"There's little more to be learned tonight," Charles said. "Tommy, your cover's blown. You might as well come home with us."

Tommy stretched his arms. "Loath as I am to accept favors from you, Fraser, I can't say I'll quarrel with a night in a featherbed rather than camping out in the Highland wilderness."

Gisèle pulled Andrew's coat round her shoulders. "I need to check on Ian."

Andrew got to his feet. "I can—"

"I want to see him." Gisèle met Andrew's gaze with a hint of the defiance she frequently showed Charles. "You can come, too, if you like."

Charles pushed his chair back from the table. "I'd like to talk to him. And Mélanie should have a look at his wound."

In the end, they all decided to visit the wounded smuggler. Andrew suggested they go through the underground passage, which would be faster than the route aboveground.

"I'm sorry, Charles." Gisèle turned to her brother by the kitchen table while Andrew was hunting for the torches. She lifted her gaze and looked him full in the face, equal parts schoolgirl confessing to a peccadillo and soldier owning up to a breach of conduct. "I'm sorry I lied to you."

"I'm sorry, too." Charles looked down at her, face serious but eyes soft. "I'm sorry you didn't feel you could tell me the truth. But I'd be an even greater idiot than I've already proved myself if I blamed you for that." He paused. "I'm glad you felt able to confide in Andrew."

Gisèle fingered the lapel of Andrew's coat. "Andrew's a good friend. He's always been kind to me."

Tommy lifted his brows at Mélanie, as though to say *I can't for the life of me make sense of what's going on between those two.* Mélanie was inclined to agree.

Equipped with torches lit at the kitchen fire, the five of them went through the concealed opening in the lodge's book room and along the passage to the main house. The library was the only room in Dunmkyel that was actually built into the original thirteenth-century keep. It jutted into what had once been the Great Hall on the keep's first floor. A side door in the library gave onto the turnpike stairs that led to the next level of the keep. Charles opened it, holding his torch aloft. They stepped into close air, heavy with the expected smell of dust and damp and inactivity. And another, unexpected smell—sickly, sweet, choking. The smell of battlefields and hospitals and scenes from her own past that Mélanie would never be able to blot out.

"What the devil—" Andrew said.

Charles shifted his torch. The light spilled over the steep granite stairs and onto a crumpled form lying at their base.

Gisèle gasped.

"Stay here, Gelly." Charles gripped her arm, but Gisèle pulled away from him and ran forward. Charles followed her. Something made Mélanie hang back, as did Tommy and Andrew. Brother and sister bent over the body.

It was Gisèle who spoke, in the same flat voice Charles used when emotions threatened to overwhelm him. "It's Father."

Chapter 30

A bizarre mosaic of images swam before Charles's eyes. A tuft of graying light brown hair. The gleam of midnight-blue superfine. The red-black sheen of blood—spilled over the floor, spattered on the steps, clinging to the remnants of hair and coat and twisted limbs.

Someone had bashed in Kenneth Fraser's skull, reducing the sardonic features to a pulpy mass. The congealing blood told its own story, but Charles dropped to his knees and reached for his father's wrist. Cold, dead flesh, no trace of a pulse. Charles got to his feet and pulled his sister away from the wreckage on the ground before them. "Yes," he said, "it looks as though it is Father. He's been dead for some time."

Gisèle's breathing sounded like cracked ice. She spun round in his hold, flung her arms round his neck, and buried her face in his cravat.

Charles stroked her hair. "We should move him. Andrew—"

Andrew touched him on the arm. "Belmont and I can see to it."

"It's all right, I'm—"

"You're not 'fine,' Fraser." Tommy brushed past him. "You

wouldn't be human if you were. Last I checked, you were still human. Barely." He bent over the body, as did Andrew.

Mélanie squeezed his shoulder. "Darling." It was all she said. It was all he could take. He managed a brief glance into her eyes. He could handle the others, but he feared Mélanie's comfort would shatter him. "Mel, can you take Gisèle—"

"I'm not a baby, Charles. Don't." Gisèle jerked out of his arms. "I have to go check on Ian."

"I'll go."

"You can come with me." Gisèle started up the stairs.

Charles ran after her. "Examine Father," he said over his shoulder to Mélanie. "See what you can learn."

He followed his sister up two flights of turnpike stairs, worn by centuries, to the old solar. The light of his torch showed the old wooden ladder still in place beneath the trapdoor that led to the top level of the tower. He caught Gisèle's hand. "Let me go first. Just in case."

She looked at him for a moment and then nodded and stepped aside. "Don't be alarmed, Ian," she called as he climbed the splintery ladder and pushed open the trap door.

"Miss Fraser, are you all right?" said an anxious voice from above. "I heard—"

The voice died as Charles climbed another rung of the ladder and lifted his torch into the close damp of the top tower chamber. A startled pair of eyes looked at him from across the room.

"You must be Ian," Charles said. "I'm Gisèle's brother Charles. We haven't met, at least not since you were a boy. It's all right, Gisèle told me what happened last night."

Some of the tension drained from the young man's face. He was probably no more than seventeen, with pale skin gone paler from shock and clear eyes that gleamed green even in the shadows. His right leg was stretched before him at an awkward angle, bound round with several lengths of lint, the lower half of his trouser leg cut away. "I'm sorry, Mr. Fraser. I told Miss Fraser she shouldn't involve herself—"

"My sister is a very strong-willed woman." Charles climbed into the room, ducking his head beneath the low ceiling. The ladder creaked as Gisèle followed.

Ian's gaze darted to her. "I thought I heard voices down below. I couldn't make out the words, but they sounded angry. Then there was some sort of crash. I thought Wheaton had come for me. Then I was worried something had happened to you. I tried to get to the stairs, but I couldn't manage with my leg."

"It wasn't Wheaton." Charles knelt beside the young man. "Someone bludgeoned my father to death at the base of the stairs."

"God in heaven." Ian's gaze went back to Gisèle. "I should have got downstairs if I had to roll all the way."

"He'd have been dead before you could have got down," Charles said. "How long ago did you hear the crash?"

"Three hours. Perhaps four. I haven't much sense of time since I've been here."

"Could you tell if the voices you heard were male or female?"

"I thought they were men. But truth to tell, I couldn't swear to it."

"Let's get you downstairs, lad. The cold won't help you heal, and my wife should look at your leg."

Between them he and Gisèle got Ian down the tower, Charles half carrying him a good part of the way. The need for action, too strenuous to leave room for thought, was a welcome tonic.

Andrew and Tommy had lain Kenneth Fraser on the sofa in the library, wrapped in Tommy's coat. Mélanie was kneeling beside the body. "I'd guess he's been dead about four hours," she said. "Judging by the marks, the weapon looks to have been a rock or something jagged rather than a cudgel. The initial blow probably knocked him out."

Charles nodded. Perhaps later, when he was capable of feeling, he'd be relieved that his father hadn't suffered. "You should look at young Ian," he said, pressing Ian into a chair.

Gisèle walked over to the sofa with deliberate steps. Andrew moved toward her, but she put out her hand to stop him. "No. It's all right." She looked down at their father. "They didn't let me see Mama after she died. I always thought it would have been easier if I had. It never seemed real somehow." She drew a breath. "This is real."

"Yes." Charles squeezed her shoulders and was surprised when she leaned into him for a moment. They stood together looking at their father's body in the room in which their mother had died.

"Do you want to wake everyone?" Andrew asked. "Or wait until morning?"

"To begin with," Charles said, "I want Glenister."

Gisèle looked up at him. "You're going to tell him about Father?"

"I'm going to show him," Charles said.

"Without warning him? Charles, that's monstrous."

"So's murder," Charles replied.

Glenister responded to Charles's knock at his bedchamber door with a quickness that suggested he hadn't been sleeping. Sick dread filled his eyes. "It isn't Evie?" he said. "Or the boys?"

"No." Charles took pity on him thus far. "It isn't anything to do with them. Come down to the library, sir. There's something I want you to see."

Glenister followed him downstairs without attempting to press him for more information. He paused on the library threshold, taking in the assembled crowd, then strode into the room and stopped short at the sight of the body on the sofa. He stared down at the man who had been his—friend? enemy? lover?—as though he could not take in the sight before him. Then he spun away. "Good God, what happened?"

"I thought perhaps you could tell us," Charles said.

"You think I had something to do with—"

"I think it's past time we discussed certain questions. Would you prefer to do it here or in private?"

Glenister held Charles's gaze for a moment. Without another word he turned on his heel and strode into the study. Charles followed.

Glenister crossed to the velvet-curtained windows, putting as much distance as possible between himself and the library. "Some-one killed him."

Charles leaned against the closed door. "That much seems obvi-ous. He was overheard arguing with someone."

Glenister's hands closed into fists. "Why the devil would I kill your father?"

"Among other things, because you admitted you'd hated him for years in this very room just hours ago."

Glenister drew in his breath as though to let lose a stream of invective. Then he sighed and regarded Charles with the look he'd used to wear when he'd stopped by the Dunmykel nursery with a box of chocolates. "For God's sake, use your head, lad. Why the devil would I admit I'd sunk so low as to try to use my own niece to get my revenge on Kenneth and then turn round and kill him?"

"Perhaps because you blamed him for Honoria's death."

Glenister's eyes turned tiger bright. "Are you telling me Kenneth killed her?"

"Do you think he did?"

"If I was sure of it, I'd have broken his neck last night. You must believe that."

Charles advanced a half-dozen paces into the room. "Who was the man in the secret passage last night?"

"I haven't the least idea."

"He was here to meet someone. I'd wager a guess that someone was Father or you."

"It's your father's house."

"In which you and Father have indulged in games for more than a quarter-century."

Glenister dropped down on the sofa, pulling his dressing gown close round him. "I thought you believed this man couldn't have killed Honoria."

"I do. But he may well have killed my father. It's time you told me the truth, sir."

"The truth about what?"

"The Elsinore League."

Glenister's fingers closed on the silk at the neck of his dressing gown. "What the hell is the Elsinore League?"

"I was hoping you could tell me. Mr. Wheaton—"

"Who?"

"Wheaton. A smuggler who ran errands for you and my father. He says you drank and whored—"

"Damn it, of course we—"

"And smuggled works of art." Charles flicked a gaze at the Gentileschi painting of Cleopatra.

"If that were true, we wouldn't be the only people in Britain to do so. Damn it, Lord Elgin was hardly aboveboard with those marbles of his."

"Aunt Frances thinks you were lovers."

"*What?*"

"It's a reasonable assumption," Charles said. "David would like to think acts of debauchery only take place between people of the opposite sex, but I'm not so naïve."

"Oh, for God's sake. I didn't even like your father."

"As Aunt Frances would say, liking has very little to do with it. And then there's Castlereagh, who thinks the Elsinore League were a spy ring begun by French revolutionaries."

"I'm not a traitor."

"That doesn't precisely answer the question."

"The question is a bit of damned impertinence I shouldn't have to listen to from my godson."

"Do you deny you were part of an organization called the Elsinore League?"

"I could deny it if I wanted, but I see no reason to do so." Glenister spread his fingers on the sofa arm. "Kenneth and I were certainly never lovers in any form of the word, and we never did anything to betray our country. The Elsinore League was a sort of club your father and I formed at Oxford."

"For what purpose?"

Glenister turned his head and let his gaze drift over a Fragonard oil depicting a young man about to unlace a young woman's bodice in a garden lush with ripening spring. "All the amusements one might expect of young men with healthy appetites."

"So you chose the name Elsinore because something was rotten at its core?"

"Let us say because it seemed to our undergraduate ears to symbolize indulgence in vice. We used to have house parties. At one or the other of my estates. Here after your father bought the property."

"I think I found the rooms Father built for the purpose. In the caves off the secret passage."

Glenister's brows lifted. "You're quicker than I thought. I suppose we should have been grateful you never stumbled across them as a boy. Though the door has a lock. Rather a good one."

"I have a set of picklocks. Rather good ones. Not all the League's members were English, were they?"

"Some of our Oxford friends were foreign born. We met others when we made the Grand Tour who became part of the Elsinore League. As might be expected, they ended up on various sides in France in the war. But neither Kenneth nor I ever did anything to betray our country."

"Were any of your fellow Elsinore League members involved in the French Revolution in any way?"

"As far as I know, lad, you're by far the most radical thinker ever to grace your father's door."

"Was your brother a member of the Elsinore League?"

"Yes. But Cyril's revolutionary sentiments were too romanticized to be taken seriously. And most of the time he knew better than to drag politics into convivial gatherings."

"Was the shooting party where he died one of the Elsinore League's gatherings?"

Glenister's face twisted. "A gathering I wish to God we'd never held."

"Who else was present for it?"

"William Cathcart. Billy Gordon. Tony Craven, I think. I'm not sure of the others."

"Aunt Frances thought two of them might be French."

Glenister stood and took a turn about the hearthrug. "Yes, all right. A couple of the members had slipped over from France on one of Wheaton's smuggling runs. It was after the war started, so they had to come under assumed names. No harm in revealing the truth now, I suppose."

"What were their names?"

"Du Bretton. They were brothers."

"Aunt Frances also remembers an Irishman with cold blue eyes."

"Christ, I haven't seen some of these men in ten years. I couldn't tell you their eye color. Arthur Donnell may have been there. He was Irish."

"You're sure there wasn't another Frenchman present called Coroux?"

Glenister jammed his hands in the pockets of his dressing gown. "Never heard the name."

Charles couldn't be certain of whether or not his godfather was telling the truth. "What about the man you and Father had smuggled out of France a fortnight ago? Who was he?"

"I don't know what you're talking about."

"Wheaton remembers receiving the orders quite clearly," Charles said, neglecting to add that Wheaton's account of the events had not included Glenister.

Glenister wandered over to the card table and absently turned over one of the cards. "I had nothing to do with smuggling anyone out of Paris. I don't know about your father, though I can't imagine why he would have done so."

Which meant that Glenister wasn't going to fall for the bluff. Or, just possibly, that he was telling the truth. "Do you think it's possible any of the members of the Elsinore League could be Le Faucon de Maulévrier?"

"Le who? You mean that butcher from the Revolution? My God, if that's the sort of thing Castlereagh's going about saying, he has less wit than I credited."

"You admit some of your friends ended up on the opposite side during the war. You can't know what they were all up to during the Terror."

"The era of the Revolution was our salad days when we were in closest contact."

"But you can't rule out one of your friends being Le Faucon for a certainty?"

"There's very little in life that I can rule out for a certainty. I thought you were the one who was supposed to be getting to the truth of the matter."

"I'm endeavoring to do so. What were you and my father afraid of Honoria discovering?"

Glenister stiffened. "There's no reason Honoria should have learned of any of this. Gently bred girls—young women don't concern themselves with such matters."

"One of the things we seem to have established today is that Honoria didn't play by the rules. She was asking questions about you and Father and possibly about the Elsinore League. She thought the whole thing had something to do with her father's death."

Glenister stared down at the card clutched between his fingers. "Cyril's death was a tragic accident. An accident for which I blame myself, but only because as his elder brother I should have looked out for him. As an elder brother yourself, I'd expect you to understand."

Charles saw the accusation in Gisèle's eyes in the lodge kitchen and the horror beyond her years when she'd looked down at their father's body. "I understand that. It doesn't explain what you were afraid of Honoria learning."

"Honoria liked to pry into things. Sometimes I think she imagined things that weren't there. Precisely as you're doing now."

"How can you be sure I'm imagining things if you're not aware of the full story yourself?"

The muscles in Glenister's neck tensed. He dropped the card as though it burned him. "That's enough, Charles. I'm going to bury Honoria tomorrow beside my brother. And then I'm taking Evie and my disgraceful elder son and my even more disgraceful younger son and going back to London."

Charles stepped between Glenister and the door. "Last night you wanted to know who killed Honoria. You don't care anymore?"

"Of course I want to know. But not—"

"Yes, sir?" Charles said into the silence.

"It's been twenty-four hours since Honoria's death, you've learned nothing, and someone else has been murdered."

"I've learned a great deal. Just not who killed Honoria."

"Nor will you, if you waste your time asking impertinent questions." Glenister stepped past Charles.

Charles grasped his wrist. "Do you really think David and his father will let the question of who killed Honoria drop? Do you think I'll let my father's killer go unpunished?"

Glenister pulled away from Charles's grip. "Such a display of filial devotion. Kenneth would be impressed. Especially since he wasn't even—"

"Remotely fond of me," Charles finished for him.

Glensiter stared at Charles for a long moment. "Quite."

But they both knew that that wasn't what he had been about to say.

As most of the house party knew of Kenneth Fraser's death, Charles decided it would be better to wake the others—Lady Frances,

David, Simon, Evie, Val, and Quen—and tell them as well. Once again they gathered in the Gold Saloon, supplied with plentiful coffee. Mélanie presided over the coffee urn, still dressed in her breeches and grubby coat, uncombed hair spilling over her shoulders, a bruise beginning to show on her jawline. She managed to look as in command of the scene as if she wore muslin and pearls and white gloves.

The company greeted the news of Kenneth Fraser's death with the numb horror of those who have been half prepared for some other calamity to befall and are only rather surprised that this is the form it took.

"But—" Evie stared round the room as if her brain had ceased to function. "Did the same person who killed Honoria kill Mr. Fraser?"

"Not necessarily," Charles said. He was standing in front of the fireplace, where he had stood with his father and Glenister and David less than twenty-four hours before.

David stared into his coffee cup as if he wasn't sure what it held. "Surely it's stretching coincidence for the two murders to be unrelated."

"Probably," Charles agreed. "But that doesn't mean the same person killed both of them."

Lady Frances fingered a fold of her dressing gown. Her eyes were like glass. "The bastard. The bloody, careless, inconsiderate bastard. He was always miserable at good-byes." She dashed a hand across her eyes. She was, Charles realized, the first of them, including himself and Gisèle, to express any grief over Kenneth Fraser's death.

Quen leaned forward, chin resting on his clasped hands. "So what happens now?"

"Honoria's funeral will take place in the morning as planned." Glenister spoke before Charles could do so. He was standing by the windows, as far from Charles as the width of the room allowed. "Then you and I and Val and Evie will return to London."

"*What?*" David sprang to his feet. "We had an agreement, sir. No one leaves until we know who killed Honoria."

"This changes things. There may be danger."

"You're turning tail and running because you're afraid?"

"Of course not. But I've already lost one niece. I have to think of Evelyn—"

"Evie can return to London with her maid if you wish. But so help me, sir, if you leave with this matter unresolved—"

"You'll what?" Glenister surveyed the younger man, gaze cold with contempt.

"I'll refer the entire matter to Bow Street."

"You wouldn't dare."

"Try me."

"I think your father will have something to say about that."

"My father will want to know who killed Honoria. And why his co-guardian didn't stay to face the consequences."

"Your father won't want his niece's name dragged through the mud any more than I do. We've already risked—" Glenister let his gaze rest on Val for a brief, angry moment. "I'll call on your father as soon as we return to town."

"No."

The word, spoken with quiet emphasis, came not from David but from Quen. He, too, was on his feet, staring at his father.

Glenister's gaze rotated slowly in his eldest son's direction. "No, what?"

"I can't stop you from leaving, sir, but I have no intention of doing so myself until we learn what happened to Honoria. And to Mr. Fraser."

"Quentin—"

"I'm not leaving."

"Nor am I." Evie went to stand beside Quen.

"Nor I." Val got to his feet as well. He seemed rather surprised at himself for having spoken.

"Right." Quen reached for Evie's hand and cast a brief glance at his brother. "We're all staying. Assuming Charles will have us. It's his house now."

The words brought Charles up short. In the midst of everything else, he hadn't yet considered this. "Lord Glenister knows that I'd prefer to have everyone stay."

Evie went to uncle and took his arm. "I know you're worried after losing Honoria, Uncle Frederick, but surely the least we owe to her memory is to find out what happened. Think how shocked I'd feel if you made me the excuse for running off to London."

Evie Mortimer knew how to handle her uncle. She'd neatly undercut the one creditable argument he could make for leaving. Run now and he looked like a coward. Or a guilty man.

Lady Frances pressed her hands over her lap. "I suppose you want to know where we all were last night."

"It's possible Father was killed by someone from outside the house, but yes, I do."

Not surprisingly, they'd all been alone in their rooms. That much established, the company scattered to dress for the day. Mélanie walked over to Charles, put out her hand, and then dropped it to her side without touching him. "David's going to have more questions."

Charles nodded. "I think it's time for another council, one that includes Gisèle and Tommy. You talk to them. I want to go through Father's papers before anyone has a chance to tamper with them."

"Charles—"

He summoned up the best approximation of a reassuring smile he could muster. "I'll take Andrew with me. He'll make sure I don't have a nervous collapse. And he knows the accounts better than anyone."

She scanned his face for a moment with a gaze like a lancet. Then she nodded and went to gather up the others.

He and Andrew walked to the study in silence. Charles struck a spark to the Chinese porcelain lamp on the desk and turned it up so the light fell over the tortoiseshell marquetry and gilded green leather of the desktop. His father's desk. His father who was lying wrapped in a coat on the library sofa, who would never again flay him with his tongue or cut him with a cold stare or slice the ground from beneath his feet with the lift of his eyebrow. Or answer any of his questions.

Charles pressed his shaking hands down on the desktop and turned to look at Andrew. There was at least one dilemma revealed tonight that he could sort out. "Andrew. What Quen said—it's true. Father never got round to changing the entail, so Dunmykel's mine."

"Yes, of course, as it should be."

"And more important, I'm Gisèle's guardian."

Andrew tugged open a desk drawer and took out a stack of papers. "That's good. She needs you. She has for a long while."

"Yes. And while I don't know her as well as I should, a few things were painfully obvious tonight. My sister is head over heels in love with you. And though you seem to have managed to convince her that you don't return the sentiment, you can't deceive your oldest friend. I can't imagine a man I'd rather have as a brother-in-law."

Andrew listened to his words with a face that was as closed and set as the fifteenth-century marble bust in the corner. Then he slammed his hand down on the desk, spattering ink from the ink pot and knocking the penknife onto the floor. "Jesus. You really don't know, do you?"

"Know what?" Charles bent down to retrieve the penknife.

"There's no reason you should, I suppose. I didn't myself until—" Andrew strode across the room, gaze moving over the paneling, the curtains, the Gentileschi Cleopatra, the Fragonard oil, anywhere but Charles's face. "Gelly—Gisèle—visited Dunmkyel with Lady Frances last Christmas. She was very concerned about how the tenants had been faring since the Clearances. She put Christmas baskets together and she wanted to go with me to deliver them in person. At first I didn't think much of it, she always used to follow us about when she was a child and she was always kindhearted, when she wasn't—"

"Being a pest. It's all right, I can say it. She's my little sister."

Andrew swallowed. "Yes. Then I started to notice that she wasn't just being Lady Bountiful with the tenants, she was asking some very keen questions. She'd come to see me in my office and we'd end up talking for hours and I realized—"

"That she's not a child anymore."

"No, she isn't." Andrew stood by the fireplace, shoulders hunched as though he were struggling against the force of some burden that was too great to bear. "You told me once—one of those nights when you were home from Oxford and we sat up drinking my father's whisky—that you didn't believe you were capable of falling in love. I thought that was a bit bleak. I never doubted I could feel it. I'd seen it. My—parents—loved each other. But I'd never felt it for myself, until—" He shook his head, his eyes dark with unvoiced longing. "It's a funny thing when it finally happens. And when you know you shouldn't—I tried to pretend it wasn't happening. I tried to think of her as my employer's daughter, my friend's little sister." He stared into the cold grate. "I'm older than she is. More than ten years. I should have been stronger."

Andrew had always had scruples, but Charles was surprised at the torment in his friend's voice. "Andrew, if this has something to do with your guilt over Donald Fyfe's death—"

"That's the least of it. Let me finish." Andrew's voice had the bleak scrape of an iron shackle. "One night Gelly and Lady Frances dined with my mother and me. It started to snow during dinner and Gelly wanted to see it. We took a walk. She was wearing a white wool cloak and snowflakes caught in her hair." He drew a breath as though about to confess to a mortal sin. "I kissed her. My mother caught sight of us from the sitting room windows. After Gelly and Lady Frances had gone home, she told me—she explained why it had to end at once."

"Whatever she might have feared Father would say—"

"It isn't that. Or not for the reasons you think." Andrew moved to the window and stared at the sliver of night-black glass between the curtains. "Didn't you ever wonder that Maddie and I look so completely unalike? We always used to be embarrassed because people would take us for sweethearts rather than brother and sister. She's my twin and yet we don't even look like siblings."

"A lot of siblings don't."

"But you can see Mother and Father in Maddie. Mother's mouth and eyes, Father's nose and hair. They're knit into the fabric of who she is. Now you can see it in her children as well. I look like I belong to another family. Which makes sense now. Mother wasn't pregnant with twins, Charles. She didn't give birth to twins. She went away to have Maddie. To stay with her parents, the story was. But the truth is she was paid to leave Dunmkyel and have the baby in secret. And to bring back two babies and claim they were both hers."

"Who?" Charles said, though the answer hung between them, poisoning the air. "Who paid her?"

"Can't you guess? The same person who gave her the second baby and paid her to raise it as her own. Your father. Gisèle's father." Andrew turned and looked Charles full in the face. "My father, brother."

Chapter 37

Charles stared across his father's study at his oldest friend. "Knowing Father, I don't know why I'm remotely surprised."

"That's all you have to say? Jesus, Charles, I almost—with your sister. Our sister." Andrew pressed his hand over his eyes.

Charles moved round the desk, watching the man who, like Quen, might be Kenneth Fraser's son. "Andrew, there's something you should know. Actually, I'd have thought you already did know it, given the gossip."

"Charles, nothing can—"

"Hear me out. From my earliest memories, my parents could barely be in the same room without baring their teeth. Gisèle was born twelve years into the marriage. Mother and Father had stopped sharing a bed long since. None of us knows exactly who Gisèle's father is, but it's almost certainly not Kenneth Fraser."

Andrew lifted his head to look at Charles. Hope leaped in his eyes, then was ruthlessly quenched. "Almost," he echoed. "You can't know for a certainty."

"I'm as certain as I can be." Charles leaned against the desk. "Certain enough to have no qualms about you and my sister."

"And if the truth got out?" Andrew strode back to the fireplace. "Even if you're right, the world assumes Kenneth Fraser is Gisèle's father. If Gelly and I married"—his voice caught for a moment, like rope frayed raw—"and then there was gossip about Kenneth Fraser being my father as well, what would that do to Gelly? What would it do to any children we might have?"

"There's no reason the world should ever know Kenneth Fraser fathered you. It's remained secret for thirty-odd years."

"It's remained secret because I've been out of the way of the world. If I married the Duke of Rannoch's granddaughter, people would pay attention. Secrets have a way of working their way to the surface at inopportune moments. The past twenty-four hours have proved that."

"Gossip can't destroy a marriage. Not if two people—"

"Really love each other?" Andrew's shoulders shook with bitter laughter. "Christ, Charles, this ought to be funny. You arguing for the power of love to overcome all obstacles."

"It depends on the people involved. You've been steadfast in your loyalties for as long as I've known you, and Gelly showed tonight that she's a lot more mature than I believed her to be. Don't you think she should have a say in this?"

"Brilliant, Charles. How exactly would you suggest I explain it?"

"So you haven't told her any of this?"

"You think I'd tell her that the man she fancies herself head over ears in love with may be her own brother?"

"So instead you told her it couldn't go any further between the two of you and didn't offer an explanation."

Andrew's jaw clenched. "More or less."

"Which has her thinking that you love someone else or that she's in some way inadequate. It can be particularly painful to be nineteen, Andrew. Even imagined slights hurt like salt on a wound."

"Do you think I haven't wanted to write to her these past months?" The words seemed to be ripped from Andrew's throat. "Haven't picked up the pen and written only to toss the letters on the fire? Haven't tormented myself with imagining what might have been? My God, you don't know how sickeningly happy I was when she arrived at Dunmykel just now. I had to do something—any-thing—to push her away. Even letting her think I cared for Miss

Talbot. Because when I'm with her a part of me doesn't care that
there's no hope for us. A part of me wants her anyway. Even believing she's my sister."

"And now I'm telling you she's not your sister."

"Think, Charles. Even if it weren't for my parentage, what do I
have to offer Gisèle? I'm an Edinburgh lawyer turned estate manager. Not to mention a former smuggler. She's an heiress, a duke's
granddaughter. She could—"

"Oh, for God's sake, don't go all lending-library novel about the
disparity of fortune bit. Gelly's got enough money for both of you."

"And you don't think people would comment on that?"

"Is that what you're letting stand in the way of my sister's and
your happiness? That people would call you a fortune hunter? I
thought you were tougher than that."

"Are you so sure marrying me would make her happy?"

"Gelly demonstrated that fairly convincingly this evening."

"I'm not talking about tonight, I'm talking about five years from
now. Ten years from now. She's nineteen, Charles. I'm almost two-
and-thirty. Her family was smashed to bits when she was eight years
old. It hurt her more than anyone realizes when your mother died
and then when—"

"I left."

"Yes." Andrew looked him full in the face. "I understand why
you did, but Gelly doesn't. She's got used to people leaving her.
Sometimes I think she's grabbing onto me like a spar in a shipwreck.
How long would it be before she realized what she'd thought was
love was really infatuation, before she decided she wanted someone
closer to her age, someone who moved in the same world, someone
who could let her be a grand London hostess—"

"Someone like Val Talbot?"

Andrew grimaced. "Someone of good character who could offer
her all those things. Jesus, what kind of a man would I be if I married her knowing I can't give her what she deserves?"

Mélanie's face the day he'd asked her to be his wife flickered
before Charles's gaze. He had spelled out precisely what he was
offering her—protection, his name, care for her child. A cold substi-
tute for what she deserved. "You don't know you can't give her what
she deserves, Andrew. You can't know it."

"What the hell do I have to offer her?"

Charles recalled the way Andrew had looked up at Gisèle when he recovered consciousness in the cottage, his gaze stripped naked with vulnerability. "Yourself."

Andrew gave a mirthless laugh.

"Don't scoff. It's a damnably difficult gift to give."

"Damn it, if you're such an expert on marriage—"

"What?"

"Look, Charles. I know you just found your father's body smashed to pieces. I know this must be hell for you. But I saw how much it hurt Mélanie in the tower just now when you could scarcely even look at her."

Only someone who knew him so well could strike so effective a blow. Charles swallowed, tasting the emptiness inside himself. "I said giving yourself was a great gift. I never claimed to be much of a success at gift-giving myself." He scraped a hand through his hair. "I hate to see you and Gelly unhappy."

Andrew shook his head. "Same old Charles. You still haven't learned that you can't fix things for everyone." He strode back to the desk. "Let's look at your father's papers."

"Our father's."

"He never—" Andrew cast a glance round Kenneth Fraser's study. The paintings Kenneth had collected hung on the walls, the bronzes and marbles stood on the desk and tables, the smell of the snuff Kenneth had blended in London lingered in the air. "I can't think of him that way. I had a father."

"A far better one." Charles moved back round the desk.

Andrew stared down at the blotter. "I told you Father never confronted me about the smuggling. But not long after he lied to the excisemen for me, I overheard him say to Mother that he'd always worried blood would tell. I didn't understand it. Not then."

"I saw him with you, Andrew. He loved you. The way a parent should love a child."

"I think he did, though God knows I didn't give him a lot of reason to in the last years of his life. The devil of it is, I'll never be able to ask him about any of it now." Andrew opened a ledger. "What do you want to look at first?"

Charles stared down at the columns of figures in the ledger. Routine estate expenses, but the dates made him realize something about Andrew's story. "Father didn't own Dunmykel yet when you were born."

"No, it still belonged to his godfather." Andrew ran his finger down the page. "But he must have been familiar enough with the estate to realize my parents would be good people to take charge of his by-blow."

"He hadn't yet come into his legacy from his uncle in Jamaica, either. He was a London barrister without much to his name in the way of fortune."

Andrew flipped the page. "Frankly, I'm surprised he went to the trouble of providing for me."

"So am I. Father wasn't one to take his responsibilities seriously in my experience. Not at any expense to himself." Charles stared at an entry for replastering the Gold Saloon. "Do you know who your mother was?"

"No. I didn't even ask at first. I know who my parents are. Whom I'll always think of as my parents. But I did finally ask Mother who was—who'd given birth to me. She didn't know. Mr. Fraser brought me to her when I was a week old."

"If your mother—the lady who gave birth to you—had been a country girl or a maidservant, one would think Father would have simply paid her money to raise you herself. The fact that he found surrogate parents for you, under such secrecy—it sounds as though your mother was a lady of fashion. Who lacked a husband or wasn't in a position to pass you off as her husband's child."

Andrew stared down at the ledger, gaze fixed and glassy. "Does it matter now? We're supposed to be investigating Miss Talbot's death. And Mr. Fraser's."

"Precisely."

"You think this has something to do with it?"

"I think anything to do with the secrets my father kept may have something to do with why he died. The question is which pieces are important. And how. Let's have a look at Father's dispatch box."

· · ·

At David's suggestion, Mélanie gathered the oddly assorted band together in his bedchamber. She glanced round the circle of people clustered within the green-trellis-papered walls. Gisèle sitting on a jade satin settee, pleating the fabric of her skirt between her fingers. Tommy lounging on one of the shield-backed chairs, David sitting bolt upright on the other. Simon leaning against the wall by the window. Charles's sister, Charles's friends, Charles's colleague. It was, she realized, the first time she'd presided over such a gathering without her husband present. Yet they were all looking at her with that air of expectancy with which they looked at Charles. The barricades between her and her husband might be stronger than ever, but she seemed to have crossed over a line with the other people in his life. That was something. At least it should be.

Everyone present knew bits and pieces of the evidence uncovered in the past four-and-twenty hours. It took a little time to fill them in on the parts they didn't know, but they were patient and refrained from unnecessary questions. Though the latter might have been due to shock as much as tact.

"You lot don't do anything by halves, do you?" Tommy said when she finished speaking. "I know every family has its secrets, but—" He shook his head "It occurs to me that I may have been unfair to Charles. In this household, he's lucky to have grown up sane. Though come to think of it, I've accused him of insanity on more than one occasion."

"Our family's attitude toward scandal is a bit like Vanbrugh's ideas about architecture," Gisèle said. "Nothing's so perfect it can't be improved upon by excess." Her bright, brittle voice was an echo of the tone Charles had used in the Gold Saloon. "And it looks as though that applies to the Talbots as well. Unless we're all so tangled at this point that we count as one family. How odd that we never knew Quen is Father's son."

Tommy gave her one of his rare smiles that was kind rather than mocking or flirtatious. "Surprised you have another brother?"

"Not really." Gisèle twisted the grimy green ribbon at the waist of her gown. "I mean, I don't really have another brother. Everyone knows Father isn't—wasn't—really my father. You see what I mean, Mr. Belmont? We're straight out of a Greek tragedy, except not nearly so mythic and profound."

"More of a Jacobean drama," Simon murmured.

David was staring across the room at Tommy. "Just exactly why did you ask Honoria to meet you yesterday?"

Tommy crossed his legs. "I told you, I wanted to make sure she was happy."

"Why would the happiness of a girl you'd met briefly in Lisbon six years ago seem important enough to risk jeopardizing this secret mission of yours?"

Tommy returned the fire in David's gaze with the steadiness of a seasoned campaigner. "A gentleman doesn't talk, but I think in this case the facts speak for themselves. I don't blame you if you want to call me to account, but might I suggest you wait until Miss Talbot's and Mr. Fraser's murders are resolved? We really can't afford to have anyone else get killed just now."

David sprang to his feet. "By God, Belmont—"

"Oh, for God's sake, David." Gisèle snapped a length of the green ribbon off in her fingers. "If you're going to defend Honoria's honor, you'll have to resign your seat in Parliament, because confronting Honoria's lovers will be full-time employment." She glanced round the circle of faces. "Mélanie put it as delicately as she could, but I can add the pieces together. It's obvious how far Honoria and Val's games went." She looked at David. "If you want to thrash Val when this is over, I won't have any objection. In fact, I'll help." She turned to Mélanie. "Does Charles think the man who shot at him in the secret passage is the same man who killed Father?"

"He thinks it's possible," Mélanie said. "The man was here to meet someone last night, perhaps Mr. Fraser. He could have come back to see him tonight."

"But why would he kill him?" Gisèle looked at Tommy. "Could the intruder be this Faucon de Maul-whatever-it-is?"

Tommy rolled his eyes at the public nature of his once-secret mission. "Perhaps. It sounds as though he's the man Wheaton brought over from France and Giles McGann escorted up the coast."

Simon crossed to the cabinet in the corner. "It sounds as though Le Faucon de Maulévrier—or whoever the man was who Wheaton ferried over to Britain and McGann brought up the coast—was blackmailing Kenneth Fraser to see to his safety." He opened the satinwood doors of the cabinet and retrieved a bottle of whisky. "There's that bit Wheaton remembers about old debts coming in handy and what Miss Fraser overheard her father and Glenister say about 'the members' helping them tidy up a mess of some sort. But if this man was blackmailing Kenneth Fraser, it's hard to see why he'd kill him."

"Perhaps he doesn't need Father anymore now that he's out of France," Gisèle said. "If Father was the one person in Britain who knew who he really was, he'd be a liability."

"And Honoria?" David said. "Where does she fit in?"

Gisèle leaned forward, elbows on her knees. "If she was poking into the past, and she stumbled on something concerning Le Faucon and whatever nasty thing the Elsinore League swept under the carpet years ago—"

"She was killed by someone in the house," David pointed out.

Gisèle blinked. "The only people in the house who would have been afraid of her investigating the Elsinore League are Father and Lord Glenister, and Father couldn't have killed her, so . . ."

"We don't know that she was killed because of the Elsinore League," Simon said. He was pouring the whisky into a variety of drinking vessels—glasses, mugs, a coffee cup he'd brought up from the Gold Saloon.

"But we know Soro claimed they'd killed at least once and we know Honoria was poking her nose into their business," Tommy said. His voice had its habitual drawl, but his hands were balled into fists.

Mélanie felt herself softening inside as though she were looking at her son rather than her husband's former colleague and frequent rival. "Whyever she was killed, it wasn't because of anything you told her when you met her in the churchyard, Tommy. You said yourself you kept talking at cross-purposes."

"If I'd got her to explain why she was suddenly so interested in the past—" Tommy shook his head.

Mélanie accepted a glass of whisky from Simon. "She wanted to know about her father. We keep coming back to him and the Elsinore League."

Gisèle scowled into her whisky. "What is the effect Honoria has on men? I know she is—was—pretty, but that's not enough to explain how she could make all men besotted with her. Even Charles—" She glanced at Mélanie and drew a breath. "I mean—"

"It's all right." Mélanie took a sip of whisky to cover the fact that it wasn't all right at all. Beneath the smoky taste, something lingered on her tongue, like an afterthought.

"She didn't actually mention her father's death when we met," Tommy said, "even though we were standing in the churchyard right beside his grave."

"Yes, but—" The afterthought clicked into place in Mélanie's head. "Don't drink."

"What is it?" Gisèle said

Mélanie set the glass down. "Laudanum."

Chapter 32

W hat is it?" Andrew said as Charles lifted a worn brown
leather volume from Kenneth Fraser's dispatch box.

"It seems to be a ledger." Charles set the volume on the desk and
opened the front cover. "Recording payments of some sort." He
scanned the dates, entered in a bold script that was clearly his
father's. Like a blow to the gut, it hit him again that the man with
that decisive hand was gone. Dead. Reduced to a wreckage of blood
and bone.

"April of 1780 to—" Charles flipped through the entries. The
writing stopped well before the last page of the ledger. "October
1785."

Andrew leaned down to read the entries. "A thousand
pounds. Two thousand pounds. A thousand again. Three thousand. Good God, there's a small fortune here, even by your
father's standards."

Charles turned the pages of the ledger again, more slowly. A few
a year, but not at regular intervals. All varied between one and three
thousand pounds. Except for the last.

"What the devil was Kenneth Fraser paying twenty-five thousand pounds for?" Andrew said.

"He may not have been paying it out. He may have been taking it in. These dates are before he came into his inheritance. Before he bought Dunmykel."

Andrew frowned down at the ledger. "Your father always insisted I record the details of any transactions. He was meticulous about it, for all he was often an absentee landlord. Yet there's nothing here to indicate what these amounts mean, not even if they're incoming or outgoing. He must have thought whatever it was too dangerous or damaging to record."

Charles nodded. "And he kept the ledger locked away, which implies—"

His words were drowned out by the creak of the door being thrown open. "Charles." Mélanie hurried into the room. "Someone put laudanum in David's whisky."

"*David's?*"

"I know, it doesn't make any sense, but there's no doubt. I tasted it. Though I might have missed it if we hadn't tasted the laudanum in Miss Talbot's brandy so recently."

"My God," Andrew said, "is some lunatic drugging all the drinks in the house?"

"We checked," Mélanie said. "We checked all the whisky, brandy, sherry, water, anything liquid any of us had in our rooms. David's is the only one that's been doctored. And before you ask, David says the last time he had a drink from the bottle was the night before last. Before Miss Talbot was killed."

"Where are the others?" Charles asked.

"In the old drawing room. I didn't think there was enough room for all of us in here."

"Right. Andrew, bring the dispatch box."

Gray predawn light leached round the white-painted shutters in the old drawing room. The candle sconces by the fireplace and the lamp on the rosewood table created islands of warmth in the cool shadows of the room. Tommy and Gisèle sat on one of the cream silk sofas. David was pacing up and down at the far end of the room. Simon stood beside the pianoforte, staring at a musical score as though it held answers to why someone might be making an attempt on his lover's life.

"I don't understand," Gisèle was saying when Charles opened the door. "Why on earth would anyone want to kill David? I mean, he's—"

"Completely irrelevant." David halted his pacing. "At least as far as everything we've learned about Honoria's death and the Elsinore League."

"Except that you're standing in for one of Honoria's guardians." Charles closed the door and moved into the room.

"We are assuming the same person who drugged and strangled Honoria drugged David's whisky, aren't we?" Gisèle said.

Charles pulled one of the canvaswork chairs away from the rosewood table and held it out for Mélanie. "We can't be sure of anything, but I'd say the odds are extraordinarily high that the same person drugged Honoria's brandy and David's whisky. On the other hand, it's not at all clear that the person who drugged Honoria is the same person who strangled her."

"Oh, for God's sake, Fraser," Tommy said. "How many villains do you think are running about this estate?"

"An obscenely high number by any count."

"But why would someone have drugged Honoria if it wasn't part of the murder?" Gisèle asked.

"I don't know." Charles dropped into a chair beside Mélanie and then wondered if it had been a good idea. If he stopped moving for too long, he feared he might not be able to get started again. "I still can't work out how the killer could have planned the murder without having known Honoria would be alone in Father's bedchamber. Or else having known Father's bedchamber would be empty so the killer could move her there after she was dead."

Mélanie rested her arm on the table and leaned her chin on her hand. The bruise on her jaw had turned a dark purple. "I can't figure out how the killer could have counted on Miss Talbot or David drinking the brandy or whisky on any given night. I suppose Miss Talbot might have always been in the habit of taking a drink at bedtime, but we know David isn't. The whole thing seems incredibly chancy."

"Not to mention that David might have shared the whisky with—oh goodness." Gisèle sat up very straight. "Could the killer really have been trying to drug *Simon*?"

Charles cast a quick glance at his sister. "Clever girl, Gelly." He turned to David. "If you'd had a glass of whisky, the odds are Simon would have as well, aren't they?"

"Yes." David's gaze moved to Simon, dark with concern.

"Whichever one of you was the target, the killer would have wanted to drug you both," Mélanie said. "To ensure that you both slept through the attack."

Simon flipped the musical score closed. The flutter of the pages echoed in the still room. "I can think of several actors and at least one manager who would quite like to see me dead. But none of them happen to be at Dunmykel."

Tommy lifted his gaze from a contemplation of the scrolls in the carpet. "You're French, aren't you?"

"My mother was French. I spent the first ten years of my life in Paris. How did you know?"

"Your voice. One gets used to reading accents in my line of work." Tommy scanned Simon's face. "You look to be about my age. You must have been born just before the Revolution."

"My father went abroad to study painting and married an artist's model. My mother."

Tommy leaned back on the sofa and crossed his legs at the ankles. "Could your father have had anything to do with the Elsinore League and Le Faucon?"

"Good God, no. My father certainly wouldn't have been in Glenister and Kenneth Fraser's set. As for the Le Faucon—my father was a painter with mildly revolutionary views, but he never went much beyond speaking his mind in cafés. He's the last man to be involved in something like—" Simon drew in his breath and looked across the room at Charles. "I suppose you'd have said the same about your father and Lord Glenister a fortnight ago."

"But even if Simon's father had been involved with the league, why attack Simon?" David said. "How could Simon pose a threat now?"

"Perhaps because of something from his childhood." Mélanie

looked at Simon. "Something the murderer's afraid you'll re-member."

Simon aligned the edges of a loose sheaf of music on the piano. "Are you asking if one of the men I handed cups of coffee to in my parents' salon or met walking with my mother in the Bois de Boulogne or having ices with my father in the boulevards could have been Le Faucon de Maulévrier? As I said, I suppose any-thing's possible. But I don't see how the devil I could work it out now. And no, I don't remember anyone in particular with cold blue eyes."

Gisèle scowled at the torn flounce on her skirt. "Besides, we still aren't sure that Honoria's death had anything to do with this falcon person. If the man who attacked Charles is Le Faucon and he killed Father tonight, then someone else killed Honoria."

Charles rubbed his hand over his eyes. His gaze seemed to have stopped focusing properly several hours before. Perhaps with his first glimpse of his father's body. "A lot of ifs," he said. "But yes."

David strode forward and rested his hands on the sofa table. "What now? The one thing that seems clear is that the killer may be planning further mischief."

"At least there's not much chance of either of us sleeping through anything now," Simon said.

David glanced at him over his shoulder. "That's not exactly enough to reassure me."

"We'll take it in turns to watch the upstairs corridors outside the bedrooms tonight," Charles said. "In teams of two."

"It shouldn't take two," Tommy said, "it's not much of a—oh, I see. Insurance in case one of us is the killer."

"We can't afford to overlook the possibility."

Uneasy silence filled the room, like the gathering light that seeped round the shutters and pooled on the oak floorboards.

"We ought to go dress," Gisèle said in a voice that echoed off the carved ceiling.

David stared at her as though to ask how she could think about clothes at a time like this.

Gisèle got to her feet. For a moment, in the half-light, she might have been Lady Frances. "It's only a few hours until Honoria's funeral."

Mélanie didn't go upstairs with the others. She could change from her breeches and coat to suitable mourning attire in ten minutes if necessary. Through the years she'd mastered a number of tricks for making a quick toilette. Instead she accompanied Charles and Andrew back to the study. Though she knew there was little she could do to comfort her husband, she felt better when she could keep an eye on him.

She surveyed the two men as they followed her into the study. Charles's face seemed to have been scoured to nothing but sharp bones and gray hollows. When she inadvertently brushed against his hand, his skin felt like ice, as though he had shut down inside and encased himself in numbness. Yet she had the sense that if she tried to break through the frozen fortifications, it would be like putting a match to gunpowder.

Andrew looked as though he was locked in some internal battle he was determined to win. He'd scarcely spoken during the scene in the old drawing room, and though he'd smiled at Gisèle when she left the room he hadn't attempted to go near her. Now he crossed the study, set the dispatch box back on the desk, and stood to one side.

"We found a ledger," Charles told her, lifting a worn brown volume out of the box. "Records of large sums of money, but nothing to indicate what they're for or if they're incoming or outgoing, so— wait a bit." He ran his fingers along the inside cover of the ledger. "Hand me the penknife, will you, Andrew?"

Charles took the ivory-handled knife and cut away the inside binding of the ledger. A corner of something paler showed against the dark binding. He peeled the binding back to reveal a slim sheaf of papers.

"Good Lord," Andrew said.

"It seems I had a few more things in common with Kenneth Fraser than I'd like to admit." Charles laid the papers out in the light of the lamp. Mélanie and Andrew stood on either side of him.

Spread before them were a series of notes written on heavy cream laid paper stamped with a crest.

April, 1780
Fraser,
As agreed.
G.

June, 1781
Fraser,
This settles matters between us.
G.

October 1782
Fraser,
Pursuant to the matter discussed.
G.

February 1784
Fraser,
Once again, in regard to our last meeting.
G.

"G?" Andrew said. "Glenister? That's his crest, isn't it?"

"That's the Marquis of Glenister's crest, yes," Charles said.

Mélanie flipped through the yellowed pages of the ledger. "The dates on the notes all correspond to entries in the ledger."

"So Glenister was giving Mr. Fraser money?" Andrew said.

"Not the current Lord Glenister." Charles ran his finger down the ledger entries. "Look at the dates. Frederick Talbot didn't become marquis until 1796. These notes are from his father."

Andrew turned a bewildered gaze from the ledger to Charles. "Why the devil would Glenister's father have been giving money to Mr. Fraser? Did they even know each other well?"

"Father and Glenister became friends at Harrow. Father wasn't much given to telling me tales of his boyhood, but presumably he spent some of his school holidays with Glenister's family. I do know that as an orphan he was constantly being shuffled about among relatives. Visits to a titled family must have been appealing." Charles stared down at the notes as though trying to absorb hidden clues from the brief wording. "I can think of two explanations that would account for the secrecy and the wording of the notes. Father was an intelligent young man with no fortune of his own at this time. Either old Lord Glenister had some secretive and probably underhanded business that needed to be attended to and he engaged Father to handle it for him. Or Father was blackmailing him."

"Or both," Mélanie said. "If Mr. Fraser undertook some underhanded business for old Lord Glenister, that could have provided Mr. Fraser with the means to blackmail him."

"But even if Cyril Talbot was working with Le Faucon or was Le Faucon himself, the dates are too early for this to have anything to do with that." Charles flipped to the last entry in the ledger. "All the entries are about the same amount. Then there's this one for twenty-five thousand pounds. In October of 1785. It was in late 1785 that Father received the legacy from his uncle in Jamaica."

"And the legacy was twenty-five thousand pounds?" Mélanie said.

"Near enough."

Andrew's eyes widened. "But—surely this uncle in Jamaica wasn't a fiction?"

"No, but 'uncle' was a courtesy title. He was a second cousin of Father's mother. Packed off to Jamaica in disgrace forty-some years before and estranged from the family. I always thought it odd that the man chose to leave a second cousin he'd never met such a large legacy."

"If he'd been in Jamaica for forty years and was estranged from his family here, there'd be no one to question where the money had really come from," Mélanie said.

"Convenient, isn't it? The other thing I've always thought odd is that Father didn't come into the money until two years after his cousin died. I think there was some story about a misplaced will resulting in a delay of the legacy." Charles looked down at the final entry in the ledger. "Without this money, Father could never have bought Dunmykel and stood for Parliament. Without Dunmykel and his parliamentary career, Mother would never have looked twice at him." His gaze moved from the Laurano marble and the Fragonard oil to the oak paneling and leaded glass windows of the house itself. His father's legacy that was now his, even though in the end that wasn't what Kenneth Fraser had wanted. "So the question," Charles said, in a voice as falsely bright as the gilt paint on scenery at the Tavistock, "is what unsavory act did Father commit in exchange for this money? And what does it have to do with why he was killed."

Chapter 33

Honoria Talbot was laid to rest beneath a sky as gray as the salt-scarred granite of the tombstones in Dunmykel's churchyard. A light drizzle began to fall midway through the service. Mélanie tugged at the silk-lined brim of the bonnet Blanca had trimmed with black ribbons for the occasion. The damp chill on her skin was a reminder that she was alive. A welcome reminder as she stared down at the lacquered dark wood that held the remains of a girl who had been many things, but who no one could doubt had been vibrant and vital.

She turned her head to look at her husband. His gaze was fixed on the casket, but Mélanie didn't think he was seeing the shiny black wood. She couldn't guess what visions haunted his gaze. Honoria as a child? Honoria in his bed in Lisbon? Honoria as his wife and the mother of his children? Perhaps all of them. Perhaps others that she couldn't even guess at. But whatever he was feeling, he was doing his damnedest to suppress it so he could keep watch on the mourners. The suspects. He was doing a very good job of suppressing it, too, which was good for catching the killer but not for his own health.

They hadn't talked about his father's death. She doubted they ever would. On the walk to the chapel, it had occurred to her that the one place she could count on being able to make Charles feel something was in bed. Which was a pity, because they didn't seem to be doing much sleeping lately, let alone have leisure to indulge in any other activities in their bedchamber.

The sound of Lord Glenister's ragged breathing punctuated the droning of the minister. Glenister's eyes were bright and his face red from more than the cold air. Evie stood beside him, her black-gloved hand curled round his arm, her face thin and somber. Lady Frances was at his other side, holding his arm in a way that was oddly maternal, for all they were much of an age. Her rouge stood out like spots of vermilion on her pale cheeks, but Mélanie suspected her grief was more for Kenneth Fraser, whose body still lay in the chapel, than for Honoria Talbot.

Glenister's two sons stood with their shoulders almost touching, in a greater display of unity than Mélanie had ever seen from them. Quen stared at the coffin as though to keep his gaze focused on it throughout the funeral was a test he had to pass. Val looked at the toes of his boots, the wind-tossed yew branches that overhung the churchyard, the darkening slate of the sky. Everywhere but at the wooden box that held the body of his cousin and lover and of their unborn child.

David was white-faced but wore the determined expression of one who has been trained from the cradle to do his duty on formal occasions. Only his eyes, shadowed by grief and fear, gave him away. Simon looked as though he wanted to put his arm round him but knew David wouldn't let him. Much as Mélanie felt about Charles.

Gisèle's brows were drawn in concentration. She would neither look away nor pretend to a grief she didn't feel. Every so often her gaze moved to Andrew Thirle, standing alone on the opposite side of the grave, as though she was torn between fear of seeing grief for Honoria Talbot in his eyes and a need to comfort him if the grief was there. When Andrew met her gaze, she gave a determined smile. Andrew smiled back, a brief lift of his mouth that did not touch the pain in his eyes. Charles had explained the story of Andrew's parentage as they were dressing for the funeral, so Mélanie did not find Andrew and Gisèle's behavior as inexplicable as she had the night before.

Tommy also stood alone, scowling at the coffin with a fierceness that betrayed the fact that keeping up his detached façade required as much concentration as a sword fight to the death against two foes at once (in which Mélanie had seen him engage on more than one occasion).

The children were not at the funeral, but Aspasia Newland had come to pay her respects to her former charge. Like Andrew and Tommy, she stood a little apart from the others. After one brief glance at Quen and another at Evie, she kept her gaze on the coffin. But her expression, more than any of the others', was impossible to read.

The minister fell silent. The service was over. Charles touched her arm and jerked his head at Glenister.

Aspasia Newland paused beneath the lych-gate and looked over her shoulder at the funeral party. Charles Fraser had crossed to speak with Lord Glenister and Lady Frances. Fraser was always a difficult man to read, but Aspasia would swear she'd seen the ache of grief and the sting of guilt in his gaze as he looked down at Honoria's casket. Now, however, he closed in on Honoria's uncle with the relentlessness of a swordsman moving in for the kill.

His wife had gone to join David Mallinson and Simon Tanner. Mr. Belmont was speaking with Miss Fraser. Mr. Thirle, who had turned to go, lingered by the yew trees, frowning as he watched Mr. Belmont touch Miss Fraser on the shoulder and murmur what were probably condolences. Aspasia had not realized there was anything between Andrew Thirle and Gisèle Fraser, but even across the churchyard she could read the physical ache and mental torment in Mr. Thirle's posture. The pain of giving up what you most want. A pain lessened not one whit by knowing one is acting for the best.

A similar stab cut through the tightly buttoned fabric of her bodice. At last, because she had made up her mind that she had to do so, she looked at Quen. He was standing between Evie and Lord Valentine, tension radiating off the set of his shoulders and the line of his back. He turned his head in her direction. All this time, and she could still draw him with a glance.

Quen murmured something to his brother and cousin, then came over to join her. A thousand memories washed over her as he crossed the rain-spattered ground. The blood rushed to her skin and her body hummed with a wave of pure animal need that she should be long past at her age.

He stopped about three feet away. Droplets of rain clung to his skin and his coat and the glossy beaver of his hat. His eyes were black, the way they got when he was angry or in pain. Or in the throes of passion, his fingers twisted in her hair, her name a ragged gasp on his lips.

"Val's seeing Evie back to the house," he said. "Or rather Evie's seeing Val back. As usual, she's the strongest one in the family, and Val's picked this rather inconvenient time to display genuine feelings. You wanted to talk?"

His face seemed thinner. He'd aged in the five years since she'd left Glenister House, but he seemed to have aged more in the two days since Honoria's death. The lines that bracketed his mouth were deeper and his voice had taken on an added weight, as though it had gone from cello to double bass. "I'm so sorry, Quen." She suppressed the impulse to put out her hand. "I haven't had a chance to tell you."

He swallowed. For a moment, the newfound maturity was gone and he was as young as Chloe. Then his gaze hardened. "I know Honoria made you leave Glenister House. She told me a month since."

"Yes." Aspasia smoothed the black ribbon she'd tied round the sleeve of her spencer. "Mrs. Fraser explained it to me."

"You must have hated her." He gripped the gatepost and avoided her gaze. "Honoria."

Her fingers clenched involuntarily. "I confess to not feeling particularly charitable at the time. In truth, I didn't feel very charitable when I saw her again in Scotland." She swallowed a welling of anger that stripped her throat like acid. "But she didn't deserve to die. I'm sorry for the pain her loss causes you and Evie, and your father and Lord Valentine."

Quen frowned into the distance, as though he was searching for something in the curtain of mist that blanketed the landscape. "She was—lately I didn't like her very much. But I did love her. And I miss her."

"She was your baby sister in all but name."

"Though Val seems to have taken the relationship in a rather different direction." His fingers tightened on the wood of the lych-gate. "Damn her, why couldn't she stop her infernal meddling? If she had she might still be alive."

Aspasia drew a breath. Her lungs felt weighted with lead. "You can't know that." She nearly added "my love" and bit the words back just in time. "You can't blame yourself. Honoria had been—"

"Oh, Christ, don't start in with the bloody platitudes." The lych-gate shook beneath the force of his grip. "Not you, Aspasia. You've always been better than that."

"She was right about one thing at least, Quen. She was right when she told me to leave Glenister House. We couldn't have continued as we were."

"No, of course not." He dropped his hand from the gate and fixed his gaze on one of the posts. "That's the way of love affairs."

She curled her gloved fingers inward to stem the impulse to put her hand on his shoulder. Touching him had always been like holding a brimstone match to hot coals, ever since that moment she'd stumbled on the library steps at Glenister House and found herself in his arms. An accident that truth to tell hadn't been so very accidental. "It wasn't fair to Honoria and Evie. Any scandal concerning their governess would have reflected on them. I should never—I was selfish—"

"*You* were—" He started to look at her, then glanced away. "Oh, God, what does it matter now?"

"It matters because it ended badly."

"As opposed to all the illicit love affairs that end well?"

"I'm older than you, Quen—"

"As you never tire of holding over my head—"

"And I should have been sensible—"

"Why?" He spun round, the burning gaze of the boy who had been her lover set in the stark face of the man he had become. "Love isn't sensible. Love's a fire that can't be contained. Until it burns itself out. Bloody hell, I sound like a bad poet."

The fire, which should have turned to ashes long since, warmed her skin beneath the sensible governess-gray bombazine of her gown. "But whatever else I did," she said, "perhaps my worst sin was cowardice. I had to leave, but I shouldn't have left as I did. At the time it seemed the only prudent course, but I didn't want you to think—my dear, I didn't say good-bye because it would have been too painful. I hope you know that."

"I—" He looked away again. "I did wonder."

The rain must be getting worse, because she could feel it through her gown and spencer. Either that or her senses were keyed to feel everything more intensely. "I learned long since that happiness isn't a permanent state. One has to take it in bits and pieces." She felt a smile, faint but real, break over her face. "There were a lot of bits and pieces in our time together. More than I've known before or since. However selfish it was, I'll always be grateful for that."

He looked at her then, really looked at her for the first time in five years. "I never thought—I—thank you, Spasy."

The sound of the pet name that no one else but her now scattered family had ever used brought a welling of hot tears to her eyes. She blinked them back and tried to pretend she was standing in front of a schoolroom slate.

"Will you be all right?" Quen's voice stroked along her nerve endings like a caress.

"Of course. It must be the last two days. In general I'm not overset so easily."

"No, I mean—if Lady Frances finds out—"

She'd forgotten how chivalrous he could be. She glanced at her employer, who had gone to speak with the minister. "Lady Frances is a very tolerant woman. But even if she should dismiss me, I'll manage. I've been managing rather well for nearly forty years."

He gripped her arm. "If you're in trouble, come to me."

"Quen, I could hardly—"

His fingers dug into her arm. "Promise."

She managed a smile. "Are you offering me a position as governess to your daughters?"

He gave a short laugh. "I'm highly unlikely ever to set up a nursery. Respectable girls tend to run a mile from me."

She put her hand over his own before she could think to restrain herself. Her throat tightened with a pang for the loss of something that had never been hers to keep. "As a governess, I know to my sorrow that respectable girls find disreputable young men indecently attractive."

He grinned, with the sort of tenderness one shows not for a lover but for a former lover when the bitterness has passed. "The glamour would soon wear off if they had to live with me. Evie could vouch for that."

Aspasia shook her head. Really, it was a wonder. How could a man with such a keen understanding be so blind. "Oh, my dear. Evie's been head over ears in love with you for years. Haven't you noticed?"

"Evie?" Quen dropped his hand from her arm. "Evelyn, my cousin?"

"Who's followed you about the room with her eyes since I first came to Glenister House when she was thirteen."

"But—"

"I know, in every other way she seems a highly sensible young woman. But then what were you just saying about love not being sensible?"

"But she's only a chi—"

"Oh, for God's sake, Quen. Chloe's a child. Evie is two-and-twenty. And even at thirteen, she was the most mature person in Glenister House."

Quen tried to run his fingers through his hair. His hat thudded to the ground. "Evie knows me. Probably better than anyone, though I hope to hell she doesn't realize half the things I've got up to. She couldn't possibly—"

"Love you?"

He bent down to retrieve his hat. "As more than a cousin-brother, she has no choice but to put up with."

"If you won't take my word for it, you'll have to work it out for yourself. And then see what you want to do about it."

He shook the raindrops from his hat and stared at it for a moment, as though the dark fabric held visions of a future he'd never considered. "I should get back to the house. I don't want to leave Evie to cope with Val for too long." He set the hat back on his head. "You've always been good at reading people, Aspasia. But Evie and I didn't stumble out of the pages of one of Mrs. Radcliffe's novels."

Yet a thoughtful frown gathered between his eyes as he walked away. Aspasia watched him go. A cold ache spread through her that had nothing to do with the rain. Evie could be the making of Quen. Aspasia knew she'd done the right thing. The fact that she was quite failing to feel any of the comforting sense of virtue that should accompany that realization might have something to do with her inherent selfishness.

Of course, it also might have something to do with the part she hadn't told Quen about. The fact that she wasn't nearly so sanguine as she had managed to appear. That even now she could not think of his murdered cousin without feeling bitterness.

Not to mention guilt.

Charles crossed the rain-spattered churchyard to join Glenister and Lady Frances. His godparents, he realized. Lady Frances was holding Glenister's arm and murmuring softly to him. They looked more like a couple than Charles's real parents had ever done.

At his approach, both went still. He stopped a few feet off. "It does little good once again to say I'm sorry for what happened to Honoria, but I am. More than I can possibly express."

The red-rimmed gaze Glenister turned to him had a core of steel. "You aren't in the diplomatic corps anymore, Charles. What do you want?"

"I need to talk to you."

"Here?" It was Lady Frances who spoke. "For God's sake, Charles, Honoria is—"

"Barely cold in her grave is the usual term, I believe. And whoever put her there is still loose. Time isn't on our side." Charles looked at Glenister. "I thought it might be easier to talk away from the house."

"There's nothing easy about any of this." Glenister's gaze said that he had taken the gloves off last night and had no intention of putting them back on. He glanced at Lady Frances. "It's all right, Fanny."

She nodded, flashed a frowning glance at Charles, and moved off toward the minister. Glenister jerked his head toward the birch coppice and the path back to the house.

They walked a few steps in silence. "Well?" Glenister said.

"Why was your father paying money to my father?"

"Why—" Glenister swung round to look at him. "What the devil are you talking about, boy?"

Charles looked through the rain-filmed air at the man who had been both friend and enemy to Kenneth Fraser. "I found a ledger in Father's dispatch box recording payments, and notes from your father that accompanied the payments."

Surprise or fear or perhaps both flickered in Glenister's gaze. "That's ridiculous. Father would have had no reason to give money to Kenneth."

"Which beggars the question that he seems to have done so. Why?"

"I haven't the least idea. You should know better than anyone that a son isn't always in his father's confidence."

"No, but in my experience friends usually confide in each other. Father was your friend in those days."

"Your father's and my friendship wasn't based on those sorts of confidences." Glenister strode on, boots thudding against the damp leaves. "Kenneth was a barrister, don't forget. There are plenty of reasons Father might have engaged his services."

"If Father had been pleading a court case for your father, surely you'd know of it. And payments to a barrister for pleading a case wouldn't be locked away. Nor would they culminate in a payment of twenty-five thousand pounds."

Glenister stopped in his tracks. Either his shock was genuine or he was a better actor than Charles had credited. "How much?"

"Twenty-five thousand pounds. You've never found a record of it in your father's papers?"

"Good God, no." Glenister put up a hand to knock a birch leaf from the brim of his hat. "That's as much as Kenneth's legacy—"

"I suspect it may well *be* the legacy. The one that was supposedly from Father's cousin in Jamaica. The one he bought Dunmykel with."

"Don't be ridiculous. We know where the legacy came from."

"Do we?"

"Kenneth would have told me—"

"He would have told you about the legacy, though he didn't tell you about the payments from your father?"

Glenister stirred a pile of rain-soaked leaves with the toe of his boot. "You may find this difficult to believe, Charles, but most men from time to time find themselves involved in entanglements from which it is difficult to break free. Kenneth was clever and discreet and ambitious. And ruthless, as I know to my cost. Father might have engaged him to negotiate with one or more former mistresses."

"To pay them off? Or perhaps to look after children he'd sired?"

Glenister looked at Charles sharply but made no comment.

"Did your father have by-blows?" Charles asked.

"None that I know of. But as I said, I was hardly in his confidence."

"Did your father have anything to do with the Elsinore League?"

"Of course not. We hardly wanted our parents to observe our antics. The Elsinore League was Kenneth's and my friends from university."

"And a few more you met abroad."

"A few."

"Did your father know about the Elsinore League?"

"I sincerely hope not. Good God, would you have wanted Kenneth to know if you'd—"

"I seriously doubt I ever did anything my father would have found remotely shocking."

Glenister gave a short laugh. "You've always been honest, I'll give you that." He started walking again. "Whatever the reason, surely any payments my father made to Kenneth can't have anything to do with Honoria's death. They're ancient history."

"Like the Elsinore League?"

"Precisely. Look, Charles, the Elsinore League was a young men's club, an excuse for drinking champagne and claret and making outrageous wagers and sampling the pleasures of the demi-monde. Whatever fancies you may have in your head, that's the truth, pure and simple."

"I'm no longer sure any of us is capable of telling the truth," Charles said. "Or that I'd recognize it if we did so."

. . .

Quen paused inside the drawing room and stared through the French windows at the slender, chestnut-haired, gray-gowned figure on the terrace. Evie. As familiar as the taste of whisky, the turn of a card, the rattle of dice. As familiar, but as pure as a whiff of Highland air amid the smoke and scent and liquor of a gaming hell. Surely, *surely* he'd have known if her feelings for him were more than cousinly. Yet could he claim to have known Honoria? Or Val?

He turned the handle and stepped onto the terrace. "You'll get wet."

She looked round and smiled, though her eyes were dark. "I like the fresh air. It clears away the unwelcome ghosts."

He joined her at the balustrade. "Where's Val?"

"I persuaded him to lie down. I don't think he slept more than an hour or two last night."

"Nor did you."

"Yes, but Honoria wasn't going to have my baby." She cast a sidelong glance at him. "Did you know? About Honoria and Val?"

"Not until Val told me last night. I seem to have been the only one in the family not in on the secret." Quen's hands tightened on the granite. "I wanted to thrash Val, but he seems to have picked now of all times to grow a conscience. I couldn't do anything to him worse than what he's doing to himself." He looked down at the pale curve of Evie's cheek beneath the close-fitting plaited straw of her bonnet. "How long have you known?"

She stared at her black-gloved hands, resting on the balustrade. "I've suspected almost from the first. I've been certain for two years at least. I—"

He started to touch her shoulder, unconsciously as he would have done before Aspasia's words in the churchyard, then dropped his hand. "You couldn't have controlled Honoria, Evie. No one could."

She stared out across the gardens at the gray, churning sea. "The last thing Mama said to me when she put me in the carriage to go live at Glenister House was 'Be a good girl.' I nodded so solemnly, as though it was as simple as remembering to clean my teeth or put on fresh linen every morning."

"Evie—"

"No, listen, Quen, you don't know. You don't know me. I'm not sure I want—but the last few days have been so precarious. I'm afraid if I don't tell you the truth now I'll never get a chance."

"The truth about what?"

She drew a breath. "When I first came to Glenister House, I'd hear the gossip and the whispers. I'd try to sort out the entanglements in the Glenister House set, who was sharing whose bed. It was years before I realized it didn't matter. Sooner or later everyone slept with everyone else. Even then it never occurred to me that I—oh, God, Quen, I'm so ashamed."

"Why?"

"Because when I realized what was happening between Honoria and Val, my first reaction wasn't shock or horror or even concern for Honoria." Her hands tightened, pulling at the fabric of her gloves. She kept her gaze fixed straight ahead. "It was why couldn't this be Quen and me."

Truth. Clear, incontrovertible, and devastating. He stood still, robbed of the power of speech or even thought.

Evie drew a sharp breath and leaned into him, and he closed his arm round her.

Chapter 34

Colin cuddled up against Mélanie on the nursery window seat and lifted his dark gaze to her face. "Did Grandpapa die the same way Noria did?"

"Not exactly, darling. We're not sure why either of them died."

"But one must have something to do with the other, mustn't it?" Chloe, curled up at Mélanie's other side, twisted the end of her hair ribbon round her finger. "I mean two mur—two people dying in two days can't be a coincidence."

"No, it's probably not coincidence," Mélanie said. "But we're not sure what it means."

Colin wrinkled his nose. "I'm sorry Grandpapa's dead. But he didn't like me very much."

Mélanie swallowed. That, as Tommy would say, was a poser. "Colin—"

"He didn't." Colin sounded more matter-of-fact than upset. "He always looked at me like I'd been naughty, even when I hadn't done anything."

Chloe shifted her position on the window seat, rustling the

chintz cushions. "I don't think he liked anyone much. Except sometimes I used to think he liked Mama, and she didn't know it."

Mélanie cast a swift, involuntary glance at Lady Frances's daughter. Chloe looked back at her with an unblinking blue gaze.

Colin tugged at Mélanie's sleeve. "Did Daddy cry? Grandpapa was his father. I'd cry if Daddy died."

Mélanie's throat closed. "Daddy's had a lot to worry about. He hasn't—"

"Had time to cry," Charles said from the doorway.

Colin grinned, started to get up and run to his father, and then sat still. "I'm sorry," he said. "I'm sorry your father's dead."

Charles crossed the flowered nursery carpet and knelt before the window seat. "I'm sorry, too. But I hadn't seen much of my father in a long time. Not all fathers and sons get on as well as you and I do. As I hope we always will."

Mélanie felt Colin relax against her. As usual, he seemed to find the truth far more reassuring than sugar-coated lies.

"Mama looked like she'd been crying when she was here this morning," Chloe said.

Charles touched his young cousin's arm. "She'd known my father for a long time. Longer than any of us."

Chloe nodded, again unblinking.

The children asked fewer questions than they had when Mélanie had told them of Honoria's death. Even Chloe seemed a bit worried about the possible answers if she probed too deep. Miss Newland, returned from the funeral with a composed face but eyes rather brighter than usual, proposed to take the children for a walk.

"Let's go back to the study," Charles said when they had seen Miss Newland and the children off. "I want to look at the ledger again."

He didn't meet her gaze as they walked down the stairs. Gray shadows of fatigue drew at his face. Last night she'd thought that the only way he could go on was to suppress everything. Now she wondered how far he was from the inevitable collapse.

"In a lot of ways," she said as they rounded the corner on the half-landing, "Colin is a remarkably insightful child."

"Of course, he's your son." Charles paused, his hand on the newel post. "Oh."

"He's quite right," Mélanie said, her gaze on the grisaille painting of Terpsichore. "You haven't."

"Cried? Why should I?" Charles released the newel post and continued on down the stairs. "Losing Honoria meant something. Losing Father—how can losing someone you never knew mean anything?"

She gathered up the folds of her gown and hurried after him. "Because now you've lost the chance to ever get to know him."

"There wouldn't have been a hope in hell of that if Father had lived to be a hundred. I faced that fact years ago." He cast a swift glance at her, as closed as an infantry square. "It's all right, Mel. You don't need to keep worrying about me."

"I thought if you didn't want to talk to me, you might want to talk to David. Or Andrew?"

He started across the hall, his footfalls hard and erratic on the marble tile. "Why should I talk to anyone?"

"Because at some point this is all going to hit you, and we really can't afford to have you collapse. Not until we've caught the person or persons who are going about murdering people."

"I'm not going to collapse."

"Darling, you can't know that. When my father died it was days before it really hit me what had happened—"

Charles spun round, his hand on the knob of the study door. "When your father died you were nineteen, you lived with him and you loved him and you knew you were loved by him. I'm nearly thirty, I haven't lived under Kenneth Fraser's roof for ten years, and even then we rarely inhabited the same house." He held the study door open for her. "And there's no sense pretending I loved him any more than he loved me."

Mélanie moved past him into the room. "Point taken. Except that last."

He crossed to the desk and took the key to the dispatch box from his pocket. "Not very filial of me, but true nonetheless."

"Charles, you can't—"

"You weren't here. You didn't watch me growing up. You know a lot, but you can't know what it was like. You can't know what Kenneth Fraser meant to me, when I don't even know myself."

"That's precisely why—"

He dropped the key on the desk. It clattered against the penknife. "What the hell is this, Mel? Now that we're living in Britain you suddenly think you have to go all wifely and fuss over me?"

"I've been fussing over you for years. You always complain about it."

"You fuss over me when I have a bullet wound or a knife cut or a blow to the head. You don't fuss over—"

"Your soul?"

He gave a sharp laugh. "I wouldn't worry about my soul. It has a nice protective layer of scar tissue."

"Damn it, Charles, you don't need to prove you can handle everything on your own."

"So says the woman who deliberately allowed herself to be beaten black and blue a few hours ago."

"That's last night's argument, darling."

"Which is still relevant this morning. Speaking of injuries—" He grasped hold of her chin with a gentle touch that belied his harsh voice and turned her face to the light from the window. "You should put some ice on that bruise."

She tugged away. "I'm fine."

His gaze moved over her. "It's always worse the morning after a beating like that."

She folded her arms, ignoring a twinge of protest in her ribs. "I told you, I'm fine."

"I'm supposed to take your word for that?" His gaze turned gunmetal hard. She could feel the pressure against her bruised throat and jaw. "If you're so keen on soul-baring confidences, perhaps we should try it the next time you have one of your nightmares."

The air round them was suddenly filled with mines and mantraps and unsheathed knives. She swallowed. "A palpable hit. Though lately I'm not the only one who's been having nightmares."

"No." He picked up the key again but went still as his gaze moved to the box. "Someone's tampered with the lock."

Mélanie leaned forward and saw what he'd seen—scratches round the brass of the lock, the sort made by attempts to pry a lock open without the correct instruments. "You're sure those weren't there last night?"

"I made special note of it." Charles unlocked the box and pushed back the lid. "And I made special note of how I left the contents. The notes were perpendicular to the lid, not parallel."

They lifted out the contents and went through them item by item. Nothing was missing, but some of the papers showed smudges that hadn't been there the previous night.

"Anyone could have done it with a hairpin and enough time," Charles said. "The question is, why search now."

"Because with your father dead, you'd be going through the papers. Someone feared what you'd discover."

"Something more than the notes and the ledger, or the lock-picker would have taken them. Something Father had concealed away. Something Honoria might have stumbled across looking for information about her own father?"

They regarded each other across the dispatch box, the tension of a few minutes before washed under the safer waters of the investigation. "We went through her room meticulously," Mélanie said.

"And I'd swear we searched every corner of the study last night," Charles said. "I'll have Addison go through Father's room." He flipped open the ledger. "Glenister claims not to know anything about his father's payments to Kenneth. He suggested Kenneth was negotiating with one or more of old Lord Glenister's former mistresses who were proving difficult."

"Do you believe him?"

"I think he's hiding something. Exactly what he's hiding and how much of the truth he's told us are open to debate."

Mélanie looked down at the dates in the ledger. "Did Glenister think your father might have been arranging for the care of old Lord Glenister's by-blows?"

"He said he didn't know of any bastard children of his father's, but it was possible."

She flipped to the last entry in the ledger and stared at the yellowed paper and black ink. "When was Andrew born?"

"August. The fifteenth."

"Of what year?"

"Seventeen eighty-five. Oh, Christ."

"The last payment to your father is less than three months after Andrew's birth."

Charles frowned at the entries. "According to Andrew, Father went on paying for his upbringing for years. There's no record of later payments in the ledger."

"Perhaps your father stopped recording the payments. Or perhaps he had an understanding with old Lord Glenister that he'd take the money for Andrew out of the twenty-five thousand pounds."

Charles grimaced, the way he did when he was cursing himself for being a fool. "I wondered how the devil Father found the money to pay for his bastard before he came into his legacy."

Mélanie smoothed her finger over a scratch in the leather of the desktop. "Lord Valentine said Miss Talbot was keen to play their game with Andrew at first. Then the night of the murder she told him Andrew wouldn't work. If old Lord Glenister was Andrew's father and Miss Talbot learned the truth of Andrew's birth, she'd have known Andrew was her uncle."

"And she drew the line at incest?"

"Most people draw the line somewhere."

Charles leaned against the desk and turned sideways to look at her. "If old Lord Glenister was Andrew's father, there's no particular reason anyone should have wanted to keep it secret. Unless, of course, the identity of his mother is a matter of secrecy."

"It almost has to be to explain why Andrew was smuggled away."

"A married lady. Or an unmarried girl of good family. Potentially scandalous. But enough to still cause a scandal thirty-odd years later? So great a scandal someone would kill to conceal the truth?"

"Was old Lord Glenister's wife alive in 1785?"

"No, she died giving birth to Georgiana, Evie's mother."

"So at the time Andrew was conceived, Glenister senior would have been a widower."

Charles's gaze sharpened as if he were focusing on a rifle target. "A secret marriage?"

"Do you think it's possible?"

"Anything's possible. But I'm not sure where it gets us. Andrew being old Lord Glenister's legitimate son wouldn't threaten the current Lord Glenister's inheritance. He'd still be the firstborn."

Mélanie pushed a thick wave of hair back from her forehead. She'd managed to pin it up in a chignon, but it was stiff with sweat and salt from last night's adventures. She couldn't remember when she'd last had a bath. "What if old Lord Glenister isn't the Talbot who fathered Andrew?"

"You mean what if old Lord Glenister hired Father to deal with his son's mistress?" Charles paused a moment, the idea taking shape. "Or his son's wife?"

"Suppose Glenister, the current Lord Glenister, had made a secret marriage when he was young. Perhaps a ring and marriage lines were the price of one of his seductions. A shopkeeper's daughter from Oxford. A tenant on one of the family estates. He managed to keep the marriage secret, but eventually she became pregnant and he told his father. Was old Lord Glenister particularly particular about the family bloodlines?"

"So much so that he'd pay the lady to go away and foster the child out rather than have a shopkeeper's or tenant's grandchild as the future Marquis of Glenister? Possibly. He cut off Evie's mother's inheritance when she eloped."

"If the lady was still living when Glenister married Lord Quentin and Lord Valentine's mother, the prior marriage would bastardize them."

"Which is ironic considering Quen apparently is a bastard in any case." Charles drummed his fingers on the desk. "If Honoria discovered her uncle had made a prior marriage—"

"Theoretically it gives Lord Quentin a motive to get rid of her. But—"

"I can't see Quen killing her to protect his inheritance. Or Glenister killing his beloved niece to protect the inheritance of the son who isn't his anyway. Besides, what would Honoria have had to gain from revealing the information?" Charles frowned at the leaded glass panes of the windows. "Oh, good God."

"What?"

"Honoria kept asking Tommy about her father. But suppose she wasn't thinking about revolutionaries being smuggled out of France. Suppose Cyril Talbot didn't have anything to do with Le Faucon, or at least Honoria didn't know anything about that part of his life. Suppose her father's intrigues with the Elsinore League involved an unsuitable woman whom he—"

"Married." Mélanie stared at her husband as the idea locked into place in both their minds. "If Cyril Talbot made a secret marriage and fathered Andrew, then Andrew would be Miss Talbot's brother. Which would certainly explain her deciding she couldn't seduce him."

"And the truth could bastardize Honoria and take away her inheritance. Which gives Honoria a motive to kill someone else, but I can't see how it could motivate anyone to kill her."

Mélanie sighed and leaned against the desk beside him. "It's all speculation in any case. That any of the Talbots fathered Andrew."

"Andrew has Glenister's coloring. More than he resembles Father." Charles ran his hand through his hair. "I wish to the devil we could prove it, even if it has nothing to do with the murder. It might convince Andrew to stop being so pigheadedly noble where Gisèle is concerned."

"Have you thought about having Lady Frances talk to him about Gisèle's parentage?"

"All she could do is reiterate that Gisèle almost certainly isn't Kenneth Fraser's daughter. Andrew would just say what he said to me—that we can never know the truth for an absolute certainty. And that even if we could be sure, he doesn't deserve to be happy, that he's bound to make Gisèle miserable because she's nineteen and can't know her own mind and he didn't go to the right schools. 'The hind that would be mated by the lion.' Why the devil can't he see that what they have is—"

"Special," Mélanie said. Charles's gaze flickered to her face. "I saw them last night," she added.

He turned, his back to the desk, and folded his arms across his chest. "The way they looked at each other. Like—"

"Romeo and Juliet."

He cast a sidelong glance at her, then looked away. "I want Gelly to be happy." He fiddled with a silver paperweight on the desk. "I want her to have—"

"What you'll never have yourself." Amazingly, her voice was without bitterness. She couldn't blame him. Neither of them had ever promised the other anything more.

He turned a surprised gaze to her. "I want her to have what *you* deserved to have." He glanced down at his fingers, curled round the paperweight. "When I saw the way Andrew was looking at Gelly, all I could think—I'm sorry I never looked at you that way."

Her throat closed. "I can't see you climbing a balcony, darling. Unless it was to steal documents from the room beyond."

"You deserve someone who could—you deserve a Romeo."

She touched his hand where it lay on the desk between them. "I'm not much of a Juliet myself, Charles. At least not for a long time." And she didn't really want a Romeo. Even if Charles was able to make such protestations, she was scarcely the sort to believe them. And yet—she had engraved a quote from *Romeo and Juliet* on the watch she'd given him their second Christmas together.

> *My bounty is as boundless as the sea,*
> *My love as deep; the more I give to thee,*
> *The more I have, for both are infinite.*

She hadn't realized how true the quote was until she visited Scotland with Charles three years ago and walked along the beach at Dunmykel Bay with him and Colin. It had hit her then, how indissoluble her tie to him had become. Even then she'd scarcely let herself use the words. And she'd thought she could be content with what he had to offer to balance his own side of the equation.

Now she looked at her husband's familiar face and saw the selfish, desperate depths of her own greed. She wanted total surrender. *By yonder blessèd moon. Love, lord, ay, husband, friend. Soul's idol. I love you with so much of my heart that none is left to protest.*

His fingers tensed beneath her own. "I—"

"Oh, good, here you are." Tommy strode into the room and pushed the door to behind him. "The others are all in the dining room. Miss Fraser's organized a sort of dinner. She's nearly as coolheaded as you are, Fraser, and a good deal less annoying."

Charles turned from the desk to face Tommy. The vulnerability was gone, closed over by layers of hard-won scar tissue. "Is Glenister there?"

"Large as life, though he's keeping to himself. I don't know what you said to him, but he looks as though he'll plant a facer to the next person who tries to talk to him. At least he's stopped threatening to leave, probably because his sons and Miss Mortimer are acting as though there'll be another murder if he attempts to do so." Tommy hitched himself up on the corner of the desk. "Look, you don't have to tell me any more family secrets or nonsense about who slept with who thirty years ago—"

"Whom." Charles leaned against the paneled wall.

"What?"

"Who slept with whom."

"Right. Who slept with whom and who happens to really be whom's father or mother. I already know more than I ever wanted to about the liaisons of the Fraser and Talbot families." Tommy's gaze sharpened like the point of a swordstick. "But if you've found anything in that dispatch box that has to do with Le Faucon and this Elsinore League business I need to know."

"We haven't," Charles said. "At least, nothing we can be sure of."

"Spare me the verbal fencing, Fraser. What about what you can't be sure of?"

Charles and Mélanie exchanged glances. Difficult to gauge how much to reveal or not reveal when it was impossible to know how the pieces fit together. "Glenister's father was paying money to my father," Charles said.

Tommy's eyes narrowed. "Why?"

"We're not sure."

"But presumably because of something they both wanted to keep secret."

"Quite."

"Let me guess." Tommy picked up the silver paperweight and tossed it in the air. "It could have to do with more of these who was sleeping with *whom* details, which is why the two of you are looking so reticent. Or it could have to do with the Elsinore League."

Charles folded his arms over his chest. "That's it in a nutshell. According to Glenister, the Elsinore League was a club of young men sowing their wild oats and had nothing to do with Le Faucon de Maulévrier. Even assuming Glenister's telling the truth, Le Faucon could still have been a member of the league. But we can't connect Glenister's father to the Elsinore League. Can you?"

"Not based on what Castlereagh told me. Of course, Castlereagh doesn't seem to have told me the whole of it."

"Old Lord Glenister was a political force," Charles said. "More so than his son."

"He was a Tory?" Mélanie asked.

"A conservative Whig. But he opposed the Revolution."

"Other than Cyril Talbot, the only one we can link to revolutionaries so far is Simon Tanner's father," Tommy said.

"We can't link Simon's father to anything. Save that he supported the Revolution."

Tommy swung his leg against the side of the desk. "Perhaps—"

A rap at the door cut into his words. Charles straightened his shoulders, instinctively braced against intrusion. "Come in."

The door opened. A man with bushy white hair and thick brows stepped into the room. Mélanie felt more than saw Charles's sudden stillness. He and the white-haired man regarded each other for a long moment, choked with memories.

"Hullo, Charlie," the man said.

"Hullo, Giles," said Charles.

Chapter 35

Charles scarcely moved a muscle, but Mélanie read a host of emotions in the tightening of his jaw and the widening of his eyes. Relief that Giles McGann was alive. Surprise at his reappearance. Fear of what was to come. Bitterness at the bite of betrayal.

McGann regarded Charles in silence. He had piercing blue eyes set in a lined face that retained a hint of boyish mischief. "I heard about your father," he said at last in a rough, musical voice. "And Miss Honoria." He drew a sharp breath, his gaze clouded with grief. "I'm sorry."

Charles swallowed. Mélanie suspected he was struggling to find his voice, though when he spoke, he sounded normal enough. "Did you know we were looking for you?"

"Not for a certainty. But I guessed."

Charles sucked in a breath and released it. "You bastard. I was afraid you were dead."

"Yes, I'm sorry about that. I couldn't—"

"Take the risk? Or my father couldn't?"

McGann's eyes darkened to cobalt. "Charlie—"

Tommy sprang off the desk. "Loath as I am to interrupt this

touching reunion, would you mind telling us where the devil you've been, McGann? You are Giles McGann, aren't you?"

"Thomas Belmont," Charles said. "A diplomatic colleague. And this is my wife, Mélanie."

"Mr. Belmont." McGann nodded at Tommy and then turned to Mélanie with the same appraising gaze she received from everyone in Britain from London duchesses to the Dunmykel grooms. On the whole, though, the servants and tenants were friendlier than the duchesses, and McGann was friendlier than most. "Mrs. Fraser. I'm pleased to meet you at last. Charlie wrote that you were beautiful, but I see he understated the matter."

"You're a very kind man and a charming liar, Mr. McGann." Mélanie tried not to stress the word *liar,* but it seemed to linger in the air. "Knowing Charles, I'm sure he didn't write anything of the sort." And yet it seemed he had written to McGann after they were married. Still without making any mention of his old friend to his wife.

McGann's eyes glinted. "Let's say I've learned to read between the lines when it comes to Charlie."

Tommy coughed. "As I said, I'm loath to interrupt—"

"You want to know where I was. Or rather, you want to know why I disappeared."

"Because Father asked you to, I presume," Charles said.

McGann raised his untidy brows.

"Why else would you return now that he's dead?" Charles's gaze hardened. "I wasn't aware you and my father were on such close terms."

"There's a lot you don't know, Charlie."

"So I've come to realize in the last few days." Charles regarded McGann with the wariness he would accord an enemy agent.

McGann took a turn about the hearthrug. His gaze lingered on the Fragonard oil, luminous in the shadowy light from the window. "Your father always did have a fondness for beautiful things. Like me and my books. It was the one way I ever felt any sort of kinship with him. Only your father has—had—more blunt to spend. If it wasn't for that—well, let's say the last thirty years might have been very different."

Charles leaned against the wall and tracked McGann's every movement with his eyes. "Different how?"

McGann tugged at his frayed coat. "A lot of his friends like to collect as well. Picked up a taste for it on the Grand Tour, I dare swear."

"We already know about Wheaton and the smuggling ring," Charles said. "You worked with them."

McGann flushed but did not shy away from Charles's gaze. "So I did. You've been gone from Dunmykel for a long time, Charlie. You were a clever lad, but even as a boy I don't think you quite realized— times have been difficult for a long while now, long before your father's Clearances."

"Smuggling was a way to hold off starvation."

"For some. I can make no such claim. For me it was a way to buy a few more books, an extra bottle of whisky. And perhaps to have a bit of adventure."

"The lure of danger?" Tommy cast a sidelong glance at Charles. "We wouldn't know anything about that, would we?"

"What did you do for the smugglers?" Charles said.

"Nip down to the cove every now and again and pick up a parcel from a fishing boat and keep it for a week or so."

"Who came to collect them from you?"

"Your father himself, more often than not. Lord Glenister once or twice. Occasionally some other of their friends. I didn't know them all by name. We'd have a code word for the exchange. Characters from Shakespeare usually. Funny, a grown man knocking on one's door in the dark of night and muttering 'Peaseblossom' or 'Bardolph.'"

"How do you know the parcels contained works of art?" Tommy asked.

"For a certainty? I suppose I don't. The parcels were the right size and shape and once or twice the wrapping slipped and I got a glimpse of a bit of bronze or the corner of a frame."

"Which doesn't preclude other things being hidden in the pictures or the statues," Tommy said.

"I suppose not, but why the devil would anyone—"

"You didn't just collect parcels." Charles watched McGann with a stillness that gripped like a vise. "You traveled to the south recently. To escort someone to Dunmykel."

McGann's eyes narrowed. "You've learned a great deal."

"Not nearly enough. Who was he?"

"I don't know. He called himself Jean Lameau. The only thing I'm certain of is that that wasn't his real name."

"Had you seen him before?"

"Oh, yes. He'd been a guest at house parties your father gave at Dunmykel. Back in the early days. I hadn't seen him for close on twenty years. But he had the sort of eyes one doesn't forget. The sort that seem to be able to see into any dark corner he chooses."

Tommy took a step toward the door, probably to block the exit in case McGann had any thoughts of bolting. "Tell us everything you can about him."

"I very nearly have, Mr. Belmont."

"Was he French?" Charles asked.

"He wanted us to believe so. Wanted us to believe it a bit too badly, I'd say. Either that or he was trying too hard to put on a gentleman's accent. I don't think the voice he spoke in came naturally to him. But I couldn't guess what his true voice would sound like, or what it would reveal about his origins."

"What did you talk about?" Charles said.

"Books, oddly enough." McGann touched his fingers to the leather binding of a volume on the card table. "At first he tended to look at me as though he was more interested in the view past my shoulder. But then he came down into the cabin and found me reading and we struck up a conversation. He wasn't averse to talking, provided it was impersonal."

"What sort of books did you discuss?" Charles asked.

"Oh, for God's sake—" Tommy said.

Charles flashed a look at him. "It might be important."

"Shakespeare," McGann said. "The Greeks. Dante. A few seventeenth-century poets. He avoided anything overtly political."

"You think that's why he was leaving France?" Charles asked. "Because of politics?"

"Isn't that why most people have left France in the past three decades, one way or another? But exactly what Lameau's politics were or why he was forced to flee France or what he'd been doing in London before I picked him up, I couldn't tell you."

"Did he ever say anything at all that stood out to you?" Charles said.

"No, he—" McGann frowned. "There was something, though I never could make head nor tail of what it meant. Just before we disembarked, apropos of nothing at all, he said, 'Do you think it really is possible to pawn a heart, Mr. McGann?'"

"'Pawn a heart'?" Charles repeated.

"Those were the words. I said it was difficult enough to give a heart in my experience. I'd never thought much about pawning one. Lameau smiled and said giving might be simpler. Pawning could create debts that came back to haunt one."

"What do you think he meant?"

"I assume it was a quote. I thought it might be from Shakespeare, but I'm damned if I can say where." McGann shook his head. "I enjoyed talking with him. But I wouldn't care to meet him on a dark street with a knife in his hand."

"What happened when you reached Dunmykel Bay?"

"He thanked me, said he'd like to disembark first, and asked me to give him a half hour before I left the boat. I did as he asked. I returned home, but a few hours later your father called at my cottage and told me to make myself scarce."

"Why?"

"He said you were likely to come asking questions and it would be easier for everyone if I wasn't there to give the answers."

"Have you heard of the Elsinore League?" Tommy asked.

McGann nodded. "I suppose you'd call them a club. Something Mr. Fraser and Lord Glenister and their friends started up at Oxford."

"To do what?" Charles said.

"You'd know the sorts of things young men get up to at Oxford better than I would. Drinking, gaming, wenching—" He coughed. "Your pardon, Mrs. Fraser."

"Believe me, Mr. McGann, you haven't said anything one doesn't hear stories about in Mayfair drawing rooms. Was Mr. Lameau a member of the Elsinore League?"

"I assume so. He was a guest at Dunmykel on more than one

occasion, though not for close on twenty years, as I said. I'd caught glimpses of him, but I hadn't heard him called by name until I was asked to escort him to Scotland."

Charles's gaze moved over McGann's face. "What was your connection to the League?"

"I didn't have any connection to speak of. I knew about them, that's all. A lot of the members were the men I retrieved parcels for."

Charles began to pace up and down the end of the room, his gaze intent. "Why would anyone be afraid of the Elsinore League now? Why would they be a source of danger?"

"Who says they are?"

"A friend of mine who was shot to death in London two weeks ago."

"Good God. By whom?"

"We aren't sure. But his last words were a warning about the Elsinore League."

Tommy tugged something from his coat pocket and strode forward, holding it out. Mélanie recognized the paper with the falcon stamp that Tommy had taken from McGann's desk. "What about this?"

McGann glanced down at the paper. "Unless I'm very much mistaken, that came from my desk, Mr. Belmont."

"You were missing. I had reason to believe you might have information of vital importance to the Foreign Office. What is this?"

"What it looks like. Instructions about a delivery."

"From?"

"One of the Elsinore League members. He used that signet stamp to sign his papers."

"What was his name?"

"I don't know. He always used the stamp instead of a signature."

"Who collected his parcels?"

"Mr. Fraser."

"Could the man who used this signet have been Jean Lameau?" Charles asked.

"Possibly. As I said, I couldn't put any of their faces with that mark."

"Could the Elsinore League have been more than a club of débauchés?" Tommy said.

"What are you suggesting, Mr. Belmont?"

"I'm not suggesting, I'm asking."

McGann was silent for a long moment. "I told you, they were secretive. I never actually attended meetings. I could only guess at the membership based on who used the Elsinore League seal and who was about Dunmykel when they were having their gatherings. I could only guess at what they did based on rumors of debauchery."

"Did you ever hear mention of a man named Coroux?" Charles asked.

"Oh, yes. He was one of the members. One whose name I did know. Frenchman. He visited quite often in the early days, before the war. Later his visits were more scarce, and he'd use an English name, but there's no doubt it was the same man. It must be close on twenty years since I've seen him, too."

"What about Honoria Talbot's father?" Charles said. "Was he part of the Elsinore League?"

McGann was silent for a fraction of a second. "I assume so. Like Lameau and Coroux, he was at a number of their gatherings."

"Was he friendly with Lameau and Coroux?"

"Not particularly more than any of the others."

Charles folded his arms over his chest. "Andrew said you were fond of Cyril's wife. I hadn't realized."

Memories glinted in McGann's eyes. "One doesn't confide such things in children. I suppose Andrew heard it from his mother. Catherine Thirle always had sharp eyes." He passed a hand over his hair. "She was a lovely girl. Susan—Lady Cyril as she later was. I never—we came from different worlds, of course. But she deserved better than Cyril Talbot."

"In what way?"

"She deserved a man who loved her. From aught I could make out, Lord Cyril never did. When they'd been married less than a year, he brought his light-o'-love with him to one of the Elsinore League gatherings."

"Who was she?" Charles asked. "This mistress of Cyril Talbot's?"

"Opera dancer by the look of it. Skinny, brown-haired creature. Not near as pretty as Susan."

"Did the liaison last a long time?"

"Not so far as I could tell. He brought three or four different birds of paradise to Elsinore League gatherings through the years."

"Did he have a lady with him at the shooting party where he died?"

"Not that I saw. I believe any women at that gathering were smuggled in from the village."

"Were Lameau and Coroux at that house party?"

"Yes." McGann's voice had the cautious note of admitting no more than was strictly necessary. He shifted his weight from one foot to the other. "It was the last time I saw Lameau until I brought him up the coast. I saw Coroux once or twice more."

"Did the Elsinore League have anything to do with Cyril Talbot's death?" Charles said.

McGann turned to the fireplace and stood still for a long moment, his shoulders slumped as though beneath the weight of a burden. "How much do you know?"

"His death wasn't simply a drunken accident with a gun." Charles's tone made the words half statement, half question.

McGann gave a grunt of acknowledgment. "Your father was right. You're too damned good at putting the pieces together."

"You were present when Cyril Talbot was shot," Charles said.

"That's a clever guess, Charlie. You can't possibly know for a certainty."

"Why not?"

"Because I'm quite sure none of the others who were present would have admitted it to you."

"Who were they?"

McGann sighed, as though even now weighing the wisdom of saying more. "Me. Cyril Talbot himself. Your father. And Lord Glenister."

"But not the rest of the house party?"

"No. He died away from the house. On the beach."

"What were the Talbot brothers, my father, and you doing on the beach in the middle of the night?"

"I'd come to the house to deliver a parcel for your father. A drawing, I think. Your father grabbed me and insisted I accompany them. He said I was sober and wouldn't talk and they needed another man present if the thing was to have any semblance of honor."

Tommy let out a low whistle. "Four men. Good God, it was a duel."

McGann flicked a glance at him. "You think quickly, Mr. Belmont."

"My father shot Cyril Talbot in a drunken parody of a duel?" Charles said.

McGann shook his head. "Your father was one of the seconds. I was the other. The duel was between Lord Glenister and Cyril Talbot."

It took a great deal to shock Charles, Tommy, and Mélanie herself into silence, but for a moment they all stared at McGann.

"What the devil was the duel about?" Charles said.

"I don't know. The challenge had been issued and accepted long before I came on the scene."

"But it was serious? It wasn't some sort of game gone awry?"

"Oh, no. Glenister looked—" McGann shook his head. "Glenister looked ready to murder his brother. Which I suppose one could argue he did."

"Did they both fire?" Mélanie asked.

"Lord Cyril's shot went wide. Difficult to say if it was drink or deliberate, though I'd guess it was deliberate. Glenister aimed straight for his heart. The fact that he didn't kill him outright I attribute to the amount *he'd* had to drink."

"Christ." Tommy shook his head. "Your families just keep getting odder and odder."

"What happened after the shots were exchanged?" Charles said.

McGann closed his eyes for an instant, as though picturing the scene. "Your father and I ran over to Lord Cyril. Glenister remained where he was. When I looked up he was just standing there with the pistol dangling from his fingers. He said, 'Is he dead?' He sounded as though it wasn't a matter of very great moment whether his brother lived or died."

"He was in shock," Mélanie said.

"Very likely. He turned and walked back to the house without us. Mr. Fraser and I carried Lord Cyril through the passage into the library. The others were there—Lameau or whatever his name really is and Coroux and Sir William Cathcart and Mr. Gordon and Mr. Craven and another Frenchman whose name I've never been sure of. Mr. Fraser told them that there'd been an accident. Glenister stumbled over to the sofa where we'd laid out his brother. It was as though he'd suddenly realized what had happened. Tears were streaming down his face. He said, 'I'm sorry.' Lord Cyril said, 'Take care of her.'"

"Her?"

"Miss Honoria, I assume."

"What did Glenister say?"

"'I will. I swear it.'"

"And then?"

"Your father told me to make myself scarce. I think he was afraid I'd reveal the truth of what had happened to the other guests."

Charles walked forward and rested his hands on the desk. "What was the duel about?"

"I told you, I don't know."

"I know what you told me. I'm not asking what you know. I'm asking for your best guess."

"All I can say is that it must have come about quickly. I'd seen the two brothers out riding earlier in the day and they appeared to be on perfectly good terms."

"Then I'll ask you again—what do you think the Elsinore League had to do with Cyril Talbot's death?"

"As far as I know, only that the duel took place during one of the Elsinore League's parties. The quarrel between the brothers seemed to be personal."

"But you can't be sure it was?"

"I can't be sure of anything. Save that Glenister fired the shot that killed his brother. And that he meant to do so."

Charles held McGann's gaze with his own, as though searching out whether or not this was the extent of the truth.

Tommy drew a swift, frustrated breath, but before he could speak, another knock sounded on the door. "Yes?" Charles called.

"Sorry to interrupt." Lord Quentin stepped into the room. His face was pale, his gaze focused and intense. "But I thought you should know at once. It's Father. He's left Dunmkyel."

Chapter 36

Charles met Quen's gaze across the study. The look in the younger man's eyes reminded him of soldiers who've returned from their first battle. "When?" Charles said.

"We're not sure exactly." Quen pushed the door shut. "I saw him pour himself a glass of wine when we first went into the dining room. Everyone was milling about the sideboard. It was nearly an hour later that Evie realized he wasn't in the room and went to look for him. Apparently when he returned from the funeral he gave orders to have the carriage readied and had his valet pack a bag. I'm sorry, Charles. I should have guessed he might try something. But it never occurred to me he was a coward as well as a criminal."

"You think your father killed Honoria? Or my father? Or both?"

"Why else would he have run?"

"Because he didn't want to answer further questions."

"For fear he'd implicate himself."

"Or someone else he cared about."

Quen's eyes narrowed. "You think he might be protecting me? Or Val or Evie?"

"Or Aunt Frances or just about anyone else in the house given the right circumstances. Especially if he feels responsible." Charles touched his fingers to the ledger on the desk. "What do you know about your uncle's death?"

"My uncle?" Quen passed a hand over his face. "Oh, you mean Honoria's father. I was only five when he died. I don't remember much, save that Father came back from Scotland looking as though he'd simultaneously lost a prizefight and suffered a bout of influenza. He told us our uncle Cyril was dead and Honoria was going to be our sister now." Quen glanced round, as though for the first time taking in the presence of Mélanie, Tommy, and McGann. He peered at McGann. "Giles?"

McGann inclined his head. "I'm sorry about your cousin, Lord Quentin."

"Thank you. So am I." Quen's gaze whipped from McGann to Charles. "What have you learned?"

"You'd better sit down, Quen," Charles said.

"Look, Charles, I know I'm still a suspect. You just said as much and I'm not stupid. But I can help you better if I understand. And if I was guilty of one or both murders, presumably I'd know whatever it is already."

"Only the relevant bits."

"And you can't be sure which are relevant."

"Quite. For your own sake I'd rather you never had to hear any of this. But too many people know too much of it now to keep it quiet."

"Then you'd better tell me."

Charles watched Quen for a moment longer. He had an image of the bright-eyed little boy he'd taught to hold a cricket bat. His throat went tight with the difficulty of choosing the right words, the way it had when he'd had to explain to his son that people who were sick didn't always get better. How to judge how much was important, how much Quen would learn anyway, how much Quen had a right to know. How much Quen would want to know. In Quen's place, Charles realized, he'd want to know all of it. That, in the end, decided him. Without further prevarication, he recounted the story of Quen's birth as he'd been told it by Glenister and Kenneth Fraser.

Quen scarcely moved a muscle. He remained standing and

watched Charles with a fixed gaze that grew darker and more intense as Charles unfolded the story.

When Charles finished, Quen was silent for the length of several heartbeats. "I should be more shocked than I am. I never suspected, but—I always used to wonder why Father favored Val." He drew a long breath, the sort that shudders through bone and muscle. "This explains it. It's not as though we're the first family this has happened to. Everyone knows old Lord Melbourne didn't father William Lamb and they manage to rub along—" He swallowed as though forcing the revelations down his throat. "My mother died when I was in shortcoats. I didn't really know her. She—"

"Was a pawn in a nasty game Kenneth and Glenister played," Charles said. "Don't blame her, Quen."

"Does Val know?"

"None of us has told him."

"I see." Quen gave a curt nod, though his eyes contained a world of burdens still to be dealt with. "That's my problem in any case." His gaze flickered round the company. "What the devil does this have to do with my uncle Cyril's death?"

Charles exchanged a glance with Mélanie. "Nothing that we've yet been able to determine."

"But Giles told you something about him? Something to do with his death? Oh, Christ, don't tell me it wasn't an accident? Did Father—"

"You're very quick," Charles said.

Quen looked back at him with a gaze from which all feeling had been bled. "In the past few hours I've come to believe my father— Lord Glenister—capable of anything. How did Uncle Cyril die?"

Giles McGann repeated his account of the midnight duel on the beach. Quen listened with the air of one who has overflowed his capacity for shock.

"Do you have any idea what the duel might have been about?" Charles asked.

Quen shook his head. "I have vague memories—Father and Uncle Cyril on horseback. Arguing about politics. Laughing together in the drawing room when we were brought in to say good night. They'd try to outdo each other, but that's much the way of it with brothers—" He frowned and turned to McGann. "Uncle Cyril said 'Take care of her' to Father? He didn't use Honoria's name?"

"No. No, I'm sure of it."

Quen looked at Charles. "I said they tried to outdo each other. The way Val and I do. Riding, sparring, fencing. Women as well, I don't wonder."

"You think the 'she' Cyril wanted Glenister to take care of was a woman they both loved? A woman they fought over?"

"It fits the facts, doesn't it? They were all drinking at this house party. Uncle Cyril let slip that he'd seduced Father's mistress. Father insisted on fighting him. Later Father was apparently overcome with remorse, and Uncle Cyril begged him to look after the woman with his dying breath." Quen's mouth hardened. "Honoria learned the truth and Father killed her to cover up his crime. Your father—oh, Christ, my—Kenneth Fraser guessed that Fath—Glenister—had killed Honoria and so Glenister killed him to keep him quiet."

"It fits the facts on the surface," Charles agreed. "It doesn't explain why Glenister was eager to have Honoria's murder investigated until Father's death and then suddenly became so eager to avoid questions that he turned tail and ran." He flipped open the ledger. "Do you know of any reason why Kenneth Fraser would have received payments from your grandfather?"

Quen's mouth curled. "You mean from the late Marquis of Glenister? My grandfather is apparently Kenneth Fraser's father. No, I don't. Was he receiving payments?"

Charles explained about the ledger.

"I can imagine either Uncle Cyril or Father being entangled in a secret marriage," Quen said in the same sort of strangely matter-of-fact voice they'd all been using to discuss such revelations. "Oh, Lord, I suppose that could bastardize Val and me, but as I seem to be a bastard in any case—" He rubbed his hands over his eyes. "You think that's why they quarreled? Uncle Cyril was asking Father to look after a woman whom he'd secretly married? But if the whole thing had been hushed up over a decade earlier, why did they suddenly quarrel at the house party?"

"Perhaps Lord Glenister didn't know of the marriage until the house party," Mélanie suggested. "Perhaps as you suggested, they both loved the lady."

"Have you ever heard of the Elsinore League, Quentin?" Tommy asked.

Quen shook his head with no sign of fear or recognition. "No. Are they important?"

"Very," Charles said. "Though we can't determine just the hell how. Apparently they're an organization Kenneth Fraser and Glenister started."

"Father—Glenister—wasn't much in the habit of confiding in me."

"Nor was Kenneth Fraser in me."

Quen gave a nod that was at once curt and tinged with fellow feeling. "What now?"

"We continue the investigation."

"Can you learn the truth?"

"I can try," Charles said.

Quen nodded again. "Evie and Val are upset about Father. I should tell them—something. If you don't—"

"It's all right," Charles said. "We can talk more later."

Quen moved to the door, then turned round, his hand on the doorknob. "Charles? When all's said and done, I'm rather glad you're my brother."

Tommy watched the door close behind Quen, then spun round to look at Charles with the gaze Charles remembered from the cricket field at Harrow. "You can't tell me that's all it was. Two brothers quarrel over a woman or a secret marriage and one kills the other? That's what they've been so desperate to cover up? Where does Le Faucon fit in?"

"Perhaps Le Faucon knew the truth of what happened and used it to blackmail Mr. Fraser and Lord Glenister into helping him escape France," Mélanie suggested.

"And then he killed Mr. Fraser? So why did Glenister run? He seems to be the one man who might know where the hell Le Faucon is. I'm half tempted to chase off after him, but I'm afraid Charles would learn something and not have the grace to share."

"How well you know me, Belmont."

Tommy scanned Charles's face as though it were an encoded document. "To quote Quentin, what now? This might be a good time for the investigative equivalent of the St. Crispin's Day speech."

"I'll talk to Aunt Frances. She's known Glenister and Cyril and Father longer than any of us. She was at Dunmykel when Cyril died."

"Not exactly the stuff that inspires the happy few, but I suppose it's a start." Tommy moved to the door. "I'm going to search out some dinner. Or at least a drink."

"I'd like to look in at my cottage," McGann said. "But I can come back and help keep watch tonight."

Assuming you trust me. He didn't add that, but the thought was evident in his tone. "Thank you, Giles," Charles said. "We'd be grateful for it."

McGann's gaze filled with a mixture of relief and worry at what was to come. He inclined his head to Mélanie and followed Tommy from the room.

Charles stared at the door. "Quen took that better than I expected," he said without looking at his wife.

"A combination of stoicism and shock, I suspect."

He nodded, gaze still on the polished mahogany. Without planning, he found himself saying, "I'd like to claim Quen for a brother. But I'm not sure—" He drew a breath and added in a rush, "Did you ever wonder if part of Hamlet's problem was that he suspected his father wasn't his father at all?"

He could feel the thoughtful shift in Mélanie's gaze, though he didn't look at her. "You think Claudius might have been his father?"

"Who's to say when Gertrude and Claudius became lovers? If young Hamlet suspected that his actual father wasn't the man demanding vengeance but the man he was being told to wreak vengeance on . . ."

"Your father doesn't have a brother," Mélanie said.

"No."

"But you wonder if someone else—"

He looked out the window at the rain-spattered lawn. "For years, I think. But I haven't admitted it until now."

"Why now?"

"Because I can't run away from him or any of it. And because of the viciousness of what Father did in seducing Glenister's wife. Perhaps I'm giving Father too much credit, but I think something more than the thrill of the game was behind it. If Father knew or guessed that his own—that I—was illegitimate, then Glenister's calm certainty that no gentleman would foist a bastard heir on another would have particularly rankled."

"You don't think Glenister—"

"Fathered me? No, or I doubt he'd have spoken to Kenneth as he did. I'm afraid I haven't the least idea who got my mother pregnant."

"Darling—"

He'd said too much. He fell into that trap with Mélanie. The moment he let his guard down, confidence tumbled upon confidence until his defenses were shattered like the walls of Badajoz. He moved to the door. "It's academic, really. Father or not, my relationship with Kenneth Fraser is a blank. And I still have to discover who killed him. Let's talk to Aunt Frances."

It was still light outside—the clock had just struck eight—but Mélanie lit a number of candles in the old drawing room. At this point they needed to illumine the questions asked in any manner they could. Lady Frances's hair shone golden in the candlelight, and the figured lilac sarcenet and Valenciennes lace of her skirts shimmered against the sofa. A queen, condescending to listen to the questions of a troublesome foreign ambassador.

"You're asking me to remember whom Glenister and Cyril Talbot were bedding nearly twenty years ago?" she said when Charles finished speaking.

"At the time of Cyril Talbot's death," Charles said. "Hardly an insignificant moment."

"My dear Charles, I can barely keep track of the romantic intrigues of my friends from week to week, let alone dredge up details from two decades ago."

Charles gripped the back of one of the canvaswork chairs. "This isn't drawing-room gossip, Aunt Frances. Two people are dead. And there's no reason to be certain it will stop there. Seventeen ninety-seven. Christopher was a baby. The Directory was in power in

France. Pitt was Prime Minister. The French had landed at Fish-
guard in February. Fox retreated from active politics. Tell us what
you can remember."

She smoothed her hands over her skirt. "I can't be sure of the
dates," she said at last, "but I think Glenister was still in the midst of
his intrigue with Lady Bessborough. Cyril probably had one of his
opera dancers in keeping—yes, he did, I remember seeing him driving in the park with her not long after I emerged from my lying-in
with Christopher. I'm not sure of her name—I need hardly say we
were never introduced, and he kept a whole string of them. Even if I
had known their names I couldn't have told them apart. They were
all the same type. Curly chestnut hair, blue eyes, delicate features. I
always suspected Cyril was trying to replace his first love, whoever
that might be."

"Mr. McGann didn't think Lord Cyril had been in love with his
wife," Mélanie said.

"No," said Lady Frances agreed. "Of course one can never say
exactly why any two people choose to marry, but I always thought
there was something a bit perfunctory about Cyril allying himself
with Susan Mallinson. As though he'd made up his mind to marry
and she was the most convenient choice at hand. Susan was fair-
haired, like Honoria. None of Cyril's mistresses were blondes."

"Do you think it's possible Glenister and Cyril competed for the
same woman?" Charles asked.

"Given the way they both behaved, it would have been a wonder
if they *hadn't* pursued the same woman at one point or another,"
Lady Frances said. "But I know of no specifics."

Charles walked to the piano and stood staring down at the keys.
"Do you think Cyril Talbot could be Andrew Thirle's father?"

"*Andrew's?* Good heavens, have we come to question *everyone's*
paternity? Catherine Thirle isn't at all Cyril's type."

"Apparently Mrs. Thirle didn't give birth to Andrew," Charles
said, and proceeded to tell the story of Andrew's birth, the ledger,
and their suspicions that Glenister or Lord Cyril had made a secret
marriage.

"Old Lord Glenister was an appalling high-stickler," Lady
Frances said. "He cut off poor Georgiana—Cyril and Frederick's
sister—without a shilling when she eloped with a man he deemed

ineligible. Of course, it didn't help that she gave birth to Evie a scant five months after the elopement. Her reputation never recovered." She shook her head. "When I think of the way Frederick and Cyril carried on their affairs with impunity while their sister suffered miserably for one love affair—which ended in marriage—it's enough to make me take that Wollstonecraft woman seriously."

"Quite," Charles said. "But if Frederick or Cyril had actually married a girl their father had deemed unsuitable, he wouldn't have been able to look the other way."

"No. I wouldn't be a bit surprised if old Lord Glenister had tried to cover up such a marriage. Or if he turned to Kenneth for help in doing so."

Charles ran his finger over the keys. "The sort of woman you say Cyril favored has Andrew's coloring."

Lady Frances pursed her lips. "I would have barely been out of the schoolroom when Andrew was born. I never heard any gossip about Cyril having a by-blow. But if you're asking if Andrew looks as though he could be the son of the sort of woman Cyril favored— yes. Very much so."

"Did Father ever say anything to you that would indicate payment from old Lord Glenister was the real source of his legacy?"

Lady Frances fingered her diamond bracelet. "He hated to discuss the legacy, which in itself may be suggestive." A fold of her lace overskirt had caught on the diamonds. She disengaged it. "Though he did once say—it was late one night. We were at Dunmykel. In the library. We'd just—suffice it to say, Kenneth was in the condition in which gentlemen are likely to make confidences."

A spasm crossed Charles's face, as though he could have lived without this image of his father and his aunt engaged in such an act in his favorite room at Dunmykel. "And?"

"I was looking at a Caravaggio drawing Kenneth had just bought. I said he'd been lucky to have acquired a fortune that allowed him to indulge his tastes. Kenneth turned his head toward me and said, 'Wise men make their own luck.' Which doesn't precisely fit with his fortune being founded on a legacy that was a lucky chance."

Charles nodded. He moved to the door as though done with the conversation, then turned back to his aunt. "Aunt Frances, did Father ever—"

"What?"

Mélanie felt the air quicken between her husband and Lady Frances.

After a seeming eternity measured by the trickle of wax down the tapers on the mantel, Charles shook his head. "Never mind. It doesn't really matter now."

Gisèle twisted round on one of the two straight-backed chairs on the first-floor landing to look at Mélanie. They were taking their turn keeping watch over the upstairs corridors. The long-case clock by the stairhead had just chimed out a quarter past one. "How on earth did you get Charles to agree to sleep? I'd have thought he'd insist on sitting guard all night."

Mélanie shifted her position on the chair, conscious of the weight of her pistol in the pocket of her gown. "Even Charles knows his limits. Though he's constantly testing them."

"What about you?"

"I know my limits." Mélanie twitched her gray jaconet skirt smooth. "I slept a few hours earlier. Charles will do better without me."

Gisèle studied her as though she were a half-deciphered text. "I used to not be able to make sense of the two of you. You don't act romantic in the least, not the way one expects lovers to act—"

"We're not lovers. We're married."

"But then you do that thing."

"What thing?"

"The thing where you have a whole conversation just looking at each other, without talking at all," Gisèle said, as though Mélanie was very slow not to have realized what she meant.

"That's what happens when you live with someone for a long time."

Gisèle shook her head. "I've seen lots of married couples. I've never seen anyone quite like the two of you. And then there's the way Charles looks at you when he doesn't think you're noticing."

"How?" Mélanie asked before she could stop herself.

"Like Romeo gazing up at Juliet on her balcony. I hoped—" Gisèle drew in her breath, so sharply that Mélanie felt the stir of air. "If I can't have that, I think I'd rather not be married at all."

Mélanie looked into her sister-in-law's eyes, bright with the reflected flame of the candle on the table between them. Any answer she might have made seemed to stick against painful truths in her throat. What could she say to a girl of nineteen ready to turn her back on love? It's all an illusion? She'd have said that once. Did she even believe it anymore? Could she believe in anything more lasting?

She was spared the necessity of speech by Simon's appearance. "I'll take over." He touched Gisèle on the shoulder. "Go get some rest, Miss Fraser."

"Oh, goodness, I'm not Charles. I couldn't sleep a wink tonight. I'll look in on Ian. Andrew and Evie are sitting with him."

Simon watched Gisèle walk off down the corridor, then sat beside Mélanie. His brows were drawn and an unvoiced fear lurked behind his eyes.

"What is it?" she said.

"I found something tucked away behind David's whisky bottle. I'm damned if I can explain what it means, but I think I know who drugged David's whisky."

"Who?" Mélanie said.

Simon uncurled his clenched palm to reveal a strip of ice-blue silk. "Honoria Talbot."

Chapter 37

S mall arms closed round his neck like a vise. Panicked breathing thudded against his chest. Molten flames shot up about them. He glanced round for a means of escape. He couldn't feel the heat of the flames. Glass enclosed them, protected them, imprisoned them. The flames beat against it.

What's happening, Charles? Honoria's voice sounded in his ear, desperate and insistent.

Charles sat up in bed, digging his fingers into his scalp, caught between sleep and waking. He could still feel Honoria clinging to him, though he knew she wasn't there.

The black streaks of the bedposts. The shadowy mass of dressing table and chairs. The lingering scent of his wife's perfume. He was surrounded by his room at Dunmykel, yet the pounding of his heart and the sweat pouring through his hair made the dream world as vivid as reality.

Mélanie. He wanted to run to her and pour out his fears into her lap. But he couldn't burden her. He couldn't lay himself open. He pushed back the bedclothes, pulled on his boots, and stumbled to the door, dressed in the shirt and breeches he'd been sleeping in. Mélanie was to the left, in the central corridor, where she could keep watch on all the occupied bedchambers save their own, deepest into the north wing. He ignored the tug of her presence (insistent, battering, seductive, like the notes of the sonata she loved to play) and turned to the right, toward what he knew he had to face.

The far end of the north wing. The day nursery, smelling of chocolate and buttered bannocks, filled with ghostly shapes in the darkness. He crossed to the windows by instinct, tugged back the curtains, jerked open the shutters. Cool black glass. Protecting, imprisoning. As it had in the dream. As it had when he was a boy of nine and looked out the window of another nursery to see a molten glow on the lawn beyond.

The memory, buried for years, returned in a flood. He'd been staying at his grandfather's. He'd woken and looked out the window of the nursery in his grandfather's house to see the glow of flames out the window. Not a fire, but the lamps and flambeaux of a carriage arriving late at night. He'd looked down and seen the Marquis of Glenister ascending the steps of his grandfather's house, shoulders stooped beneath a burden the ten-year-old Charles had not understood.

What's happening, Charles? Honoria had slipped into the nursery and tugged at his nightshirt, demanding an explanation he couldn't give. All he could do was hold her close, imparting a comfort he feared was as false as his own mother's promises.

The nursery door had jerked open. The thud of the oak and the rattle of the hinges reverberated through his memory. A dark figure had half fallen into the room. *Dear God.* Glenister's voice, hoarse but still recognizable. He'd wrenched Honoria out of Charles's arms and buried his face in her bright hair. Tears spilled from his eyes. Charles had never seen his father or any of his father's friends cry before.

Sweetheart. Glenister had stroked Honoria's hair. *I'm so sorry. So very sorry. But I'll make amends. I swear it. I'll take care of both of you.*

Charles, aged nine-and-twenty, stood alone in the day nursery at Dunmykel, picturing Glenister holding Honoria only days after he'd killed her father.

Both of you?

.   .   .

Mélanie fingered the strip of silk. "It's definitely Miss Talbot's. I saw her dressing gown when Charles and I searched her room."

Simon nodded. "It's the one she wore to my room and dropped on the floor. The question is, why the devil would Honoria have drugged David's whisky? If she was trying to drug me and thought she'd have a better chance at having her way with me if I was unconscious, she knew less about men than I thought."

Mélanie stared at the shimmering silk. "She could have been planning to seduce David. But again, I can't see what she'd have to gain from drugging him unconscious first. It doesn't make sense."

"No. I wish to God I knew what mischief she'd been planning, but it doesn't get us any closer to knowing who drugged Honoria herself."

"Quite. The two may be completely unrelated."

Simon stared into the shadows in the arched recesses between the wall sconces. "If Glenister killed her, David won't let it go."

"Neither will Charles."

"I can't stop David. I wouldn't want to stop him, truth to tell. But it can be a dangerous thing, trying to bring down a peer." Simon turned to look at her. "How long can Charles keep this up?"

"I don't know."

Simon's gaze lingered on her face. "He's always driven himself hard, from when I first knew him at Oxford. I used to be amazed at how long he could go without sleep and still render a coherent argument. Sometimes in Latin." He gave a faint smile, but his eyes stayed serious. "Later, after his mother died, I couldn't believe how he could go on devouring Ludlow and Hume and Suetonius and sit up arguing politics in a coffeehouse as if nothing had happened. But— in the end none of us are truly immune to feeling."

For a moment Mélanie thought he meant to say more, but instead he tented his hands together and stared at his fingertips.

She looked at the first of the grisaille paintings on the stair wall. Erato, the gray shadings of her form washed golden by the candle-light. In the flickering light, she almost seemed to be moving. "Simon. Did you ever wonder if Hamlet might have feared he was really Claudius's son rather than the king's?"

Simon raised his brows but didn't question the change in subject. "Anything's possible. I staged a production of *Hamlet* once where

Laertes insisted on playing the part as though he was driven by an incestuous passion for Ophelia, which has about as much or as little textual evidence. I told him it was an interesting thought, but we weren't doing *'Tis Pity She's a Whore* this season. What's the matter?"

Mélanie was on her feet, her thoughts tumbling with possibilities that chilled her to the bone and quickened her blood. "I've just thought of something. Simon, I'm going to fetch Mr. McGann to keep watch with you. I'm sorry to desert you, but it's important. You could say it's the key to everything."

Charles opened the door of the day nursery and stepped into the corridor. He started to turn to the left, toward his and Mélanie's bed-chamber, but sensed a stir of movement to the right, more a prickling of his nerves than a sight or sound. The door at the end of the north wing creaked softly. Someone was slipping down the servants' stairs, away from the sharp gazes of those keeping watch in the central block.

Charles made his way to the end of the corridor and down the servants' stairs, grateful that all the creaky treads were still ingrained in his memory from childhood. He could hear faint footfalls ahead. He reached the base of the stairs and inched through the archway into the corridor in time to catch a glimpse of pale hair and a black coat vanishing into the library. Tommy.

Charles walked down the corridor and eased open the library door. No stir of movement, no exclamation of surprise. He found a flint and lit the nearest lamp. The room was empty. Tommy must have gone down the secret passage. Charles extinguished the lamp, put the flint in his pocket, and took one of the tapers from the mantel. There was nothing for it but to follow.

"Mélanie." Gisèle looked up at the opening of the door to the room that had been given over to Ian. Her smile changed to a look of concern. "Is something the matter?"

"No." Mélanie closed the door and schooled her features to cheerful ordinariness. "Mr. McGann was chivalrous and gave me a brief respite. I thought I'd see how the rest of you were doing." She looked from Gisèle to Evie, who was perched beside her, to Ian, lying in the sickbed, and Andrew, sitting on the opposite side.

"I'm sorry, Mrs. Fraser," Ian said. Mélanie was pleased to see he had a little more color than he'd had the previous evening. "I keep trying to think if there's something more I can remember from when I worked for Mr. Wheaton."

"So do I." Andrew's mouth tightened. "But I'm afraid I wasn't important enough for Wheaton to reveal secrets to."

Mélanie dropped down on the end of the bed. "Did you ever get the sense that the smugglers might have had special hiding places?"

"Hiding places?" Ian and Andrew asked, almost in unison, in the same surprised tone.

"For especially valuable objects or papers." Mélanie glanced round the circle of faces. The lamplight shone off four puzzled gazes. "Charles and I suspect Mr. Fraser may have had some important papers that weren't in his dispatch box. Papers that Miss Talbot had discovered, papers that may have to do with why she was killed. I was wondering if Mr. Fraser could have hid the papers in the rooms off the cave."

"Rooms off the cave?" Andrew shook his head. "I'm sorry, I don't mean to keep repeating things. But I didn't realize—"

"I though you must know. Mr. Fraser built a set of hidden rooms off the cave the smugglers used. Through a panel in the rock, much like the one in the library." Mélanie smoothed a wrinkle in the quilt. "It would have been the perfect place to hide something he didn't wish to have discovered." She waited a moment, just to make sure the words had sunk in, then reached out to feel Ian's forehead. "Oh, good. No fever."

Charles traversed the passage, mentally calling himself every type of fool imaginable. How the hell had Tommy got downstairs without being glimpsed by Mélanie and whoever else was keeping watch over the first-floor corridor? No, that was a foolish question. Eluding attention was Tommy's stock-in-trade, just as it had been Charles's own. Damnation. He'd come far too close to trusting his erstwhile colleague. He should have remembered that Tommy was working for Castlereagh, whose loyalties and motivations with regard to the Elsinore League were still far from clear. He should have remembered that above all Tommy was always committed to winning the game. Of course, he still wasn't sure what the hell game Tommy was playing.

No footfalls sounded ahead. Tommy was moving silently. At the fork in the passage Charles hesitated a moment, but he could think of no logical scenario for Tommy to have gone to the lodge, so he continued on toward the cave.

He inched into the cave as he had the library. When no sound greeted him beyond the pull of the waves, he lit his taper. The cave was as empty as when he and Mélanie had visited it two nights ago, the crates still stacked as they had been. He went to the mouth of the cave and shone the light of the taper over the sand. No footprints. Which meant that either he'd been wrong and Tommy had gone to the lodge for God knew what reason. Or that Tommy had triggered the panel to the supposedly secret rooms.

Charles pressed the depression Mélanie had found in the granite and blew out his taper as the panel slid open. This business was better accomplished in the dark.

The inner passage was as quiet as that from the house, leading Charles to wonder if perhaps he was on a fool's errand. But then he rounded a corner and saw a blur of lamplight that warmed the granite. The door to the secret chambers, with its intricate rose lock, had been left ajar. He stepped through the open doorway. Tommy stood with his back to the door, a lamp on the table beside him, fingers moving over the gauzy folds of the gown Juliet was half wearing in one of the paintings.

"Looking for something?" Charles said.

"Christ, Fraser." Tommy spun round. "I should have known it was no good trying to give you the slip."

"So you should." Charles advanced into the room. "How the hell did you get past Mélanie?"

"Slipped out my window and went along the outside of the house. You and Mélanie should have thought of that. Civilian life's making you soft."

"You should have realized I was following you. What the hell are you doing here, Belmont? How did you even know where these rooms were?"

"It wasn't hard to figure out how to find them once you mentioned they existed. You aren't the only one with picklocks."

"And your reasons?"

"It doesn't take a genius to deduce that if your father had any papers too dangerous to keep in the dispatch box, this is the most likely hiding place. I suppose to be sporting I should have come to you and we could have searched for the hiding place together. But we're not at Harrow anymore. The playing fields of Europe are a bit more complicated."

Charles set his unlit taper down on the table. "Have you found anything?"

"If I had, I'd hardly have been running my fingers over Juliet's charming frock. I prefer my women flesh and blood rather than painted. Since you're here, I've no objection to searching together."

Charles scanned the room. "Have you tried the Hamlet paintings?"

"I checked Gertrude and her trio of gallants. I hadn't got to Hamlet and Ophelia."

Charles picked up the lamp from the table and held it up to the painting of the Prince of Denmark and the far-too-insipid-looking Ophelia. The couple were surrounded by shadows, but the lamplight revealed no hidden clues in the dark recesses of the picture. The light bounced off the filmy white of Ophelia's gown. The texture appeared remarkably real. The artist had not been without talent. Like Juliet, Ophelia was half wearing the gown. It was pushed down to reveal her shoulders and breasts and the skirt was tucked up, but a jeweled girdle encircled her waist. Charles lifted the lamp higher. "Look at that."

"What?"

"The clasp on the girdle."

"It looks like some sort of design, but—"

"I think it's the castle from the Elsinore League seal, tilted on its side. Hold the lamp."

Charles dragged one of the Holland-covered chairs over and climbed up on it. The clasp on Ophelia's girdle was the Elsinore League seal, or a simplified version of it, tilted on its side and unrecognizable unless one looked closely. He ran his fingers over it. Plots within plots, secrets within secrets, hiding places within hiding places. With a click, a piece of the painting sprang open to reveal a narrow aperture. Charles reached inside and felt the cool, dry crackle of old paper.

Tommy let out a low whistle and set the lamp down on the table. Charles lifted the papers out, sprang down from the chair, and walked over to the lamplight. A bundle of letters bound with pink silk ribbon and fastened to other papers with a plainer, buff-colored ribbon. He caught the date on the top letter, October 1784, and the words *My dearest Cyril* in a round schoolgirl hand. He moved closer to the lamp.

"I take it back," Tommy said. "Civilian life hasn't robbed you of your talents. But you were always too trusting. Set the papers down and step away from the table."

Charles turned his head. Tommy was standing three feet away, a pistol in his hand.

"I didn't realize Castlereagh was so desperate for information," Charles said. "Or so lacking in trust in me."

"If you think I won't fire because I'll have to answer to Castlereagh, think again. This doesn't have anything to do with our esteemed Foreign Secretary. Put the papers down, Charles."

Charles set the papers on the table, aware that Tommy's gaze was focused on his right hand as he so. At the same time, with his left hand, he eased the flint from his pocket. Tommy reached for the papers. As he tucked them inside his coat, Charles hurled the flint at his right shoulder.

Tommy flinched and his arm jerked. Charles sprang at him as he pulled the trigger on the pistol. The shot went wide, as Charles had calculated it would. He and Tommy crashed through the archway into the next room. Tommy tossed aside the spent gun, spun away from Charles, and reached behind him. Something silver glinted in his hand. A rapier from the basket of props. The blade sliced through Charles's shirt and across his left shoulder. Charles twisted away, stumbled to the basket, and snatched up a second rapier. He whirled round and smashed the rapier blade against Tommy's sword.

They backed into the main room, blade meeting blade in a deadly parody of their Harrow fencing matches.

"Careful, Charles." Tommy circled round, blade gleaming in the lamplight, eyes harder than the steel of the rapier. "I've been practicing all these months you've been lounging on a parliamentary bench and scribbling speeches."

Charles circled in the opposite direction, gaze trained on Tommy for the smallest flicker of intention in the other man's face. "How long have you been working for them?"

"For whom?" Tommy's eyes glittered like dark glass. Sweat glistened on his forehead.

"The Elsinore League. Or Le Faucon de Maulévrier. Or both. Did you meet with Le Faucon in London? Or did you come to Dunmykel to see him?"

"My dear Charles." Tommy danced to one side, blade extended. "You should know better than to think a man in Le Faucon's position stayed within reach of Dunmykel once he disembarked."

"So it wasn't Le Faucon in the library the night Honoria was killed. It was you." Charles moved to counter him, dodging away from the trap of the table. "For God's sake why, Tommy?"

"Let's say with the war over I needed a new scope for my talents."

"Doing Le Faucon's dirty work? Did you kill Francisco Soro for him?"

Tommy edged away from the lamplight. "What makes you think that?"

"Because I doubt Le Faucon, whoever he is, would have risked his neck taking shots at the Somerset Place terrace. And I know your talents as a sniper."

"You flatter me, Charles. If my aim was better you'd have been dead that night and we'd have been spared this bout of swordplay."

"Did you kill my father?" The words came out with a desperation Charles hadn't intended, as though the answer could somehow expunge nine-and-twenty years of distance and uncertainty. As though he owed a debt to the man who probably hadn't been his father at all.

Tommy's fingers tightened on the rapier handle. "That question's a bit more complicated than you might think."

"The question of who bashed Kenneth Fraser's head in isn't complicated at all." Charles stepped to the side, so he had open space at his back. "If you're planning on killing me, there's no harm in telling me the whole truth."

"Oh, no, Charles. I've learned never to count on my plans working in advance," Tommy said.

Then he lunged for the kill.

Mélanie slipped into the library, moved to a wing-back chair in the corner beside the fireplace, and blew out her candle. Nothing to do now but wait and see if she was right, though her throat ached and her stomach churned with the fear that she was.

The cold seeped through her gown and shawl. The stillness pressed in on her. She was beginning to hope she was wrong when the hinges of the door creaked and the air stirred. She willed herself to immobility.

A slight, dark figure slipped into the room, stood still for a moment, then started across the room with determined steps and the stir of kerseymere.

"Hullo, Evie," Mélanie said.

Chapter 38

S pasy, wake up.”

"Quen.” Aspasia sat up in bed, blood pounding, thoughts atumble. “What's happened? Is Chloe—"

"Everyone's fine. My God, what we've come to.” A desperate laugh underlay his voice. “You never used to scream when I came to your room in the middle of the night.”

"Are you mad?” She tugged the sheet over the serviceable linen of her nightdress. “I have no intention—"

"It's all right, Spasy. I haven't come here to seduce you. I have more important things to think about.” The flame of the candle he carried wavered as though his fingers were trembling. He set the candle on her bedside table. “You were right. About Evie.”

Her throat closed. “I won't say I told you so. I'm glad you talked to her.”

"I didn't bring it up. She did, though not in so many words. We were talking and then suddenly she was in my arms.”

She wanted this. She knew it was right. So why did it feel as if a knife was twisting beneath her ribs? “That sounds like effective communication.”

"It's the devil of a mess."

"Quen, if you'd only stop these Corsairlike delusions that you're not fit to touch the hem of her gown—"

"It's not that. That is, I'm certainly not fit to touch the hem of her gown, but that's not the problem." His hand clenched on the quilt, crumpling the moss roses. "I love Evie. But I'm not in love with her. I thought perhaps—but the moment she leaned into me, everything was clear."

"If you think—"

"Will you be quiet for two seconds together, woman? This isn't one of your schoolrooms. I'm not in love with Evie, and I don't think I ever could be. I don't think I'm capable of loving anyone else so long as I'm still in love with you."

For a moment, she was sure she'd never breathe again. "Oh, my dear. I won't pretend I'm not—that a part of me isn't flattered. But you will get over—"

"That's just it." He placed his hand over her own. His fingers were warm and firm and oh so familiar. "I don't see why I should want to."

She tugged her hand away. "Because of what we said earlier today. We can't go back."

Quen stared down at a frayed thread in the quilt. "I learned a number of things today. Including the fact that apparently Kenneth Fraser fathered me."

She'd thought no revelation about the Glenister House family could surprise her. She'd been wrong. "Quen—"

"I've spent five-and-twenty years either trying to live up to my father's expectations or trying to prove I could go merrily on my way to hell and not give a damn what he thought of me. Or sometimes both at once. One way or another I've let my entire life be shaped by a man who isn't even my father, a man who may have killed Honoria. What's the sense? I'm through with playing by other people's rules. I'm going to rough-hew my own destiny. I don't want to go back, Spasy. I want to go forward."

She felt the pull of his words like a tug to the marrow of her bones. "I can't, Quen. I can't be your mistress again. It was madness the first time. Sweet madness, but I can't repeat it."

"I don't want you to be my mistress," the future Marquis of Glenister said. "I want you to be my wife."

. . .

"Mrs. Fraser." Evie turned from the library fireplace, her face a mask of shadows. "I came down to look for a book."

"In the secret passage in the dark?"

Evie stepped away from the carved Fraser crest that triggered the opening to the passage. "Silly of me, I suppose. Ian fell asleep and Gisèle seemed to want a moment alone with Mr. Thirle. I gave up any hope of trying to sleep myself tonight. I was thinking of what you were saying about the hidden rooms and I wanted to see them. I never have."

"Exploring the passage with a killer running about could be dangerous," Mélanie said. "Didn't Simon and Mr. McGann ask you what you were doing?"

"I told them I was going to get a book. I wasn't thinking very clearly, truth to tell. I just wanted to be doing something."

"You wanted to find the papers I said might be hidden in the secret rooms."

"No. Well, yes, of course, if I could. It would help if we had them, wouldn't it?"

"If I'm right that they contain a secret Honoria was killed to conceal, then yes, very much."

Evie's eyes widened. The whites gleamed in the darkness. "You think that's why Honoria was killed? Because she knew something dangerous?"

"And was trying to use the knowledge to blackmail someone." Mélanie crossed the library and lit the lamp on the gateleg table in the center of the room. "What was it, Evie? Did she try to force you to slip into David's bed? Some sort of revenge for Simon rejecting her?"

Evie drew back against the paneling. "Mrs. Fraser, I'm not sure what you think happened, but I can tell you've got it hopelessly twisted round."

Mélanie studied Honoria Talbot's cousin, only a little over a year younger than she was herself. One of the few people in Britain who'd accepted her from their first meeting. "It was the earrings. I should have thought of it earlier."

"The earrings?" Evie repeated, as though Mélanie had taken leave of her senses.

"You said Honoria came to your room the night of the murder because she wanted to borrow your coral earrings. But Fitton said Miss Talbot told her she wanted to wear her striped lilac sarcenet and her violet spencer the next day. Honoria had an impeccable sense of style and color. She wouldn't have worn coral with lilac and violet."

Evie burst into laughter that echoed off the dark reaches of the ceiling. "That's what you're basing this on? Mrs. Fraser, I know you're desperate to find answers—we all are—but surely you realize Honoria might have changed her mind about what she meant to wear the next day?"

"She might. But then I started considering the other facts. Simon figured out that it was Honoria herself who drugged David's whisky. Not the way to embark on another seduction attempt. But what better revenge than to have Simon's lover caught in bed with a woman, an unmarried young woman whom David would be in honor bound obliged to marry. David's father would insist on it—in fact, he'd be only too happy to see David with a wife."

"David can stand up to his father."

"But David's own sense of honor would compel him to make the girl an offer rather than see an innocent pawn face ruin."

Evie shook her head. Wisps of chestnut hair fell about her face and clung to her forehead. "You can't imagine I'd ever agree to such a scheme."

"Not without a great threat being held over your head."

"What could possibly be—"

"We all have an ultimate weakness, something that can push us over the edge." Mélanie glanced down at the lamplight on the red-grained wood of the table. She knew, none better, how to search out those weaknesses and turn them to her own advantage. "Power, fortune, a cause, the need to protect those we love." She lifted her gaze to Evie's face. "Lord Quentin said you think it's your job to look after everyone in the family. Miss Newland said you were practically running Glenister House at thirteen."

Evie's gaze held the sort of confusion Mélanie saw on Colin's face when he couldn't follow the logic of an adult conversation. "I'm sorry, I must be being very stupid. I thought you were accusing me of killing Honoria. And now you're saying I killed the girl who was practically my sister to protect my family?"

"The rest of your family. Because the knowledge she'd acquired endangered all of them."

A spasm crossed Evie's face but her eyes remained as clear as spring water. "I don't understand."

"Your grandfather, old Lord Glenister, paid Kenneth Fraser to tidy up problems for him. Thirty-two years ago, he paid Kenneth Fraser a particularly large sum, so large a sum that Kenneth Fraser was able to stand for Parliament and eventually purchase Dunmykel. At roughly the same time, Mr. Fraser paid Mr. and Mrs. Thirle to raise a baby as their own baby daughter's twin. Andrew."

"You're saying Andrew Thirle is Mr. Fraser's son?"

"Andrew believed so, but Charles and I think Kenneth Fraser was acting as your grandfather's agent in the matter."

"You think my *grandfather*—"

"We couldn't determine who had fathered Andrew, though we suspected it was a member of your family. We also learned that at some point in the past, the current Lord Glenister and Mr. Fraser embroiled their friends, both here and on the Continent, in something dangerous, something personal, something Mr. Fraser and Lord Glenister feared Honoria learning the truth about to the day she died."

Evie ran her hands over the thick gray folds of the gown she'd worn to Honoria's funeral. "Mrs. Fraser, my uncle and Mr. Fraser and their friends did many things I'm sure they'd have preferred Honoria never to learn. Need I elaborate?"

Mélanie turned up the lamp so the light spilled between them. "And we know for a fact that twenty years ago this autumn, the current Lord Glenister and his brother, Lord Cyril, had a sudden falling-out at a house party at Dunmykel. Kenneth Fraser was present, as were a number of their friends, friends they'd known since university and the Grand Tour. Lord Glenister insisted on challenging Lord Cyril to a duel and mortally wounded him."

Fear flashed in Evie's gaze, like a ripple in a stream. "Uncle Cyril died in a shooting accident."

"That was only the cover story. When he was dying Lord Cyril begged his brother to 'take care of her.'"

Evie wet her lips as though her mouth were dry. "Honoria. Of course Uncle Cyril would have wanted Uncle Frederick to look after her."

"So I thought at first. But Honoria's guardianship was already arranged to be shared by Lord Glenister and Lord Carfax, all the legal documents drawn up. Lord Quentin suggested that Lord Cyril might have been referring to a different woman, a woman both brothers had loved. Andrew Thirle's biological mother, perhaps? Lady Frances said Lord Cyril kept a succession of mistresses of the same physical type—chestnut-haired, blue-eyed, small-boned. She suspected they all resembled his first love. I think she may have been right and that that first love was Andrew's mother. Then I realized the chestnut hair and blue eyes fit someone else." Mélanie surveyed the young woman before her. "I expect you look very like your mother, Evie."

Aspasia stared into the dark eyes of the man who had been her lover. "That's not funny, Quen."

"It wasn't meant to be. Do you want me to go down on my knees?" Quen's gaze glittered with a fire that would spill beyond the confines of any grate. "You always laughed at that sort of thing in novels, but I'm happy to oblige."

"I'm fifteen years older than you."

"Charles is six years older than his wife. Thirle's thirteen years older than Gisèle and that doesn't stop them from looking longingly at each other."

"It's different—"

"With women? For shame, Spasy. I thought better of you."

She drew back against the headboard, resisting the pull of his gaze and the false promise it held, bright as paste jewels. "You can't marry a governess."

"You've suddenly become a believer in the social divide?"

"We can't ignore realities. We'd never be—"

"Accepted? By a pack of dowagers we don't care a rush for anyway?"

"Your family—"

"You mean the father who isn't really my father? For what it's worth, I think Val will come round. Evie"—a spasm crossed his face—"Evie won't turn her back on us. She's made of stronger stuff than that. Father may cut off my allowance. Are you afraid to be poor?"

"I've been poor all my life. But you should have a family—"

"You don't want children of your own?"

She turned her head away and blinked back tears. "You don't even know if I can have them."

"Well, for that matter, I don't know if I can, either. We certainly went to rather uncomfortable lengths to prevent finding out five years ago."

"Quen—"

"Do you love me?"

"Unfair."

"Do you?"

"It's not that simple."

"You're afraid we'll make each other miserable? I don't know about you, but I've been fairly miserable these past years without you. I really don't see how marriage could make the situation worse."

He gripped her shoulders and put his mouth against hers. "I need you. I'm lost without you. But don't marry me because of that. Marry me because you need me, too."

Evie scarcely moved, but the revulsion in her gaze was like the kick of a musket. "What are you saying? That it wasn't Uncle Cyril's indiscretion Mr. Fraser was paid to cover up? It was my mother's?"

The weight of a still-unvoiced past thickened the air between them, like the smell of damp and leather and old parchment that filled the library. "A friend of Lord Glenister's and Mr. Fraser's recently blackmailed Mr. Fraser into helping him escape France," Mélanie said. "I suspect he had helped Mr. Fraser conceal the truth of Andrew's birth. He asked Charles's friend Giles McGann if he believed it was possible to 'pawn a heart.' We knew it was a quote, but none of us could place it or determine its relevance. Until just now, when Simon made a reference to *'Tis Pity She's a Whore*. And all at once I realized where the quote came from and why the man had referred to it."

"For God's sake, Mrs. Fraser, I know how Charles is about plays, but if you're going to base this on earrings and quotations—"

"'I have . . . killed a love, for whose each drop of blood I would have pawned my heart.' *'Tis Pity* is the story of a corrupt society in which the only pure love is the incestuous passion between a brother and sister."

All the blood fled from Evie's face. "That's monstrous. You're implying that my mother and Uncle Cyril—"

"Were lovers when they were young. I can only guess at the details, but I can tell you what I think happened. Your mother became pregnant—she must have only been seventeen or so. At your grandfather's request, Mr. Fraser—who had undertaken other secret errands for him—arranged for her to go away, probably to France, to have the baby in secret and then brought the baby to the Thirles. No doubt he sought the help of friends in France to make the arrangements."

"But even if that were true, Uncle Frederick would have known—"

"Perhaps not. Perhaps it was only Mr. Fraser and his friends who were involved in the arrangements and they kept your Uncle Frederick in ignorance of his sister's plight. Or perhaps he knew the truth of the matter and forgave his brother because he was so young. What he didn't realize was that Lord Cyril and your mother had resumed the affair and your mother found herself with child again. Only this time she eloped with an impoverished army officer and passed the baby off as his. Somehow the truth came out at that house party twenty years ago. Whatever he knew of the past, Lord Glenister couldn't forgive Lord Cyril this time. He insisted on fighting him. When Lord Cyril begged Lord Glenister to take care of 'her,' he wasn't talking about a mistress or about Honoria. He was talking about his other daughter, the daughter he couldn't claim. He was talking about you, Evie."

Evie drew a long, harsh breath. "Mrs. Fraser, I grew up in Glenister House. I'm scarcely naive. But I don't know whether to be more shocked or offended at what you've just implied about my mother. Not to mention my uncle Cyril."

"It takes something shocking to motivate a murder."

"But even if this fantastic story were true, why should it have motivated me or anyone else to kill Honoria?"

"Because Honoria had been curious about her father's death for years and she'd stumbled upon the truth. Probably in papers Mr. Fraser kept hidden. Papers that we have yet to discover. Papers you tried to find in Mr. Fraser's dispatch box."

"How on earth could I—"

"Someone picked the lock on the dispatch box. It can be done with a hairpin, though it's a bit time consuming. But these papers aren't in the dispatch box. You believed me when I suggested they might be in the secret rooms."

"Of course I believed you. It would never have occurred to me that you were playing such a fantastical game." Evie regarded Mélanie in much the way Rosencrantz or Guildenstern might stare at Hamlet when he spouted his most fantastical nonsense. "I still don't see why you think I killed Honoria."

"Because Honoria, who turned all information to her own ends, threatened to reveal the story if you wouldn't go along with her plan and hide in David's bed. Which would have led to you and David being forced into an unhappy marriage of convenience. And Honoria would have had a hold over you forever and a way to bring unhappiness to those you loved."

"Honoria wouldn't have dared reveal such a story even if it were true."

"Could you risk that?" Mélanie pressed up against the hairline cracks in Evie's composure with a relentlessness that was as automatic as the cut and parry of a sword fight. "Your mother's happiness, your uncle's, your own . . ."

"There's no risk if the story isn't true."

"Your uncle feared the truth of the past coming out. That's why he fled rather than face Charles's questions."

"It's absurd." Evie spun away, then turned back to face Mélanie. "I scarcely know where to begin, the story is so absurd. All other things aside, how could I have known Honoria would be in Mr. Fraser's room?"

"Because she told you." Mélanie turned her deductions against Evie like the edge of a blade. The words came easily, but nausea bit her in the throat, like last night when the smugglers had beaten her. She wondered if Charles would forgive her for destroying another of his childhood friends. She wondered if she'd forgive herself. "Other than Val, you're just about the only person Honoria might have confided in about her plans to seduce Mr. Fraser. I suspect she did come to your room the night of the murder. Or summoned you to hers. Not to borrow your coral earrings, but to talk about her plans for David. She may have meant for you to slip into David's bed that night or that may have been a plan for the future. But I'm quite sure she told you she meant to go to Mr. Fraser's room herself later that evening. Perhaps she knew he'd gone off with Lady Frances and she said she planned to be waiting for him when he returned. If so, you'd have known she'd be alone in Mr. Fraser's bedchamber."

The slash of the accusations showed in Evie's eyes, but her gaze did not waver. "Honoria was drugged."

"With laudanum. Probably the laudanum she kept in her own room. You must have known about it—it was part of the plan for David. Either you managed to drug her brandy in her room two nights ago, or you'd done so earlier."

"And then I went to Mr. Fraser's room and strangled her with the bellpull? My cousin? My almost-sister?"

"Who couldn't be stopped in any other way," Mélanie said.

Evie stared at her with a gaze that was battle worn and bleeding but still defiant. "You're mad, Mrs. Fraser."

"Quite possibly. That doesn't mean I'm not right."

The heavy oak door thudded open.

"Mélanie, thank goodness." Gisèle ran into the library, a candle tilting in her fingers. "It's Charles. I went to check on him and he's not in his room. He didn't come into the main corridor, so he must have gone down the back stairs in the north wing. Do you think he went to the secret rooms to look for the papers?"

Hell and the devil. Mélanie had been trying to draw Evie out with her theory about the papers, but the papers could well really be in the secret rooms. Charles must have concluded as much. Damn the man, why had he gone off without her?

Mélanie moved to the panel. "I'll check."

"I'll go with you," Evie said.

Mélanie looked into Evie's bright, steady gaze, checked her instinctive retort, and nodded. Better to keep the girl where she could watch her. And if Charles had discovered the papers and they contained what Mélanie suspected, better to confront Evie with the proof away from the others.

"Shall I come, too?" Gisèle asked.

"No, stay and help keep watch upstairs. Let David and Simon and the others know where we've gone."

Gisèle's gaze skimmed over Mélanie's face. "Charles will be all right, won't he?"

"I should think so. Charles can take care of himself." Mélanie pressed her fingers to the crest and released the panel. "Most of the time," she added under her breath.

Charles parried Tommy's sword thrust and spun to the side. Pain screamed through the cut in his shoulder. He brought his sword up in a counterattack. Blade whipped against blade. The world shrank down to the point of a sword, the flick of another man's wrist, the advantage of a foot of ground, a split second of time, an inch of steel.

Tommy pressed the attack, driving Charles against the table. Charles fell back as though he had stumbled, snatched the pewter lamp from the table behind him, and hurled it at Tommy's head.

Glass shattered. Metal struck flesh. The room was plunged into darkness, filled with the smell of coal oil and singed hair. Charles lunged forward, sword extended to slash at where Tommy had been standing. His blade met something solid. Tommy gave a muffled curse, followed by a stir of movement and then the slice of his blade against Charles's own.

Charles could barely pick out the darker form of his opponent in the shadows. They dueled the length of the room again, but this time it was like fighting a phantom, relying not on the treacherous evidence of one's eyes but on the stir of booted feet on the Aubusson carpet, the whip of a blade through the air, the smell of the other man's sweat.

Charles stepped to the side, round where he thought the sideboard stood. The second it took him to judge the distance gave Tommy the opening he needed. He flung himself forward, pinning Charles to the wall with his body. Their blades twanged together overhead. White fire ran down Charles's shoulder.

He pressed his arm against Tommy's, scrabbling for an inch of

advantage. Steel whined against steel. Then candlelight spilled
through the open door. Tommy stumbled back, blade still aimed at
Charles.

"I suggest you stop trying to run a sword through my husband,
Tommy, unless you want a bullet through the heart," Mélanie said.

Chapter 31

Mélanie looked into Tommy's brilliant blue eyes. He was watching her with much the same flirtatious mockery as when he was about to ask her for a waltz. Damn it to hell, she'd *liked* him. But then she should know friendship was no guarantee of anything. "Drop your sword on the ground, Tommy. And step away from it."

"My dear Mélanie—"

"Now. You know at this range I could choose between shooting you through the heart or between the eyes. Or in the stomach and watching you die slowly."

Tommy uncurled his fingers from the rapier hilt and let the weapon clatter to the ground. With the leisurely grace of a man crossing a ballroom floor in search of champagne, he took a half-dozen steps away from the fallen weapon. Out of lunging distance. His gaze moved to Evie. "Quite a gathering. I didn't realize you had a taste for intrigue, Miss Mortimer."

"Are you all right, Evie?" Charles asked. Sweat dripped from his forehead and plastered his shirt to his chest, but he didn't, to Mélanie's sharp eyes, appear to be seriously hurt.

Evie nodded. She was standing by the door, hands clasped

together. Charles shot a brief look at Mélanie. Mélanie flickered back an it's-too-complicated-to-explain-now look.

Gun trained on Tommy, Mélanie set her candle on the table. It cast a small circle of warmth on the unbleached cloth. The four of them stood in the blue-black shadows on the edges of the light. Mélanie glanced at Tommy. He was standing quite still, but even unarmed she knew he was as dangerous as a lit cannon. "What exactly is Tommy's interest in the matter?"

"I'm not sure," Charles said. "He's been working for Le Faucon and the Elsinore League. Or perhaps ultimately for one against the other. I'm quite sure he killed my father and Francisco and hired the man who attacked Manon in Covent Garden." Charles's voice was cool, but his eyes sparked with molten rage in the darkness. Her fair-minded husband wanted nothing better than to run his sword through Tommy Belmont. "He came back here tonight for papers Father hid in these rooms. He has them tucked inside his coat."

"My, you have learned a lot, haven't you?" Tommy studied the pistol in Mélanie's hand, like an archaeologist examining a potsherd he'd never seen before. "I must say, this is an interesting dilemma."

"There's no dilemma at all." Evie pulled a pistol from the pocket of her gown. "The papers, Mr. Belmont."

"Evie—" Mélanie said.

"Put your pistol down, Mrs. Fraser. I don't want to hurt anyone, but if what you suspect about me is true, you know I'll use this."

The room went still. Confusion, fear, and the dawning of under-standing shot through Charles's gaze. "Evie," he said in the quiet voice Mélanie had heard him use under sniper fire, "whatever else has happened, we're all on the same side when it comes to Tommy."

Evie spared him a brief glance. Memories flickered between them for a moment, the way they only can between people who've shared hobbyhorses and cambric tea in the nursery and first ponies. Then her gaze went hard in a way Mélanie would not have thought possible, even during their confrontation in the library. "We haven't been on the same side since Honoria learned how to twist you round her finger, Charles."

"For God's sake, Evie, this isn't about Honoria."

"Oh, Charles, haven't you learned anything? Everything's about Honoria. Even in death. She always saw to that." Evie's hand tightened on the trigger. "Mrs. Fraser." Her voice cut with insistence. Her fingers trembled. Her eyes glittered with the look Mélanie had seen on the faces of soldiers about to rush into the breach at the end of a siege.

Fear could make people do crazy things. Five years ago, Mélanie might have defied Evie's ultimatum and played dice with her own life. Five years ago she hadn't been a wife and mother. She looked from Evie's shaking fingers to her overbright eyes and then set her own pistol down on the table.

"Step away," Evie said.

"Evie, we aren't—"

"I mean it, Mrs. Fraser."

Mélanie moved away from the table, toward her husband.

"Throw your sword down by Mr. Belmont's, Charles."

"You've known me all your life, Evie," Charles said. "You must know I'd never—"

"I think the past two days have proved we can't be sure of what anyone might do. Throw the sword down, Charles. I know I could only shoot one of you, but you can't be certain whom it would be."

Charles stared at Evie a moment longer, as though measuring her resolve, then tossed his sword to clatter against Tommy's.

Evie walked toward Tommy. "The papers."

Tommy was staring at her, eyes dark with realization. "You killed her."

"You're not exactly in a position to make accusations, Mr. Belmont."

"In God's name, why? What petty, absurd jealousy—"

"I'm not the jealous sort, Mr. Belmont."

"My God, all that life, all that brilliance—you blotted it out."

"You see, Charles," Evie said, her gaze not leaving Tommy's face, "everything *is* about Honoria. I suppose I should have guessed you were in love with her, too, Mr. Belmont. Most men were."

"You coldhearted bitch, how dare you—"

"I believe I asked you for the papers."

Tommy regarded her for a long moment that seemed to stretch like a rope pulled to the breaking point. "Unfortunately, you leave me little choice, Miss Mortimer. You're a more resourceful woman than I would have thought. Or, it seems, than Mélanie would have thought." He reached inside his shirt, drew out a packet of papers, and held them out to her.

Evie had to walk close to him to take the papers. Mélanie calculated how many seconds it would take her to snatch her pistol from the table and what would happen if Evie panicked with Tommy close enough to grab her gun.

Evie's slippers whispered against the carpet. The papers crackled as her fingers closed round them. A second later, she collapsed on the floor, a knife hilt protruding from her chest.

Tommy snatched up Evie's gun and pocketed the blood-spattered papers. "Careless. She should never have got so close to me." He backed toward the door, the pistol extended toward Mélanie and Charles. "Don't look at me like that, Fraser, you wanted Honoria avenged as much as I did, but you'd never have had the guts to do it."

Mélanie dropped to the ground and pressed her shawl over Evie's wound, in a hideous repeat of their last moments with Francisco Soro.

"What the hell's in those papers?" Charles said. "Whoever you're working for, you aren't just trying to cover up romantic indiscretions. There's more, isn't there?"

"My dear Charles." Tommy put his hand to the door. "More than you'll ever know."

The door swung shut and the bolt slid into place.

Evie was struggling to draw a breath. "It's all right, sweetheart," Mélanie said. The endearment came to her lips as easily as if she were speaking to her children. "Don't try to talk."

"Quen—Val—tell them—sorry."

"I will."

Charles dropped down beside her. "Lie still, Evie." He touched his fingers to her cheek.

Evie's clouding gaze fastened on his face. "Honoria—there wasn't any other way."

Charles's face tightened with equal parts rage, grief, and guilt. But he merely said, "We'll get you out of here."

"Have you got your picklocks?" Mélanie asked. She pressed her shawl over Evie's chest. She could feel the chill spreading through the girl's body.

"No. I came hideously unprepared."

Mélanie pulled a pin from her hair. "Can you do it with this?"

"Given time." He glanced down at Evie.

"There isn't time." Evie caught at a fold of his coat. "Stay."

"Of course." Charles settled beside her and folded her hand between his own.

A smile twisted her lips. "Look after them for me, Charles."

"Quen's getting quite good at looking after himself."

"He shouldn't be alone. He'll make a shocking mull of things." Her gaze moved over the shadowy paintings—Hamlet and Ophelia; Romeo and Juliet; Olivia, Viola, and Sebastian. "What an odd place to die," she said, and went still.

Chapter 40

It was a variation on the aftermath of Honoria's murder. Mélanie went to get David and Simon. Charles went in search of Quen. They had placed Evie on the library sofa, as they had Kenneth the night before.

They gathered in the old drawing room, where Gisèle and Andrew, who had been in the library when they returned to the house, were already waiting. Quen brought Miss Newland with him. "We're going to be married," he said without preamble.

In another set of circumstances, it might have been a surprising announcement. As things were, Mélanie was merely conscious of a vague happiness for them, overlain by all the sorrows of the night.

Numbness encased them all, like the white-painted walls and linenfold doors of the room. Later, Mélanie thought, when the reality of Evie Mortimer's death and what she had done in life had gnawed its way through their consciousness, it would be worse. For now, that numbness was the only thing that allowed them to listen to the truth of what had happened.

They sat round the unlit fireplace, and she and Charles once again recounted the facts, past and present, that had come to light in the past few hours. Cold facts that could not begin to explain the feelings behind the events or the feelings that those events would now stir.

Strangely enough, it was David who protested that it couldn't be the way they said, who questioned every detail, who made them go over the story again and again. Quen sat by in frozen silence, eyes glazed not with shock or horror but with grief.

"David, don't," Quen said at last, his voice like a lash. "Questioning won't change the facts."

David, who'd been pacing, turned from the fireplace. "You believe it?"

Quen drew a breath, as though he had to sift the air through the mesh of everything he'd learned in the past two days. "It makes a sort of horrible sense," he said. "That's the thing with all these revelations. Honoria and Val, Kenneth Fraser and my fath—Glenister—and my mother. None of the revelations has been half so surprising as they should have been."

Miss Newland gripped his hand. He looked at her for a moment. What he saw in her eyes seemed to steady him.

"Yes, but—" David shook his head. "The idea that Honoria wanted Evie to be caught in my room as some sort of revenge for Simon—" He couldn't even say it. "It's preposterous. And she should have known I'd never—"

"Wouldn't you?" Simon, leaning against the piano, turned to fix his lover with a hard, even stare. "If Evie had been publicly caught in your bed and faced social ruin, you'd have felt in honor bound to offer to marry her. Don't deny it. You wouldn't be the man I lo—you wouldn't be yourself if you'd done otherwise."

David looked back at him. "But why the devil would Honoria—"

"Pique." Quen scraped his hands over his face. "Honoria couldn't abide being made a fool of. I knew that, even if I didn't—even if there was a lot about her I didn't understand."

Andrew had said nothing at all. He was staring at the candlelight on the swirls of green and gold on the carpet, as though answers lay in the intricacies of the pattern. Now he raised his gaze to Charles's face. "If Cyril and Georgiana Talbot were my parents—Evie Mortimer was my sister. They both were. Miss Mortimer and Miss Talbot."

"At least by blood. Not in the way Maddie is."

"If I'd known—"

"But you didn't," Mélanie said. "None of us did, until too late."

Gisèle spread her hands over her skirt, stained with dust and dirt and blood that must be Evie's. When they'd brought Evie into the library, Gisèle had knelt beside her for a long interval. "She was crying," Gisèle said now. "The night of the—the night Honoria was killed. Evie almost never cried. I should have known something was wrong."

Charles crouched beside her chair and squeezed her hands. "You couldn't have guessed this, Gelly. It takes a great deal to drive someone over that edge. You couldn't have known Evie was teetering on it."

"But she was my friend. I should have—" Gisèle rubbed her hand across her eyes. "Evie'd always do absolutely whatever she thought necessary to sort a situation out. She'd always seemed so sweet and reasonable, but she could be quite ruthless, really. I suppose she must have decided—"

Quen nodded. "She never shirked what she thought needed to be done. I loved her for it. I never guessed—" His hands went white-knuckled. "I don't think I can even remember ever seeing Uncle Cyril and Aunt Georgiana together. But there's a painting of them at Glenister House. Uncle Cyril must have been seventeen or so, Aunt Georgiana would have been sixteen. They're in a garden, laughing together. I'd always look at that painting and think how happy they looked, so much more at ease with each other than most siblings. I never thought—"

"That they were lovers," Andrew said.

Gisèle wrinkled her nose. "It seems so—I mean, no offense, Charles, but I can't imagine anyone *wanting* to—"

"Who's to say what drove them?" Charles squeezed Gisèle's hands again and got to his feet. "The lure of the forbidden? The comfort of the familiar? The fact that perhaps they saw each other little enough that they didn't really feel like brother and sister? If the intrigues of their parents' generation were anything like their own, it's always possible they really *weren't* brother and sister, at least not by blood. But whatever bound them together, it seems to have drawn them back to each other for years."

"From my conception to Miss Mortimer's," Andrew said.

Gisèle stretched out her hand to him, then let it fall in her lap.

"Uncle Cyril went away to school when he was eight," Quen said. "Aunt Georgiana would have only been seven. After that they wouldn't have seen much of each other. I suppose at some point he must have come home and—"

"They looked at each other and didn't see a brother and sister anymore," Andrew said. "I think—I think I can understand how it might have happened."

"But—" Gisèle's eyes darkened the way Charles's did when he was piecing evidence together. "Oh, Andrew, did you think Father—did you think I was—is that why—good God, why didn't you *tell* me?"

Andrew looked back at her without flinching. "That was only part of it. There are a lot of reasons why it would never work, Gelly."

"There aren't any that matter," Gisèle said.

Quen stared at the flame of one of the tapers on the mantel. "I said I'd kill whoever took Honoria's life. It seemed so simple. But if Evie were still alive, I don't know what the devil I'd feel—save relieved to have her back."

"They were both in my charge," Miss Newland said. "I should have—"

Quen gripped her hand and shook his head. "No."

Simon tore his concerned gaze away from David. "Tommy Belmont—he was working for Le Faucon?"

"He as good as admitted as much and that Le Faucon was the man Wheaton conveyed from France to London and McGann escorted up the coast to Dunmykel."

"I still can't make sense of it," Quen said. He seemed to find it a relief to focus on the Elsinore League rather than Evie. "Le Faucon, the Elsinore League, my father—the man I thought was my father—and the man who apparently really is. Can you explain it, Charles?"

"I can try, though a lot of it's speculation." Charles walked to the fireplace and wiped a trickle of wax from one of the candlesticks. "Our fathers—Glenister and Kenneth Fraser—formed a club at Oxford called the Elsinore League. We can't be sure of the exact membership, but I imagine it included a number of wealthy and powerful young men from Britain as well as foreigners they met at university and on the Grand Tour. They drank, they whored, I expect they gambled. Expensive habits. Kenneth Fraser was probably one of the poorer members of the league at this time. But he'd come to the notice of his friend's father. Old Lord Glenister started employing Kenneth to do secret errands for him when Kenneth was still at Oxford. Kenneth kept a ledger recording the payments he received from old Lord Glenister, and he concealed the notes he received with the payments in the binding of the ledger. The notes are cryptic, but I imagine old Lord Glenister employed Kenneth to tidy up his sons' peccadilloes. And possibly his own as well. But none of these tasks could have been as serious as the predicament old Lord Glenister brought to Kenneth in 1785. His seventeen-year-old daughter Georgiana was with child and arranging a marriage with the baby's father was impossible, as the father was his own younger son."

Andrew drew a swift, hard breath. Gisèle moved to the sofa where he sat and placed her hand over his own.

"Kenneth arranged for Georgiana Talbot to have her baby in secret," Charles said, "probably somewhere in France."

"I think Aunt Georgiana did travel on the Continent at about that time," Quen said. "Before she made her debut. What about my fath—the current Lord Glenister? Did he help Kenneth Fraser hush up Cyril and Georgiana's affair?"

"I suspect so," Charles said in a tone that was classic Charles Fraser—cool, concise, all the facts marshaled, all feeling held at bay. "That would fit with what Gelly and Honoria and Evie overheard him say to Kenneth about involving the members in something personal. I'm quite sure Kenneth turned to some of his fellow Elsinore League members for help in making the arrangments for Georgiana's stay abroad and her accouchement. A Frenchman named Coroux and another man who may or may not have been French but who later became known in France as Le Faucon de Maulévrier. Meanwhile, Kenneth arranged for Catherine Thirle, who was also pregnant, to go away from Dunmykel for her own delivery. After Georgiana gave birth—after you were born, Andrew—Kenneth brought you to Mrs. Thirle. Mrs. Thirle brought you back to Dunmykel as her daughter Maddie's twin brother."

"And Georgiana Talbot?" Andrew said.

"Returned to her family," Quen said. "Made her debut in society in due course. But though by all accounts she had a flock of suitors, she didn't marry for a long time." He looked at Charles. "You think she and Uncle Cyril resumed their affair?"

"Then or later. What seems certain is that whatever force held them together endured. Eventually Cyril married. Perhaps he was trying to cover up his affair with his sister. Or to find a refuge from it. Aunt Frances said she thought he chose Susan Mallinson because he'd made up his mind to marry and she was the most convenient choice. He continued to keep mistresses who strongly resembled Georgiana."

"My poor Aunt Susan," David said. "She wouldn't have understood any of it. And she died giving birth to Cyril's daughter."

Charles nodded. "Her death may have been the catalyst that drove Cyril and Georgiana back together. In any case, not long after Susan died giving birth to Honoria, Georgiana found herself pregnant. This time she took matters into her own hands. She eloped with Captain Ronald Mortimer, who evidently loved or wanted her enough to ignore the fact that she was four months pregnant with another man's child. Whether her father guessed the baby was really Cyril's or whether he thought Georgiana had been Mortimer's mistress, he washed his hands of her and cut off her dowry."

"A cold devil, my grandfather," Quen said.

"Quite." Charles's mouth tightened. "Georgiana and Captain Mortimer were left to live off his half-pay in the obscurity of Ramsgate. Meanwhile, Kenneth Fraser had done very well off the payment he received for covering up Georgiana's first pregnancy. He'd entered Parliament and bought Dunmykel and married my mother. The Elsinore League gatherings continued, though perhaps not as frequently as when the members had been younger. Some of the members had been caught up in the French Revolution and one had become Le Faucon de Maulévrier. Perhaps Cyril Talbot was involved in Le Faucon's revolutionary activities. Or perhaps he and the others didn't even know this man was Le Faucon. In any case, Le Faucon was present at the Elsinore League gathering Kenneth hosted at Dunmykel in the autumn of 1797. Colonel Coroux was there as well, as were Cyril Talbot and the present Lord Glenister, who by this time had inherited his father's title. Whatever role Glenister had played in hushing up Georgiana's first pregnancy, I'm quite sure he didn't know Cyril and Georgiana had resumed the affair or that Cyril was Evie's father."

"Until the house party?" David said.

"Yes." Mélanie took up the story. "Somehow Cyril revealed the truth—a slip of the tongue made in a drunken stupor, perhaps, or a desperate confession, or a bit of both. Glenister may have been able to forgive his brother for the initial affair with Georgiana when Cyril was eighteen, but he couldn't forgive him for resuming the liaison and for getting Georgiana pregnant again. He insisted on challenging Cyril to an impromptu duel and he killed him. With his dying breath, Cyril asked his brother to look after Evie."

"Glenister rushed to my grandfather's to see Honoria and repeated the promise," Charles said. "I heard him, though it wasn't until tonight that I understood what he meant. Kenneth tried to keep the duel secret from the others at the house party, but Coroux and Le Faucon must have overheard something. They knew about Georgiana's first pregnancy. They were probably able to piece together something very close to the truth."

"And then, after Waterloo, in the face of the White Terror, they realized how useful that truth could be," Mélanie said.

"Quite. Colonel Coroux found himself imprisoned in the Conciergerie as a Bonapartist officer. Le Faucon, whatever his original nationality, seems to have been living in France as well. We know that the current Vicomte d'Argenton was trying to uncover Le Faucon's identity. Both Le Faucon and Colonel Coroux needed to escape France and both tried to blackmail Kenneth Fraser and Glenister into helping them."

"So Francisco Soro was working for your father and Glenister?" David said.

"Indirectly. I think Kenneth and Glenister once again turned to their fellow Elsinore League members for help. According to Glenister, members of the Elsinore League wound up on both sides in the war in France. I suspect Francisco was hired by Royalist members of the Elsinore League in Paris who were acting as intermediaries between Kenneth and Glenister and Coroux and Le Faucon. Francisco and Manon were carrying messages to Coroux in prison as Coroux negotiated for his escape. Francisco may have been in communication with Le Faucon as well. The coded letter he gave me could have been from either Coroux or Le Faucon, threatening to reveal the truth about Cyril Talbot's death if Kenneth and Glenister didn't get him out of France. And who would Kenneth and Glenister most fear learning the truth? Cyril's daughter. Glenister's beloved niece, the girl Kenneth wanted to marry. Francisco must have heard the Royalist Elsinore League members he was working for say that the men Coroux and Le Faucon were blackmailing 'feared most for Honoria.' "

"So it was our fathers—Glenister and Kenneth Fraser—who had Colonel Coroux killed?" Quen said.

Charles nodded, his mouth hard. "They must have decided it was safer to have Coroux killed than to get him out of prison. I suspect it was his death that made Francisco turn on them and flee for England."

"And you think Tommy Belmont followed him and killed him?" David said. "How the hell did he get mixed up in all this?"

"We can only speculate. Perhaps his father or one of his uncles was a member of the league. They'd have been at Oxford with Father and Glenister. Perhaps after Castlereagh employed Tommy to investigate the league, Tommy decided it was more of a challenge to work with the league than to expose them. The closest he came to explaining himself was to say that with the war over he needed a new scope for his talents."

"My God," David said. "Belmont was always a cynic, but surely he had some sense of loyalty—"

"Tommy is addicted to risk," Mélanie said. "It's what made him a good agent. And what made him restless in peacetime." She cast a glance at Charles. "It isn't easy, learning to live in a world that doesn't teeter constantly on the edge of chaos. There's a wonderful freedom in never having to think beyond momentary survival. Whatever drew Tommy to the league, I suspect he was caught by the challenge of a new game to play. He can't resist dangerous games. In that sense, he's very like Honoria Talbot."

Charles looked back at her for a moment, gaze steady with understanding, then turned back to the others. "I'm not sure when Tommy became entangled with the league, but I suspect he had something to do with Colonel Coroux's death and Le Faucon's escape to London. Tommy admitted that he followed Francisco to London and killed him. But meanwhile Le Faucon had decided Father posed a danger to him."

"Why?" David asked. "If they'd kept each other's secrets all these years and your father had helped him escape Paris—"

"I'm not sure. Perhaps because only Father knew where Le Faucon had gone to earth in Britain. We don't know that Glenister or any of the others knew the details of his escape. Glenister may have deliberately stayed out of it. Or perhaps because of the papers Tommy was at such pains to retrieve from the secret rooms."

"The papers Evie died for," Quen said. "What were they?"

"I only got the briefest glance," Charles said. "On top was a bundle of love letters from Georgiana to Cyril, which Father probably got his hands on when he was covering up her first pregnancy. But there were other papers that weren't part of that packet. Papers that I suspect hold the truth about Le Faucon's identity. It would have made sense for Father to keep all his various forms of insurance together."

"And Honoria found them?" Quen said.

"She must have done. We know she was looking for information about her father's death. And perhaps she thought it would be handy to know any secrets Kenneth Fraser possessed in the event he ever learned the baby she carried wasn't his. She must have learned about the secret rooms somehow—perhaps from one of the servants. Once she found them she would have been able to discover the papers."

"Which Tommy Belmont was also after," Simon said.

"Yes. As best I can guess, Le Faucon contacted Tommy after he reached Britain and engaged Tommy to kill Father and retrieve the incriminating papers."

"So it was Mr. Belmont whom you found in the library the night Honoria was killed?" Gisèle said. "He'd come to see Father? Was he planning to kill him then?"

"I believe so. He'd probably sent Father a message saying they needed to talk. Father went back up to his room after his—interlude—with Aunt Frances. No doubt he intended to change and then go down to meet Tommy. But instead he found Honoria and all thoughts of Tommy fled. Tommy arranged the meeting again for last night and—" Charles's eyes went dark. "We all saw what happened."

Quen stared at Charles, the weight of his family's past sliding over his face. "Do you think Tommy will come after my father—Glenister?"

"I doubt it. If Tommy had wanted to get rid of Glenister as well, I think he'd have asked both Father and Glenister to meet him and dispatched them at the same time. But we can warn Glenister of what we've learned. Then he'll have to decide for himself how to proceed."

David frowned as though he were trying to make sense of a complex set of Parliamentary maneuvers. "What now?" he asked.

"As I said, I expect Glenister will deny knowledge of any of this. So, I imagine, will Tommy's family, who will probably give it out that he's gone to India or Jamaica for a protracted stay. I'm quite sure Castlereagh will refuse to talk, and I'm not sure how much he knows in any case. The two agents who were supposedly infiltrated into the Elsinore League worked for Tommy. They'll probably disappear. If they even existed in the first place. We can confront Wheaton—in fact, it will give me great pleasure to do so—but I doubt even he knows more than he told us, save perhaps that Tommy was working for Father at one point."

"And Evie?" Quen said.

A shadow crossed Charles's face, though the candlelight didn't waver. "Glenister and David's father should know at least part of the truth about what happened to her and to Honoria. I leave it up to you and David to decide how much."

Quen exchanged a look with David and nodded slowly. "My aunt Georgiana will have to know something as well."

Andrew, who had fallen to staring at the carpet again, looked up at him. "Miss Mortimer's mother? Oh, God, she's my—"

For the first time, he seemed to realize that the woman who had given birth to him and Evie Mortimer was not simply a name with a tragic history, but a very much alive human being. The full impact of what the evening's revelations implied about his own life seemed to break over him. He went completely still, his face drained of feeling, as though to feel or think anything at all would be to shatter in pieces.

Gisèle put her arms round him. Mélanie expected him to draw away. Instinctively, she braced for rejection on Gisèle's behalf. But instead Andrew leaned into Gisèle and clutched her tightly. Gisèle smoothed his hair. "It's all right, love. I'm here."

"I'm sorry," Andrew said. "I—"

"Don't talk, dearest. Not now." Gisèle glanced at Charles and then led Andrew from the room.

Quen helped Miss Newland to her feet. "We'll talk more tomorrow, Charles. I'm afraid—I can't think further tonight."

David gripped Charles's arm for a long moment. "It had to be done. We had to know. Thank you. And you, Mélanie."

Charles shook his head. "There's no thanks for this."

"There's always thanks for the offices of a friend."

David turned and touched Mélanie's arm. Simon squeezed her hand, and then they, too, left the room, Simon's arm round David's shoulders. The various lovers scattering to different parts of the house in a sort of dark version of the end of *A Midsummer Night's Dream:* "Jack shall have his Jill; Naught shall go ill."

Mélanie turned to look at her own lover. No, not her lover, as she had told Gisèle. Her husband. A tie at once closer and farther removed.

Charles was standing by the fireplace, one hand on the mantel, his head bent, his face hollowed out by the candlelight. There were soot marks on his cheeks and jaw. His shirt was streaked with dirt and blood. She was going to have to get him to let her examine the sword cut on his shoulder, which he'd been endeavoring to keep hidden from her.

Without looking up, he said, "I'm sorry I went to the secret rooms without you."

Her breath stuck in her throat for a moment. "I went to confront Evie without you."

"If we'd—"

"We can play it out a hundred different ways, Charles. I should have guessed Evie might have a pistol. We should have guessed Tommy might have a knife. But God knows what Evie might have done in desperation if she'd stayed in the house while we confronted Tommy. God knows what Tommy might have tried to disarm us if Evie hadn't been there. We can't ever be sure."

Charles nodded, still without looking at her. "She was scarcely more than a girl."

"Not in the end. She was a woman, forced to make hard and desperate choices. But she did choose."

"It's a damned bloody waste. Both her and Honoria." He swallowed. The candlelight shot through the linen of his shirt and picked out the pulse beating just above his collarbone. "I wasn't in love with Honoria," he said a low voice. "But I loved her. She was my friend. She was beautiful, yes, and of course there were times when I couldn't help but notice it. But that wasn't the sum of it. That wasn't even the most important part. Why does every relation between a man and a woman have to come down to the carnal?"

"Perhaps because that's the easiest for people to understand."

"A sad commentary on humanity. I don't think David's ever been remotely close to being in love with me. Why should everyone assume that I could only care about Honoria if I was in love with her?"

"Difficulty looking beyond the obvious. I was the worst offender of all." Mélanie found herself staring at the gold circle of her wedding band. She'd cast Charles's relationship to Miss Talbot in terms of romance and desire from the moment she overheard them in the library at the Glenister House ball. "I was jealous." She let the word linger in the air with all its implications. "But of all the sorts of intimacy, perhaps what happens between two people in bed was the one I had the least cause to be jealous of."

She looked at her husband. Charles's gaze was as unreadable as the Elsinore League's codes. "In the end I scarcely knew Honoria," he said. "You can't be jealous of an intimacy I shared with a woman who was a stranger to me."

"I can be jealous of what you shared with the woman you thought she was." Mélanie gripped the hard gold of her wedding ring. "You and Miss Talbot came from the same world. Whatever your feelings for her, you could scarcely avoid imagining the sort of life you might have had with her."

Self-mocking laughter glinted in her husband's eyes. "Christ, Mel, you've read the way my Parliamentary speeches are received in the press. I don't belong in the world I was born into. I never have. If I'd married Honoria she'd have wanted to see me Prime Minister or at the very least Foreign Secretary. We saw the world in different ways. I understood that even before I learned—everything we've learned about her. I'm not even sure who she was anymore. I don't think I'll ever understand how she could play dice with other people's lives. And yet—I can't believe she couldn't have been more than what we've learned these past days."

Mélanie felt something twist in her chest that might have been regret or fear. Or guilt. "That's the wonderful thing about you, Charles. You always think people can be better than they are."

Charles stared at his hand where it gripped the mantel. "I'm glad Quen's going to marry Miss Newland. Perhaps Andrew and Gelly will be able to salvage something from the wreckage."

"I hope so."

"Odd how we latch onto marriage as the only sort of happy ending to balance the scale."

Mélanie's nails scraped against her jaconet skirt. "I suppose it's some sort of affirmation of hope for the future. If one does it for the right reasons."

"Assuming one knows what those are." He dug his fingers into his hair, his gaze still fixed away from her. "Suppose Hamlet had married Ophelia, instead of trying to send her off to safety in a nunnery. Would he have been impossibly selfish?"

Her fingers tightened, snagging a thread. She didn't pretend to surprise at his change of subject. It wasn't really a change at all. "I'm quite sure that if Ophelia had been raped and left pregnant, Hamlet would have offered her marriage to protect her. That wouldn't have been selfish. That would have been heroic."

"Would he have made her happy?"

"I suspect in a few years she wouldn't have been able to imagine life without him." She swallowed, pushing air and words past the tightness in her throat. "Better to ask, would she have made him happy? And would he ever have been able to believe he had any right to be happy?"

Charles stared at his fingers spread on the golden oak of the mantel. Without any change in inflection, he said, "I tried to kill myself once."

She couldn't control her intake of breath. Other than that, she sat absolutely still.

"After my mother died," he continued. "After she put a bullet through her head. Not immediately after. I went through the motions of finishing up at Oxford. By that time, I knew I'd lost my brother as well. That we'd never be the friends we'd been, though I didn't understand why. I still don't. And I realized my father would never—not that I ever thought he would. Or I should have known better than to think it. And I didn't begin to understand what Gisèle needed from me. Not then. Perhaps if I had—" He shook his head. "I don't know what triggered it, what sent me over the edge. Why I was suddenly standing in my rooms in the Albany, trying to slash my wrists. Not very effectively."

"Thank God for once there was something you didn't have a talent for."

He gave a faint smile. "David found me. He and Simon wouldn't let me out of their sight for a fortnight. David got his father to arrange my post at the embassy in Lisbon. I let him bundle me off. I let him connive at my running away."

"He probably saved your life."

"Perhaps. If I'd been stronger—Gelly needed me. I should at least have tried to explain to her. The Dunmykel tenants needed a voice raised on their behalf, not an absentee heir across the sea.

Running away may have given me a respite, but it didn't solve anything."

It had led him to her and to their children, the one he had given his name to and the one they had created with their own bodies. But she didn't say any of that. She didn't dare.

"I thought if I could learn who killed Honoria, if this time I could actually confront things instead of running—" He dropped his hand from the mantel. "But we seem to be left with a worse mess than ever." He took a turn about the hearthrug, as though it were an enclosed space. As though he wanted to break free but couldn't. "There'll be things to do. Andrew and Quen are bound to have more questions come morning. We have to decide how much to tell the others. And we need to arrange for the funeral—both funerals—Father and Evie—"

"Darling." She got to her feet. "We don't have to do any of it tonight."

He spun round to face her, his gaze raw. "I have to." The words thundered against the oak ceiling. "Because if I stop and think—"

He broke off. She waited in an eternity of silence. The tapers guttered on the mantel. The smell of beeswax drifted through the room.

"Last night, when Wheaton's men had you, I was terrified," he said.

It was the last thing she'd expected to hear. "You can be ridiculously overprotective, Charles."

"No, not that." His voice was rough, as though he were trying to pick his way through an unfamiliar tongue. "It was sheer bloody selfishness. I was terrified at the thought of losing you. I couldn't imagine—I need you, Mel."

She stared through the shadows at him, robbed of speech.

"Oh, God, Mel, I—" He took a half step toward her, and then stumbled into her arms. She held him, his head against her shoulder, his chest shuddering against her own.

He clutched her as though he was afraid she'd be wrenched from his arms. He sobbed into her hair. Sobs that bridged years and worlds, lies and deceptions, words they had never spoken and perhaps never would.

"Don't let me go."

She smoothed his hair. They didn't live in a fairy tale. They couldn't ever forget what they had both seen of the world. They could only hold each other in the face of it. "It's all right, darling. I'm here."

In the end, perhaps, that was the most anyone had.

Historical Note

Once again, I am indebted to the libraries at Stanford and the University of California, Berkeley, for their wonderful research materials. I am also indebted to the many kind people at castles, country houses, and museums (not to mention the helpful staff at hotels and restaurants) in Scotland and England for answering my endless questions and to the Frick Collection and the Metropolitan Museum of Art, which provided the inspiration for Kenneth Fraser's collection. I would not have been able to create the world Mélanie, Charles, Simon, David, Gisèle, Tommy, Quen, and the others inhabit without these invaluable resources.

The Elsinore League is fictional, as is Le Faucon de Maulévrier, though the rebellion in the Vendée, in which I have grounded Le Faucon's history, was real.

Lord Castlereagh is the only real historical personage to make an appearance in this book (though several other real people are mentioned, such as the Duchess of Devonshire, Lady Bessborough, and the Lamb family). Obviously Castlereagh's involvement in the events of the novel is fictional, but I have endeavored to portray him in a manner consistent with the historical record of the complex man he was.